Her machete arced and dropped, and reeki vines slumped, spraying sap. Sal took a breath, took a step. Her sled crept forward at her back, and she took another night-blind swing at the trail-blocking fall of reeki vine.

Whiool. Raschad's whistle froze her in mid-swing. She vaulted onto her load and grabbed her long rifle, then belly-hugged the canvas and stared downtrail. The faintest glow of moonlight sifted through the tree canopy, revealing a shadowy lump atop the other sled. Raschad.

Whee-a. Wait, the whistle said. So she waited, sweat pooling, the night gummy hot, fear chilling her spine. Everything was unnaturally still, but something stirred up top. Heart thundering, she fixed her eyes on a moonlit slit in the high canopy.

A shadow slid across it ... and another.

Mistwalkers. Her lungs emptied. Going to lose the loads, forfeit the contract—if she lived. Twoteeth had said the mistwalkers were roused. Mad mistwalkers she didn't want to meet.

More shadows above. Their musk carried to her, diluted by reeki stench. She'd never seen so many mistwalkers at once—moving spooky silent, the way they always moved. She held her breath as they rustled past. How had Raschad spied them?

Be still, she wished him. Be still and wait ...

Look for these Del Rey Discoveries . . .
Because something new is always worth the risk!

DEMON DRUMS by Carol Severance
THE QUICKSILVER SCREEN by Don H. DeBrandt
A PLAGUE OF CHANGE by L. Warren Douglas
CHILDREN OF THE EARTH by Catherine Wells
THE OUTSKIRTER'S SECRET by Rosemary Kirstein
MIND LIGHT by Margaret Davis
AMMONITE by Nicola Griffith
DANCER OF THE SIXTH by Michelle Shirey Crean
THE DRYLANDS by Mary Rosenblum
McLENDON'S SYNDROME by Robert Frezza
BRIGHT ISLANDS IN A DARK SEA by L. Warren Douglas
THE RISING OF THE MOON by Flynn Connolly
CHIMERA by Mary Rosenblum
THE IMPERIUM GAME by K. D. Wentworth
THE HELDAN by Deborah Talmadge-Bickmore
MISTWALKER by Denise Lopes Heald

MISTWALKER

Denise Lopes Heald

A Del Rey® Book
BALLANTINE BOOKS • NEW YORK

To my parents and the Slide Mountain Writers

A Del Rey® Book
Published by Ballantine Books

Copyright © 1994 by Denise Lopes Heald

Library of Congress Catalog Card Number: 94-94038

ISBN 0-345-38890-9

Manufactured in the United States of America

First Edition: July 1994

10 9 8 7 6 5 4 3 2

Chapter 1

Fear climbed his spine. Sweat burned his eyes. The jungle steamed, the air too thick and hard to breathe. Mud caked him—balled between his thighs, hanging in green mudcicles from his pack. He fought a scream, fought instinct, held still—no running, no striking out. Feather-light hands whispered against his face, patted his chest, tugged at gear and clothing.

Old fears protested the intimacy. Human instinct cringed from six-fingered touches. But he held himself by force of will. Beneath the soft fur and raspy fingertips lay poison claws.

Vines writhed upward, twining shaggy tree trunks and disappearing into verdigris vapor. And dark ropy stems dangled from the mist as if rooted in green sky, the world turned upside down. More Aireils descended from cloud and phantasm. Mistwalkers, the greenies called them.

Wisps of gray-green fur rippled like skeins of hoary moss. Forms blurred, the creatures seemed merely coagulated mist, animated tendrils of vapor. But grounded, they became substantial, stood balanced on the curved sides of long-toed feet. Lithe bodies towered over his and bent in ways he couldn't—their spines curved once more than a human's. Hips rolled and listed, ropy limbs flexed.

So much articulation disconcerted the senses. He closed his eyes. His heart thumped. His breath came short and quick.

The beasts chittered and clicked, hissed and hummed. Burning, oily sweat seeped into his eyes and started tears that dripped off his chin.

The enclosing understory spun and wavered. Hands grasped. Alien musk—a coagulation of rot, sap, and animal oils—engulfed him, overpowering the stench of his own fear. Dizzied, his mind tried to slip free. But a howler shrieked high above, setting him

1

trembling, and that shock reached them. Chittering faded to chirring, gentle, soothing in spite of everything.

Hands dropped away. But a tug at his hair, where it had come loose from his greasy bandanna, and a touch on his brow forced him to look up. The creature's eyes, narrow and slanted, shone from within deep folds of wrinkled mist-green flesh—everything on this planet was green and green. Hair wisped from its chin and the sides of its otherwise naked muzzle and stood straight up from the pointed crown of its head. Old, old eyes—their expression wary, contemplative, saddened—chilled his heart.

The chirring deepened. His lungs stuttered. The song broke off on a single click, and between one bleary blink and the next he stood alone, the surrounding jungle empty and dripping.

He drew a shuddering breath, waited, and sensed nothing of the creatures. His hard-used legs shook.

He chanced a step, then another and another, and stumbled at last from the clearing, fear roiling his stomach, his load weighing him into the mud, Tumble Town so far away.

His lungs ached. The mist settled lower, still suffocating. Mud sucked at his cleated boots; brush snagged his clothes and tore flesh. Pallid fleepa faces flashed in the undergrowth, their big eyes round and startling, looking like lost babies in blue fur nighties. Their unnatural silence warned him.

He fought panic in that hush. Rot stench rose from mud. Insects whined against his face netting. Reeki sap stiffened his hair and clothes. Stinking, it deflected the bugs and turned him as green as the planet Ver Day's human natives. Vines dangled about his head and slithered beneath his boots. Preposterous insects—eyes too big, legs too long, bodies built of tiny triangular segments—dropped on his shoulders. A rotund bomb beetle burst against one arm, and the burning explosion wrung tears from his eyes.

Going to die. Going to die. The litany obscured distance and pain. Poor Mother, waiting across space and void for word that he had come through safe one more time. His load of crystals thumped his back with each frantic move, flogging him for his failures. He'd let them do this to him, let too many people do too much. He should have died. But Aunty had taught him to fight, and Academy had taught him to kill.

Flashes of light erupted against the red-streaked blur of his vision. Reeki stench twisted through his wavering sanity, and the jungle bled.

He stood, weapons raised. Sarel and Mickel hid with Mother.

Screams sounded. But nothing stirred in the hallway. Flames crackled. Smoke eddied. Shot charges whined . . .

He stumbled on a root knee and blinked back to the jungle. Tears tracked the reeki muck on his cheeks. He had stood useless while everyone died. But if he had left Mother's door, he'd have no family left at all. He shuddered. Survived that to die on this mud-suppurating planet?

A white blur blinded him and a sucking mass smacked his face. He screamed into silken folds, then through crossed eyes watched as the nurse flower withdrew, bobbing on its trigger vine. He touched his cheek, fingers trembling. His face had been vacuumed clean. Sweat and jungle's breath trickled on his spine. Netting flopped loose about his neck.

Going to die. He tugged his face net straight and stumbled onward. Going to die, and his sister and brother would die with him. He strained, pushed his plodding pace.

He'd worked in the green five days short of two months—the latter the exact limit of Grandfather's patience. He had to reach Tumble Town, report in, prove he was still alive to be the family's heir but too far exiled to be an immediate threat. If he missed a contact . . . *Live*, survive this stinking hell.

He forced himself up a slope coated with reeki vine. Pools of water glinted with the plant's green oils, and his boots slipped and slid. His knees found rock. He gripped a vine—browned with age and peeling thready fibers—and hauled himself upward to the mound's crest, his hands friction-burned, his lungs laboring. Bracing his palms against his knees, he gagged and spit.

An unfortunate miscalculation. Grandfather's voice echoed and gnawed at him. Don't you tell me that, old man.

You've failed, all of you. I married your mother to a Tarsian because they were rich, and popular with the Emperor. Fools. Couldn't hold on to a fortune, couldn't bend those proud knees to be ruled. Their fault, not mine your father was assassinated and no one even claimed vengeance. The Emperor wanted the fool dead.

I want you all dead. Spittle splashed his cheeks. No . . . his own tears. He fought free of nightmare. He wasn't on MB-2, couldn't stand in the muck dying.

His boots struck dry ground. He staggered into a vine-strangled tree trunk with a lung-stunning jolt, and his mind slammed him naked against the wall of Grandfather's study. *Run or I kill you.* The old man's eyes glowed red between powdery folds of wrinkled flesh. *Run.*

Grandfather melted to green. He walked, cold even with the jungle steaming all about. His vision blurred.

Stars glittered in his mind in a matrix of fathomless space. Safe. Instinct steadied his legs. Reflex propelled his feet. He stumbled on through the sappy, greasy green.

Bodies flowed from limb to vine, vine to limb, following the mudslugger. Thoughts eddied and merged—sensation and vision. The mudslugger moved. Fear stink rose from it. Thoughts coiled and bunched. Young ones hung poised to chase it.

But this mudslugger glittered. And the old one's curiosity held them watching. Tendrils of the mudslugger's presence wafted to them—a strange bitter taste on the tongue, strange chill-prickling scents, a quivering in hidden gills.

Chase it.

But senses shifted. Its glittering glowed brighter, soared through a vision clear and shining perfect. Where was that?

It saw something. In its mind, it saw ... free, endless, filled with glittering. What was that?

The jungle rose in a steaming crest from the base of the hill, crowding upward—green and rank and daunting—leaning toward the settlement as if contemplating how best to erase the humans' clearing. Sal studied the vine-entangled wall of scrub, trees, and treetops and watched the roaks lift and reel, black specks against a white-hot sky.

Their keening chorus grew louder. Someone coming.

She shifted for a better angle at her boot, and Morrie's weathered, scrap-wood porch rail creaked beneath her weight. Humming softly, she picked mud from her boot sole, caught in the afternoon's lazy disinterest. Insects shrilled in the scrub, and a scarlet sow beetle gnawed a porch corner. She let the fist-sized bug be, in no mood for a fight.

Morrie sat on the shack's rotted steps, his age-thinned shoulders humped beneath a shirt faded to white except for grime and thin spots where his skin showed through. One bony kneecap poked from the torn leg of mud-green jungle pants, and a scarlet millipede the length of her thumb stuck squashed to his scarred boot toe. His was tinkering with the fuel feed on her burner—Sal's one big sin, a hard-tech possession. But metal burners just worked better than anything made of botafab. Morrie tossed the burner's fire wand aside and disconnected the hose from its tank. He had patience for tech things, which she didn't, and there was no hurrying him. She picked at her boot and watched the scenery.

Smoke rose behind Toh's Bar, burners firing back the jungle, preserving the bit of space and light in which Tumble Town survived. Holding back the reeki vine was like staving off a flood. The big legume would feed, house, even clothe a body if anyone got that desperate. Ripe reeki wands were oily enough to light as torches, and most other parts of the plant had turned out useful, too. It started out like a pea vine, turned fibrous and woody as it matured, developed a trunk like a tree when old—and a greenie's hard life could turn impossible without it. But sit still for long on the edge of the scrub, and the reeki would grow right over you.

If Toh was paying, Sal might join the burn crew, earn enough to pay Morrie for the fix-it. If he ever finished.

The roaks' keening grew louder, and a nearer section of the colony rose in a flurry.

She glanced up the wide mouth of Tumble Town's curving main street. Traffic from the Pike and River trails fed north here past the town's bars, shops, and hotels-with-bars. For just sitting and watching, she had the best seat in town. But this time of day little stirred; most everyone except the burners was either drinking or napping.

A couple of kids played in front of Bwashwavie's produce stand, flinging mudballs across the street at three littler ones beneath the wooden porch of Greta's Laundry. Their throws were low, their arms too weak for the distance. But they single-mindedly kept trying anyway.

More roaks lifted. Somebody coming for sure.

Engines whined on the government flight pad atop the hill straight back from the shack—govies ruining the jungle's peace again with their tech. The whine cut off, the mechanics just tuning a skid flier's jets.

She jabbed at her boot sole.

"Flight-day tomorrow. Reckon there'll be four, five skids landing this time 'a year." Morrie spit on her burner's hose and squeezed the tube around the spit globule, checking for air leaks. "Don't 'magine it worries you none havin' more supplies arriving for delivery just now."

Levering a mud clod from her cleats, she let it fly in the old man's direction. She needed to hit the trail before her next load of freight bulked up, but Morrie's digging at her didn't find muscle to pull it. The Pike was a two-sled draw, like it or not.

"Summer's always busy." Her back ached just thinking about

it. With the trails the driest they'd be all year, people ordered up supplies against the monsoon season. Once the rains fell steady, nothing could move.

A door slapped open on the abandoned tent house neighboring Morrie's, and a fat, knee-high green midas waddled out. Pronged tongue flicking, the lizard lumbered onto the walk in front of Greta's and switched to the street's patchwork of cobblestones and potholes when it ran out of planks. Its wedge-shaped head held high, splayed feet toed in, elbows pointing straight out from its body, it padded across boggy mud to the Bwashwavie's produce stand. A swing of its broad blue tail knocked over a mud-flinging kid. Outweighed, the brats tackled the lizard anyway.

Sal traded boots and dangled one leg off the porch, all her weight resting on the rail. Just dare break.

Roaks exploded from the nearest tall trees. About here now. She shaded her eyes. The birds banked in a screaming flurry, and as they passed over the shack, droppings hit the roof like heavy rain.

"Morrie . . ." The old man swiped at a plop on his pate and kept on tinkering. "Shrike."

She dug out a ragged blue bandanna, stretched, and wiped green slurry from his wispy white hair. Refolding the rag, she watched the jungle's border of scrub trees and brush. Reeki vines mounded the low growth, their three-lobed, hand-sized leaves spread wide to the sun, their hardening seedpods dangling like lumpy fingers, nearly ready to gather.

"We could eat a salad. The reeki's purpled up nice." Young reeki leaves were tasty raw, if a mite greasy.

"Get some if you want." Morrie kept on working.

She might—might dig roots, too. Bugs, bogs, and heat didn't make digging a fun job, but boiled reeki was good free eating. City livers didn't know what they missed—except reeki stink.

Another band of roaks lifted. Sal kept her eye to the jungle verge.

"Somebody makin' prog-er-ess out there." Morrie spat on the burner hose again.

"About time you noticed."

"I noticed before you give me this burner."

Liar. Sal watched the jungle.

Scarlet bruk poked red blossoms above the reeki vines' green tangle, and farther into the scrub, a mass of parasitic whiskey-root threads coated a stunted tree with a golden veil. Fleepas scolded and scampered in the towering tree canopy. Orange-billed roaks flapped black-feathered wings, dislodged and disgruntled.

What you see? she wondered at the birds, and dug her scopes from a belt pouch.

Raising the MagEyes—one piece of tech, along with her burner, that she allowed herself—she focused on a white spot so high and far away she nearly lost it raising the scopes. In the magnified rounds of her lenses a solitary muumuu dangled by its scaly tail from a corker branch. What a sight a body could see from up there. Silver fur ashimmer, the slack-bodied nectar feeder basked in the sun, eyes closed, undisturbed by disgruntled fliers or noisy climbers, hanging so still that glitterwings floated through the blossoms about its head and gathered on its nose like wisps of yellow confetti.

She twisted on the rail, scanning farther, and nearly fell into the mud—hard hips slipping on hard wood. Her arm flung wide, the MagEyes dropped, and a jungle tramp trudged into sight.

"Shrike if I know who that is." Her boot hit the porch. A rotten board cracked.

Morrie glanced up, squinted. "Meesha Raschad."

"Haia?"

The old man just tinkered, ignoring her.

Out in the mud, the big tramp trudged nearer. Roak squat dappled the battered leather hat he wore clamped over a dirty bandanna, streaked his muddy shirt, and spotted his reeki-plastered bushwhackers and pants. Leather leggings protected his calves and shins. Mud bulged from his heavy jungle boots. Muck and netting hid his face, and whoever he was, she didn't even recognize the way he moved.

"Don't reckon you know where he come from." Couldn't be local, Sal thought. After twenty years of growing up in and around Tumble Town, she knew everyone from this part of the green.

"Could of fell out'a spacer and into the Bog for all I know. I don't ask." Morrie's pale blue eyes rolled. "Been in and out, maybe a year now."

"I ain't seen him before."

"Ain't surprising. You been lording it north since last spring." Morrie's reedy voice snapped. "Afore that you was way east. Be gone three, four months at a time, you misses things, missy." His bushy white eyebrows arched.

Sal stuck out her tongue. Morrie didn't approve of her ambitions or like her expanding her pack contracts until she couldn't handle them alone anymore. But she had to pay for the new sled somehow. And if she hadn't bought it, she'd have lost the Pike run. The load this trip proved that point—it was just too big these days for a single sled.

Too many people were living in the green, some of them ignoring the Terms of Settlement and building where they had no right, using tech that was illegal by her interpretation of the Terms. She'd put up with that pack of Liberalizer newcomers, and then here was Morrie, probably saving all spring to surprise her with a stranger he knew and she didn't.

The tramp passed them, angling cross-street toward Boojie's, the nearest bar. His shoulders sagged, and he was stiff with the weight of accumulated mud and a bulging pack. No doubt Boojie's looked good to him, scabby pink paint and all.

"Don't look like no *Meesha* I ever seen," Sal said. Sounded like a fancy woman's name.

"Might soo-prise you." Morrie cackled to himself.

"Not if I can help it."

"Don't be so fast. You been lookin' for muscle to help pack." She stared at Morrie the same as she would a big roacher.

"Listen now." Morrie spread his hands, palms up. "When Raschad comes in, it's likely he's broke out of supplies, looking for wages to pay his refit. I hear he works fair." Morrie bent back over Sal's burner. "Suits yourself."

"That fixed yet?" She watched his gnarled hands work.

"Oh, aia. Been fixed five secs after you give it to me. But t'ain't half clean."

They glared, short with each other by old habit.

"Think I'll buy me a brew. You could be till tomorrow." Sal unfolded from the rail, straightened her shoulder holster, swiped mud from the thighs of her worn jungle pants, and jerked on a limp-brimmed felt hat that covered all of her hair and the tips of her ears.

"Have fu-u-unn." Morrie's grin exposed widely separated teeth stained a dark green by years of eating a poor man's diet of reeki. Scowling, Sal stumped into the street, sensing the old man's smirky smile following her.

Boojie's ran long, dark, and narrow inside. The crowd amounted to one short-hire docker, two townies who scrubbed clothes for Greta, a boar herder with manure-caked leggings, and the jungle tramp.

"Brew, Jimmy," Sal called.

Jimmy waved from deep in shadow.

Leaning on the bar, she left room for privacy between herself and the tramp. Fat Al, Boojie's old gray-hided midas, took that as invitation and waddled up. His purple tongue flicked the thigh pocket of her pants, and she swatted a roacher off the bar. The lizard slurped the bug and waddled stiff-shouldered into the shadows, hunting a cool spot. Midases grew real warm-blooded for lizards.

Dim green light, bleeding from shallow ceiling-level windows, created an illusion of coolness in the taproom. Two ceiling fans stirred sluggishly, adding to the illusion. But the air hung thick and humid, ripe with the combined stench of the boar herder and the reeki-coated tramp. Her brew arrived.

"Feels like you got lizards on your vents, Jimmy."

"Been chasin' them all day." The barkeep ducked and came up holding three little emerald-colored midases by the tails. "The other three are likely on the back vents. They're free."

"Naia. I ain't got time for training a pup. Don't Fat Al know where these wrigglies come from?"

Jimmy shook his bald head and snorted. "Al don't care when their mama done rolls her scaly behind." The pups squealed and snapped. "Here now. Get on out."

Jimmy moved around the bar, opened the front door, and pitched the wriggling babies into the street. Then he caught the rest of the lizard litter in the back of the room and pitched them out with the others. Cleared of obstruction, the bar's floor vents breathed cold air from the cavern-cum-cellar below Boojie's, pushed heat out the taproom's high windows, and lifted sweat from the nape of Sal's neck.

"Now for Mama." Jimmy grimaced and headed for the bar's storage room.

Sipping her brew, Sal studied the jungle tramp's reflection in the pockmarked mirror on the wall above the liquor racks. Morrie claimed that Boojie's, though never big, had once been nice, with polished floors and crystal chandeliers. But the guano mines had dug out their allotment of roak squat and closed years before, and the bar had never looked better than this in her lifetime. Scars dented the hand carved bar. All the chandeliers were long gone, and sawdust coated the floor.

The tramp looked to be on a par with Boojie's usual clientele, and drank like it, too. Surfacing from a mug, he tugged a muddy rag from one pocket and wiped muck from his face and hands before hefting a bowl of stew and gulping it without the nuisance of using either spoon or fork. She knew *that* feeling—shaky, desperate to fill a hollow stomach. She let him be and just watched, watching everyone in the room, everyone watching her.

Jimmy strode out of the back room, his muscled arms wrapped about a bright green female midas, her pale belly glittering in the sunlight from outside. The boar herder's eyes followed him. Sloppy-fat, the woman sat with six empty mugs ringing her table. Likely she'd just sold her sty herd for shipment to Capitol. A squeal sounded beneath the woman's table—starter piglets all bagged up and safe.

Sal swallowed, relishing the cold trickle of brew down her throat. Herding was a living, but she'd rather starve on reeki. And this time of year, that did happen. Fools thought themselves fed so long as their stomachs were full, and lazy people wouldn't hunt nuts and roots to stay healthy. Once the various jungle fruits rotted or gigis staked them out, and the morel and other molds dried up, staying alive took work. Reeki alone wouldn't keep a body alive forever, and it stunted the brain. But raising porkers was wrong by Sal's standards—just another Liber stretching of the Terms. Bootleg smelters, backyard smithies, and imported animals didn't belong out here ruining the green any more than off-planeter newbies belonged out here stealing it from greenies.

"Haia." The tramp's deep-voiced hail drew her attention.

Lizards rousted, Jimmy slammed the front door, collected the man's waving trade chit, and carried off the tramp's stew bowl for a refill. Sal had wasted enough time on a fool's poke; she wanted to take a stranger packing about as much as she wanted one of Boojie's pups. But this time of year, muscle went scarce, and she was desperate. Damn Chic—if the idiot had to spawn, couldn't she have waited until the end of haul season?

Gripping her mug, Sal waded through the watery green dimness toward the tramp. At least the man looked jungle-tempered and carried the proper size for pulling a heavy sled. Jimmy was just setting another serving of stew beneath the tramp's nose. Elbows on the bar, the stranger scooped up a spoon this time around, his eyes watching her in the mirror.

Just beyond grabbing distance, she rested her mug on the tortured old bar and leaned against its blackened rail.

The tramp peered at her over one arm, gravy on his chin, jaws working. A medicine patch rode behind his right ear—no good news. Must be a Liber to use tech medicine. Which was why Morrie had been on about the man falling out of a spacer. But geared up the way he was, come packing out of the jungle like this, he didn't look Liber, and he didn't carry enough tech for it, either. Shrike, Morrie'd no more send her after a Liber than he'd send her chasing a newbie.

She pushed her hat back, arched her eyebrows and leaned toward the stranger. "I'm Sal Banks. Know it's pushy, catching you barely in, but old Morrie says 'times you're for hire."

He blinked and ate. She waited. He chewed. Too pushy. Best leave. Cheeks warming, she half turned.

But his spoon dropped. He guzzled into his mug again, and that sight held her a breath longer. His head came up, chin dripping foam, gravy washed away.

"Talk 'morrow." Snorting, he retrieved his spoon.

"Ta'marraw's feen." She added accent to let him know she was good and local, nobody to put off.

He blinked and scooped a poodle spider off his shoulder. She hadn't noticed the fist-sized black leggy amongst all the other muck he wore. "Here." He held it out to her.

Were his eyes odd-shaped? She couldn't see their color in this light. Was that a city accent he spoke with?

His hand shook. The spider cringed into a ball. She scooped the delicate thing from harm's way.

"Ta'marraw, then." She hoped he still remembered their conversation by morning.

He stuffed a hunk of bread in his mouth. She didn't expect he noticed the mold, but she'd watched him eat for long enough.

Meesha Raschad sat on the edge of a listing plank bed, stared at his soggy boots, and didn't know what to do about them. He wanted them off. That ranked right up with taking a shower. But neither was going to happen. He didn't have the strength, didn't remember leaving the bar, wasn't sure how much he'd paid for this room or what name he'd used at the desk. Didn't matter.

A biting fly circled him. He rested on residual equilibrium, then slumped sideways. Planks creaked. Sap and mud soaked the worn mattress ticking. He snored softly, safe.

Chapter 2

Sal woke early and went out early—her habit—walking the length of the settlement to check the depot board for jobs. Nothing new. Wandering back, she stopped at Mary's for breakfast—roak eggs and big lumpy slabs of pan bread, sour and chewy the way she liked it, with toddberry jelly. Busy cooking, Mary waved from the restaurant's kitchen. Sal waved back.

Mary and Ma had been friends. Ma would finish cleaning at the Sundowner or up to Heaven's Rest, then stop to gossip while Mary turned reeki this and reeki that into food. Sal could remember running between Mary's thick legs while the woman laughed, sweated, and stirred giant pots of stew and roots. But one day, with Pa off in the green, Mary came with George—who'd been sheriff in Tumble Town near all Sal's life. They told her—thirteen years old and all alone—that Ma was dying. Mary held her then. George held her much later.

Aching full, Sal paid Deni, the countergirl—shouldn't have spent the money. Giving Mary a parting wave, she clumped outside to stand on the plank walk and watch Tumble Town start another day.

People crowded the muddy street, shopping, selling, and queuing for a wash. If a body wanted a scrub but didn't have the means or sense to collect and store clean water or space to use it, then they'd best not be late for the showers in this town full of transient packers and mud-poor gatherers. Herself, she'd used a can and washtub last night at Morrie's, with the old man locked outside, trying to peek through the knotholes. Old somabitch, the sight would kill him.

She stepped in at the Hill House's door. Keeping her muddy boots off the cleat-scarred but freshly scrubbed ku-soo wood floor, she balanced on the boot grill. Mud rolled off her soles and fell through wooden slats into a tray that was emptied twice a day or it overflowed into the lobby.

"Got a big ol' tramp here, Cally?" she called to the desk clerk. "Come in yesterday afternoon?"

"Not here, Sal." Cally smiled. "You huntin' a partner?"

"Naia. Just short hire." A tramp like Raschad she didn't need around, and she and partners never got along long anyway.

"I heard you've a big load waitin' up top."

"Waiting, and contract getting short. I'd best move."

Cally waved, and Sal ducked back outside. The tramp might be at Toh's. The barkeep rented the cheapest rooms in town, and Raschad hadn't been fit to climb far uphill yesterday.

Passing the Pannier's big display window, she flinched at the price of new leggings. Best make her own. But she stopped anyway and studied a carving on a stone pedestal. The banban wood from which the predatory scriar was formed was sanded so smooth and polished so fine that the big jungle animal's crouched body, tensed to spring, shone like a real black pelt. Everything about the carving was picked out in exact detail: the humped, muscle-rippling shoulders, saber fangs, curved claws, stumpy tail, and the flat head with narrow tapering eyes set above a snarling muzzle. This would be Danner Nolson's work, or maybe Keet Barren's. Sal shuddered. The piece, tiny as it was in comparison to a living scriar, was too real.

"Fight!" A kid's squawk shattered the rhythm of the town's morning clatter, and twisting around, she saw the street brats lit up like Holiday and headed for the showers. "Fight!"

Stepping to the edge of the raised walk, she saw people gathering along one side of the showers. Shouting and jigging, the crowd hid the attraction from her. But she spotted George's white shirt at the shower's front gate. Twisting the arms of two scrawny towel attendants, he looked too distracted by the fight to concentrate on the job before him.

A stranger hesitated near George, and Sal thought the stocky woman meant to lend a hand. But the packer moved on, more interested in the larger commotion. So Sal waded into sticky slick street slop, and by the time she reached George, he was sitting on one runt with the other's face jammed in the mud.

"Don't imagine you need any help, Sheriff."

He grinned, a lazy white smile beneath his drooping black mustache—a smile that warmed her soul, among other things.

"Naia, me. But this one's not breathing right." He shoved the kid's head deeper in the mud. "Cuffs are on my belt."

She bent down and dug around George's middle, embarrassed to paw at him in public. That she knew exactly what was under his pants, and every soul in town knew she knew, embarrassed her the more. Worse, she had the feeling George didn't mind at all.

Cuffing the two attendants, she dragged them off George just as the fight crowd broke into booing. Bodies parted and she saw a muddy figure squirt from the grip of a big brawler and plunge free. A string of brats chased the coward off downhill.

"Got'em?" George asked her.

"Aia."

"Keep an eye to the gear." George nodded toward the shower gate, where a big jungle pack spilled its contents in the mud.

"Got it."

George disappeared into the crowd. Seeing him go, some people's attention shifted to the spilled pack.

"Haia!" She waved, and two shave-headed, barefoot brats danced away from the gear, acting innocent.

Glancing from prisoners to pack to the crowd, she saw folks already wandering off. George emerged, wrestling a big, muddy, half-naked body. He didn't look happy, especially when he and the mudball both slipped in the mire from the shower drain. George felt it his professional duty to present a clean and neat appearance, and his starched shirts had become near the same as a uniform in people's eyes over the years.

"Easy there." George shoved the muck-coated skinner up beside her and spit to one side. "Says he's working for you."

For her? The mud man wobbled back a step, and she sensed something familiar in the idiot's stance.

"You under all that, Raschad?"

"Aia." He hugged his gut, panting.

"We was interviewing." Sal spoke aside to George, studying the jungle tramp. "*Maybe* he's workin' for me."

"I heard you need muscle," George said. Was there anyone who hadn't? Sal wondered. George gripped Raschad's elbow, steadying him. "He looks to be the victim here." Blood stained the tramp's muddy face, and it would take tending to keep infection out of the mud-packed wounds.

"That your pack there, son?" George called most everyone *son*, though he wasn't much over forty.

"Aia." Raschad's expression went grimmer beneath his muck mask. "What's left."

"Figured." George nodded toward the cuffed shower attendants. "These boys were *attendin'* to it while you were distracted. Sorry

I didn't help you sooner, but I can count on catching someone thieving any time there's a shower brawl."

Raschad grunted and eased toward his pack, his bare feet uncertain in churned mud. George's critical eyes followed him, and everyone in the crowd was also taking his measure. In particular, Sal noticed the stocky stranger who'd passed George by earlier, studying Raschad as if the big man were edible.

"Got to do something with him." George pitched his words low. "The one that jumped him took off."

"I seen that," Sal said.

"Well, the squat couldn't handle this tramp. Or the coward figured he'd given the kids time enough to work their side of the deal. But they didn't. So maybe he'll come back with a knife, catch this one alone after dark. That tech of his is tempting. Someone else might decide the man looks easy and go for him. He ain't standin' real straight."

George was asking if she wanted Raschad in jail or was willing to take him herself. Shrike, the man did look pathetic down in the mud wearing only his knee-length undershorts, holster slipping off one shoulder as he crammed his pack back together. A shriking big, power-butted weapon rode in that holster—big enough for him to take care of himself, though she couldn't place its make. Still, she needed muscle, and where else would she find it now?

"Let me talk to him."

George shrugged. She skated through the mud to Raschad.

"I hear you're still interested in my job offer." Strapping his pack closed, the man nodded. "I'll tell you straight, then." Sal squatted, picked a pair of socks out of the mud and handed them over. "I run two packer sleds, working govie contracts. Deliver light goods up the Pike onto the Plateau and clear down to Oofall. I got a contract running short for pickup now. The route aims up the Pike to Noca Tana, around on the Ebbid Trail through D'arnith's Wood, and clear in a circle back here. It'll be a fast, hard pull and naia fun."

"Aia." His grunt was breathy. "Need it."

"All right, then."

"Didn't finish my shower." A split lip slurred his words.

"Do it down to my place. You've worn your welcome thin here, I reckon." She stood and stumped back to George, who still held his two prisoners.

"I'll take him." She nodded to Raschad. "Need a packer."

"That ain't what he is, Sal."

"What?"

George jerked his prisoners down the street. "Best get him out of the mud."

"Haia?" But George kept going, hands full.

Raschad limped up, shoulders hunched, wearing only his slicker over his mud-slathered body, one arm wrapped around his middle. His boots were untied and squished with every step.

"Ain't you a sight." Shaking her head, Sal slogged downhill, feeling like a parade master.

Morrie stood up off his front steps and smiled like a midas spying a sow beetle as she hiked up with Raschad in tow.

"We need water here, old man."

"Need more'n that. I'll get the scrub brush and soap."

"You don't even remember what they are." She glared at Morrie. He snorted and disappeared into the shack. "Around here." Sal led Raschad to the shack's back porch and lifted a wood pallet down onto the moss patch next to the steps. "I'll fetch water."

Raschad sank onto the porch and levered one boot off with the toe of the other. By the time she'd hauled water from the rain barrel, he'd hung his slicker beneath the shack's eaves and was standing in its scant shelter in only his shorts. She caught an impression of long solid legs, narrow hips, deep chest, broad shoulders—real likely muscle.

She strode onto the porch. Even at her ample height, that only put her at head level with the man. Dumping water over him, she kept the slicker between them, and the big tramp crossed his arms, scrubbed his shoulders, and swiped at his face.

Mud dissolved and ran. He threw his head back.

And her heart stopped. Sucking a breath, she force-started her pulse and grabbed his hands away from his face.

She knew before she did it. But she reached out anyway and lifted the long hair from his neck, exposing clean, untanned skin, skin as pale and golden as noonday sun.

"Morrie!"

Raschad's expression flashed startled, wary. "You knew." He sucked his bloody lip. "You knew?"

She shook her head side to side. Up close, facing him in full sunlight, she saw eyes as lavender as the blush on budding reeki—alien eyes; too, too pretty eyes.

Where was her brain? No wonder those boys at the shower had tackled a lunk like Raschad and expected to get away with it. No wonder he packed big tech, probably hard tech. Why'd she let that answer slip from George?

Because she couldn't believe Morrie would send her hawking after a newbie. Because Raschad had never looked up while they talked at the showers and hadn't said five words to her at a time ever, none of those spoken clearly enough to catch his accent until now. Who would believe the tramp she had seen hauling out of the green yesterday, looking like damnation afoot, could *be* a newbie?

"I'll go." He sucked in a ragged breath. "No trouble." He reached for his slicker.

Her jaw worked. She'd best say something, but . . .

His feet slipped on wet wood. His hips dropped, and an arm shot out. He caught himself on the porch post. Color drained from his face. Bruises rode his cheeks like storm clouds.

"Mor-rie." She grabbed Raschad.

"B-Be fine." Wheezing and grunting, he doubled over.

She slapped a biting fly off his shoulder.

Eyes clenched shut against muck dribbling out of his hair, he tried to straighten up. "Give . . ." Pack galls and bruises calicoed his shoulders, and he looked to be holding his ribs together from the outside. "Give me my slicker." He took a strangled breath. "I'll go."

"Naia." She gritted her teeth. "I gave my word to hire you. I don't back out on that."

Her gut twisted. But she'd made a pact, and her name rode on keeping it—even with a newbie. See how Morrie liked this fix. But if she tossed Raschad out now, the whole town would know. Whole town probably knew he was newbie from the first and never said a word, just George rolling his eyes and acting strange. *That ain't what he is, Sal.*

Morrie clumped onto the porch at her back. "Didn't know's you was such good friends a'ready."

Sal cranked her head around and glared. "Get Dancer." Her growl melted the sly smile from the old man's face. "He's hurt. And if my arms weren't full, I'd hurt *you*."

Raschad dropped, and his weight slewed her around. She grabbed with both arms, and he sat straight down on the ragged edge of the porch boards, dragging her with him.

"Shoo." Morrie braked to her side. "Thought you'd lost him." He bent over next to the newbie's ear. "You a'right, son?" No answer, except a little wheezing sound from Raschad's chest. Morrie's forehead wrinkled. "I'll get Dancer."

"That's what I said."

"Who minds you." Morrie stumped off the porch and around the shack, leaving her alone holding a wet, naked man.

"Reckon we might finish getting you clean."

Raschad's head bobbed against her shoulder. She tested whether he'd stay sitting without her support; he did. She scooped up the scrub brush and soap Morrie had dropped and dragged a second bucket of water within reach.

"Looks like that bullyby hit you kind of hard." He nodded, making it such a tiny movement that he didn't even disturb the stream of water dripping from his chin. "I'll hurry."

Teeth gritted, she scrubbed his hair with tech soap oily enough to break loose lice eggs, rinsed that out, and shampooed him again with homemade bar soap. Tackling the rest of him then, she tried not to look at, tried not to feel, his muscled alien body.

"Here." She grabbed a rag, wiped wet hair away from his eyes, and dried his swollen face.

He blinked up at her, finer-looking by the breath, his fair hair darkened by water, the shape of his face clean and angular—so pretty, bruises and all, that she regretted looking at him. *She* should be half as pretty. A newbie like this . . . what kind of damnation did Morrie wish her?

"Stay."

He sat, head hanging. She went inside to find a blanket and towel, carried them out, and dried him, beating bugs away as she worked. His skin felt like silk, smelled morning sweet, and he had the softest feet she'd ever met.

"Newbie?" She wrapped the blanket around him. "Raschad?"

No answer. Going to die right here. Her stomach took a plunge and she dropped on the porch behind him, spread her legs, scooted against his back, and tugged him onto her shoulder. He whimpered, slumped, and left her sitting like an idiot, arms braced behind her, imitating a chair back.

He woke in darkness, blank with fear, uncertain where he was, whose bed, or if it *was* a bed the way it swayed and rocked. A light came on, dim, floor-level—a handlight.

"Newbie?"

He remembered her resonant voice, remembered a bucket bath, sunlight, and her strong arms holding him.

"Bad dreams, I reckon." She spoke with the typical greenie aversion to asking a direct question.

"Aia. Nightmare." He put a hand to the wall and stopped the ceiling-hung cot from swaying.

"Got food if you want, whatever else you need." A spate of wall-shaking snorts erupted outside the shack's door. "Don't mind Morrie." She glared at the front window. "His noise and stink keeps the bugs away."

Heart quaking, he concentrated on the snoring, tried denying his stomach's rumbles. But one meal in three, four days . . .

"Hungry," he admitted, though he didn't want her getting up in the dark to fix him food. He didn't need debts, and she'd done more already than she had reason to do. He should have guessed when she approached him in the bar that she hadn't realized he was a newbie. But even now he found it difficult to focus a coherent thought.

She rolled out of her hammock, tall and broad-shouldered in the shadowy light, a long shirt floating about her muscled body. Watching her tug on a pair of loose trousers, he was reminded of Aunty suiting up in armor.

"Here." The greenie woman brought a cup of water. "Safer than gov'ment supply."

While he drank it all at once in a soothing rush of wetness, she crossed to a rickety cupboard hung above the low plank counter that fronted the shack. He tried not to watch her, tried not to think about eating . . . She returned, arms loaded, and dumped food on his feet. Then she held the cot steady while he sat up beneath the sleep netting, wearing nothing but a blanket.

"Rest. I'll fix things." She sat on a log round and began to slice bread and cut cheese. "Only thing else we have is reeki."

"That will be fine."

Eyeing him as if he lied, she poured preserves into a chipped pottery bowl and handed it to him beneath the netting. For the time of night and the state of his stomach, the reeki tasted finer than Mother's most exquisite banquet. Flamed roast, shellfish, creamed sweets served in crystal—none of those dishes ever tasted as good as this one.

"Thank you." Chewing strained his bruised jaw, but it was a minor pain compared to the gnawing in his stomach.

"You'll earn it."

"This is more than money."

"So, you owe me." She shrugged. "Ain't bad on my side."

"You don't have to hire me. There's no need to be stuck with a newbie you don't want."

She looked tempted to agree. But her jaw set.

"I told you. I keep my promises." She met his stare. "Besides, I need muscle now." She shoved a slice of bread at him and swatted back a swarm of gnats. "But since you have your doubts of me, I'll tell you clear how I feel. Newbies are a waste. You'll live a bit yet, thanks to George and Dancer, but not long enough to pay Ver Day back for your keep."

Her jaw worked. Round golden eyes met his gaze head-on, neither ashamed of her opinions nor worried about hurting his feelings. Though he knew better, knew greenie pride, he stood up to her glare anyway. And that set her off.

"I know what you're thinking. Newbies always figure they know better than greenies." She slapped a roacher from the netting over his legs. "And this planet's settlement looks young by human standards—a couple hundred years, nothing compared to, say, Noxibillie's four thousand generations." Her eyes dared him to call her ignorant.

"I know that before the Coolvein Rebellion, people on Ver Day was all newbie, everyone using only the cheapest, poorest tech they could steal from Didionia before sneaking off that old dirty planet and running to here. They scrambled to learn the green and survive without destroying the place for their kids, wanting to leave it as green as they found it. You probably know all this." Her eyebrows arched, her expression angry and stone serious.

"Some of it."

"Well, not enough. Because the only thing newbies know better than greenies is dying faster. You don't know about living all your life in the green, and there's ways off of Ver Day for newbies. But when the Coolvein Rebellion stopped immigration onto this planet ten, fifteen generations back, there wasn't any choice left for people here. They survived or they didn't, but no one was comin' to help.

"And no off-planeters brought in new hard tech or broke the Terms of Settlement, nor harmed things with either poisons or medicines. Since then, Ver Daians have been different, because the physical stuff it takes to survive this jungle is as uncommon as common sense. And all in two, three generations, we e-evolved ge-genetically."

Raschad sensed her stretching for terms only tentatively within the grasp of her vocabulary, reciting a lesson.

"Only folks strong enough or strange enough survived and raised kids. And of them, only the kids that could eat reeki and stand the bugs lived to breed up the next generation. Shrike, after eighty years passed and the Coolveins lost their fight and off-planeters come dribbling onto Ver Day again, lookin' for paradise, we was all green from eating reeki, being raised in reeki-tainted wombs, drinking green milk.

"The green made us strong, gave us immuno ..." Her eyes darted; her jaw tensed. "Immuno ... whatever." She waved a hand in frustration. "Anyways, so we didn't get sick so often anymore, didn't die of fevers right and left. And our tech was all green, either hand built from wood or clay or tech-grown bot-an-i-cal may-ter-ticks ..."

"Matrix."

Her eyes flared. "They give you this speech when you come on planet?" she asked outright, intentionally insulting him.

He shook his head negative.

She compounded her insult. "Why'n hell not?"

"I'm sure Immigration assumed I'd find out."

"Assumed?" Sal's jaw clenched, unclenched. "This shriking government don't care lately, except about its own greedy grabbing. They *want* you off-planeters here, want you showing off tech and bragging about it. They figure greenies will start wanting hard tech so much, like your big old cannon, that we'll forget our common sense. They've even written up a little proposition they call the Liberalization Act, a real simple thing. It's only supposed to put the Terms of Settlement into modern language and set up a way to amend them. The act itself doesn't do anything, they say.

"But I like the old language the Terms are written in, and I figure *amend* means change. And if newbies are the kind of change Governor Wally's backing, then we'd all be fools to agree with him. Because newbies don't live long enough to be more than a waste, catch fevers just from touching the mud, starve with reeki and morel growing all around, rile the gigis, and spook the mistwalkers."

His heart did a little skitter dance, and her eyes narrowed, not missing the slightest change in him.

"I agree." He spoke around a mouthful of reeki preserves and bread. Her eyes rounded. "I didn't immigrate here." He swallowed. "I worked a ship out this far, then my officers decided they didn't need me and spaced away. I hadn't credits enough to buy passage anyplace else."

"Lots of other working ships land here."

"None that wanted me." He'd already said too much.

"But you can pull a sled from here to Noca Tana and back?"

"Aia." He'd better be able to haul her sled after digging nothing but junk crystal the last two months. He'd have to send everything to Mother and Sarel.

"And you still want to work for me, knowing I hate everything a newbie is?" Again she insulted him, trying to drive him away, or maybe just warning him.

"Aia." He needed this job to reequip and return to digging, if the mistwalkers let him. He nodded, sweat chilling.

"Ribs must be sore." Her voice softened.

"They're better." He rubbed a hand across them. "Nothing broken. I'm just worn down."

"We all been there." Her implied sympathy threw him. What was she thinking?

She caught his chin, and he endured her too close examination. The sight and the smell of her, strange and earthy—a deep jungle-green greenie—unsettled him.

"Dancer does a good job mending folks."

Raschad assumed she meant the crazy old woman who had bandaged him earlier.

"She's a friend of Morrie's. Relative, sort of." Sal leaned back. He let his breath out. Her mouth twitched. Embarrassed?

"Reckon you weren't expecting a fight this morning," she said.

"The bullyby just tackled me, shoved me through the canvas into the mud." He took a bite of cheese. It tasted of the reeki the milk bov had grazed.

"They was after your tech."

"Aia. My own fault, should have seen it coming. I was too wobbly, looked easy."

Her eyes widened. He couldn't begin to decipher her expression.

"Town's going to squat." She slapped bugs off his bare shoulder. "Would be squat if it weren't for George."

"The sheriff?"

"Aia, the sheriff. Would think you'd met him by now."

"No." He swallowed. "I try to be unobtrusive in town."

"Un-op-trues-eve." She laughed, and the curve of her mouth made her almost pretty, green tan and all. His cheeks warmed. "Whatever that means, maybe you'll do better at it tomorrow."

Looking up into her smile, his stomach full, someone watching over him, he didn't expect tomorrow could be better than this. He closed his eyes, meaning still to finish the bread.

Sal slipped the crust from his limp fingers and put the lid on the last of the preserves. A newbie that ate reeki? She'd seen it all now, and breakfast would be poor pickings in this shack. Brushing crumbs from the cot, she studied him in the dim tech light. He hadn't gotten any uglier. Long hair curled around his sleep-softened face, and he looked hardly older than herself.

He reminded her of Ma that last day, all muscled, yet so limp and pale. She shook that off.

But how did she face a person still breathing, yet already dead? Maybe that described everyone, just not so immediate. But avoiding newbies and hating them were a single thing in Sal's mind. And dealing with him just set her off, broke the dam, set her jabbering a storm about First Settlers and all—proving to herself again, she guessed, why greenies hated newbies.

You had to hate them. Liking a newbie was the same as liking tech you didn't need—it betrayed the green.

Still, this one wasn't an idiot. He could have blasted those kids at the shower, but he didn't, and didn't end up in George's jail, either. For a newbie, he showed sense—even ate reeki. Hope that didn't kill him. Squat, he was alien.

She raised a clenched fist, aware of the absence of Morrie's snoring, and shook it at the black square of netted window over the counter. She heard the outside hammock creak.

"Your day's coming, you old drunk." Sal spoke low, so as not to rouse Raschad.

Forgetting Morrie, she shooed bugs off her *guest* and sealed the dirty netting over his cot. What a waste.

If protection agreements with the Allies forced Ver Day to accept off-planet immigrants, why not keep them in the city? Newbies made cheap, smart labor in the Industrial Zone tech plants that turned out things such as her sleds, her handlight—a present from George—her scopes and her burner. Counting both sleds, that made five tech things she used. But except for her burner, her tech was all botafab; left in the green, it would melt down within two months, just so much fertilizer. Off-planet tech laid around forever or until it leaked poison.

Hard tech didn't belong in the jungle. And, reconsidering, she supposed off-planeters didn't belong displacing Ver Daians even in the city. Jobs came hard these days. For certain, newbies didn't belong out here dying in the green. Let the Governor's pack of liars argue, but newbies were wrong.

Sal ungritted her teeth and blew out a long breath. She hated politics. Still, everyone had a vote, and she hated wasting hers by not knowing who lied and who told the hard, uncomfortable truth. She just prayed the First Settlers got a handle on the Liberalizers and their stretching of the Terms of Settlement before Governor Wally cut loose and clear-cut the whole planet for export just so he could buy fancy tech toys.

You're the problem, newbie, she thought—the little grain of grit that wears a bearing lopsided, upsets the balance of what should be. And by that light, making sure aliens didn't survive in the green was patriotic. Some did just that, too—made sure. Staring down at Raschad's pretty face, she flinched.

The government lied to these ignorant people. Damn the government. She didn't want this man dying here. But he might; he would die some place soon anyway. Just a waste. Only a miracle would put him on his feet strong enough to pull for her on this run. She prayed against it.

Morrie had tricked her into a real mess. What had got into the old man?

Chapter 3

Rain bathed the jungle at dawn—no unusual thing, and it brought no miracles. Raschad slept like the dead and looked dead, too, except for the rise and fall of his chest. Morrie came in soggy from the front porch, peeked at the newbie, and hunkered near the fire Sal had lit in the mud oven.

"Looks some better." Morrie pitched his voice low, his expression thoughtful.

Gazing over the top of the old man's head, Sal studied Raschad. Pallor showed beneath his tapestry of bruises, and she wondered what color would be properly healthy for him. At least he didn't seem fevered. Dancer's doctoring had kept infection out of his wounds so far—or maybe the tech medicine patch he still wore had helped; constant dosing was a common practice among newbies. Anyway, he seemed healthier than yesterday.

"Hard to believe this pretty man's tramped the jungle all this summer." Sal eyed the newbie some more.

"They say he's mean. Shrike, you saw him come out of the green day afore yesterday, making a way where most off-planeters and some on-ers can't find one." Morrie shook his head.

"Aia. Well, I'm wondering how come his toes ain't tore up and rotted off if he come so far."

"Newbies got tough feet."

"Gigi squat." Sal poked the fire. "They got tough nothing. And it's strange that all a sudden you let a newbie sleep on your own blankets."

"My fault you brung him."

"Aia, which don't put him on his feet for the Pike run. Maybe you'll pull a max-loaded sled for me."

Morrie hunkered and ignored her baiting. And still it surprised her that he didn't raise more fuss about the newbie taking his bed. What was he thinking?

She lifted the brew can from its nail and hauled out the tea tin. Opening a packet of trail biscuits and the last of the preserves, she let her eyes wander back to Raschad. A week wouldn't see him strong, even if she had a week.

"Food time, you old hiss." She hefted the teapot, swung a leg over a log round—Morrie's best chair—and filled their battered tea mugs as she settled on the stump. Slow with morning stiffness, Morrie waddled over and curled his knob-knuckled hand around a mug. His scowl commented on the meager meal.

"I know." She nodded at him to take first helpings. "I was stupid enough to bring an extra appetite home. But you started this. I'm tempted to let you starve."

"I told you plain out he might of fell from a spacer."

"Then sent me after a newbie anyway, knowing I didn't believe you," Sal gulped hot tea.

"Not my fault ya fell on yer head young."

She grabbed three of his four trail biscuits—which was four of the six in the package—off his plate and swung to her feet.

"Going to check the boards." She lifted her slicker off a nail. "I'll bring food." She glanced at Raschad.

"Get," Morrie groused. "I'll sit the babe, ain't goin' nowhere in this muck this early."

Her little finger rose, and she stepped out quick before he threw anything.

Unaccustomed cool greeted her, a relief from days of temperatures and humidity nearer scalding. Rain drizzled through the porch roof, and the street ran with a slithering sheet of green mud. Across it, Boojie's looked black and abandoned, its roof peak hidden by lowering mist—more gloom and doom.

Stepping into the street, she hunkered into her moldy slicker hood. The clouds rode so low this morning that it felt as if they perched on her shoulders, weighing her into the mud. But all her life she'd lived in this jungle. A little rain didn't scare her.

Working her knees loose, she skated up the street. Quiet held the town; the showers were abandoned, their soggy canvas sagging. Shutters hid the Pannier's displays, and only a curl of smoke rising from Mary's chimney lent any cheer to the scene. The mud thickened, sucking at her boot soles, and she passed the Apothecary—closed—then the Sundowner. Even the brothel sat quiet and drear this morning, all the divine ladies still abed. Rain was apparently inhospitable to the divies' spirits.

Big and fancy, Heaven's Rest sat off to the right of the wide bend before Vos's Grocery. A white veranda and white shutters softened the gray of the hotel's quarried stone walls, and a moss lawn swept down to the street like a blanket of velvet. She'd never gone farther inside than the hotel lobby—and only done that once, during high summer, when George took her in just to cool off in the Rest's fine deep-rock chill. It gave her the creeps, made her feel like she'd crawled inside a cave. But where most other places in town were wont to sink into the pits that cooled them, the Rest stood safe.

Bucolic Jordan had designed and built the fancy retreat to sell the govies excitement. So after picking the solidest point of rock in town, he had run pipes into the hill and then vented the pipes into the hotel's high and dry basement. Sal had thought of trying the trick at Morrie's. But she wasn't much for drilling rock, and the whole shack was like to disappear into a sink if she did. Smiling, she climbed past Vos's up to the depot.

Solarstrip lights glowed inside the shipping office at the head of the docks, and more tech lights shone from the communications office higher on the hill. Next to the CommO, as the govies called it, sat the assay office and guard box that held the government jail and barracks.

Not a guard showed his face this morning, and the flight pad and skid hangars above and behind the depot buildings' storage and service yards were quieter than a grave. Govies didn't like the rain much; it ruined their flight days. Sal only hoped it ruined this one good—any more freight arriving would overload her sleds. And she wasn't in the mood for the squawking mess the skids caused on landing.

Every flying thing—roaks, sheerwings, nightbabies, buzzards, and the rest, bird, animal, and bug, large and small—declared war everytime they spotted a skid. They mobbed the machines, fouled the airflows, knocked the tech fliers off course, and made life in town miserable—people kept glancing up for fear of dead birds or dead govies falling on their heads. That was why depots always sat on freestanding hilltops, so the skids could sail in high enough above the low jungle to avoid attack, then pop up quick to a landing on the hill, maybe before any critters up top spotted them. At that, flight days were kept to only two per month, limiting damage and wear on nerves.

Sal turned her face to the rain, and a cool clean trickle down her neck made it under her shirt and between her breasts. What could be finer than nature's own way? She might make her living hauling freight for the govies, but she didn't have to like them or their dirty tech.

The docks stood as empty as the guard's porch; all the govies were inside, dry and comfortable. She stumped onto the main landing and surveyed the contract boards outside the shipping office. Side runs from a regular route could make a trip more profitable. But she only checked now to see where everyone else was running—she had no room for extra freight this trip.

Standing at the edge of the wooden platform, she kicked mud out of her soles, swatted rain flies, and slowly deciphered the posted route names and contracted packers.

"Sal'ai."

Boots thumped the board steps behind her, and Mooli Toon, a longtime packer on the south and west jungle trails, nodded. Like Sal, Mooli and her daughter, Nike, kept the private mail and light goods moving through the jungle. Government fliers hauled heavy equipment and govie supplies, but everything else delivered in the jungle had to be broken down small enough and light enough to ride human-powered sleds. A few tech-driven heavy haulers worked the main roads, but they ran no farther into the green than Tumble Town.

"Goin' ooute soon, I hear." Mooli lumbered to a stop.

"Soon's I have working muscle." Sal pitched her voice to show she had time to talk. News from Mooli was worth hearing.

"Ya b'fare de trails. Strange lots folks south trail. Lots o' mistwalkers afoot."

Mooli pronounced *south* as "soothe," *foot* as "fote," and her thick jungle tongue challenged Sal's ears even after all these years hauling into the deep green. For Sal, one advantage of being raised in town was that she at least spoke the same dialect as the govie contractors. Nike had to do the dealing for Mooli.

"Goin' up the Pike." Sal caught herself falling into deep jungle drawl. "Into Noca Tana. Don't much see strangers that deep of the green."

"Naia." Mooli shook her head. "Ya b'fare, still. Us run up a body Mafeezie's Junk-choor."

A dead body at the junction was no unusual news; that area was about the limit of most city people's endurance.

"Newbie?" A thing like this was best discussed straight out. But Sal shivered, remembering Raschad.

"Naia. City rat. Me guess mistwalkers done 'em."

"City folk comin' out farther every year."

"M'are t'is yar," Mooli said.

More this year, for certain. Nodding, Sal knocked her heels on the edge of the dock again. Mafeezie's Junction sat nearly all the way to the River Trail, and even city livers might reach Tumble Town if they got that far. Then what would this place become? Times were, she found the Plateau and some unnamed deep green hollow real attractive. If she had to, she could live off gathering and fishing. But packing was in her blood, and it kept her around this stinking depot.

She glanced uphill. Above the low-slung roof of the CommO, Government House's white tile roof shone among towering burntwoods and soggy lorri trees.

"Da Sup'visor sit rael feen o' der, don'e."

The Supervisor sits real fine up there, don't he.

"That he does." Sal nodded. "Spouting the Governor's politics don't hurt your advancement even if you're tech-poisoned dumb. Tikey O'hoorahan says when every Supervisor is a member of the Liberalizers, Old Wally can strangle us all until we vote in his Liberalization Act."

"M'die fairst."

Mooli had voted First Settler all her life, the same as her Toon ancestors. So had Sal. Greenies believed heart and soul in the Terms of Settlement, or they wouldn't be in the green. The silence stretched, politics too uncomfortable a topic for long conversation, and Sal stared across the street at the Slackets' Garage pasted to the edge of the cliff face.

The building's outlines showed vague in the sheeting rain, and with its little ditches—part of the constant war between the elements and the Slackets—running full, its footings stood hidden by muddy water. Why the twins insisted on maintaining their bird's perch where others wouldn't stand, let alone build, they had never quite explained. The location did give them good money, being this near the depot. But what gave them peace of mind, living behind the garage and facing that long, long drop to the Yava Valley floor, who could guess. They said they liked to watch the farmers working guano into their fields come a clear day. But the nearest wheat farm was fifty sectors west of here.

"I 'ear ya 'ired on dat newbie tramp what was fittin' atta sha'wrs." Mooli knocked her boot heels against the dock's edge, sending mud flying and vibrations rivering up Sal's legs.

She glanced at the big woman. Did Mooli sound uncommonly interested? Hard to tell through her drawl.

"Maybe." She wanted to say more. But no sense making it harder for Raschad by telling folks he might not make it onto his feet in time to leave. Mooli waited silently. "I ain't dealt with newbies before. He might not haul."

"Aia."

Most greenies only hired newbies to work the bastards to death or scam them broke. Sal couldn't conscience that.

"I'zs talkin' ta Chofl Norris las' ni'." Mooli knocked her other heel. " 'E say da boy na' bad. Say boy works, learnin'."

High praise from Norris. But why were Mooli and Norris discussing the tramp? "Morrie said as he'd heard the man worked, or I'd not have spoke with him at all." She scraped her boot toe along the platform edge, scaling gunk from between sole and toe.

"Um." Mooli rubbed a hand through her thatch of gray-streaked, kinky hair. "Me 'ired 'im onced."

Mooli hired a newbie?

"Short time," the big woman added. "Runup o'im ooute of Liikiiki's. Wer starved. Fed'im. Let 'im work off 'elpin' finish ta pack. Doone good, watchet me. Smaert. Tha' ben close a y'ar n'alf. Cain't spek fer 'im personal, but 'e muscle."

Ran up on him out of Liikiiki? That was near as far south as Oofall and right down in a hollow of the Big Sandy River where fever took newbies quick. He worked good, Mooli said, watched her and learned. Well, Raschad had shown sense yesterday at the showers. But a year and a half ago? How long had this newbie been in the jungle? And what did Mooli mean she couldn't speak for him personally, yet stand and claim he was good muscle? Had the man gone after Nike? Nike after the man?

"Reckon I ain't got a choice—" Sal hunched her shoulders. "—but to take him. I offered before I knew he was newbie. All the same, I offered. If he gets up in time."

Only fair now to tell the woman a bit in return and maybe get an extra word herself. Mooli shrugged meaty shoulders.

"I'zs wonderin' 'ow 'e doin' afta dat mud bout. But'e ben'ere long 'nuf, eemagin'e gettin tug, naia sa papery."

Meaning, he was tough and might even survive to get out of the jungle. *Paper people* were throwaways, free to be used up. Out here, all newbies were paper. Mooli meant Raschad was useful. Which meant he hadn't gone after Nike.

"Etting time." Mooli lumbered off the dock.

And Sal watched the big packer plow downhill. What had their conversation been about? Trail news you could expect from Mooli. But discussing mudpots and tree falls was different from telling other people's business. Mooli didn't gossip. So what had set her talking about Raschad? Shouldn't have mentioned Governor Wally and his tricks. That always brought newbies to mind.

Sal dropped off the side of the dock and splashed toward Vos's. Maybe when the mud settled, things would come clear.

Vos's interior hung thick with shadow, little light making it through its two wall-sized front windows on a morning like this. In the gloom, plank shelves circled the walls, filled with a mixture of goods. Three containers of tech-labeled jams stood beside a pyramid of jars of locally stewed, tender young reeki pod preserves; toddberry jelly; nipple jam; and the like. Waterproof bags of fine blue imported azuli wheat flour sat beside sacks of reeki meal, and jars of salted ear beans and frae fern shoots butted against replacement parts for burner tips.

Yardage filled a front corner; climbing rope and cheap reeki cordage hung from the rafters. And on the floor, barrels of scarlet pog beans, tiny white wing peas, heavy grained golden rice—from the lowland ponds below Liikiiki—whole brown reeki peas, hard as gravel, and ground reeki grits shared space with barrels of pickled roots, sacks of dried scrub pods, and bundles of syrup cane.

Lean and wiry, hair slicked down like a govie's, Earl, Jr., was working the counter today, half hidden in shadows in spite of a handlight hung above his head. At his back, dip jars of spices— ground bark, dried leaves, pods, whole seeds, powdered seasoning roots, and shaved tubers—rose from floor to ceiling. And jumbled scents and aromas set Sal's stomach rumbling and gnawing.

"Morning, Banks."

"Morning, Earl." What had put the man off? Earl had called her Sal since she was big enough to walk in the place. "Just a measure of rice and pog beans this morning."

Earl barely looked at her, all business. But whatever nagged his hide, he didn't let it hurt trade, just set a weight in one scale bowl and filled the other bowl with rice until the arm balanced out. She watched him work, as fascinated by the scale now as she had been coming in here as a child with Ma.

"Thanks much."

"Be two and half coins."

She'd meant to tack it on her tab, but the way he stood said he wanted cash. Just lucky she carried enough. What *had* set him off?

"Reckon you ain't much on newbies, Earl."

"Be two and half coins."

The slime. After all these years of taking her money, she couldn't believe he'd turn cold just because she short-hired a newbie. She swallowed hard, her face hot, jaw clenched, and paid up with a wince—shouldn't have splurged on breakfast yesterday.

But mad as she was, she clumped out of Vos's and right down to Mary's anyway. She just needed a friendly face.

"Haia." With the breakfast crowd lighter this morning, Mary came out to chat.

"Haia, Mary. You have any cheap bread?"

"For you?" Mary smiled, red cheeks glowing. "Always." She waddled to the end of the counter—she was getting softer these days than her baking. "Good thing you come before it got too gray."

Sal hoped Mary was teasing. Mary was. The two bluish loaves of yesterday's bread that she brought looked fine.

"Mary."

"Aehh." The woman laughed, even her squeals soft. "You must be hungry if you can't take teasing." Sal cringed. "That man must be eating you out of the shack."

Couldn't hide a breath from this town. "You know tramps and newbies never get enough food on their own." Sal shrugged as if hosting newbie company was common trade. "A newbie tramp is pit'ful."

"Aia, I know." Mary laughed. "Now an' again one even touches my heart."

Mary rolled her eyes, and Sal's face heated. They touched more than Mary's heart. But though Sal didn't hold with whoring, she supposed there were worse ways to earn a meal than pleasuring Mary's motherly body.

"You should let one touch yours, aia, Sal."

"Damn, Mary." She tugged the bread out of the woman's hands.

"Coom'on. Do you good, from what I hear of him, though I don't know certain, him not having touched my heart . . . yet."

"Mary!" Sal tossed a coin on the counter, ears burning, and left. Mary's laughter followed her out the door.

The whole town must be giggling about Raschad sleeping in her shack. But what did they think could happen with Morrie underfoot, even if she was inclined? Which they knew better than to think, with a newbie. Her morals didn't run that loose. She'd hired him to pack, for gigi's sake.

Damn Mary. Sal knew the woman had been flat relieved when, not even seventeen, she had taken up with George for a time. But when that didn't resolve itself into anything permanent, Mary pushed other men her way. So far she'd fended them off, but

Mary never quit. What had the woman heard about Raschad? All Sal needed was *friends* pushing him at her.

She peeked in her sack at the bread. It smelled good enough to eat right there. But buying ready-made baking was extravagant enough without hogging it for herself. And she wasn't baking in this muck and heat. Morrie might cook up some reeki pan bread, but he worked on his own schedule. So she had to feed the newbie something or he'd never get out of the shack. And remembering the way he ate during the night, she wished she'd bought more rice. But she wouldn't head back to Vos's on her soul. Earl, Jr., could be narrow-minded as a whip.

She skidded and skated through the mud. With the rain stopped, the sun popped out and set everything steaming. Sweet wood smoke drifted around her, smelling of roasting galls and other jungle treats. Her stomach rumbled again, and before her brain could stop them, her feet headed for Ernesto Chi's smokeshop.

Ernesto's smelled like paradise. Morels and doeheads, stump midgets and log warts, hung cured and smoked from the shop's rafters. Wrapped sausages, cheese, and meal cakes lined the shelves. And a big glass-fronted chillcase filled the back of the shop, packed with pricey tree galls and imported meats.

Short and swarthy, his black mustache just showing gray beneath a prominent nose, Ernesto was weighing out a bright red bov steak for Winter Appenheimer. Winter owned the Pannier's building, lawyered out of an office above the store, and could afford such delicacies. But the sight half turned Sal's stomach and made passing up wrapped rashers of sliced purple klimie easier.

She did love klimie. But she wasn't rich or a govie, and outside of fish—which studiers claimed weren't natural to Ver Day anyways—she didn't hold with killing creatures just for the pleasure of their taste. The green provided food aplenty without poaching and slaughtering. Greenies generally followed that inclination, and the Terms included an injunction that limited the taking of wild game to the monsoon season—when no one could get out to hunt anyway. Besides, wild meat made you sick more often than not. But Heaven's Rest bought whole sides of farm meat from Ernesto for its hightown visitors.

Winter nodded to her as he paid and headed out. She nodded back, wondering if the man's eating habits or her own memories made her most uneasy with the lawyer. George and Mary had taken her to Winter after Pa's death, and the educated man filled out papers changing Ma's property to her name. Every time she'd signed a document, concentrating on the curves and the straights

harder than she ever had before in her life, she'd felt herself another stroke alone.

"Sally-aia." Ernesto smiled, nearly hidden behind jars of brui
gall jerky. "I've fine hard morel cheap today." He drew a sausage
roll from under the wood counter he used for wrapping purchases.

"I've five coins to spend, Ernesto. That's it."

"We get you a bit." He peeled the hard sausage and sliced off
a chunk. "That be a fightin' newbie you hired, I hear."

"For a newbie."

She slapped her coins on the counter and Ernesto made change,
lips skewed sideways as if afraid to say more, his eyes laughing
at her. Jungle rot, didn't people have better things to worry over
than some newbie?

By the time she hit Bwashwavie's for beeshu nuts and mi
fruit—about the only fruit not rotted this time of year—and made
it back to the shack, she was hot, mud-slimy, broke, and mean-
hearted. Every eye in town had followed her all morning,
everyone smirking behind her back.

She stomped onto the porch, shook herself off, took one step—
and a damned board broke with a *crack*. Her leg dropped through
half to the knee. She lurched sideways and down, arms too full to
windmill, and only her boot top and a miracle—at last—saved her
from breaking bones or shredding her shin.

"*Shriking hell.*" She yanked her leg free—madder than a bomb
beetle in a crock—staggered off-balance, and slammed against the
door, knocking it inward with the load in her arms.

The shack shook. An arm-stunning thud blocked the door's inward arc. And a yelp froze her. The door bounced back, hit the
rice, and tore the bag.

Sal just stood there, her eyes trailing rice grains down to a
shirtless Raschad on the floor. A large white welt marked where
the door latch had caught him square in the back, and the man
sucked air as if dying.

Ain't even noon yet, she thought, a twinge stabbing behind her
right eye.

"Squat, Sal." Morrie exploded across the room, shirt aflap like
tattered wings, and knelt beside the newbie. "You got the manners
of a gigi."

"I only opened the damn door."

"Like you was comin' to kill."

"Shrike. He don't belong in front of the door."

Raschad made feeble rising motions. "I'm fi—"

"Qui-et. I'm trying to learn her manners." Morrie turned on Sal. "Ain't nowheres else for anything his size in a hole like this."

"I'm—"

"Hiissh!"

"Morrie!" She dropped the bread and morel to save the rice. "Let him talk."

"Put that junk down an' help me."

"I'm fi—"

"Shat up and catch your breath."

"Mor-r-rie."

The newbie sucked air. She dumped the rice in the slop bucket on the counter—a safe enough spot for it, there not being food enough lately to *have* slop—and reached to help.

"Here." She stooped, slipped an arm about Raschad, and gripped a belt loop. At least he had his pants on this morning.

"Up now, son." Morrie caught him from the other side.

They steadied him to a log round, and Morrie sidled away, leaving her imitating a chair back again, bracing Raschad, her face heating. Couldn't he at least stink?

"I'm . . . fine," he panted, face just blank enough that she knew he hurt.

"Sorry."

"H-Heard you." He shivered. "My fault." His bare chest rose and slowly fell. "Should have moved."

"You got that right." Morrie tossed a blanket, and *she* had to wrap it around Raschad. "If'n you hears her coming and don't move, you got slow re-flex-es and less sense."

"I've been told that now and then."

Morrie snorted. "I bet you have, in this jungle."

Raschad laughed, the last thing Sal expected, and the sound carried warm and rich in the bleak little shack.

"You manages for a newbie, I guess." Morrie shook his head and pawed through the groceries.

Steadier now, Raschad sat forward. Freed, Sal moved around the table and found that most of the spilled rice had caught in a pile on the coarse reeki-weave sack Morrie used to stuff the crack under the door. With a little rinsing, they wouldn't have lost too much dinner through knotholes and gaps in the floor.

Just a fine morning. Newbies always brought bad luck. But when she glanced up and caught Raschad's sky-pretty eyes on her, it was harder to think that.

"Sorry." His voice rasped low.

She made a sour face. "My fault, busting the door in."

"Aia, it is." Morrie grumped. "I'll get a pot."

"May I help?"

May I. She cringed at Raschad's proper off-planeter accent, more perfect than the govies spoke.

"Don't fret about it." Morrie tossed a cooking pot at Sal. "Just ease those ribs. Best check his shoulder, gal."

She glared at Morrie from floor level, but he grabbed the morel slab and started slicing.

Shrike. Dumping salvaged rice into Morrie's pot, she carried it to the table, bugs, dried mud, and all.

"You sort this mess, and I'll look at your back."

Raschad nodded, nervous, as if he were at fault here. Which made her feel the fool again. She could imagine what he thought of the way she and Morrie carried on. Well, she was what she was—which at least wasn't newbie.

But as she moved behind him and he slid the blanket off his shoulders, head down, shy as a kid, keeping himself partly covered and paying a lot of attention to the rice, his manners shamed her for thinking ill. He tried to please. And the finger-length splinter sticking from between his shoulder blade and his spine embarrassed her. Idiot. Index finger crooked, she lifted bloody curls aside and squelched a shiver.

"Have to dig a bit."

"Aia." He kept sorting, tossed a rusty rail on the table.

"Shrike, Morrie. You could sweep once in a while." She glared at the old man.

"Piss on it." But Morrie's return glare wavered as she drew her belt knife. "My cleanin' ain't that bad."

She stuck the knife in the open side of the mud stove, shoving its blade into coals—instead of in Morrie's hide. Morrie snorted as if he'd known all along what she was about.

"Reckon you ain't got any such thing as a clean towel."

The old man dug under the counter, tugged a strip of white sheeting from a sack, and threw it at her.

"I got anything I want, if I want it bad enough."

She ignored Morrie's sass, retrieved her knife, turned to Raschad's back—and all that pale, pack-galled skin stopped her. She'd touched men before—Sonny, George personally, Morrie in extreme need—but naia a newbie before yesterday.

She chewed her lip. "You ready?" He nodded. "Will hurt."

"I'm fine."

"Aia." She hesitated again.

Might catch a blight from fresh blood. No telling what human subspecies he was, what planet of origin he claimed or the diseases he'd suffered. Truth, though, with him cleared by immigration, she was safer from him than he from her.

She caught Morrie watching them. Damn cuss could have done this. Biting harder on her lip, she brushed Raschad's silky hair out of the way and slit the skin over the top of the splinter.

Blood welled and ran, its iron scent filling her sinuses. Memory welled with the blood, and she swallowed hard, steadied, and fought down the shakes.

The newbie sat stone still, and she dug her blade under the wood and lifted.

"Shrike." She flipped the splinter at the stove. "Tip broke off."

Raschad didn't budge, didn't protest. She held her breath and put the knife to him again, glad at least that she hadn't tried to pull the splinter. But now blood hid the wood. The newbie's hands clenched and his breath caught. She'd make more noise than that over a blister. A lucky dig flipped out what she hoped was the last hunk of wood.

"Morrie, got that stuff Dancer used yesterday?"

"Aia."

The old man wasn't amused anymore. Rotten wood, like mud, was no light matter for anyone in the jungle, all too nice a breeding ground for every invisible beastie.

Sal bled the cut clean, conscious all the time of hard muscle close beneath the newbie's skin and the fine curve of his arched neck. Morrie donated a hidden jar of mash-brewed liquor. She rinsed the tear with it, and the bleeding quit completely when she applied Dancer's salve. Bandaging the cut, she caught Morrie watching her again. What a matchmaker.

"You got an extra shirt, Raschad?" She wiped her hands on a rag. "Your yesterday's isn't dry yet."

"Aia. I'll get—"

"I'll get it." She held him down.

"Just grab my pack."

Her concern made him visibly nervous, and when she passed his pack to him, he took it so fast their hands brushed. His touch was cool and electric all at once.

Without meaning to, she found herself staring into his eyes. And the damn man blushed. She looked away. He dug out the shirt. She helped him into it. The only one who didn't seem relieved when he was dressed was Morrie—dirty-minded drunk.

The day settled down then. At noon they ate rice spiced with nuts and wild greens, which Morrie'd foraged, and morel gravy sopped up with bread. It tasted good, and with a word or two of encouragement, Raschad emptied every pot.

"Gal." Morrie stared at her, but nodded at Raschad. "You best get this one in the jungle. Teach him how to dig."

She laughed, and Raschad looked uncomfortable—which was fine. It shouldn't always be her feeling in the wrong.

"Washing up'll be easy." Morrie gathered empty dishes.

"I'll help," she offered.

"Naia, be fine." Morrie batted ragged eyelashes at her, arched bristling eyebrows, and winked.

"I'll help." Raschad knew what the old wart was implying.

"Naia. You rest."

Morrie scooped crockery off the table, clattered dishes into the wash bucket on the counter, and added water—heated by the last of the cooking fire—from the pot on the stove. Scratching the gnat bites around his wrists, Raschad glanced at her.

"I want to thank you." He shrugged.

"Forget it. We already talked about this. You rest and get ready to work it off."

His scratching switched to his shoulder, his eyes still on her, his expression unreadable beneath his purpling bruises and swollen eyes. "I pay my debts."

"Fine. You want the cot or the hammock?"

"Which has the fewest bugs?" He scratched his chest.

"Take the cot." She shook her head. "Morrie's stink runs off everything."

"I heard that," Morrie grumbled.

"Big deal, old man." Sal levered off her stump round and headed for the porch. "Maybe I'll hunt up some wood for that hole in the porch after my nap."

"Promises."

She shut the door on the rest of Morrie's comments. But the old man knew her. Faced with the hole in the porch, two in the roof, and several in the hammock, she didn't fancy either carpentry or napping. Even Boojie's looked a better choice. So she stumped off the porch and slogged across the street.

Inside, three dockers and a couple of gatherers sucked on mugs and listened to Marta Woozniack promote her fiddlehead beer. Marta's brewery sat uphill behind the Gigi's Eye, the biggest greenie bar in town, right up against the cliff below the depot. Her chilling cellars, dug back into a big cavern, were the finest in town next to the Rest's, and she could deliver to the local bars without her brew ever heating up again after its final cook. Marta sat swapping drinks and stories with Mike and Tiny Slacket.

Being male and female, the twins weren't identical, but telling them apart when fully clothed—in grimy matching bib overalls—was a test of observation. Tiny's upper torso bulked out just as big and flabby as his sister's, while Mike carried her weight waist up and thigh down, with hips as hard and narrow as her brother's. They had identical haircuts, too—thin strands slicked to their scalps, white half-moons over their ears every six months—and dirty mechanics caps crammed on top.

Sal didn't like tech, but she enjoyed Mike and Tiny, and they'd grown up together, her the younger by maybe four years. Great talkers they weren't, but they made a fine audience, which pleased Marta just now.

"Haia, Sal."

"Marta. Hear you're gettin' rich off Capitol trade." Sal glanced down at Marta's scuffed boots and up past shiny pants knees and the brewer's worn shirt. As much business as Marta turned without ever spending an unnecessary credit, how wealthy was this woman?

"Money don't buy me happiness." Marta's broad smile was toothy and warm. "I'm workin' too hard." She ran a hand through short hair, and Sal noted a first touch of gray. "Them tech lovers suck more brew every day. And First Settlers think it's their duty to drink greenie product. Jimmy, a brew for Sal."

"It's a mercy, gal," Sal said. And it was more generous than Marta's norm. Marta smiled again, and Sal knew she'd made a mistake, put herself in debt to conversation.

"Heard you had a guest."

"Boarder, more like it." Sal kept her voice casual, hoping Marta would let things drop.

"Heard he's workin' for you."

"Soon as I can put him to work."

Marta's mouth twisted and her eyes danced. *What now?*

"Aia. I heard he earns his money." Smiling, Marta turned back to Mike and Tiny as if Sal had left the room.

She stared at Marta's sloping shoulders and wanted to throttle the woman. What did Marta mean? What did Mooli and Mary and everyone in town have to say about this newbie that they never quite said?

Chapter 4

Sal hid in Boojie's half the afternoon, too mad for hunting muscle—would find none anyway. After leaving, she patched Morrie's porch, then pulled a sled into the scrub, and hauled back stones to brace her woodwork. The shack stood shadowed as she entered. Raschad sat alone, looking out a back window.

"Where's Morrie?" She spoke low in the evening stillness.

"Said he was thirsty."

"Ain't he always. Hungry yet?"

"No. Not accustomed to regular meals."

If two meals in two days was regular, no wonder his ribs rode so near the surface. "I reckon Morrie wouldn't bother inviting you along." Sal tugged off her gloves.

"I'm not much of a drinker."

"Well, he don't frequent the most congenial dumps anyway."

"I received that impression when he said 'newbies don't come out alive.' "

"Didn't have to say that."

"True," Raschad shrugged.

"I'd like to talk about that."

"Being newbie?"

"Aia."

"Sure." His tone carried no enthusiasm.

She propped herself on the table edge anyway. "People will tell you I hate newbies. I already explained it ain't a lie. I hate stupid people, which you are, just for being here. But you claim you're desperate more than stupid." She arched a tired back. "Which means you're even likelier to die quick. But I hear you've haunted the green longer than any newbie I ever heard of before, and I ain't never seen a newbie come tramping in the way you did a day ago." She stared into his bruised eyes. "So maybe you're a miracle. But I doubt it."

"I'm not still here because I decided Ver Day was paradise." He shook his head. In the shadowy light, she couldn't read his expression. "And I'm not a criminal by any local standards." Which meant he was somewhere. "I have . . . family problems." He shifted on his log round, shadows deepening about him. "I've earned enemies here, but only for staying alive." And the longer he survived, the more greenies would hate him. "I won't bring you other problems in the jungle."

"Fair enough." She backed off, her instinct telling her to believe him. "Sorry I pushed, but people talk about you, which they don't bother over most newbies."

If he worried what people said about him, he didn't show it, just gave a slow nod and curled up off the log round, using the window jamb for support. He looked as stiff as the floorboards and took his time straightening to his full height.

"Hope I didn't pop a rib for you with the door."

"I'm fine—just should have moved around more today. Be all right by tomorrow."

"Won't be strong, though, not even by the day after."

"That your schedule?"

His bad manners grated, but she let it go. "Even leaving then leaves things close."

"I'll hurt. But moving will take it out."

"I hope so." Better yet, she hoped he stayed stiff and down. But then who'd pull for her?

He made a "humph" sound and shuffled toward his pack. Retrieving something from it, he slumped onto Morrie's suspended cot, braced his feet, and smeared white cream out of a tech tube onto his face and arms.

"That's strange-looking stuff."

"Insect grease." He spread it over his throat and neck, tucked some down his shirt.

"Sure smells nice." Like a city whore.

"Reeki sap works better. But this doesn't burn in cuts."

She remembered his reeki-stained face in Boojie's that first afternoon. She'd never known a newbie to bother with reeki. Newbies thought anything hard tech was better than handmade or green tech—another reason they didn't survive long.

"I best check that splinter cut."

"Morrie did before he left. Put salve on it."

"Good." Good that she needn't touch him again.

He lay back on the cot. "I think I'll take a nap."

"Do."

She settled at the window where he'd sat, and soon his breathing slowed and went deep. She wondered what besides hunger drove him out of the jungle so fast that he was worn to the bone and gut-deep exhausted. On a thought, she tiptoed across the shack and peeked inside his boots.

Silvery tech cloth lined them, looking as soft and spongy as the mair moss that cushioned her hot spots and kept her feet dry. No wonder his toes weren't rotted off. He was techy all right, just kept things hidden.

She went outside to unload rocks.

The sun set, which made it damn late on top of this hill in the dead of summer. She went inside, staring out the shack's back window again and fussed about Morrie. By now he was dead drunk—or dead. She should look for him—would have looked by now if the newbie weren't still snoring.

She hated to leave the man asleep and alone with every fool in town knowing a newbie lay hurt in this shack. What if someone decided to solve her problems for her? She remembered Earl, Junior's surliness this morning. No local would stoop to murder, but jungle greenies crowded the town just now.

Raschad stirred. She turned. He stilled, not another twitch or sound.

"Raschad?" Shadow hid him. "Just me. Banks. You're in my shack."

"Aia." He sucked a ragged breath. "Remember."

Which she thought was exactly right—he hadn't known where he lay, had needed her to call out to remind him.

"Good. Now take your hand off your tech."

"How did you know?" He asked blunt again.

And again she let it go. Her digging after his history earlier hadn't been much more polite.

"I sleep gun-ready myself." She stood. "Too many years on the trail." Remembering his mention of enemies, she wondered how many years he'd slept with a weapon in hand. "Thought I'd go for a walk 'round. Morrie hasn't come back. You're welcome."

"Will I cause trouble?"

"Not so long as you're with me."

She was an idiot to invite him. But she didn't relish leaving him awake and alone with her every belonging, not with him moving well enough now to just walk away.

"May I turn on a light?"

May I? Had to do something about the way he talked.

"Here." She switched on her handlight, a good one with a solar recharger. George hadn't shirked when he bought it.

The room lit up, and mouse-sized roachers skittered through the floorboards. Raschad gave his bed net a practiced flip, and critters of several varieties flew. Curling over, he studied the floor before lowering his feet and shaking out his socks.

"I hear you've tramped the jungle near two years."

"Three." Liar.

"You didn't start off this deep of the green."

"No. I hired a tramp to guide me into Mafeezie's Run. It seemed the most civilized area of Ver Day outside of Capitol."

"It ain't."

"So I discovered."

"Most newbies stay in the city, work the factories."

"Too many people for me."

"Mafeezie's ain't much better."

"Naia." He dropped into local accents, not patronizing her, she thought, just relaxing. "But I survived. My tramp didn't. I can't decide if his death was my fault or not. He appeared to die of a heart attack, and he predicted the day we met that I would give him one."

"Don't worry on it." She thought he smiled a bit, wasn't sure. "All the old hisses say that around here."

"Aia." He did smile then, wiped sweat from his face.

Night promised to be puddling hot. Sal watched Raschad pull on a boot and worry the bites on his wrist while he laced it. Tumble Town stood so high above most standing water that with the latest insect hatch still in the larval stage, the bugs hardly bothered her up here. The jungle floor must be hell for him.

He stomped into his other boot, kicked the bugs out of his pack, and retrieved his holster. A newbie packing tech into local bars was no good idea, but she couldn't ask him to go unarmed.

She ignored the matter and checked her own multiclip semiautomatic Camm. Add that to her tally, and she indulged in six tech things. Would the First Settlers forgive her that much? Maybe, but dealing with this newbie could wobble the scales.

She found her hat. He tucked his hair up in a tramp bandanna. "I imagine my gear is safe here." He spoke polite for once.

"We'd best stow it." No one'd steal from Morrie. But newbie tech bore strange attraction for some people.

She hefted one end of his heavy pack. He caught the other, and she led him outside to her nearest sled.

"In here." She opened the front sled locker. "I don't want any kid getting ahold of tech he can't handle."

She didn't want this newbie stripped naked, either. Slamming the locker, she worked its latch tumblers until the box sealed tight, a safeguard she never used. So already this newbie caused her to change her ways. Not a good thing.

They skipped Boojie's—the bar wasn't Morrie's favorite—and strode uphill. With both moons bulging near full, the street was lit so bright that shadows showed, and day-feeding birds still swooped after bugs. Raschad moved stiffly, but with a practiced step, managing the mud well enough.

"You walk as if you miss your pack." Sal spoke just so she wasn't strolling silent through the strangeness of the night with a strange, fine-looking man.

"Aia. Don't know how to balance without it, or when I've moved without it." A hint of unease tinged his words.

"Don't worry. No one will break into my locker even if they knew how. First, they'll figure Morrie's already stolen anything worth taking off you. Second, if they stole anything, Morrie'd find out and torch their hides. And if they survived Morrie, they'd never survive me or George. Your stuff is safe."

"I don't know when that's been the case, either."

He sounded tired. Talking strained most tramps, who grew accustomed to living solitary. Sal respected the mood; she fell into it herself after a long haul. But, him being newbie, if he'd really lived on Ver Day for three years, they were years spent alone, always treated mud low.

"Here." She waved at the Pink Garter's door. Squealing pipe music spilled into the night, mixed with cursing and yelling. "I'll just stick my head in and check for Morrie. But usually by now he's way up the street."

Showing good sense again, Raschad slipped into shadow at the corner of the bar's uneven split-log porch and settled into a waiting stance, nearly invisible against the building.

"Just a look," Sal said. She stepped through the Garter's door and gave the taproom a quick scan, half blinded by lamplight. No Morrie. She ducked back out, blinking. "Not here. We'll hit Dig's Den next. But I warn you, the higher we climb, the more the quality of things goes downhill."

His soft snort sounded amused.

Dig's was in full swing, with music louder than the Garter's, its doorway thick with smoke. A knot of bullybys stood in a pool of lantern light that spilled from the bar's windows. Swigging from a shared bottle, they watched the crowd inside and took turns feeling up an escaped bar girl.

"You stick with me this time." Sal spoke to Raschad under her breath. "Dig's is big. Use your eyes and help." She didn't add the obvious, that she daren't leave him outside in the dark alone with the bullies. Circling the bunch, she slogged through mud, hoping no one knew her.

"Haia, Sal. Join the party. Bring ya friend."

Who was it? She blinked into lantern glare and made out the speaker—a big, hairy gork perched on the windowsill. She bit her tongue and kept it civil.

"Not tonight, Frim. Looking for Morrie. You seen him?"

Raschad eased up at her back, hiding behind her—smart again. The bullybys mumbled drunkenly and gave negative nods.

"Thanks anyway." She turned for the door.

At her back, Raschad startled. She shoved on into the light and noise of the bar.

"What?" Her eyes searched the wide, smoky room.

"A very *friendly* bunch."

"Perverts." She half turned back. What made Frim think he could rag anyone, newbie or no, who was with her?

Raschad stopped her—just a touch of his hand, then away. "I've survived worse."

He was right. Folks wouldn't understand her fighting over a newbie. The thought made her gut twist.

"Come on." She steered him up to Dig's freight-crate bar and into an empty spot near the wall beside Jeff Jinkman and Gager Ko. The boys were safe company even for a newbie—so innocent and content in each other's company that just looking at them made Sal smile, and made her hurt a bit, too.

The ku-soo wood wall beside her, once pale and speckled with black grain, was darkened by grime and scarred by smoker burns. Regge Cole stood on a barrel in a back corner of the bar, playing a stringer hard and fast. At his feet, his drummer, his fiddler, and a bottle plinker raced through a wild tune.

"Haia. A mug here, Vic." She waved and plunked down her last coin. "You drink and be still, newbie. I'll be back."

Raschad nodded. Watching for Morrie, Sal eased through the late crowd of drinkers. People liked Jeff and Gager. No one would bother them to get at Raschad. But every other breath, she checked the newbie. He didn't move, just kept his head down in his brew.

"Sally-aia," a high voice pierced the noise and the music.

She spotted a thin arm, waving in the air. Tikey O'hoorahan was the skinniest packer she'd ever known.

"Haia. Gov'nor's favorite hauler looks fit." Sal edged toward Tikey.

"I'm fit and greener than he is." Tikey ran freight clear in to Capitol and back every month.

Sal caught Tikey's callused hand over the heads of her tablemates, Tikey's lads. The crews ran six big power haulers up and down the main trails and passed a lot of freight, but earned Tikey no more credit than Sal made off her pack sleds.

"Thought I seen you come in with a friend." Which was the polite way on Tikey's part to raise the subject without actually saying she was with anyone.

"Taking a man out on a quicky haul. Hard to find muscle this time of year. Don't reckon you have extra for hire."

"Naia. Tight now. Maybe later."

Tikey's voice rose, meaning she had more to say. Not again. Sal felt like asking Tikey straight out about Raschad and to hell with manners. But too many people sat at the table. She just smiled and glanced around for Morrie.

"Sit it down." Tikey kicked a chair.

The man in it stood like a shot, and the other haulers popped up as if all connected. "Time to turn in," one said, and they faded away, leaving her no excuse to ignore Tikey.

"I'm looking for Morrie. Can't sit long." Turning a chair around backward, she squatted, rested her chin on a reeki bow back, and watched Raschad, her patience strained.

"If you're going out, you watch the scrub, gal. Gigis been tearin' things up so bad south of Diz-et-el, people are talking about the year they ran clear to the wheat fields."

"They can't reach the wheat fields across Old Gorge." Regge's stringer twanged, grating Sal's nerves.

"They can if they come east through Tumble Town. You be careful. Jungle's gone squat crazy this summer."

Regge's band thumped and thrummed.

"Aia." At the bar, Raschad glanced her way then back to his brew. "Mooli Toon says there's folks wandering out of Mafeezie's, Aireils stirred up."

"Heard she found a body." Tikey's eyebrows arched. "Not

good, Sally-aia. Gov'ment's pushing too many people into the jungle, people who ain't fit to survive out here."

"But our good Governor Wally Cal Humphreys . . ." People called him Wall-eye. "Dear Wally's going to save us all with liberalization, if we only mind his preaching."

"He can preach all he wants." Tikey snorted. "Greenies ain't so reeki dumb as he thinks. His Liber Act means throwing out the Terms of Settlement, tearing up the jungle, open logging, pit mines." Tikey's jaw worked. "Coming out of Capitol last run, the air flat stunk, was all gray. They're cheatin' on the pollution maximums already. Growing botafab don't dirty the air. So what they making? Cheating on proscribed tech, too, or I'm blind. I run tech, but my haulers are clean. Not Capitol. The skies can't neutralize the factories' dirt these days. Not good. We'll pay soon or late."

"Aia. Too much tech. Too many off-planeters." Sal's stomach soured.

"I was waitin' for you to say that." Tikey glanced at the nearest tables and leaned nearer. "Look." She pitched her voice low, making Sal nervous. "I can't believe you dragging 'round that beautiful newbie. He's not your type, not your way. That be Meesha Raschad. You'll get hurt, disappointed, or both."

Sal helped herself to a half-empty brew off the table. "Don't know what you're on about, gal. I needed muscle. Morrie heard good things about the man. I've heard good things—for a newbie. But everyone says these things with a sort of *except*."

"Then you don't know." Tikey's mouth twitched.

"I *don't*." Losing her temper, Sal glanced at Raschad. He was still safe enough, and Jeff and Gager showed no signs of leaving.

"Shrike." Tikey laughed, and Sal felt like hitting her. "Gigi's ass." Tikey chortled.

Regge's strings squealed, and Sal raised a fist. Tikey swallowed hard, sucking air. Oiled with brew, Jeff and Gager peeked sideways at the newbie, smiling, their expressions curious.

"You see . . ." Tikey took a slurp of brew, choked and snorted, forced the brew down, and then sobered. "Shrike, every woman on the south trail's been after him one time or another. But he don't go for it. So they figure he's typical newbie, afraid of jungle gals. Then Mira Goontz, being what she is, offers pay. And gigis be, he lays her ugly body down and does her happy."

Sal's lips parted. She caught herself and quick closed her mouth. No wonder Mary teased her and people acted as if she was sunpoxed. She'd picked up a flat-out whore.

"O' course," Tikey leaned even nearer, "no one'd much have minded, except it's been noted he visits Gov'ment House ever' time he's in town. Usually he goes right off—until now. So people wonder what you give him to interrupt that trade."

Sal's mouth slipped wide open. The fiddle sawed higher. She caught herself and clamped her teeth, stared at Tikey, debating between killing the heavy hauler or downing Raschad.

"Then there's the matter of his temper." Tikey licked her lips. "Seems he don't take to being walked under by greenies. Some newbies is that way and die quick. But this packer name of Viak Bending, down Oofall way, claims he just tried to borrow some junk crystal off Raschad, and the newbie wouldn't giv'em. So Bending figures he'll take the load—he's greenie, crystals is from the green and don't belong to no newbie.

"But he *can't* take them crystals. Raschad put him down and near killed him. And Bending ain't the only greenie this newbie's stomped. So people don't usually mess with the man, not like those reeki-brained kids tried yesterday."

"And nobody could of told me this sooner." Sal arched up in her chair. A whore and a brawler and maybe worse—shrike, Morrie! I ain't heard of him until yesterday."

Tikey shook her head. "I forgot. You worked north all spring, must of left about the time he first visited town. Before that some say he was west out of Vicksburg. Now he's moved down again, mining a piece way south of town. Shrike, he's a hard-tech newbie mean ornery boy-slut."

Sal emptied her borrowed brew, wiped her mouth, and glared at Tikey, her temples throbbing in time with Regge's drumbeat. "Well, he ain't been healthy enough for me to question his morals even if I was a mind. His temper hasn't killed me yet, either. Reckon Viak Bending should know not to steal."

But it twisted her gut the way he'd played shy in the shack this morning, working her for a fool or worse. Bedding govies? Tikey meant no newbie tramp had any good business visiting up to the Supervisor's private residence. Supervisor Rimmersin?

Government's fault, like every other fool mess. Rimmersin came in, shipped out every govie woman on one pretense or another, left the mist-colored depot men gawking at local dark-hided gals, and so some of the city-bred spooked, deciding the backsides of the clean young city laddies working the docks looked safer. She didn't worry on a person's sexual leanings. Few greenies did care one way or the other. But upset anything's balance, and it twisted where it shouldn't.

Raschad and Mira Goontz? Supervisor Rimmersin? Hard to say which was worse. Mira was coarse, crude, and nasty. But Rimmersin was hateful and slippery, and he ran the depot like he'd rather ruin this town than deal with it. What did that man want? If Jeff and Gager took Raschad home, she wouldn't much notice. But Rimmersin dirtied everything he touched.

Her cheeks burned. The music beat faster and louder. The whole town must figure she was using him. Like Mary, they wouldn't mind so much as wonder where she'd put her brain.

Newbies brought out the worst even in good greenies. Her stomach churned. Folks didn't worry what happened to a newbie who'd just die before it mattered. Women chased Raschad, thinking him easy meat, no strings attached, do as they liked, and he wouldn't tell tales—at least not for long.

Staring at Tikey's razor-sharp, razor-scarred face, Sal thumped her empty mug on the table. This wasn't Tikey's doing. Tikey'd done her a favor to warn her. "I ain't no Liberalizer just because Morrie tricked me into hiring a newbie." Her fists unclenched. "Thanks for telling me straight. But I don't judge what he sells elsewhere, so long as the muscle he sells me is honest." She stood, kicked her chair around, and headed for the bar. Morrie wasn't in here anyway.

"Sal?"

She ignored Tikey and jerked her head at Raschad. As he stood, Gager and Jeff leaned out of his path, and people cleared out of her way. Regge's group shrieked to a halt. The swinging bottom half of the bar door slammed outward, and she plunged into moonlight, not caring if she lost the shriking white newbie. But Raschad followed quick, slogging along in her wake.

Her stomach roiled. Her face burned. She clenched her teeth, too mad to think clear. Send this boy-o back to the shack, and maybe a sherk waiting in the dark with a knife would solve her problem. Let another fool have at him.

But she turned and saw him walking head up, guarding her back. She hadn't told him what was wrong, so he didn't wait dumb for it to happen; he did everything right again—damn him—wary and smart, the kind of partner she needed on a haul. Which, she supposed, was how a newbie survived three years in the green, the yellow-pissin' pervert.

She spun about again and stomped through the mud. Up and down the street, lights glared. At her back, Regge's group blared out another song. Ahead, a squeeze organ squealed, music tumbling from saloon doors, jangling and clanging. And in the scrub, the nightly insect chorus shrilled.

Her heart thumped. Her throat ached. Shrike . . . Mud squished. She heard him slip and grunt. Breathing deep, she remembered he was stiff and sore—which served him right. She slowed down.

"Newbie." She spoke quiet, but clear. He caught up at her elbow. "You told me you haven't any special enemies, no problems to bring down on me. You still saying that?" Rude and ruder.

He stopped. She took another step. A breeze kicked up, tugged at her hair and set the trees soughing. She stopped. Bugs whined. Nightbabies wailed from the cliff face around the side of the hill, out of their roost caves on their first feeding flight. The mud made little sucking noises beneath her.

"I've been mining." He cleared his throat. "I'll cash out my take tomorrow. Pay you outright for the food, the bed, the medicine. Whatever it is you've been told, I didn't know it would be a problem. I'll clear out of the shack before you return with Morrie." The same offer he'd made yesterday morning with his arms wrapped around battered ribs—no argument.

She didn't know why it surprised her, except that he'd surprised her all day. His feet squelched in the mud as he walked away. She made herself turn around.

"You got no place to go tonight," she called after him. "And I ain't said there *is* a problem." Why'd she say that? He stopped, and she waited. He turned. "Maybe we ain't clear what you been hired for."

He stood tall, tense, balanced between coming back to her and walking away again.

"I pack." His voice carried low and emotionless. "If you want more than that, spell it out. I owe you. I'll do my best to repay. But I'm best at packing, and I have enough to survive on for now without selling more than muscle."

He spoke plain and greenie polite this time, where most newbies put names to every fault and forced words to be said that didn't have to be said, didn't have to lead to killing. Except for his skin and his proper accent, Sal could think him jungle born. He meant, if she understood newbie minds at all, that if he was starving, he'd earn his keep however need be. But he wasn't starving just now. Few folks in Tumble Town claimed any better morals. And it explained his doings with Mira Goontz.

"I been told you've missed a regular appointment up at the Government House."

"Tomorrow." Tension drained from his voice. "I have to collect my communications authorization. The Supervisor is my mail drop."

Mail drop? A smile startled onto Sal's face. You're a nasty-minded old gal, Tikey. Either he was the best actor she'd ever met, or he didn't know what she'd been implying.

"You sure company with fancy people."

"My grandfather does. He made the arrangements with Supervisor Rimmersin so I didn't fall too far out of sight."

Why did a man with family rich enough for interplanetary communications end up stuck on Ver Day? She'd be bog dead before she asked.

"Well then . . ." She turned uphill again, toward the rest of the night spots. "My apologies. But you understand I ain't known you but a day, and greenies take care of their own. Unless you come up with a worse problem than just being newbie—which ought to be enough to do you—I can't see that anything's changed in our contract." Conscience said she did the right thing. Common sense called her a fool.

She heard him following at her back, and her gut twisted.

Chapter 5

The window of the Gigi's Eye sported a yellow, slit-pupiled green-rimmed eye, dripping scarlet tears. On the bar's double front doors—thrown open now to the night—painted gigis snarled at all passers. Bony-bodied, green-furred, long-armed, short-legged, their razor-fine teeth bared, the frozen beasts prickled Sal's spine. She glanced at Raschad.

Music and stench breathed through the bar's doorway like a blasphemy to creation, but the newbie didn't turn tail. So she braved the Gigi's crowd, waded between barrel tables, one eye to Raschad at her elbow, the other searching for Morrie.

Through smoke and watery eyes she spotted him playing jinx at a table in the back of the bar. Morrie saved for these evenings as if he claimed religion. No matter that he starved later, he'd find credits to purchase an untidy glow and drag about gambling with his chums. The players tonight included Doonie Effords, Grandpa Jinkman, little Milly Chi—Ernesto's mother—Tommy Bwash-wavie, a local bullyby, and a woman wearing a packer's padded jungle-green shirt.

"Haia, Sal." A low-down bass cut through the din. She tensed. What else did someone have to say about Raschad?

But it was only Tom Bill, leaning against the bar, his graying hair thin, long, and raggedy, his grin lazy. "Haia, Mayor."

Tom'd been elected town leader eight years straight, running First Settler—which was the only political platform in Tumble Town anyway, since the govies couldn't vote local. Sal tugged Raschad to the bar, grateful to find a friendly face.

"You're late." Tom nodded toward the rowdy players at Morrie's table.

"I know. Been gabbing too much."

"Well, he ain't been no unusual trouble."

She grimaced. Tom shrugged, and his eyes followed Raschad as
the newbie hunkered at her back, elbows on the bar, trying, she
thought, to be inconspicuous. He might as well try being a sow
beetle. Tom's eyes glittered. He twirled a toothpick with his
tongue. Sal had no enthusiasm for this introduction.

"Raschad." She stepped back so the two men could see each
other. "This is Mayor Tom Bill, the best burner and town boss
around. Runs private burn crews."

"Ahh." Tom grinned. "You'll get my head swelled."

"Let it swell. We'd be living in the shadows if you didn't keep
the jungle back."

"Mas Raschad, pleased to meet you." Tom Bill *sounded*
pleased, which again did her nerves no good.

"Evening." Raschad spoke around her, and Tom Bill's smile
broadened at the newbie's too proper accent.

"Evenin' ta ya, fer sure." Tom winked at Sal, his tongue turning greenie thick. "Wouldn't encourage ya ta let 'im talk ta much
n'ere." He laughed.

Raschad's eyes snapped to the bar top, and Sal glanced around,
checking how many others had noticed she towed a newbie. Most
people were watching Morrie's table, where the bets were running
big and loud—the bullyby and the packer were at odds. She relaxed a bit. The mistake here was hers. She shouldn't have introduced the newbie so friendly to Tom, so Raschad thought himself
safe. She'd best get Morrie and get out. But the card game was
in the middle of a big deal.

"Don't know the packer." She nodded to Morrie's table. "She
looks a bit familiar."

"A load-by-load, says she's out of Oofall," Tom answered.

The packer glanced up. Her gaze slid over Sal, hesitated, then
snapped back to her cards. Of a sudden, Sal placed her. The woman'd been lechering Raschad after the shower brawl.

"You're the one was fighting yesterday," Tom Bill said, dis-
tracting her from the packer. Raschad nodded. "You looks pretty
good considering the board the hiss laid into you with."

"Thanks." Raschad spoke low, mimicking greenie this time.

She'd missed the board. No wonder the newbie ached. Tom
smiled, eyes dancing, mouth knowing. What did *he* suspect of
her?

"Reckon those are sore ribs." Tom let up on the accent, but
kept digging. Raschad nodded. Sal stared at Tom. "Go on, Sal."
His lips twitched. "I'll keep him safe. You get Morrie. Man can
fight like him is fine by me, no matter what people say."

Raschad's eyes darted to Tom's face and away. Sal's teeth gritted. Not even friends could leave it be.

She nudged Raschad's elbow. He'd be safe with Tom. He nodded and glanced from Tom to the painting hung high on the wall behind the bar. Gigis filled the canvas, mouths bloody, claws bared. Tom's eyes followed the newbie's gaze.

"That's of the ganger of '487, hit the end of summer after a real poor fruit year." Tom studied the painting. "Tumble Town was only two bars, Vos's Grocery, and some shacks back then. They tell that three gigi gangs poured into the roak grove south of town, rutting and rowdy. Then four more kited in from east, and the whole bunch stormed through here headed for the late fruit up north. Earl Senior's pa, Calvin, saved his family by barricading them in what's now the brewery cave. Choo-choo Bwashwavie's clan hid in Boojie's blow hole. Two govies survived inside a grounded skid. But forty-six people died that day, and not one building—govie or greenie—stood afterward."

Sal hated that picture. Rock and blood . . .

Leaving them, she wove through the crowd toward Morrie's table. "Excuse." She started to squeeze past two big boys.

"Haia, Banks." The back bully turned.

"Frim. You sure get around—"

"*Squat!*" A screaming roar cut her off. "You sliming gigi crud." The bullyby reared up at Morrie's table.

"And ter ya mather, too."

Shrike, Morrie. A chair rose above the bully's head. Frim's boys surged forward. Wood splintered.

A shriek pierced her eardrums. Drinks flew. Fists flashed, and a bar girl fled screeching. Morrie vanished.

The old man would be killed on the floor.

Sal lunged past Frim and slammed a fist in the gut of a fat docker who had turned on her just for being there. Slipping a roundhouse, she butted a scrawny kid, grabbed his arm, and tossed him into the woman's face.

That put her at the poker table. No Morrie. No table, just a pile of splinters. Chairs flew; bottles crashed. Screams drowned the music. Breaking glass jangled.

She dodged two drunken gatherers, staggered into a hissy little barmaid, all nails and lace, and threw the gal at the door.

Bamm! The room burst into glittering blur. Colored light squiggled her vision. Pain tore her temple.

Boom! The floor exploded into splinters. She froze, head pounding, deaf-dumb and surrounded by shocked silence.

Through the ringing of her ears, she heard, "Don't!" And the tone of Tom Bill's voice would've stopped a bull gigi.

Feet braced wide, she blinked her vision clear enough to see a big black double muzzle pointed right at her—and everyone beyond her. Behind the drunken digger holding the scattershot, Tom Bill stood with his tech drawn, one hand preventing Raschad from pulling his weapon in this greenie bar.

Her head pounded. Her eye stung. Something warm dribbled off her chin. She blinked, stared at black double O's . . . until she saw nothing at all but black.

"Sh-ut uh-p, Mo-rr-ie." The words drawled out long and slow in fuzzy red and black.

Head thumping, everything spinning from the inside out, she tried to fight her way clear. What now? Her neck didn't work. Her eyes wouldn't open. A creepy panic prowled the back of her mind, and for a long breath she couldn't think past the pain.

"Don't!" She remembered a double muzzle, Tom Bill and Raschad—the stupid damn newbie. "Naia!"

"Easy," a voice boomed in her ear.

She flinched back, sucking air and a too familiar scent—sweet, tech bug grease. Ah, gigis, Raschad was carrying her like a babe, her head against his shoulder.

Wouldn't the town talk now. She moaned.

"Taking you home." His breath puffed against her ear. "Morrie, too. Everything is all right."

Nothing was all right. She forced her head up far enough to blink one eye clear—a mistake. Morrie's whiskered chops loomed over her, and his stench sent her stomach skittering.

"Ya giv'er me, Raschad. Ya yellow-pissin' newbie."

She swallowed hard, scared she'd lose her dinner, and her head couldn't stand the pressure.

"Get on. Drunk old man." Tom Bill sounded out of sorts.

"Cain't talk'a me—" Sal flung a hand sideways and caught the old man's nose. "Squat." Morrie spit stink. "Jest die, then." And she might have, but saved herself from Morrie's brew-rotted breath by pressing her face against Raschad's chest.

"Get." Tom still sounded cranky.

Morrie yelped; mud squished. She managed a blurred glimpse of Tom Bill wrestling Morrie down the street. Then Raschad slipped. Pain hammered her skull like a gigi pounding it.

"Have . . . to rest," Raschad grunted, and something firm came up under her buttocks.

"Goin' ta bust yerself." The words slurred, but she got them in the right order.

"Ahh." Breath ruffled her hair. "Have you home soon."

"I's fine."

"Aia, sure." His arms cradled her. His breath puffed hot.

"Yer o'erheating m'head."

"You are making my gut hurt."

"Sa le'me walk."

"Couldn't pick you up again if you fell."

"Offered." The world slid away.

"She'll be fine. Got a hard, hard head this one."

Shrike, aia, she thought into darkness. Got me a real hard head. Funny how one side of it felt squishy, though.

"Keep her down as much as you can tomorrow and don't be carrying her again." Dancer spoke clipped and exasperated. "I should wrap them ribs."

Raschad's answer came so low Sal couldn't hear it above a background steam-saw roar.

"It'll keep the bugs from biting you." Dancer's tone coaxed. "Make you feel better."

"Dancer." She slurred the name between drooling lips. "What th'ell's tha' noise?"

"Ah, it's the old rat snoring—too drunk to breathe proper."

"Well ... tell'im ..." She panted around a throbbing behind her eyes. "Jest quit trying."

Gigis chased her. *Sally!* Her eyes snapped open.

Sunlight streamed through unshuttered windows and painted a lacework of webby shadows on the floor from the insect netting at the door. She sucked a breath, head pounding.

The pain eased, and she saw her arm resting in front of her on the cot. Beyond, Raschad sprawled half off a log round, the table supporting his upper body and his head resting on his crossed arms.

"New ... newbie?" The breathy weakness of her voice surprised her. "New—"

His head jerked off the table as if connected to a string, and the muzzle of his hellish big gun emerged over the top of his biceps. *Shrike, going to kill me after all this?*

"Banks?" His voice shook.

"Aia." She ran a cottony tongue around her mouth and breathed a nervous breath. "Th-Thirsty."

"I'll get it." He holstered his gun, wobbled up, and limped to the counter. He filled a battered tin with rainwater from Morrie's crock and brought it to her.

"I wanted a f-f-fancier glass."

"They must have hurt you bad." His nose wrinkled. His lips curved up. "Don't you remember this is Morrie's shack?"

It pleased her that she'd amused him. He slid his arm behind her and lifted gently, but raising her head was like dumping fire and thunder inside it. Teeth gritted, she rode out the pain and expelled her breath in a rush, blowing away the worst of the hurt. As she steadied, Raschad brought the cup up, and she curled a hand around it. Most of the water made it down her throat, the rest down her front. *Everything* ached.

"Glad you're awake, boss. Things have been lonely." His smile looked nervous. "Here." He eased a pillow behind her. She relaxed back, exploring the split in her lip with the tip of her tongue. She'd had worse. But her eye felt shriking swollen, and her hand ached.

"Where's Morrie? The old fool run off?"

"He's sleeping. Woke early, decorated the mud, and slandered my heritage when I put him back in the hammock. But he's fine."

"Thank you."

"For what?"

"Getting us home."

"Tom Bill helped. Dancer came. George checked on you after he cleared out the Gigi's Eye."

"George is a good guy. And Settlers help us if Tom Bill hadn't stopped you from drawing your tech last night."

Raschad took an audible breath. "You saw that?"

"About the last thing I saw."

"Sorry, but *I* was envisioning little pieces of you all over the floor."

"Envis . . ." She let that go, beyond deciphering his fancy words. "Just a good thing Tom was there."

"Aia."

"Aagh."

She clamped a hand to her head, holding it together. Things spotted up, and she closed her eyes. Opening them, she found Raschad down on one knee, his expression concerned.

"S'fine." She took a long breath. His hand came up, rough and huge, brushed the hair from her cheek. "Shrike, Raschad. You can't kill a greenie with a club."

"It was a chair."

"See."

"I see you are getting greener every minute. Why don't you be quiet. I'll bring more water."

Sal closed her eyes and let the pain subside. His boots thumped to the counter and back. "Better?"

"Aia."

A big arm slid beneath her head, and his body hovered close, the smell and the heat of him blocking out everything.

"Why th'ell . . ." She sipped water and swallowed. "You sure smell good."

He made a little sound, not quite a laugh, and she squinted up at him just in time to see his cheeks color. "Your head is cracked if you think this smells good."

"Wearing that bug stuff, aia."

"Aia."

"I like it. You oughta . . ." But she was too sleepy. He straightened the pillow beneath her head, and she drowsed out.

She woke alone this time, and judging from the light through the back windows, it was late afternoon.

"He-ell-pp!"

She grabbed for a gun that wasn't there and fell back, head screaming.

"Hel—" Morrie.

Cussing spouted like rain. Someone might be killing the old man, but Sal couldn't help him. Letting her head settle, she heard water splash.

"Danged fool, newbie, soma—" Morrie's spluttering choked off. Was he getting his yearly washing a little early this summer? Sal smiled.

"Scut damn! Old man . . ." Raschad's curse dropped to a growl, and she figured one old greenie was in squat-deep trouble. "You bite me again, and I'll rip off your flaky pods and feed them to the roaks."

A desperate burbling sounded, someone breathing underwater. Should she rescue the old fool after all? Naia. For once Morrie was getting his due.

Lazy, she stretched, scratched her stomach. What the . . . She half sat up. Her vision dimmed. Her stomach flopped.

When everything settled again, she eased onto her side, breathing carefully against the pain's return, and examined her *nightie*. Cloud-white silken cloth slid against her hips. Full white sleeves puffed over her shoulders, finer than anything she'd ever worn.

And beneath, she lay *naked*. Someone'd put this big loose shirt on her and nothing else. Fingering the material, so shiny and soft, she sniffed. Shriking Raschad.

"Sumabitch." Morrie was still fighting the good fight outside.

She ignored the racket, imagined the newbie wrestling her, changing her clothes, touching her when she didn't even know it. He'd no business putting anyone's clothes on her, let alone his.

Boom. She grabbed her head.

The back door banged off the inside wall, and Morrie hurtled through it—a wild-haired scrawny demon, wrapped mummy style in a blanket, way and beyond pissed. Raschad, following the old man, looked even grimmer.

"See I ever does anything nice for ya again, ya filthy newbie, off-planetin' freak." Morrie was so mad he slipped into jungle tongue.

But Raschad yanked Morrie's blanket, and the old man's cursing choked off. Sal held her head, mouth frozen between a smile and a grimace, staring at a vision. Morrie's hair stuck up in every direction, whiter than she'd ever seen it, and every bristle on his face below his eyebrows was shaved.

"Oh, Morrie! Oh, shrike!" She gritted her teeth and choked back pain and laughter. Knobby-kneed, Morrie's slug-pale legs wobbled beneath the hem of his blanket, and their grizzled hair stood straight out as if fear-shocked. "What I'd give ... for a painting of this." She choked off on a squeak.

"Well!" Morrie's snort scared a bomb beetle into flight.

"Come on." Raschad wrestled the old man onto a round. "Don't move." The big newbie's tone of voice even hushed Sal, but she smiled at Morrie as Raschad stumped out the door again.

"Ya'll get a gut tear laughin' at a poor ol' man," he grumped.

She bit down, face twisted and lips quivering. An outright laugh would split her head. "You must've really riled him."

The old man sniffed his shoulder and wrinkled his nose. "Appears he don't like public ap-sir-va-shun on his sexual pres-fran-sisses. Or somethin' like. The man jabbers strange."

"You didn't?"

"Aia." He sounded subdued at last.

"One of these days, old man, your *public ap-sir-va-shuns* are going to kill you." She didn't know whether to laugh or cry.

Morrie snorted, letting that pass, which wasn't like him, and she caught him watching her close and strange.

"Why you staring?" She tugged the big shirt's neck tight.

"Because you're breathing."

"I won't get killed in any little bar brawl." Her eyes narrowed. "I reckon you know what that was about."

The old man rubbed a horny foot against his shin and glanced at the back door. "Nothin' much. Cain't remember."

Like hell, but she didn't say a thing. Morrie had got her hurt and fretted on it, finally. Maybe he'd go easy on his drinking for a while. Boots thumped, and Raschad squeezed inside, arms full of clothes. He dumped them on the cot, burying her.

"Hey." The bundle smelled of soap, sunshine, and Raschad. "You did the wash, too." Her voice rose, and her head twinged.

"Most of it's mine. I need to retrieve my comm tonight, and they won't let me in stinking of mud and reeki sap. Thanks for the scrub board." He pulled a ragged pair of pants, a torn shirt, and some hole-pocked underdrawers from the pile and threw them at Morrie. "Here." Threat rode Raschad's tone.

"Oh, squat." Morrie's voice shook. "They're ruint! Won't be able to show m'face fer a month."

"That's a thought." Raschad smiled. But his expression held no humor at all, and the two men exchanged glares.

Sal laughed. That drew Raschad's pretty eyes to her, not glaring at all. And sitting there in his fancy shirt, she had to stop his stare. "Your arm's wearing a new bruise." She waved, desperate for distraction.

The newbie glared at Morrie, and the old man was instantly busy climbing into his clothes. "That's a gap-toothed bite."

She grimaced. "I only know one gapper here."

Morrie snorted without looking up, busy wriggling his gnarled feet through his pants legs.

"Are you all right?" Raschad sounded worried.

"Aia." Her face warmed. "Head's better." She flexed a sore shoulder. "By morning I'll want to work this out. 'Course by then we'll be another day late." She stared at Morrie.

"Shrike." The old man looked contrite, as if he expected *worse* punishment than a bath and a shave.

"Hungry?"

"Aia. Think so." She glanced back to Raschad.

"I'll cook." The man could talk so damn soft and pretty. "Then I have to pick up my comms and sell off my ore. Morrie's clear-headed enough to take care of you that long."

"Give me my Camm, and I'll take care of him."

"You are better, aren't you?" Raschad's face brightened as if a big worry had lifted from him.

"I'm a greenie, ain't I?"

She ate propped up on the cot, still wearing only Raschad's fancy shirt. He'd cooked rice with morel and greens—that he, not Morrie, had foraged—and pan bread heavy as stone. She'd tasted better. But he cleaned up afterward like a government crew—scrubbed pots, sanded the mudstove, and shined the slop pan.

"You'll ruin it." Morrie glared at Raschad, having no shame for the way he lived, though the filth embarrassed her. Usually she kept after the old man—been gone too much lately.

Raschad ignored Morrie, washed his hands, stripped off his shirt—the sight sent a shiver through her—and greased himself with his fancy bug repellent. Scars marked his arms, big scars. A long jagged white line creased his lower back, and above it the splinter gash from yesterday stood out red and angry. This man had used himself hard. He slipped on a clean shirt, wrapped a clean bandanna over his hair, and turned for the door.

"I might be late. But I'll try to hurry."

"Not on my account."

"No. Doyka Rimmersin isn't my favorite company."

"He ain't anyone's favorite company that I know. For a Depot Supervisor, he's a sorry excuse."

"A sorry excuse for anythin'." Morrie spit on the floor Raschad had just cleaned. The newbie's lips thinned.

"I'm sure you'd be a good judge of that, old man."

"Get your white hide uphill, newbie." Morrie climbed out of his hammock. "Have to make things livable for greenies again."

Raschad half turned, and Morrie raised scrawny fists.

"I intended to bring you back a brew." The newbie smiled.

Morrie's glare wavered. Sal grinned. Shrike, the newbie knew how to handle the old man.

"Get out o' here." Morrie snatched up a piece of kindling.

Raschad snagged his pack—minus bedroll and extras—and ducked through the front door netting.

"Piss." Morrie threw the kindling. It tangled in netting. "Thinks he's good as greenie." His chuckle surprised her. "He *has* got more greenie ways than a moa. Just as slippery, too."

"And you sent me to hire him." Sal rolled over flat on her back, head aching.

"Aia." Morrie moved to his hammock. "But I didn't figure you'd be stupid enough to do it."

"Shut up."

A nightbaby wailed. Leathery wings snapped next to Raschad's ear, and his fingers closed on the Morven's grip. With the weapon half drawn, he caught himself and forced his fingers apart. His heart pounded; sweat slicked his ribs. Winged snake bodies rippled against sunset as the nightbabies fed.

He swallowed hard and spun downhill. The sack of crystals on his back weighted down his shoulders and bruised his hips.

He stumped into the shipping office with his authorization—signed by Rimmersin. Two clerks chatted over the counter, and he waited to be acknowledged. If he interrupted, they'd keep him waiting all night. Finally the clerk behind the counter glanced up.

"I'd best see to this." The clerk spoke low to his friend, said something else that Raschad couldn't catch, straightened, and laughed. "Ride them easy, Scollarta." The counter clerk waved the second government worker off. "Those greenie girls will knife you for not pleasing them."

The one called Scollarta snorted and smiled, staring at Raschad now, his expression knowing yet wary. Did the men think him one of Rimmersin's bed boys? Headed for the door, the government man batted his eyelashes. Raschad flushed.

"Dump it here. You know." The remaining clerk opened a shipping crate and shoved it onto the scale beside the counter.

Slipping his pack to the floor, Raschad opened the ore pocket and dumped rose-colored crystals, still mired in stone, into the crate. The clerk weighed it out and made a show of copying the shipping directions for the crate from the authorization picked up at Government House.

Raschad's back stiffened; his ribs ached. He waited, saying nothing, giving the bastard no excuse to work any more slowly.

"Sign here or make your mark." The man knew Raschad could write. He signed. "It'll go out next flight day. You missed this one."

He hadn't, not yet. Rain had kept the fliers out. He held his expression perfectly blank, blinking against glittering motes of rage. He couldn't make Mother wait.

"I'll advise the Supervisor of my oversight." He reached for his authorization receipt, taking risks he couldn't afford.

"Well . . ." The clerk looked uncertain. "There might be room. I'll get it on."

Raschad swallowed and nodded. The man *did* think he was sleeping with Rimmersin. He caught up his pack before the clerk could see his shudder.

Entering the assay office, he still trembled with unspent adrenaline, and it was hard to wait passively again. The assay clerk sat at a desk behind the office counter, staring at an archaic datacomp. From where he stood, Raschad could hear the chimes and trills of a game of Gigi Bait. The adventure simulation had been popular on the newly introduced pay comps in the city at the time he'd left for the green; he'd played it himself. The reality of a live gigi was far different. Banks was right—city greenies were idiots.

Raschad woke her coming in, but he took such pains to be quiet that Sal said nothing. Moon shadows streaked the room. Raschad stowed his pack and went out the back door. It was shriking late, and she wondered what sort of money or fear made Raschad put up with a slimy Liber sherk like Rimmersin. The govie didn't even run the depot decent.

The bottle rested heavy against Raschad's thigh and weighed heavy in his hand. Liquor burned his throat and jolted tears from his eyes. Maybe the tears were already there. He pressed the chill bottle against his cheek and shuddered.

How many times could he walk up that hill? He didn't drink, but here he was sucking down rot to fight off old panic. He'd probably kill himself before the jungle did.

Visions of pale, slender fingers filled his mind—fingers that fluttered to his knee then away, then back to his thigh, never lingering long enough for complaint—teasing while Rimmersin voiced subtle threats in a soft, genteel voice. Had Grandfather put the man up to these antics? Once Axial had sent a naked whore to Father at Mother's birthday service.

Bugs circled and whined. Nightbabies cried. Mold and rot rode the soggy air. Swallowing another long swig, Raschad watched a broad-winged shadow—not a nightbaby, but a meat-hunting windrider—glide through twofold moonlight out near Morrie's clothesline. *Squeak.* The shadow stooped. Through the insect drone he heard a tiny death cry.

Him—that was him out there dying, another piece of him, every day, every step, every visit to Rimmersin wearing away another layer, until tonight he oozed raw. Part of that was the woman's fault. Her fairness threw him off balance now that he'd come to lean on greenie hate—something dependable in a confusing world. He sucked a breath and a swallow of liquor.

His head spun, and his stomach threatened. He'd waited, his back cramped, while the assay clerk lost at Gigi Bait, waited while the man turned the few small stones Raschad had saved back for himself into native coin, paying him just enough to cover shipping, no more. He couldn't reequip without Banks's promised job. How many times would he let them cheat him? How many insults would he take before he struck out at one of these official bastards and got himself killed?

The assay office was so small and close—its doors sealed against insects—that he'd nearly gone mad and dashed himself to tatters like the great silken moths batting against the windowpanes. Riding space galleons or piloting fighters, he'd found small spaces comforting. But he'd loved the vastness of the deep, and thought that leaving space would kill him. Now, forced down here . . . If his grandfather only knew, he wouldn't bother with check-ins and Rimmersin. This Raschad had become landbound. What could be vaster than the intricacies of the green? The jungle had crawled into his pores, and the very thought of lifting for space knotted his stomach. Love, hate, hate, love—Ver Day tore at his sanity.

He took two hits from the bottle. The moonlit yard blurred. He licked sweat salt from his lip, liquor searing his already nerve-blistered gut, and glanced up at the depot's lights.

All this way, league after league of jungle, and he'd found himself back where he'd begun; the hike up and down this hill was just a shorter version of his long journey out from the city. The depot ran on Capitol's doomed technology—solar-gel generated power, botanically based fabrication materials, information streamers and security grids. But every step down this hill left such luxuries farther behind. From the grocery store and Heaven's Rest to the whorehouse, the showers, and down through the town's string of bars, manufactured technology thinned out, mimicking Ver Day's planned transition zones between city, truck farms, jungle settlements, and wilderness.

He'd liked the truck farms—they reminded him of MB-2's massive greenhouses. But the farmers didn't want newbie help. He'd walked on into jungle slum, where he'd found the poverty of ignorance and the desperation of starving immigrants, the cities' unwanted population tricked into a land they didn't know, left to live or die on the frail strength of their own bodies and the jungle's whim.

Lights circled the rim of Depot Hill like a tiara, marking Government House's garden terrace. Did Rimmersin sit up there laughing at him? Who did the bastard work for? The Supervisor reported to Grandfather Raschad. But who paid Rimmersin the most? Maybe the old man's enemies. Every comm Raschad received from Mother sounded more and more confused. Either her mind was failing or someone censored the letters before they reached him—probably both. She was frightened. So was he.

His gut ached. Bugs gnawed his arm. He slapped and rocked, slapped and rocked, hugging himself, dry-eyed, too helpless for hope. Mother had sent medicines again. Keeping him alive was insurance on his brother's life.

Inside the shack Banks's cot squeaked. Banks, Banks. What did she think behind those hard golden eyes?

A click roused her. She shoved a cricket away from her ear and rolled over. A breeze stirred through the room.

Slap. She started, wide-awake.

Slap. Slap. What the shrike? She swung her legs off the cot and half sat up. The cot rocked and the room spun. Outside, leaves rustled on the banban tree that sheltered the shack.

Slap. Slap. Howlers hooted in the distance.

Slap. A breeze found its way through the door netting and lifted sweat from her face, the stirring air redolent with the scent of Raschad's insect repellant. *Slap.*

What was he doing out there? She sniffed, and her nose told her. Another drunk—just all she needed.

She found her boots, shook them out. A weight *thupped* on the floor and skittered. Shoving her feet in the boots, she eased upright, shuffled across the room bare-cheeked, and peeked out the back window.

Bathed in moonlight, Raschad sat in Morrie's stick rocker, slapping bugs. They liked his *repellent* as much as she did. After every slap, he took a swig from a tall bottle. Except for the slapping, he looked comfortable, his drinking serious and solitary. What had gone on tonight at Government House to set him drinking like this? *Was* there truth to what they said around town about him? None of her business. She turned toward her cot.

Slap! Slap! She'd never sleep with that going on. And what if the ignorant newbie fell off the porch and got snakebit? She turned back and brushed aside the door net.

"Raschad?" she called softly, half afraid he'd shoot.

"Aia." His voice was slurred.

"Best come in before you can't. Bugs will carry you away if you don't, and I'm not hauling you out of the mud."

"Aia."

He stood straight up, and the porch creaked and quaked. He eased past her and dropped the bottle in her hands, so she took a swig. Old stock mi-mi slid down her throat, easy as dawn.

"Shrike. You've fine taste. I'll put it up for you."

"Naia." He really slurred now. "I've had enough for this year. Get rid of it."

She looked at the bottle, then looked at his back where he'd inexplicably stopped.

"Aia." She took another swig. "Reckon you like standing in just this spot."

"It's better than falling."

"Shrike."

She caught his arm, none too steady herself, and led him to the cot—couldn't wrestle a big drunk into a hammock. He was asleep before he landed.

Morning found Morrie the better-looking of the three of them, and the most congenial. Raschad wasn't surly, just mute. When the outhouse door was locked, it took Sal a banging fit to draw enough sound from him to learn the dump was occupied.

Morrie cooked breakfast. *That* Sal was ready for, but Raschad ignored the food, emptied the water jug down his throat, and carried the dry jug outside.

Sal watched the newbie through the door netting as he worked the well pump. "He say anything to you?" she asked Morrie.

"Naia a word. Visiting Gov'ment House ain't bad duty, eh?"

"I don't think anything pleasant set him drinking."

"Well, you weren't there."

"Old man." She shook her head. "He didn't get drunk up to Government House. He got drunk on your own back porch. I'm amazed the scent didn't rouse you from the dead." She smiled, feeling mean. "I got me a quarter bottle of fine old mi-mi out of helping him to bed."

"Did you now?" Morrie's face slid right past shocked to cunning. "That's too rich a stuff for your blood."

She gave him a thin, slit-eyed grin. "You even look for it, and I'll sell your hide off to the guano miners come fall."

"Mean, hard woman you are. Don't know how I raised you so."

"*Raised* me?"

She'd lived with Morrie off and on since Pa died. But though he'd been a saving grace for a little girl orphan, he'd no wise *raised* her, even if he had put a roof over her head—which she patched the day she moved in—and food in her stomach until the Shoogs moved up from the south and hired her to guide them.

Ma and Pa had both seen that she knew the jungle. So she led the brothers where they needed to go, and they, more than anyone, had finished her raising. Then Bob died of fever, and Cab married a rich woman. Cab sat on the porch of his wife's hotel in Diz-et-el now just getting fat. He'd earned the right, packing all those years. And he'd sold her their route contracts before leaving.

"Old man, you're a sorry . . ." The room spun. She steadied her head with the heel of one hand. "Shut up."

"Wha-at? You must wants to hear about George's visit night afore last. Right interestin' it was."

She glowered around her fist. Morrie smirked.

"Should've woke up to seen it. George come checking on you, and here's Raschad, helping Dancer. George's eyes narrowed and his mustache twitched. Raschad went strange—though it's hard to tell with him—and backed off, guilty like."

Sal hid her squirm. No use giving Morrie any more satisfaction than she could help.

"It was rich. Two big studs prowling like the other was a moa. And you lying senseless and half ne-ked." The old man cackled so hard he didn't notice she was staring past him.

Raschad stood at the back door. "We were debating what to do with your stinking hide, old man."

Morrie's face blanked, and popping crackles sounded as his head whipped around. Raschad pushed aside the netting and stepped through with the filled water jug on his shoulder. Floorboards screeched. Morrie stared, silent. Raschad settled the jug on the counter and straightened.

"I would appreciate"—the newbie spoke in a near whisper—"if you would keep your voice down, Morrie. Noise is hard on my nerves this morning, and though I thank you for receiving me in your home, my nerves could be hard on you."

Sal watched as the newbie ducked out the front door. Morrie's breath hissed. It was rich—a newbie putting Morrie in his place!

Chapter 6

Head hammering, Sal made it to the front porch hammock. Raschad sat slumped on the hard slick bed of her lead sled, his head between his knees. He'd napped on the hauler all morning.

"I come out to save you from sunpox."

"Too late." His voice was hoarse, sleep-sluggish.

"Well, get in the shade now, idiot."

Stretching, Raschad caught the splintered edge of the porch and swung from sun to shadow, landing on the porch boards with a moan and a thud that shook the shack.

"Ain't much of a drinker." Sal shook her head.

"A little goes a long ways."

"Guess your head feels like mine."

"Hope not, for your sake." He rolled onto the porch, grabbed a post and levered himself to his feet. "Thirsty?"

"Aia."

He brought back two tin cups, hands shaking, water dripping. A splash caught her bare thigh below the cut-off leg of her home-fashioned jungle shorts. "Burr. Feels good." She directed a few drips onto her wrists. "Heat's a'rising."

He nodded, opened his free hand, licked a small white tablet off his palm and chased it with water.

"What's that?" It startled her rude, him taking tech drugs right in front of her.

"Vasodilator."

"What?"

"For headache." He ate a second tablet.

"Thought that came in a patch."

"These are cheaper. Want one?"

"Naia." She didn't hold with using tech medicines any more than she used other tech. A little niady root worked just fine.

Still, offering expensive med was generous. But he was only being polite; he didn't act as if he'd expected her to accept.

"Morrie?" she called through the window netting. "Got more breakfast tea?" Morrie'd mixed some niady in it.

"I'll bring it soon's I finishes your boots, princess."

Raschad sat on the edge of the porch again. Morrie hobbled out with her tea, making a big show of waiting on her.

"Does its temp-a-shur suit you, mas?"

"A degree warmer, and I'd say you pissed in it."

Morrie sniggered. "Wish I'd thought of it." He dropped on the front step in the shade.

Raschad slid off the porch, squatted, and peered between her sled's treads at the hauler's undercarriage.

"Look at the newbie." Morrie glared at the big man. "Plannin' to turn that into a power hauler."

"I've never had a chance to study a sled's design." Raschad's head swiveled. "Do you mind, Banks?"

"Look all you want. Haia." She scooped up a roacher and bounced it off Morrie's shoulder. "Explain it to him, old man. Some sherk caused a terrible ruckus up to the Gigi last night, and my head's aching."

"E-x-plain?" Morrie growled, pale naked jowls quivering. "Why the yellow—"

"Raschad, I don't exactly know how often you've pulled," Sal said.

"Exactly . . ." He counted on his fingers.

She scooped up another bug—a fat milk beetle off a patch of moss on the windowsill—and threw it at him. The insect's brown wing covers lifted. Its fist-sized white parachute blossomed, and the newbie's eyes rounded. Six double-footed legs dangled in midair, and the milker floated away like a flower on the wind.

"I've pulled twice." Raschad sucked a breath, eyes wide— startled by a little ol' bug. He dropped onto the porch again.

"Twice is good," Sal said. Twice? Idiot.

"For a full day each time."

"Mooli Toon said she hired you."

"I pushed her sleds through a stretch of bogs."

"Shrike. Morrie." She held her aching head. "Mind your tongue and show wonder boy the parts of a sled, so I at least know he can work the brakes running downhill at my back."

Morrie glared, but crabbed off the step and limped around the porch to Raschad. "This here's a standard trail sled made entirely of botafab materials, double axle, moves on four separate crawl-

ers, is about a third narrower and shorter than a power hauler."
Morrie paused as if waiting for the newbie to contradict him. But
Raschad sat quiet, all attention. "Well." Morrie cleared his throat.

Sitter and baby-sitter—whichever was which—appeared to be
occupied for a while. Morrie enjoyed nothing more than explaining tech. He might not like working with the big stuff, but he
liked understanding how it worked. And it pleased him when Tiny
or Mike asked his opinion on repairs.

Sipping her tea, Sal spied a gangly figure headed her way.

"You know what steering bars are?" Morrie lowered the two
arms that angled the sled's front treads. "This here's the brake
lever." He pointed to the right bar. "Squeeze her and a slab of
botafab does the stopping. The harder you squeeze, the sooner
you'll stop—most times." So far Morrie's explanation wouldn't
confuse a three-year-old. "This button's the willy worm."

"I want to see that."

"Get a jack."

Tom Bill strode off Greta's plank walk and across the open
space in front of the derelict tent cabin next door.

"Haia, Mayor."

"Haia, Sal. You look to be feeling better."

"Haven't felt so good since I got hit by a chair."

Tom Bill trudged into the shade of the shack and up onto the
porch. That tech medicine must have worked on Raschad's headache, Sal noticed, because the newbie was jacking up one side of
her sled.

"Hope you don't have problems." Tom nodded to the action.

"Lessons."

Tom's eyebrows arched. He took a seat on the porch rail. "Your
contract's running short, I hear."

"Aia," Sal said. "But I'll be up tomorrow."

"The willy's tucked up in that cylinder." Morrie squatted in the
mud beside Raschad, both of them peering under her canted sled.
"If you're movin' too fast, spin cranks the cylinder over so's the
willy falls out a slot and drags ground, which slows the sled."
Morrie turned the cylinder by hand, showing Raschad the quivering fringe on the willy. "Slow enough, and the weights quit
spinning fast enough to hold the slot open. The willy pulls back
as the weights drop and the cylinder spins over, closin' the slot.
All automatic, just spin and gravity, no other power."

Sal shook her head at Morrie's enthusiasm. Tom Bill smiled.

"Thanks for guarding Raschad for me the other night."

"My pleasure." Tom nodded, amused. "I enjoy talkin' to newbies. Can't fight the devil without knowing his ways."

"You're broader-minded than me."

"I don't know." He motioned off the porch, still smiling. "Looks to me like you're treatin' him just fine."

"Don't the feet tangle?" Raschad ran a hand through the willy's feathery tentacles.

"That's the idea, you idiot newbie. They catch, slow the sled, but break off, don't stop it."

"What if the drag isn't enough, and it's running away?"

"Do-or-die time," Morrie said. "Look here."

Sal rested her eyes, her thoughts spinning. Today and tomorrow, then the next day her contract ran out. And she sat here while Morrie taught her muscle to work a sled. She sipped tea, hoping it would ease her headache. It only soured her stomach.

"Sal?" She opened her eyes, realizing she'd drifted. Tom Bill cocked his head, peering beneath her chopped bangs. "I can come back another time. Just thought you might want company." He shrugged and tilted his head in Raschad's direction. "Then, too, it's an unusual chance to learn things."

"Watch that newbie all you want. Just don't mind if I nap."

"Rest easy. I won't let them piece apart your sled."

"Thank you." She meant it.

"You hit the do-or-die lever." A steering bar creaked as Morrie worked it. "See it move under there?"

Raschad grunted. Sal closed her eyes, hearing Tom Bill move to the edge of the porch nearer the sleds.

Time to run back in the green. She needed out of town, away from people. Give her trail and trees bigger than her heart, taller than anyone's soul, give her silence within the jungle's yammer and sunlight-piercing leaf canopy like a golden waterfall. Give her Glory's Roost and the emerald slither of snakes up a vine. Spitting, red-eyed moas couldn't be deadlier than sitting in this town with everyone worrying at her like gigis.

"It's just a big clamp." Morrie's voice faded to a murmur. "The bar rotates. The claw hits the axle, clamps down, sinks that spike on its trailing edge into the mud. Do-or-die."

She listened, half dreaming. Morrie explained the fanny strap attached between the steering bars. Leaning on the strap braked a sled without wearing out either hands or arms.

"The cen-ter-rif-ug-al reserve builds drag. Winds on the downslope, unwinds going up, gives you a boost. This here . . ."

The throb behind her ear eased. She dreamed—gigis, dead city folks, mistwalkers, Raschad—and woke sweating.

"Look at me."

Perched on Morrie's cot, she stared up at Raschad, feeling the fool if there ever was one.

"I didn't faint." She'd gotten up ready to pack.

"Your knees hit the floor."

"Have to bend down to light the stove." This morning wasn't turning out as planned. His fingers probed the healing cut under her eye. "Guess it's rot awful."

"You'll wear it for a while." He blinked his own yellowing eye. "Wish I had a Chilcloth."

"Wish for dry weather, while you're at it." Morrie cackled.

Sal studied Raschad's expression. Here was a man used to tech helps, who still noticed doing without. A dangerous thing. Wanting soured the soul. But he hadn't mentioned Chilcloths when his own face was bashed. Remembering that changed the color of her thoughts—if not her eye. She liked people who found not wanting for themselves easier than not wanting for others.

"You aren't packing today."

"Aia." She massaged her temple. "Aia."

Easing back on the cot, she startled as he caught her feet and lifted. Head spinning, she lay miserable, with a damn likable newbie nursing her and time counting. In less than a day she'd lose her contract, and the rest of her reputation with it.

Fog mounded the jungle hollows below Tumble Town's rise and wisped heavenward. Leaning against the dock, Sal watched colors wake with dawn as sunlight burned back the mists and tinged the world a thousand shades of greenish red.

Raschad squatted at her side, fitted out again in bushwackers and leggings. Looking like a greenie except for his skin, he doodled tech figures in the mud. She adjusted her own bushwhackers and didn't ask what the doodles meant.

The line at the docks was quiet this morning. The freight skidded in yesterday still needed sorting, and the loads due from the last delivery already rode the trails. So the packers in line now were either late, early, or running special loads. She reckoned she was the only one late, and was no happier about it than the attending contract man.

Scollarta broke off his conversation with a depot guard and

strolled toward her. He was figuring the quickest way to sweep her out of his way, or she didn't know contractors.

"Mas Banks," the dough-fat govie began before he reached her. "You'll never make delivery in contract time. The load has bulked up too much for two sleds."

"Scarlet, you know me better than that." She straightened, squashing rude noises from the mud and studying the man. His color ran high for a city breed, and his expression was worried, his movements nervous. Her gut knotted. Had the bastard resold her contract? She climbed onto the dock. Maybe catching a chair leg with her head hadn't been an accident.

"Bring the load out." She planted herself at eye level with the man, watching the depot guard past the contractor's shoulder. "I'll get it there on time."

Scollarta's syrup-colored eyes darted away. The guard, sensing trouble, sauntered forward, but Scollarta waved him off.

"We can't even load it on time, Banks." He refused to meet her stare, was up to something he didn't want examined.

"*I* can load it on time."

Scollarta's gaze slid past her off the dock, and his expression pinched up. A film of sweat popped on his upper lip. What now? She glanced down at Raschad, still doodling in slop. Why would the newbie spook the contractor?

"I'm sorry, Mas Banks." Scollarta took a step back from the dock edge. "I won't risk a heavy load—"

"Scarlet." She spoke firm. His eyes snapped back to her, and he swiped sweat off his forehead. "That's my legal contract. You *get* it out here and stacked. I'll put it on myself."

The depot guard walked the far end of the main dock now, nearly out of sight. In his absence, the packer line compressed toward Sal. Picking his teeth, Siam Ludlow leaned against the dock near Scollarta's feet. And Bocho Man and Dog Girl edged up, started a game of Spit. Their bush knives sailed in glinting arcs above the dock's deck and thunked into the wall of the contract office. Acting feverish, Scollarta glanced down the line of waiting packers.

Sal followed his gaze. Fifth in line was the load-by-load packer who'd played cards with Morrie the night of the fight. The woman's sour expression said she wanted no part of a squabble between locals and a contractor. Scollarta pulled out a white handkerchief and mopped his face.

"Now you know, Mas Banks, the load must be officially inspected and loaded."

She blew a breath out slow. Scollarta'd sold it. His eyes flicked to Raschad again. *Scared.* Her, too. Fool city man.

"You officially inspect it. I'll load it." She spoke between clenched teeth. If she let him get away with this, she might as well give up packing. She glared at Raschad just to keep from throttling Scollarta.

"Problem?" Raschad cocked his head.

"A bit."

The big newbie rose out of the mud in one fluid motion and flipped onto the dock, standing tall at her shoulder. She appreciated it. Newbie or not, he was one hunk of muscle to dare. Siam hissed and chuckled, a scary look on his knobby face.

"Mas B-Banks." The contractor stared past her. "Common sense insists you are beyond fulfilling your contract. I won't w-waste government labor bringing a load out when your sleds won't p-pass weight standards."

Wild-eyed, her hair like a quill fox's, Dog Girl vaulted onto the dock, scaring even Sal. But Scollarta watched Raschad.

"If I don't pass weights"—Sal leaned toward the man—"then the government's cheating on this contract."

Scollarta's eyes widened. His jaw clenched. Dumb thing to say. He was going to yank this contract now.

"Is it me you doubt, mas?" Raschad shifted forward.

The contractor's eyes froze on the newbie, and he choked. "The matter only concerns Mas Banks as contractor."

"I can send to Supervisor Rimmersin for references and status confirmation, if that would help." Raschad smiled.

Scollarta's face paled. His jaw slackened, and she sensed the fight go out of him. Bless the newbie's soul.

"That was not the question, I assure you." Scollarta backed away. "I see nothing will convince Mas Banks short of a weigh. I'll send for the load." The contractor scurried away.

"What you do?" Sal glanced at Raschad, speaking low.

"I took a chance. The clerks think I'm *friends* with the Supervisor. I'm not. Pray he doesn't send to Rimmersin."

"He won't."

"What's going on?"

"He's sold the load to someone else." She kicked a crate. "Figured I'd never pick it up on time. Maybe took a bribe, moved a name up the backup list. Maybe someone told him about me and a chair leg, or even arranged that meeting. Now he's scared, don't want anyone looking at this contract."

"Then he isn't finished." Raschad swatted the buzz suckers swarming his arms.

"Naia."

Dog Girl edged up. Raschad's gaze slid over ragged clothes, the short-grip blaster on Dog Girl's belt, and a brace of knives strapped to her forearm. Head rocked back, Dog Girl studied him in turn, notching weak spots. Raschad, always smart, backed up.

"You want, Sal, we'll watch this side while you go over t'other." Dog Girl's pale eyes followed Raschad.

"Would appreciate it."

"I'd welcome him on loan." Dog Girl bared howler-sharp canines in a smile even rarer and scarier than Siam's.

"Can't loan what you don't own, Girl." Sal swallowed hard.

"Swap you even."

Sal glanced up at Bocho Man's scarred face and flattened nose, pretending to consider the offer. Playing with the brute would be an experience.

"It's tempting." She lied for her life. "But I don't reckon I'd get Raschad back in the same shape I loaned him."

"Humphh." Dog Girl's thin lips twisted, and her face split into a grin. "I don't reckon." She made a swipe at the seat of Raschad's pants and flipped off the dock.

"Thanks, Banks." Raschad sounded the near side of amused and the far side of scared.

She nodded. "Kill yourself first." He rolled his eyes. *She* swatted his backside. "C'mon."

They lined her sleds up in front of the dock. Dog Girl and Bocho Man guarded Raschad's. As her load arrived, Sal climbed onto the dock again.

"Whay back." The lead docker bristled. "We'll pack it."

She blocked his path. The docker leaned into her. She met him chin to chin.

"You want to be wearing a crate, gov'ment boy?"

The man's eyes flicked to Dog Girl and Bocho Man, then on to Siam and Lucky Mac and Mac's waist-high kids. Jill and Bean were a team in the traces or out, and she always kept an eye to their knives. They held their hands real low now, and every greenie on the docks watched the docker. A pair of depot guards emerged from the assay office.

"Let her load." Scollarta trotted from the warehouse door, waving his men off, sounding friendly. The guards relaxed and headed uphill toward the government compound.

Scollarta was stealing bits of time, hoping to run her past her pull limit before she realized it. It was tempting to start something and draw the guards' attention again, but that would lose her the load for sure.

Sal grabbed a crate and began sorting onto her near sled, positioning the boxes by order of delivery, size, and weight, shifting out the occasional unmarked crate, extras she wasn't obligated to take—extras meant to put her overweight. If it wasn't marked with her load sign today, she wasn't taking it.

Squat, she didn't want to be on the wrong side of a contractor—might have to move to a new depot. Damn.

Why was she was doing all the loading? Glancing up, she saw Raschad at Scollarta's shoulder, watching the tally. She didn't say a thing. Truth be, she didn't read well enough to challenge a contractor. Raschad likely did, and even being newbie, just his standing there kept Scollarta honest.

"Wrong crate." Raschad's voice stopped her.

"No it isn't." Scollarta acted offended.

"The number was A2298903, not 08." Raschad leaned over the shorter man's shoulder. "That case isn't on this manifest."

Sal straightened, smiling at Raschad's letter-perfect government-style pronunciation. Setting her fists on her hips, she stared up at Scollarta. Raschad didn't back a hair. The contractor's face flushed.

"N-Now . . ." Scollarta stammered as Dog Girl took a step toward the dock. Sal'd seen it all now—greenies backing a newbie. Scollarta sucked a breath. "If you read the fine—"

"I did." Raschad scratched his ear through his bandanna. "It does not belong with this load."

Scollarta's eyes darted left and right, searching for something—or *someone*. Sal glanced around quick, but saw only greenies, all old acquaintances except for the load-by-load. And the packer looked too shabby for bribing contractors. But what was the woman doing here this morning?

"I-I'd rather c-concede the p-point than further slow this load." Crumbling beneath greenie stares, Scollarta had the case removed. What else did he plan to do to stop her?

"Now." A tremor shook the contractor's voice. "We'll proceed." Scollarta read off the next number.

She hefted the crate. Raschad walked away from the contractor and around the stack of crates marked with her sign. She thought he was counting. With a nod, he flipped off the dock and began helping her load. The rest of the pile was all right, then. Dog Girl towed off the loaded sled, and Bocho Man pulled up the empty. Falling into a rhythm, she and Raschad filled it quick.

"We'll just be to Slackets' and back," she called up to Scollarta as she cinched down the final canvas.

"There's no need. Our scale is in working order."

"I don't mind the cost." She felt like spitting on the man. "Tiny's scale's been recertified. I checked first thing."

"Do as you wish. But you have one hour to walking time. I wouldn't waste a breath."

Already hooked in, she ignored the man and pulled her sled toward Tiny and Mike's. Raschad eased alongside. "He himself would never waste your time."

She looked at Raschad sharp and decided he was smiling. She smiled back, in spite of everything. "You know, newbie, I'm beginning not to feel so bad about taking you with me."

"Don't judge hastily."

"Get on." She waved him forward, still smiling. "Watch out for Mike. She likes a cute sitter."

He made a face and pulled ahead. While he centered his sled on the scale, she signed in with Tiny, keeping the weigh record extra clean today. Raschad watched the scale reading. Mike waved. Raschad pulled off the scale, and Sal pulled forward.

And Frim Urt's bullybys showed up.

The boys flowed around Raschad's load slick and quick. The pack did muscle work for the docks when they worked at all, and she figured they were on Scollarta's salary today. If she'd weighed on the government scale, the contractor would have put her overweight. But he knew she'd go to the Slackets' scale, so he'd arranged trouble for her here, off government property.

Frim leaned on the newbie's load, and one bastard headed toward her sled. Mike stepped in front of that bullyby hefting a big wrench. He backed off.

"Haia, whore," Frim yelled at the newbie. "Ya goin' to make a load o' credit on this run?"

Sal's breath puffed out. But Raschad didn't react, didn't blink, just sat on his sled, harness loose about his shoulders, and stared through the toughs.

The bullybys shifted, restless. Sal ignored them and continued her weigh-in.

"I'm talking to ya, newbie." Frim spit at Raschad's sled. "Banks is a good ol' gal."

Aia, then why wouldn't any of the bastards pack with her? Her eyes flicked to Raschad—still no reaction.

"What ya be whoring with Sal for? I hear ya likes the white boys better."

Frim shoved forward, trying to get in Raschad's face. But the newbie sat too high for the bully to gain effective position. Raschad stared out at the depot, his expression blank.

Frim fell back a step. Newbies were ignorant about the jungle, but they didn't reach the green without knowing how to fight. A man with Raschad's confidence, carrying heavy tech, wasn't tackled lightly.

Tiny handed over her completed load sheets to Sal. Across the street a knot of guards had assembled, making sure no greenie trouble flowed onto the docks. Scollarta was nowhere in sight. Bad game the contractor played. Sal chewed a fingernail. "Thanks, Tiny." She tucked her tech waterproofed load sheets inside her shirt, slid between her steering bars, and ran her sled off the scale and alongside Raschad's. The bullybys gave way, then encircled both sleds.

"Haia, Mike." She unclipped again. Mike lumbered over as if she'd been waiting for an excuse. "You watch these brats for me? I got to use your dump."

Mike smiled, showing green-stained teeth, and chinked one of the boys with her wrench. The bastard yelped and moved. No one started anything—yet. Frim's group talked big, but acted slow. Besides, to collect their pay, they only had to keep her away from the dock clerk a little longer.

Frim's eyes followed her as she headed for the garage. But as long as her sleds stayed in sight, she figured he wouldn't worry about where she went. As if in a hurry, she trotted into an open repair bay and out again through a side door.

The Slackets' dumphouse hugged the edge of the cliff, and its hole never needed redigging. She didn't want to guess where their slop ended up, but right now didn't care. Easing to the front corner of the garage, out of sight of the bullies, she watched Dog Girl and Bocho Man take their turn weighing and run off the scales in the opposite direction from her sleds.

She still had time to spare—not much, but some. Dog Girl hauled back across the street, and Bocho Man pulled right past Sal's lookout. Dodging alongside, hidden from the bullies by the sled loads, she darted up to Dog Girl.

"Gettin' real close." Dog Girl spoke without looking at her as they parked beside the dock.

Sal glanced around. Everyone's attention was still focused on Raschad and Slackets' Garage. No one had noticed her yet, except the load-by-load, standing alone near the head of the dock. What *was* her business here?

"You pushed for time, Girl?" Sal clenched her weigh record and load sheets in one hand. "Want to trade?"

Dog Girl growled and shoved her sheets into Sal's hand. Bocho Man strode up and caught Sal's from behind.

They queued up at the dock window, again out of sight of the crowd at the garage. Sal stood second in line. Tikey O'hoorahan stalked up wader-legged at her back, the woman's crew busy watching the confrontation across the street.

The dock clerk at the counter skimmed the sheets Bocho Man handed him, noted the weight and tally, circled Scollarta's signature, affixed an official seal, and handed them back to Bocho Man. Bocho Man smiled, which should have warned anyone, but govies paid no attention to greenies.

Bocho Man stepped aside, and she moved to the window. The clerk fiddled with his visor.

"Mas Scollarta wants to see these." His eyes flicked to the growing crowd of packers at her back, and he took her load sheets without even looking at them. "Be a moment." The man left.

So did she. Sal caught her already sealed and approved manifest from Bocho Man and skimmed through the mud, headed for her sleds. Every greenie packer on the docks came with her except Dog Girl. Sal reckoned that was good news for the bullies, because Dog Girl's name came from biting real low.

The government guards watched, but stayed out of it. The Slackets' yard was Tumble Town property, not government.

Frim glanced at Sal and back at Mike. Mike smiled, thumping her wrench against a rock-hard thigh. Raschad stood up, all muscle and tension.

"No cause for you boys to get hurt." Sal smiled. "I got more time left than it'll take to clean ya'll out."

Frim hesitated, but wasn't as stupid as he looked. The bullybys eased back. Sal and Bocho Man pushed the bullies nearest them, Sal's eyes locked on Frim's.

He gnawed his lip, looked at Tikey's lads, and shook his head. His bunch backed off. Scollarta wasn't paying enough.

Sal moved in quick. The other packers followed her, pulling out the garbage the bullies had stuffed in her runners, and Raschad dug a hank of reeki vine out his tread governor. Now wouldn't that make a deadly surprise headed downhill? His eyes met hers, his expression ugly.

"I know. But c'mon. We beat them by moving out fast."

She slipped between her steering bars and clipped into her traces. Raschad cinched up.

"Burn reeki." Tikey slapped Sal's buttocks.

Hands pushed her sled, and she skimmed down the street, picking up speed before her shoulders adjusted to the weight on them. Twinges stabbed her bruised body, but she concentrated on her feet, sledding quick and quiet past the dock.

Depot guards watched the greenies streaming back toward the dock and ignored her. But she caught the load-by-load's eyes on them and figured she knew who'd been after her contract.

Scollarta was nowhere in sight, and Dog Girl waved from the depot window, still waiting. Sal smiled and tipped her hat. Once Scollarta read the name on those load sheets he thought were hers, he'd have to change his pants.

Skating on down the street, she and Raschad pulled into a delivery alley behind Vos's Grocery. The narrow lane, overhung by drooping blue-green lorri trees, led behind the Sundowner and back to the main street directly across from the East Pike trail head. Leaves crunched beneath the sleds' treads, sending up a fruity perfume, and out of the sun and hidden from view of anyone uphill, she breathed relief.

Next to the Sundowner, pulling into sunlight, she held her breath again. But no guards met them, and she put her shoulders to harness, pulled off the hill and onto the trail proper, hauling fast and hard, down and down.

Passing an old stone marker, toppled on the freshly burned shoulder of the trail, she felt a familiar sideways tug. But the green had long since taken anything worth finding out there.

She pulled into heavy scrub, figuring no govie squad would follow this far, and glanced in her load mirror. The newbie pulled head down, fighting his steering bar. She put on some speed. Her hand hurt; her hip ached. But she might as well see how much he knew. He had a lot of jungle ways and less tech than most newbies. But best he be reminded who was native here and that green tech worked best—clean and proven.

By the time she stopped, she figured she'd overdone her test of Raschad. Head twinging, shirt stuck to her sides, sweat running beneath her bushwhackers, she crooked her neck around her load to check on the newbie.

"Haia, alive?" She tried to keep her voice steady and disguise her own panting.

He dropped on his sled bumper with a hand over his ribs. She'd been watching him. He'd done all right—he'd quit fighting his steering and settled into harness as if remembering past pulls.

"Hurt?" she called back.

"No—naia." He sucked short breaths. "Soft."

"My problem, too." She slipped her traces, braced her hands on her knees and hung her head.

"Safe now?" He motioned over his shoulder.

"Aia."

"Good." He grabbed a reeki vine, broke it off, and smeared sap over his face and hands, slapping bugs as he worked.

"You're a little winded, newbie man." Sal straightened and walked back to join him.

His lips quirked, and he shrugged. She smiled. She'd be yelling if anyone worked her like that right off.

"What happens with that contractor when you get back to town?" His attention stayed on his grease job.

She was tempted not to answer him, to tell him to stop being rude. But it was just his way, and he did have lots to learn.

"Nothing, I hope." She swatted gnats off her face netting. "Scollarta could raise trouble, but the greenies will be after his ass if he does."

Raschad nodded, seeming relieved. Bugs whined, and the gum trees weeped goo. She watched him sap himself like a native. When he looked up, she'd have sworn he was greenie—except for his eyes, and except she knew better. Brought a *newbie* packing . . . forgive her for a fool. She shook her head.

"What?"

"None your business. Just—" Piss, if he could be rude, so could she. "How much you know about this side of the green?"

"Almost enough to fill a fleepa's brain."

"Settlers save us."

"Aia. And luck." He laughed, not much amused.

"Won't survive long depending on luck, Raschad. You got to use your head out here, think all the time. We're headed into Aireil and gigi country both."

"Aia." She heard a quaver in his voice.

"Scared?" He shrugged. "Well, you should be. But you can't panic. I ain't been stopped by a mistwalker in two years. But if we are, you just stand still. No running or jerking, no movin' at all. Don't breathe if you can help it. They'll feel you up a little, then go on their way. They're just curious, just test people. But if you move, you'll be another dead newbie."

He blinked. His bottom lip quivered. Shrike, newbies don't expect to survive. Or maybe that wasn't what he thought at all. How would she know?

"Raschad." She rocked on her heels in the mud. "Something I should say. I don't mean to use you. This ain't an easy trip ever, and I been warned the mistwalkers are riled on one trail and gigis're south of here. But I won't throw you away."

"Don't worry." He slipped a hand behind his head and arched his neck. "We're all used, some of us just more than others. I learned that lesson young. Now I'm purely commodity, and I've been paper for a long time and on more than one planet."

How to answer that, Sal hissin' didn't know.

Chapter 7

Tired joints creaked. Lebob palms snagged Sal's hat from above and screeched finger-length thorns against the sled's load canvas. The palms' cloying stench, even with the day cooling down, half suffocated her. Her feet burned. Her shoulders ached, and her back was all one misery. But she'd long since led Raschad past her usual camping spot, and there was no stopping now short of Klinker's Clearing—her first drop on this route. Normally, she hit the settlement her second day out. But if they kept moving, she figured to reach it by midnight.

Arms braced on the steering bars, she wrestled her overloaded sled along the darkening trail. The shrilling of insects tore her nerves and numbed her ears, and the soft flesh beneath her waistband burned where something had set up housekeeping. Sweat puddled in her boots, trickled down her spine, and dripped off her nose. And a fruit gnat had wriggled beneath her face netting.

Sled Scollarta to hell. The gnat crawled maddeningly around one eye. Even idiots would be camped by now. But with Scollarta maybe scheming to snatch her next load before she returned, she hauled past common sense. Who had the scum sold her out to? Frim didn't pack. Must be that Oofall woman. But the packer couldn't haul this contract alone.

Chewing worries, Sal dragged an untried newbie partner into the hell of a night trek. But Raschad didn't complain, didn't stop. She wished he would; it would give her an excuse to rest. But he stayed behind her just where he should, his sled treads crunching new growth and debris, his load scraping brush on both sides.

This section of trail needed burning. Three people abreast could just pass . . .

Thump. Her sled hung up. Her harness yanked her back.

Idiot, running blind, snagging what could be avoided in daylight. She tested the feel of her steering bars and traces, then tested harder with an angry lunge.

Treads creaked, and the sled canted. Her gut dropped out, and the whole big load tipped.

"Newbie!" She hit her harness clips, freeing herself, but stayed between the steering bars to wrestle the sled.

A grunt sounded. The sled steadied. "Lay on it, Banks!"

She threw her weight left. *Crack.* The sled dropped, hit level, and drove a steering bar into her gut. Lungs paralyzed, she heard Raschad scrabbling over her load.

"Banks?" He hit the ground beside her as she barked in half a lung full of air. "Scut, Banks."

She forced another half breath as his hands slid over her ribs. "S'all—" She sucked air.

He eased her off the jammed steering bar. "Banks?"

"Unh . . ." He loosened her belt and she caught another breath. "S'aright."

"Here. Up." He lifted her like a babe, for all her size.

"Gon' get—" She panted. "—'ernia yet."

"Then quit running into things."

He settled her atop the load and crawled up beside her. Sweat-wet and reeki-sapped, he didn't smell too fine now. But his touch was steady and reassuring, and she relaxed and breathed easier—except here he was nursing her again.

"How you?" She forced words past the knot in her chest.

"Tired."

She liked that he didn't lie about it. "You're—" She sucked a long, slow breath. "—doin' good. Just saved my rump for sure."

"Don't want to be out here alone." He humped his shoulders, stretched stiffened muscles. "Here." He straightened, and his hand settled on her back.

"What?"

"Work the cramps out for you?" His hand didn't move.

"Aia." Aia? Letting him touch her again?

His fingers dug into her shoulder muscles. She suppressed a shiver. He kept his touch polite, but the kneading felt good, all too nice.

"Thanks." She pulled away. Wasn't time for fun. She sat up, legs dangling off the load. "You got talent."

"Any time there's a need."

She hoped he meant it just as he said it—when she *needed*, not when she or he *wanted*. There was only politeness in his tone.

Cre-ee-ak. The sled settled another notch. Sal started to slip off into the mud.

"I'll get it. Rest."

Voice hushed, he caught her arm and dropped to the ground. Examining the sled's treads with his handlight, he trained the beam beneath the load, flicking it on and off to avoid attracting bugs, fleepas, or worse. The man did know jungle ways.

Howlers clamored above—a troop of the big squirrels settling for the night. This was no place and dusk no time to be sitting still. Her scream for help had been a fool's holler, and might bring anything stalking their back trail. Her stomach twisted.

Slap. Slap.

With bugs eating Raschad, his night would be long and miserable. Fruit gnats she could handle, but the damned tick under her belt . . . She swatted the gnat at her eye, pulled netting tighter at her throat, and tugged at her waistband.

Raschad's head rose, a dark shadow in fading light.

"Big stob. I think I can lever the sled over when you're up to pulling again. Can you pull?"

"Aia. Ain't nothing. Another little bruise."

Teeth clenched, Sal slid off the front of the sled to examine the left steering bar. Then she dug out her botafab tread mallet—well, seven tech things she used. Not that botafab was hard tech, or that anyone else would feel guilty about carrying the mallet, it being green tech. But using it meant depending on things and people she didn't understand. She shouldn't have lost Cab's old ironwood mallet; she should ask Morrie about how to make her own. But she had this one. A whack freed the bar, and she dug her headlamp from the front sled locker. The lamp was another tech tool. So make it eight. But Raschad carried plenty more than eight techy gadgets.

At the sled's rear Raschad rattled her metal pry bar—which she counted as part of the sled—out of its rack.

"Scut da . . ." Raschad's curse scaled upward.

Brush cracked. Sal drew her Camm and thumbed the power. "Newbie?"

"Snake." His voice quavered. "I'm all right—have an unusual fear of things that slither up my sleeve."

"Don't sound unusual to me." She shivered. "Moa?"

"Not likely. I'm alive." He moved to the other side of the sled. "Ready?" His voice was a whisper in the dusk.

"Aia."

"Now." The sled shifted.

She leaned into her harness, muscles aching, stomach bruised, expecting no good luck. But Raschad grunted, leaned into the pry bar, and the sled edged forward, one step, two . . . it broke free. For a newbie, he was handy.

Pulling uptrail, she waited for his whistled signal that he followed. Did he know to signal her?

Whee-ewe. His whistle carried above howler racket. Good boy. Sal pulled into darkness, guilt riding her shoulders.

Only a wrong-headed fool brought a newbie into the green. She was using him—no better than the rest. Morrie had tricked her into this, and Raschad was smart and tough. But newbies needed taking care of—which wasn't her strong point.

A gigi barked in the distance. A shiver chilled her spine. Ghosts danced in the dusk. *Going to get him killed.* But there was no turning back now.

Howler whoops and fleepas' bedding-down chatter gave way to the deep night yowls of prowling seeg prides and, once, the long chilling roar of a scriar.

The dagger-toothed hunter ranged behind them, and the roar had to fray Raschad's nerves. Sal sped up, but he whistled a stop. Crawling over her load, she found him hung up on a rock. They levered it free together, and the night wore on.

The scriar roared nearer. Raschad whistled twice. *Hurry,* he meant. She didn't blame him. Myron Klinker wouldn't appreciate them leading a blood hunter to the house. She pulled faster anyway.

Ground slid away beneath the sleds' churning treads. But in the dark it took all her attention to feel out the trail without worrying on scriars. She slowed again.

Sweat streamed her sides. Her nerves blipped and twinged. Two full moons rode the sky somewhere overhead tonight—they were the main reason she'd decided to tackle this late run. But little light reached the jungle floor. Flashing her headlamp, she pulled around a pothole and killed the light.

Halos blinded her. Wind sighed high above. Leaves pattered on her shoulders. Bushmice squeaked, and coonies crooned . . .

Raschad whistled, high and shrill. Sal braked and lunged for the rifle on the front of her sled.

Brush snapped. A snarl rose into the spine-rattling cry that gave the scriar its name. *Going to kill,* that yowling wail said. Terror shot down her back.

A blast flashed. *Boom.* A maddened roar tore the night.

Kill it. *Boom*. What kind of hell tech did he use?

She was half over the top of her load, going for Raschad in spite of running blind . . . *Boom*.

The blast flash left her a confused impression of a body tumbling into brush. She froze, glare-blind and trembling, the jungle silent as death.

"Raschad?" She swallowed panic.

"Banks." His voice shook. "How much farther?"

Her breath rushed out. "Gettin' close. It dead?" But what wouldn't be, after all that?

His handlight flicked on, off. She blinked, not certain she'd seen right. The scriar's body, as big as Raschad's loaded sled, lay there headless, its sleek black coat splattered with gore.

"You all right?"

"Cut, not bad," he answered.

She scrabbled off the end of her load. "You made a hell of a mess of it for using hand tech."

"Big load. Down its throat."

Brush raked her shoulder, and insect legs skittered off her leathers. She followed the sound of his panting and found him slumped against his load.

"I'm fine." He shuddered.

"Where you cut?" She touched his shoulder.

"Hand."

She flashed her headlamp. Blood covered his glove, but his fingers seemed intact. "Have an infection before morning."

"No." But his body slackened. She caught his arm and steadied him onto the sled bumper. "Need to move," he said, panting.

"We will when that's wrapped."

She stuck her hands inside her shirt and wiped them as clean as she could on her shoulder padding. Raschad sat still, leaking blood onto the ground, he and the scriar sending death scent into the night. *Got to get out of here.*

Sal dug her aidkit from her belt and found a length of bandage and a packet of gall paste to kill germs. "Ready?"

"Do it."

She grabbed his wrist. He jerked back. She clamped his arm under hers and squeezed gall in the wound. Silent, he shivered against her while she took a good tight wrap on his hand.

"Shrike." He flinched.

"Aia, me, too." She tied it off. And he laughed, surprising the hell out of her. "C'mon." She slapped his leg. He wobbled up and

backed between his steering bars, holding his hand to his chest.
"Can't steer that way. Here."

Using the rest of the bandage strip, she strapped the bar to his
arm so he could steer without using the torn hand. He clipped
onto his traces with the other hand.

Turning for her own sled, she tripped and her lamp flashed
down. The scriar's elongated head snarled up at her, mouth frozen
wide, finger-length fangs glittering white. The head sat on a
seven-toed paw as broad and flat as a griddle, a foot designed to
carry the long-bodied hunter over mucky ground. Its eyes shone
back yellow in the night, and she snapped the lamp off, climbed
over her load, and started pulling. Scriar claws brought money,
but she wasn't collecting tonight.

Going to pay Scollarta, dig her thumbs into the contractor's
flabby throat. Rage gave Sal strength. Get you for this, too,
Morrie. A gigi yelped, and her scalp pimpled, but the little devil
was far off. A seeg yowled nearer. She listened for Raschad's
sled, heard it, and went on into a hint of moonlight sifting through
thinning tree canopy.

Getting close now—had to be close. Had the Klinkers heard
Raschad's shots? They'd be fools to come out in the dark.

She pulled. The tree trunks thinned and the brush thickened.
She broke through into moonlight and sighted a row of jagged
black teeth against a shimmering sky—Myron's palisade.

"Never knew you to be stupid, Banks."

Sitting with Raschad's head facedown in her lap, his good arm
trapped beneath her, his scriar-clawed elbow pinned under her
knee, Sal agreed with Myron. Irrist, Myron's wife, bent over
Raschad's wounded hand, flushing the tear with jungle brew.

"Newbie?"

He grunted. She'd be screaming. But he could handle the pain,
the same as he'd handled it in Tumble Town. His fussing in the
jungle had just been nerves. Just a scared man.

"A newbie, no less." Myron stewed. "What possessed you?"

"Left town a breath before my contract run out, Myron," Sal
answered, ignoring his rudeness for now. "That's what possessed
me. I needed muscle, had to make time."

"You never run this late. A woman packed through here with
you last time."

"Aia, Chic. But it's a long story, Myron."

"Well, if you want to sleep tonight, spit it out."

"My partner come up pregnant clear up to Waterwheel."

She told them the whole maddening mess, from Chic dropping out on her to Morrie's tricks, then hiring Raschad, the bar fight, and Scollarta.

All that time, she held the shirtless newbie, her stomach in knots. Harness galls oozed on his shoulders. His chest looked even worse. Idiot—just because he could pull a sled didn't mean he was broke to harness. Whatever Sal told Myron now about not using newbies, with the shape Raschad was in, Myron wouldn't believe her. She didn't know if she believed herself.

Irrist's probing reached a little deeper than the newbie's control, and he startled.

"Easy. Easy, man." Sal blotted sweat from his face with a rag. "He ain't a bad packer, Myron, or we wouldn't have got here."

"Aia. Well, and I thank him for cleanin' out that scriar. But he won't leave in the morning, if he leaves ever. Ma learned me, 'Feed newbies, then run 'em off.' And that's what I done all my life—till now you bring him, wanting him kept alive. Naia a way to do that. You'll just weight my soul with his dying."

"I won't die." Raschad startled them both. She'd thought him too far gone to listen. "Banks." He grunted into her thigh. "Find my medkit. Front pouch. Find a blue med packet with a big M on it. That will clear up whatever reeki tea doesn't."

Sal's eyes met Myron's. *Reeki tea?* A man who believed in tech medicine and greenie cures in the same breath? She rolled an eye at Irrist.

"I'll fetch tea." Myron looked glummer than ever.

"Grab that black pack, will you, Irrist?"

The woman hefted Raschad's personal kit. Sal caught it and broke open the front pocket. Packets spilled on the newbie's chest. "Shrike, Raschad, you got a whole apothecary in here."

He only grunted. She found three blue packets, saved one out, and stuffed everything else back where she'd found it. What else did he have in there?

"Here." Myron returned, carrying a plain crockery teapot—of his own make—and a big mug. "It's not too hot."

"Put the med in the tea." Raschad's lips barely moved.

"Squat." She gagged doing it. The powdered medicine floated on the tea's oily surface, and the mixture's sight and smell turned her stomach. "Here."

She steadied Raschad as he raised his head and drank the mess in two loud gulps. His breath whooshed out, sucked in, and he looked ready to lose everything. But then he breathed out slow again. His muscles slackened, and he dropped limp on the sleeping pallet, done.

Hair wet to his head, face green with sap, old bruises yellowed beneath the grime and his mouth hanging open, he was no pretty sight. But she only cared that she *had* a partner come daylight. Which wasn't, she thought, collapsing at his side, very far off now, nor his living likely.

"Talk in the morning, Banks." Myron gathered up rags and washbasins, and he and his wife left.

Raschad moaned. Sal laid her palm against his cheek; it burned already. But sitting up with him wouldn't help, and she'd just come too far today, couldn't keep her eyes open any longer. Her stomach feeling as if she'd eaten lead, she sank down, her mind spinning. He'd just have to live or die on his own.

But she shocked awake, checked him, dozed, and startled again, her fitful sleep filled with gigis and nightmare. First she found him choked dead, choked while she slept. Next she dreamed she doctored and doctored him, but he died anyway . . .

Her eyes snapped open. She whipped straight up, Camm in hand, and thunked into Raschad's bare chest.

"Sorry." He eased back against the wall.

"You're alive!"

"Last I checked."

"Sorry." She reholstered her Camm, swallowed against a sleep-rotted mouth.

"Now we're even."

"Guess ain't neither of us used to sleeping with anyone."

He shook his head. "Are they short on mats around here?"

"Aia. That scriar you killed last night had already scared in a flock of gatherers. Myron and Irrist have a full house." She bit her lip. "Look at you—breathing, talking, making sense."

His lips quirked, almost smiled. "Told you."

"Who believes a newbie."

"I'm an old newbie." His eyes laughed at her.

She wouldn't have minded that, except the house was so quiet, and she lay there half naked, enjoying his company. Sunlight sparkled off white walls and danced halos about his head. Shrike. She couldn't take her eyes off him. He picked at a raw spot on his chest, the gall already healing.

"Whoever taught you about drinking reeki tea for infection was a smart one." Conversation seemed safer than just staring.

"Hiram, the tramp who led me into Mafeezie's, wouldn't leave

Capitol with me until I drank a cup of reeki without throwing up. It took about a week." Raschad smiled and shrugged.

"He saved your life last night."

"He saved it more often than that."

Sal nodded. "A body could miss such help."

"Aia." He meant it, and friendship between a greenie and a newbie came rare.

"Reckon you're awful sore for pulling today." She half wished he'd agree.

"Be fine," he told her. Had he thought even once about not pulling? she wondered. "The load will be lighter today."

"Naia. Myron has trade goods for farther on."

"But he'll feed us?" Raschad sounded desperate.

"Shrike." She shook her head at newbie bluntness. "You and food. Lizard, fleepa, child, or newbie, show up in Irrist's kitchen and she'll feed you. But first we visit the showers."

"Showers?" His voice quavered.

"Aia. The Klinkers make tile. Have their own water closets, too. Myron's prosperous and a bit techy." Sal eased out of their bedding, tugging down her shirt to hide bare thighs. "The story about Klinker's Clearing is that a rock miner blew a load of explosives and herself to heaven. At the same time, she blew a long, deep hole in the gravel bed that runs under the jungle here." Sal wormed her feet into her pants legs without bending over. "When Klinker's Granna and Granpa come salvaging the rockie's gear, they thought the crater such a pretty pro-pi-tious present, as Myron calls it, that they turned the hole into a leach field, set up their privy, and built this palisade. Their insight—some call it *end-sight*—made them prosperous."

"Must be a big field to last this long without pumping."

He slapped a stinging fly and flipped the stunned critter to a pink packy spider that rode its web in the corner next to his head. The whole affair was so casual, she almost missed it. This was an uncommonly comfortable newbie.

"They don't use the leach field for straight dumping." She tugged her pants up. "Everything's filtered first. Then the water trickles south into the ku-soo trees, and the woodlot soaks up what's left. Most of the gravel they keep clean, run pipes through it and pump chilled water back to cool the house."

"I appreciate their ingenuity." He stretched and sighed.

"Come on."

With heat building in her just from the sight of him, even tak-

ing a shower together seemed safer than sitting here. He wobbled
up, using the wall for support.

"Here, now." She caught his arm. "Easy." He wobbled off the
mat and stood a moment, refinding his legs, his body warm
against her side. "Got it?"

"Aia," he said. "Just stiff. I thought digging was hard work . . ."

She grimaced. "Shouldn't have run you like that the first day
out. I was worrying over Scollarta and my contract. Didn't mean
to lie about using you hard, but reckon I did."

"So long as you don't use me any harder than yourself, I've no
complaint."

"Well, you're dumber than I thought."

His lips quirked again. "Where're those showers?"

"Come along."

She opened their door into a long hallway. Tall windows
framed either end of it, and whitewashed ku-soo-paneled walls—
streaked with yellow, pink, and green fluorescent lichen—
reflected sunlight deep into the house. Everyone used ku-soo for
building, since the Aireils didn't object to seeing it cut; they
wouldn't stand for any logging of most other trees. She turned
left, leading Raschad down a wooden stairwell. He gripped the
carved banister, still moving slow.

The main house jutted into the compound's enclosed yard like
a big block stuck on the stockade's back wall. On the ground floor
a side door let them out onto a graveled path, fronting the apart-
ments and workshops that lined the palisade's interior. Above
everything ran a stockade of ku-soo logs—adzed to a point, hardened by fire, then set butt down into the compound's rammed-
earth walls. Whitewashed clay plaster coated the stockade, and
blue-green mi-mi vines and orange que pea blossoms stood out
bright and lacy around deep-silled doors and windows.

Raschad blinked in the brilliant morning light, and his eyes
wandered, his expression dazed. Sal knew how he felt—Myron's
place was always pretty.

"In here." Sal waved him toward an arched doorway.

The shower room occupied the compound's northeast corner
and sat low in the ground beneath a watch room. From the outside, it was easy to expect some dim storage cellar. But ducking
down the entrance steps, they entered an open expanse of tile
floor and tile walls. And shallow windows ran just below the ceiling, spilling light over everything.

"Oh." Raschad stopped on the bottom step and stared, eyes

rounded. "When you said they made tile, I didn't imagine . . ." He waved a hand at the empty washroom.

Standing tubs of rippling water caught the sunlight and reflected bubbly patterns on the walls and ceilings, and the tile itself shone and shimmered with soft pink and blue luminescence.

She'd hoped for company in the washroom, didn't want to strip naked alone with this man, not with her blood running hot this morning. But Klinker's people had come and gone, leaving everything spotless and sweet-smelling.

"How . . ." Raschad stopped short of his usual rudeness and simply ran his hand over the tiles nearest him.

"Klinker uses a special recipe." His attempted politeness set Sal in a mood to indulge his curiosity, especially if it kept his eyes off her. "They start with plain clay slabs. After sun-curing, the tiles are wet again and certain molds sprayed on 'em. Then they're dried again. The dead mold gives the color, I guess. I know there's some vermin resin, too, that helps the hardness and adds the shiny glaze. Klinker doesn't use firing at all, doesn't believe in cutting trees, smokin' the air, or dumping charcoal. But I never seen prettier tiles than these anywhere. Of course, I suppose fine tile is common off-planet."

"Not this fine." He stepped down onto the main floor. "This whole compound. I didn't know there was anyplace like this in the green."

"There's a lot you don't know. Folks have built other places just as pretty in their own way. That's why I don't give up the Pike run. I like it this side of the jungle."

"Why . . ." He limped to a long bench, set his personals kit down, and restarted the conversation with politer phrasing. "But you don't stay."

"Ain't my kind of life, sittin' down hard just to keep a fancy place. The green's prettier."

His expression shifted, and he looked thoughtful, as if he didn't understand her thinking—which she didn't expect, anyway.

She set her own things on the bench across from the one he'd chosen. Being in here alone with him was like sleeping and everything else with him, just shriking strange. Made her shy all of a sudden, and his eyes shifted away from her.

"If you need help again . . ." She hated to have to offer, but his hand would hamper him.

"Let me soak first, and you take your own shower. Don't rush, this looks good."

He turned his back, dropped his pants—all he had on—and slid into a bank of showers. Being prim now seemed silly after living together at Morrie's for four days. But they hadn't been alone at the shack.

Unbuttoning her shirt, Sal waited until he ducked out of sight beneath the shower spray, then quickly stripped and scooted behind a partition into a separate bank of showers. Sun-warmed water, already so hot she had to mix in cold, ran from the watch-room roof above through imported botafab pipes and out the tech shower head. The spray felt finer than any rich man's clothes, but she scrubbed fast and ducked back out. Raschad still stood haloed in glittering mist, water droplets shining about him bright as diamonds.

Shimmying into her underthings—loose drawers and a tight T-top to keep things from bouncing—she decided this was one of those times when she wished she was as scrawny and close-chested as Tikey O'hoorahan.

She tugged on her loose outer shirt, felt herself back on better footing, and wanted Raschad dressed, too. "Don't wash yourself down the drain, newbie."

He reached down a towel from the wooden hanging poles that ran above the showers and turned his back to her. Pinning the flaffiber towel with the elbow of his injured arm, he used his good hand to wrap it around his waist.

She spoke to fill the silence. "That felt good."

"Aia. Did I get all the soap out?" He ducked his head, and his long hair fell forward.

"Naia." A streak of green showed above both of his ears, and blackened sap stained the back of his good hand. "Let's finish you at the sinks." Sal motioned him nearer. "Stick your head in one, and I'll wash your hair decent."

"Thanks. I'll dig the tick out of your back in trade . . . if you like."

"You notice too much, newbie." She sucked her bottom lip.

"You've been worrying with it all morning."

"Was afraid to let Myron touch me last night. The mood he was in, he might've burned right on through."

Raschad laughed. Wrinkling her nose, Sal waved him toward a long, tiled counter inset with gray milkstone basins.

He moved across the room with the same easy flow of bone and muscle that had fooled her at the beginning into thinking him greenie. Truth be, she'd never seen a man—greenie *or* newbie—move so sure. Gigis, he was alien, and so different. But all she could think to describe his difference was *pretty*, no sharp angles—which she had everywhere—no flabby bulges, just muscle flowing into muscle, jungle-blooming pretty, though he could use more weight.

He turned the sink spigot, and water sprayed out. He ducked his head, bracing himself with his forearms. She eased up beside him, bent over his shoulder, and ran her hands through his long hair. This made twice that she'd washed it, when she'd never done George's even once. Worse, Raschad smelled of Irrist's povi-blossom soap.

"You wear your hair shaggy as a howler's." But it slipped between her fingers fine as banti silk.

"Since Hiram died, no one has been around to cut it. I keep it out of my eyes, and the rest protects my neck."

She dumped tech soap on his head and chased out a couple of crawlies. "The critters enjoy it."

"As long as they're gone now."

Her laugh sounded nervous. Embarrassed, she grabbed a cup, filled it quick, dumped the water over his head—

"Scuts!" He jerked up, spraying water.

"Shrike!" She clenched her burning hands. She'd scalded them both—damn solar collectors. "Sorry, I—"

He bumped blind into her side. Words failed her, and he froze, his bare chest in her face, the heat of him taking her senses. They panted against each other.

"Sorry, Raschad." Her cheeks burned.

He shook his head. "Left is hot. Right tap is cold."

"I can read, idiot." She grabbed his wet head, shoved it in the sink, and readjusted the tap flow. Finishing his shampoo, she leaned against his fine body, glad he was a rude fool and had stopped her from making a fool of herself. "There. That ought to hold you until we hit the trail."

"Thank you." He straightened, swiping water out of his eyes and looking embarrassed.

"Ain't going to jump you." Both of them understood the real irritation here.

"I know," he said.

"Then don't act so nervous."

"I . . . I'd rather not have Myron shoot me. If . . ."

"Aia." It hurt. But she understood. The Klinkers wouldn't hold with a newbie and a greenie getting personal right here. "I still need that tick out."

"You trust me?"

"I trust you to dig out a tick—nothing much more."

"Just let me get some clothes on."

He straightened and sidled away toward his pack, and he was rude all over, had apparently felt some heat, too. At least he wasn't just using Myron as an excuse to escape her. Sal mopped water off the counter.

"Banks?"

"What now?"

"Can't button them."

She turned. He sat next to his kit with his pants gaping and his wounded hand held in the air.

"You're asking a lot." She stepped across to his bench. "Stand up." He stood. She grabbed his fly and buttoned, her eyes focused past her hands at the floor. "Don't ask again."

At least he laughed. "Sorry, Banks."

"Aia, you're the sorriest thing I ever met."

"That tick still needs digging." He patted the bench. She wrinkled her nose, but the shriking tick hurt more than her pride. Teeth gritted, she stretched out flat on the bench and pressed her face into a wadded towel. It smelled of Raschad, which did nothing for her frame of mind.

Dropping to his knees beside her, he raised the hem of her shirt. "And you call me dumb." His fingers probed her waist. "I've seen smaller bomb beetles than this."

"A bomb beetle would have blown itself free by now."

He snorted, sat at her head, searched through his kit, and removed a tech sparker like her own. So that was *nine* tech things she owned.

"Going to hurt."

"Have at it." She did her best to breathe steady as he heated the burner's tip and bent over her back. It did hurt. She gritted her teeth. "Umph." A grunt escaped her . . . another.

"Almost . . ."

She held her breath, hating the stink of burning skin. The smell of blood always unsettled her.

"Got it." The sparker lifted off her back. She sucked a breath. "Look." Raschad stuck a bursting fat tick in front of her nose. Hanging from the sparker's tip, it was as round and red as a ring jewel. "Thought it would never come out."

"You thought! Crater feels as big as my boot." She reached back to inspect the burn.

"Wait." His hand blocked hers, and he fumbled in his kit again and dug out a strange-looking tech tube.

"What's that?" All his tech medicine worried her.

"Sealant."

"Sealant?" She twisted half around. "You didn't use it on your hand last night."

"There isn't enough for holes that large, but there's plenty for this. If I don't seal the burn, your harness will gall it, and you'll end up with it infected."

"I got too much greenie blood for infections, and you haven't credits enough to waste sealant on a tick hole." Sal bristled.

Raschad glanced away. "Family sent it."

That stopped her. She'd touched on personal matters again. But he hadn't used the medicine on either his fight cuts or hers. So he must've picked it up the night he went to Government House. Was it family sending him goods, or *was* he earning for special favors to Rimmersin? None of her business.

"Go ahead, then. Spend your tech." She lay back down, ashamed of her thoughts. Letting a newbie use tech on her? Getting soft. The only other time she'd worn sealant, she'd . . . She sucked a deep breath, fought her vision clear.

"All right?" he asked.

"Aia." Dumb rude newbie.

She breathed out slow. But the smell of sealant brought up an image of the government clinic. How had Ma ever paid off that debt? Pa's fancy rifle, bought with his sin money, had disappeared about then. Maybe the drunk wasn't a complete bastard.

Raschad's fingers hit a raw spot, and she flinched.

"Scut, sorry. Made a mess of it."

"Was a mess to begin with." She forced the words between clenched teeth. "You be more careful of your words, though."

He hesitated. "Newbie word?"

"Aia. Spacer talk."

His hand brushed her bare hip, and she shivered. Those hands could drive her crazy.

"Sorry. Can't get it spread right."

He lay the sealant tube in front of her nose and stuck a warm finger over the leaking burn hole in her hip. That left his other fingers dangling where they shouldn't.

"Sorrier." He moved his hand. "Scut."

"You said it again."

"Shrike, then. I'll try to be more careful." She flinched. "Of what I say and what I touch."

"Not a crime. Just be careful . . . of your talk." Words twisted on them both. "Just, when you're reeki-greased, you can pass for greenie if you don't talk. Sometimes that ain't bad."

"Thanks. Open this." He flipped a paper-wrapped sticky patch at her.

She peeled it open, and he stuck it over her tick hole, then wiped her hip with a towel and leaned away. She lay still, wishing he'd finish.

"I haven't had many people to talk to on Ver Day." He stuck the free end of a roll of tech tape to the bench, handed her the roll, and snipped off a piece with the sparker tip. "I should practice greenie more."

She listened to his educated pronunciation, his words flowing together so proper.

"Studying might help." She pulled out another length of tape for him. "But if you want to talk jungle, don't listen to me. Listen to Myron. Or Mooli Toon—she said she took you out. Now, *she* talks jungle."

"I couldn't understand a word she said." Raschad stuck a strip of tape over the sticky pad on her hip. "Didn't know I was hired until she threw a harness at me." He laughed. "Done."

"Good." She eased upright. "We're getting late, and I'm still not wearing pants."

Sal stood straight up, reached for her clothes . . . and saw blood on a pink towel. Little Sara in a berry-dyed dress . . .

Her head spun, and her legs disappeared.

"Whoa."

Raschad's arms stopped her wobble. The nightmare vanished. They stood silent, paralyzed, skin to skin, warm and sweet-smelling. People were wrong about Raschad and men.

"Give yourself a breath." His voice quavered. "That's a deep tunnel I dug in you." The hell, he knew.

He let go. Sal wanted to laugh, felt all crazy. But his letting go hurt, had to hurt him, too, couldn't be an easy choice for a man who tramped the jungle alone.

"Raschad?"

"Best let it be." He turned away and caught up his shirt.

Gentle as he spoke, all considerations considered, she'd just as soon be an idiot and lay him down just now. But she wouldn't ask again or offer pay. He wasn't starving. And he'd made his terms clear before they came packing.

"Wait." She wriggled into her pants. "You need tech on your harness galls."

His eyes closed tight, but he let her skim sealant on his raw chest and shoulders. She kept her mind on his open wounds, each one reminding her that just because he survived one day didn't mean he'd live through the next.

"Thank you for caring, Banks."

She looked into those eyes of his and couldn't answer a thing. Raschad pulled his shirt on in silence. She laced up his boots for him, and they headed for breakfast.

Irrist's eyes wandered from the pale blue bread dough she kneaded, and the mop-headed kids washing dishes stared at Raschad between bubble fights and towel snapping. Sitting at the head of one of three plank tables that stretched from the counter at the head of the kitchen all the way to the side door, Raschad ignored staring eyes and giggly little faces—used to such curiosity, Sal supposed—and concentrated on his roak eggs, smoked hyre gall, and pan bread. Soon enough the Klinkers were too busy wondering at his eating to worry why he didn't talk.

By the time they reached the sleds, Sal wondered how he could carry so much food in one stomach. Maybe liking jungle cooking was what had kept him alive out here this long. It still amazed her that he ate reeki. Shrike, he ate *everything*.

Myron wandered up while they were cleaning treads and checked the load job his crew had done.

"Banks." Myron shook a graying head and stared at Raschad. "He may be alive, but hauling out today ain't smart. Both of you are dragging, and he can't steer proper with that hand. You can replace a newbie, but you're like to lose a sled over it."

Sal turned slow and stared until Myron blinked. "I ain't looking to replace this newbie. I ain't looking to lose a sled. He says he can pull. I believe him. But I'll make sure he knows what he's getting into."

Myron chewed his cheek. "Tell'em he can stay if need be."

She nodded and walked quick around the sled to Raschad. "Myron's worried about us."

"Me, too."

"We could stay here another day."

"No."

"Say 'naia.' You can stay here, period. Myron thinks I'm out using you, and he'll keep you until you heal. Of course, he'll make you work it off."

"I can handle today. What's the next stop?"

"McDonnel's. I usually hit here in afternoon, unload, and pull out come morning, like now, reach McDonnel's late. But it's a good rest, good people. Loads will be lighter afterward. Myron's shipment gets off there, plus the McDonnels' order."

"Then I'll be fine. Hope my tick abatement worked."

"Your . . . oh. The hole's fine." Sal glanced sideways at him. "It's nothing to worry over, like your hand."

"I'm healing. Used some sealant while you talked to Irrist. It stuck. Last night it just would have bled out."

"You shouldn't have wasted sealant on me."

"It isn't wasted," Raschad shook his head. "I can handle the jungle, but I don't know these trails, and I can't afford to have you go down."

"Well, I don't trust tech med to prevent that." He trusted too many tech things, still. "Except for once, I managed all my life without it. Don't waste it on me again."

"Sorry." His jaw set and his expression closed down, unreadable. "I forget myself."

What did that mean? But she knew. Newbies didn't back-talk greenies. He fiddled with his steering bars, tested his hand. She just watched, off balance and feeling in the wrong.

"Here." She spoke softer than before. "I'll find some cargo strapping, fix you up like last night, save your hand. If we use a strip pin, you can break free fast if need be."

Binding Raschad to his sled, Sal thought, idiot, idiot, taking this newbie deep into the green. Both of them were crazy. But if they didn't pull out soon, they wouldn't make McDonnel's by dark. And if she didn't keep to schedule, Scollarta would win back all her contracts.

Chapter 8

"Hope you ain't fevered."

Stopped in deep jungle's perpetual twilight, Sal perched on her sled bumper, enjoying a morning breather. Seated beside her, Raschad chewed one of Irrist Klinker's trail bars. Between swallows of the fruit and grain concoction, he licked pink and white tablets out of a small tech container.

"No—naia. These are dietary supplements."

"Di-et-airy ..."

"Extra minerals and vitamins."

"Tom Bill'd find that interesting, I reckon."

Sal eyed him sideways.

"A curious man, your mayor." Raschad rolled his eyes.

"I get curious sometimes."

"The explanation is boring."

"Most of life is."

"Well, certain minerals common on my home planet are rarer here." Raschad chewed and swallowed. "So my body is designed to use these minerals differently from yours." He stuffed his mouth again, swatted bugs, and stared off uptrail.

"Certain minerals," she coaxed. He took the hint.

"Iron is pervasive on MB-2." He slurred his words around his food. "But not on Ver Day. So my body has difficulty extracting enough from what's available in local foods."

"Reckon that's why newbies get sick."

"Aia, partly." He slurped water, his chin dripping diluted reeki sap. "Every off-planeter makes some dietary adjustment."

"None of you belong here, that's all." The words tumbled out before Sal thought.

He gave her a sharp look. "Aia."

Where *did* this man belong?

"Well." She shifted, hunting for a way to heal the moment, feeling as rude as if she'd asked twenty questions. "Reckon haulin' our rumps down this trail is healthiest for both of us just now." She swatted a swarm of glistening, sap-oozing glue flies off his shoulder. "Let's get."

He crammed the trail bar in his mouth and squeezed between the sled's bumper and the wall of green scrub. Palm spears jabbed his bushwackers, and wiry rope-fern fronds brushed his shoulders. He raised his good hand to slap gnats that had snuck beneath his face net while he ate.

"Watch out for—"

His fingers brushed a trailing vine. A white blur smacked his face, and his body snapped taut. She grabbed his wrists. The nurse flower squeaked and slurped.

Raschad jerked, and holding him for the breath it took the nursie to feed on his sweat took all her strength.

The flower released with a tiny puff. Face cleaned and pale, eyes moon-round, he sucked a stuttering breath.

"Easy. Nursies don't hurt you," Sal said. It must've scared him bad. "Don't wet yourself."

He sucked another breath, as ragged as the first. Chest heaving, he shook his head.

She let go of his wrists. "You needed another coating of reeki, anyways."

"Banks . . ." His eyes focused on her, stranger than strange, lost and scared. "Don't ever pin me down again."

"Aia." Her heart skipped. "I thought you might tear it up. Can't have that. Nursies eat lots of bugs."

"I haven't killed one yet."

"Aia." Stupid—she kept forgetting he'd been three years in the green. This couldn't be his first meet-up with the big flower suckers. Her ears burned. "Let's pack."

He nodded and came out of it, tried to smile. But, shrike, he was spooky, with all in all too much she didn't know about him, and no time to learn enough fast enough.

"Banks." He stood bare-faced, netting knocked askew, and looked sick to his stomach. "I didn't mean to criticize. Just . . . be careful. I don't kill flowers. I have killed people."

Her stomach did a slow roll. She'd never seen more hurt in a soul's eyes.

They ate lunch with their sleds parked side by side in a wide spot on the trail. Raschad joined her on her bumper again so she didn't have to pass the biscuits and packaged meat they shared. Pa would wrap dried morel in a bandanna and walk away for a week in the green. *Getting lazy, Sal.*

"I assume you've never packed with a newbie before?" Raschad glanced at her over a biscuit, seeming to have forgotten both his manners and the strain of their earlier stop.

"I hardly even ever *spoke* to a newbie before." Which was none of his business. But she'd coaxed plenty of information from him, and the more they understood each other on this trail, the better they'd work together. "You watch out for my ignorance, and I'll watch out for yours."

"I appreciate it."

"You seem to be using your hand a bit," she noted carefully.

"It's better." He finished his bag of Irrist's trail bars.

"You for certain eat a lot."

"Jungle foods are hard for me to digest. I have to eat more to get the same calories as you do from less food."

He was sort of like the nursies, with their roots up in the air where they couldn't feed proper, had to scavenge extra goodies from every passing body. "Should've warned me to pack extra provisions."

"I brought extras," he said.

"That why your sled pulls so heavy?"

The muscles around his eyes tensed at her question, then relaxed. "It won't pull heavy for long," he teased her back.

"Just don't start eating on my freight. I got to account for it all come the end of the line."

"*Is* there anything edible in there?"

"Damping gel. If you wanta gobble that, it does seal all sorts of leaks."

He smiled. She punched his shoulder. He rocked sideways, and his boot swiped her feet off her steering bar.

"New—" Her rump slipped on the damp bumper. Her boots landed in a puddle, splattering mud on her chest, and she stared up, her mouth half open.

He just smiled. What a newbie—never backed down, acted tractable when it served him, scared *himself* at times—which was what she figured upset him most about the nursie's attack, that he'd come close to hitting her. But his back didn't bend.

"Get!" She swung at him, smiling just enough so he'd know he wasn't in trouble, and he headed for his own sled. "Going to be sassy, I'll just lead out at a run."

"Hell, Banks, you've run all morning."

"Lazy newbie." She closed up the near empty biscuit tin. He was eating her broke already.

"Pushy greenie." He clipped onto his sled.

"Idiot, tech-lover." Getting personal now. But both the teasing and their knowing that the other teased had a good feel—the balance between them shifting from one extreme to the other.

"You win, boss." He strapped his injured arm to his steering bar.

"Boss always wins. Lead out, if I'm running you too hard."

"Aia. I will." And, ready before her, he pulled in front of her sled, surprising her again.

"You lead me into a bog," she yelled at his back, scrambling to follow the idiot, "and I'll drown you."

"You can try." And he pulled out fast, matching her earlier pace until a herd of lipis bounded onto the trail.

The deer danced ahead of them, splayed hooves slinging mud, delicate heads raised, thumb-sized ears pricked. From the rear, the herd's hindquarters—with hair bristled wide in bull's-eye circles of burnt red and white—drew the eye and startled the senses, resembling a monstrous face or several open mouths. From a predator's four-footed vantage, the view had to be real confusing. Sal loved these dainties both for that foolery and the delicate white stars that dappled their brown backs like drops of dew.

Phee-ou—Raschad whistled a warning and slowed, giving the lipis space and time to move on. Which was the smart way to handle them. If a packer drove the herd, the deer would panic and startle into the brush, breaking legs and losing young. Raschad's friend, old Hiram, wherever he'd learned his jungle ways, had taught this newbie well.

In the lead again, late in the day, Sal strained her ears for any hint of prowling predators, strained her eyes against jungle shadow. Fleepas chittered. Muumuus squealed. A wompi bayed in the distance. Nothing . . .

A screech split her eardrums. Her heart slammed her throat. She caught herself and leaned into harness again, trudged on up the trail. Only a wherilin. She spotted the rainbow-colored hen as the bird tipped over a branch, flared scarlet tail feathers, and sent another shrieking shock wave through the jungle.

Palms covering her ears, Sal gritted her teeth. Sweat ran on her thighs and soaked her socks. Familiar aches knotted her calves. On the trail, her list of pains climbed with the heat. But the wherilin's beauty eased other woes.

Dropping her hands, she grabbed her steering bars and skirted a mudpot. A leech vine grasped at her, and she hacked the plant's head off and tossed the sucking tentacle into the bush. Shouldn't have done that—getting tired, getting cranky.

Her left rear tread hit slick mud and skidded. Easing off the steering bars, she let the sled shimmy clear on its own. Shrieking pots. She pulled into standing water. Rot and stench burbled, erupting with little splatters and hisses. A water spout like this would dry up in a day, unless a fungus colony bloomed in it. Then the whole trail might boil under.

She whistled Raschad a warning. He whistled back with an extra warble, meaning he was all right. The jungle favored them today: no gigis, no termite volcanoes erupting mid-trail. The normal troubles—bugs, nursies, mold slicks—those abounded, but nothing they couldn't handle fast.

A second whistle pierced Sal's thoughts—still nothing important. A vine caught in a tread, probably. She dawdled until Raschad whistled her on. Most times the cleats kicked it out on their own, if you worked it right. He was learning.

Sal picked up speed, thinking of how he kept surprising her. Who'd expect he'd pull so strong today after last night's hell haul, or that he'd handle the sled as well one-handed as with two? And he was using the wounded one more and more already—Irrist's stitching and his medicine were working. That sealant was handy. She didn't even feel the hole he'd burned in her this morning.

Her nose twitched. Her sinuses prickled. Almost at McDonnel's, goin' to McDonnel's. She made a little litany of the two phrases, saying them over and over to keep her feet moving. Goin' to McDonnel's and a fine, fine bed.

Franket McDonnel had never enjoyed the luck of finding a catastrophe-created clearing like the Klinkers had lucked on to. Instead, Frankie had hauled her kids to the top of the biggest zassa tree in the biggest zassa grove in the green and just survived.

That was ninety years ago, and the clan had grown until their houses spread through the grove's thick branches like strange, huge nests. They lived by harvesting spice, wild fruits, nuts, and whatever else they found markets for nearby. Thrifty and practical, they'd become a prosperous, happy family.

Sal blinked, craned her head, and lights glittered through the thick growth. She smiled. The place sat so hidden away and different from Klinker's that finding it was a matter of knowing where to look. Well, she knew her jungle.

Relief spread down her back and added a little spring to her step. Goin' to McDonnel's.

Gum trees, phia ferns, quauk brush, lebob palms, noddy trees, and towering burntwoods—this last the tree the govies wanted to turn into lumber—fell away, and the reeki thinned. The jungle floor opened up. And she spotted the first *little* zassa tree, standing near as tall as the burntwoods.

For a vertical distance twice her height, the zassa's trunk was bare and straight. But above that, knobs and lumps appeared: branches that had never erupted from the big tree's tough blue skin, but had grown instead beneath the outer bark. Higher up, stobs protruded at odd angles, limbs that had broken through after decades of growing beneath the tree's skin, only to die off, choked at their base by constricting bark. Then finally, topping every other tree in the jungle, true branches spread out, umbrellalike, thick as whole burntwoods and draped with hand-sized leaves the color of weathered moss. From the jungle floor the whole tree looked prickly. But only the old bark carried thorns; the leaves were as thick and soft as a fleepa's ear.

Almost at McDonnel's. How would they take her packing in with a newbie? What if he let loose with spacer talk? *What if*, nothing. These were gentle folks, and his manners weren't that bad. She worried what they'd think of *her* dealing with him, that was the problem.

Not that the McDonnels were the kind of religious that cared whether she slept alone or not. But they'd worry about her using him, worry that bringing in a body ignorant of the jungle's ways hurt the green. What little religion greenies held with mostly encompassed taking care of the land and maintaining the balance of nature. In that way, the McDonnels were *very* religious, and newbies always heathen.

But Raschad hadn't shown her anything in the last two days that said he would embarrass her along that line, either. He'd tolerated the nurse flower today, could have broke her hold except he'd understood what she'd wanted. And he'd taken care not to hurt the lipis on the trail, and took care in other ways, too—he carried his shovel while tending his needs, and never did that near running water. When he ate, he buried any scraps. Pulling, he kept to the trail, didn't make mud burrows through fresh growth, and to her knowledge, didn't smoke, chew, or sniff anything that would dirty the green or twist his judgment—unless his *dietary sup-pul-ments* were dream makers. He did swat bugs. But that was forgivable in anyone's religion—especially as much as the critters chewed on his hide. No, he shouldn't offend the McDonnels. Anyway, she'd find out soon.

The understory growth thinned and gave way to a scrubless flat occupied by massive silver zassa trunks. The incessant drone of insects faded, and the air smelled fresh and peppery. Walking by feel and instinct more than sight, she whistled *stop* to Raschad. Her sled treads clicked and froze. Peace settled over her; nothing much but McDonnel's lived in these big trees. The occasional scriar prowled through. But gigis, bugs, and most predators stayed clear of the smelly, thorny trees. A safer place was hard to find in the green.

Her sinuses prickled. She sneezed and laughed. Going to sleep cool, safe, and quiet tonight. They'd shriking earned it.

Rocking back her head, she let out a long yodeling whoop that ended on a yelp. Echoes danced through the grove and circled at her back. Dry duff crunched beneath her boots.

Yordl-aye. An answering whoop sounded from above, and before she could call again, kids rained out of the trees, whooping and dropping everywhere—nearly on her head—their headlamps weaving airy patterns in the dusk.

"You're late." A whip-thin girl landed laughing at her feet. "We worried." Dust puffed from the prickly duff around the child's buskins and rose like misty ribbons in the light of the headlamps.

"You worried, aia?" Sal smiled. "Me, too, now and a bit."

Two boys landed giggling and chattering next the girl. The finely woven cloth of their shirts and pants clung to them like second skins, and their crisp, precise speech, muted by dusk, reminded her that unlike most greenies, the McDonnels—who tried to educate their kids better than if they went to govie school—would appreciate Raschad's refined pronunciation.

"You're late. You're late." The grove echoed with the children's chant.

"I left town late."

Her protest, directed to no one in particular, fell on deaf ears. The constant downward arrival of little bodies dizzied her. She turned circles in the midst of happy bedlam. And behind her, headlamps encircled Raschad's sled. Grabbing her lamp off a mount on the sled's bumper, she directed its beam in his direction.

"Hey, rowdies. Let the man move it."

"Aia. Aia. *Aia*."

The kids slipped off Raschad's sled and pushed it so hard they half ran him over before he could react. Sal laughed. He aligned his load with hers and abandoned the traces, looking confused as moss moochers crowded his legs.

"Two things here," she whispered to him. "Don't mind the kids, and don't be telling you dig for a living."

"Sal!"

A tall, lithe woman dropped from a branch, followed by a man nearly as slender. Behind him, half a dozen adults grounded at once. Like the kids, all wore long-sleeved shirts and close-fitting pants dyed the deep green of zassa leaves, and buskins made from the leathery skin of woord galls.

"Mem." Sal forgot Raschad. The woman's embrace smelled of dry sky and bruised bark. "Nexis." She reached around Mem to clasp the man's proffered hand. Everyone smiled.

"Got a new partner, I see," Mem said.

Sal's cheeks warmed, but she'd best face things right off.

"You won't believe this." She shook hands around the circle of McDonnels—Helen, Bart, Colhien, Wintra, Max, Jacob. "I brought along a newbie."

Everyone stilled, then . . .

"Naia, Sal, not you!" Mem slapped her back and they laughed, tension dissipating.

These were good people. Sal half turned, including Raschad in the circle of adults.

"I got late, got desperate, and ain't sorry." She said it with emphasis, though she wasn't sure about the last. "He can pull, he can."

Smiles broadened, but remained shy, nervous. Raschad's smile was the same, only tired and dirty and hungry, which brought out the McDonnels' natural kindness. He reached for a proffered hand with his bandaged one, and Nexis caught his wrist.

"You didn't say he was hurt."

"Met up with a scriar the other side of Klinker's." Sal shrugged.

Tongues clicked. Mem hugged her shoulders.

"Come on. Come up. The trail's showing on you, gal. Get clean and comfortable and eat."

"Sound good?" Sal clipped Raschad's shoulder.

"Sounds miraculous."

The McDonnels laughed. "Over here, then." Nexis waved them on. "Don't worry about the loads."

Older kids were already pushing her sleds toward the hollow trunk of a giant zassa. They'd wash the treads and store the haulers in the tree bole, a safer parking spot than at Morrie's.

Nexis stopped beneath a mammoth zassa. Up and around the tree's bole flickering torches lit a high-climbing series of vines and pegs, a haphazard stairway into the forest canopy that avoided the tree's thorny hide. Kids swarmed past and scrabbled upward like fleepas, ignoring half the handholds, larking off in one direction or the other.

Sal smiled at Raschad. His eyes followed the kids' antics. He didn't smile back.

"Newbie?"

His eyes snapped down, and the color drained right out of him, leaving him with the same expression he'd worn after the nursie had introduced itself this morning.

"Haia." She caught his elbow as he wobbled.

"Sorry." He dropped his head between his knees.

Now what? *Your man*, the McDonnels' stares said.

"Raschad?" She stooped.

"Nothing. Be fine."

She knelt on one knee. "You don't look fine."

He trembled. "I am." Sucking a breath, he straightened.

"Plenty of rope, if you need." Mem hovered at her elbow.

Sal studied the newbie in the light of several headlamps. So much for worrying. He'd found a way to embarrass her that she hadn't even imagined.

"Partner?"

"I can climb." His expression blanked, and he steadied. "I can climb very well."

She shrugged to Mem. "I'll go up first."

"Naia." He started up the tree.

And he could climb, altogether too fast for his one-handed condition, which impressed the McDonnels. Children scooted past Sal on the lighter outer limbs, and she let those in a hurry go with Raschad. She concentrated on her own holds and steps.

Mem dawdled behind her, patient, polite, chattering about family matters and nut crops. The air grew cleaner, sweeter, the light brighter. Sleepin' at McDonnel's tonight.

"He don't hardly look newbie." Mem got brave.

"He says he's sort of an old newbie."

Mem laughed, but Sal said no more. She wouldn't lie to her friends, and if she recited his history, it would come out that he was rock mining. She didn't even want to think what their opinion would be of his other rumored means of income.

Panting, she emerged into sunset glow two-thirds of the way up the zassa. On a leaf-draped platform that served as the Mc-

Donnels' front porch, Raschad squatted, back against the massive bole of the tree, his bared face tucked down against his knees. Nexis squatted beside him, a hand on the newbie's shoulder. Sal cocked her head. Mem's man shook his.

"Newbie?" She leaned down beside Raschad.

"Hand hurts." His voice quavered.

"Let's get in, then. Get settled and fed."

He stood, his movements jerky. She caught his elbow and steered him after Mem through a maze of family waiting to greet them. Raschad nodded short and polite, but the wild set of his shoulders put her teeth on edge.

From the family rooms they wound through a series of enclosed hallways across an open balcony and onto a plank bridge suspended by cured reeki vine and draped by velvet walls of zassa leaves. The children's chatter grew fainter, replaced by the constant lulling shush of stirring foliage. Raschad blindly side-slipped dangling branchlets; his face dripped sweat in spite of a breeze fresh from the sky, untainted by rot or mold.

"Here." Mem stopped before a bark-doored hut. Sky showed above its low roof, and free fall gaped to their left. A plank walk curved right, disappearing into foliage. "No one's using this room just now. I can find you a bed with the girls, Sal—but we're always tight." The arch of Mem's eyebrows left it to her to decide whether or not to share quarters with Raschad.

"Looks great, Mem." Sal didn't dare leave him alone the way he was acting.

"See you at dinner, then." Mem's lips quirked.

"Aia. Settler's thanks."

"My pleasure." Mem backed away with a knowing look, and Sal wanted to just blow away in the wind.

Pushing the hut door open, she stepped into a ruddy glow. Two large, open windows framed sunset-stained foliage, and the hush of dusk filled the room.

Close on her heels, Raschad entered without a word or a sound. Dropping her kit on the floor, Sal turned, half afraid to be alone with him, wondering what he'd do now. He only sat . . . straight down on the reeki floor mats with a thump. His face netting, balled in one fist, rolled free.

She took a deep breath, moved behind him, and settled her hands on his shoulders. He made no objection.

"I been startled by heights a time or two," she offered as she kneaded neck muscles as tense as stone.

"Spacer, Banks." A tremor took his breath, and he hiccuped. "Very ex-spacer."

She didn't understand that, except she figured space was a place that could scramble up and down. She worked her thumbs along his spine and felt him begin to relax. The shaking started then. She reached from behind him, held on hard, and when he hugged her arms and ducked his head, she rocked him gently.

"Sorry," he whispered. "Old nightmare."

That she understood, haunted in her own sleep by old friends, dead friends. Growing brave, she hugged him nearer, turned his face against her body. He held on, but didn't take it further, just needed the comforting. And she knew better, however nice he felt, than to push it further.

Tap-tap. She flinched. A second rap sounded at the door.

They unwound. Raschad levered erect, and she straightened and stood. His hand swiped his cheek and dropped. She moved to the door, but waited until he nodded before opening it.

Nexis stood on the balcony, packing a bucket of hot water and towels. "Thought you could use these."

"Aia, you're generous."

She stood aside to let him enter. But Nexis settled his load to the floor, backed a step, and crooked his head away from the door. Raschad sat, tugging off belts and weapons. Sal followed Nexis onto the balcony, hoping the newbie wouldn't be insulted by their private conversation. But when had she ever worried about hurting a newbie's feelings?

"Granna is concerned for the man. She says she won't be offended if you eat here tonight."

"I was worried—" Sal chose her words carefully. "—that he might scare the kids."

Nexis's lower lip disappeared. "You're both welcome, if you feel up to it. But the family can be overpowering." He shrugged, embarrassed clear to his ear tips.

"Be fine." She couldn't blame him for the family's small inhospitality toward Raschad. If she had kids, she'd think five times before letting them near a newbie. "I'll settle him, then join you. I wouldn't mind the news of things."

"Good." Nexis smiled and relaxed. "We enjoy your company."

She smiled. "Fine. I'll be there."

Their eyes held. Nexis blushed, smiled, and slid away. She shook her head. If Nexis weren't taken . . .

But that wasn't true. Why were the men she liked always homebodies, comfortable living settled when she couldn't sit still a week unless forced to? It seemed a packer would suit her best. But she'd never met one she'd tie herself to if she were minded to take a man—which she wasn't. Ma killed herself working, while Pa lazed in the shack or wandered the green doing just what he wanted. Naia, she'd no use for a permanent man.

Truth be, except for George, she'd hardly ever been with a man. Sonny Doobay didn't count, and was dead anyway, poor little bastard. She flinched, Sonny's screams always just a blink away.

Turning back into the room, she let old memories go. But Raschad sat on the edge of a bed in his harness padding and sleeveless undershirt, holding his outer shirt, and the sight of him now made the feel of him that morning in Klinker's shower flash through her mind. All of a sudden the air was close and hot in spite of the high-canopy breeze stirring through the windows.

Sal closed her eyes. Maybe *time* made this newbie stranger attractive to her, for all she didn't trust him—time without a kindly human touch. Until his queeg frog Olvira had died, Morrie'd shown more affection for the pet than for her. George loved her, but suffocated her.

Then back in Tumble Town, Raschad's pretty eyes had turned on her, with never anything lecherous, conniving, or greedy about his look. And somehow between here and there, he'd suckered his way into her soft spot for caged fleepas and other needing things. Or maybe it wasn't even that deep. But holding him a moment ago had felt good in spite of his hurt.

She hefted Nexis's bucket, took down a pitcher of cold water from the high-lidded dresser, and sat both in front of Raschad.

"You first. I'm going after food."

He nodded, eyes on the shirt in his hands. At the door she glanced back. He looked thin and lonely, mean and scared.

Sitting shirtless, Raschad gulped gourd stew and munched flaky, pale blue biscuits made from expensive flour. The McDonnels might not want a newbie at their table, but they hadn't shirked on the food they served him.

He chewed and swallowed, eyes on his plate, eating without asking why she hadn't brought a plate for herself. Stomach growling, she cleaned gear and offered no explanation. The stew filled the room with a mouth-watering aroma of spices and rare jungle roots, and she pressed a fist into her gut to quiet it. Raschad finished his fried fish and cleaned his plate to a shine, sopping up gravy with a last bite of biscuit.

"Good. Thanks." He sat the plate aside, pulled the bed sheet over his legs, and shucked his pants under cover of the bed-clothes. Then he tucked up his legs, stretched out, and went limp. Leaves murmured. Boughs soughed against the hut's roof. His breathing deepened. She crossed the room, stopping at his side to study his battered body.

Today's pull hadn't added much damage. His harness galls were healing beneath a skim of sealant. The bruising about his eyes had faded. He breathed deep and steady, limp now after his earlier panic. A tough newbie, a tough man.

Turning away, she rigged a privacy blanket for her own bath and then stripped. Raschad's breathy snoring filled the room. Strands of fleepa fur braided into the reeki fiber mats soothed her itchy feet, and the bathwater, still warm, smelled of moon blossoms. Sponging chafed skin and insect bites, she felt her over-heated muscles cool—sleeping at McDonnel's.

Perched on the edge of her bed, she sank into its feather pallet and was tempted to join Raschad in sleep. But her stomach convinced her otherwise. Once dressed, she slipped from the room, feeling no guilt at leaving him behind when he surely needed the extra sleep. Besides, newbie or greenie either one, he should just be grateful for this room and this night.

Seated next to Granna McDonnel, she forced down a final bite of fruit pudding. Granna beamed. The old woman seldom spoke, but her warm smile filled Sal as much as the meal.

The platters sat empty. Fried fish and squash, mashed roots and gravy, nutloaves, biscuits, stew, steamed greens, a salad of wilted reeki sprouts—everything had been eaten. Smiling, the adults pushed back from the table and wandered to the big outside balcony, discussing weather and harvests.

Sal recited her tale of disaster in town, including Morrie's tricks and Scollarta's scheming. Eventually the children—their dinner chores completed—joined the adults, and there were songs and stories late into the night. For a longtime orphan like Sal, it was a healing time. With the moons riding high, Mem walked her back toward the hut and Raschad.

"Family never changes." Sal kept her voice low as the household settled about them.

"Just gets bigger." Mem's tone had gone serious. "I'd like to talk personal."

"I owe, and I'm willing." But with Raschad along, Sal dreaded Mem's questions.

"How you going to vote on the Liberalization Act?"

Sal stopped still on the plank walk, stared at Mem in moon shadow. "You can't be favoring it?"

"I don't know."

"*Mem!* You're greener than I am. Something's got you thinking crazy."

"Bad things."

Sal waited, not pushing, even though Mem opened this conversation.

"There's strangers running through the green." Mem leaned on a reeki vine railing. "Couldn't talk plain in front of Granna and the children."

A chill trickled through Sal.

"No one wants to see how bad things have gotten." Mem's voice dropped low, and Sal leaned nearer to hear the tree woman. "There's been poaching—carcasses only missing a few steaks— and trees cut. Even found zassas axed, random stupid harm."

Sal didn't want this kind of news.

"Don't know where these people come from." Mem's jaw bulged. "They're crazies. Forel Chaugger says he found a fresh-dug shaft just north of the Forks. The bastards blew open the mountain with tech explosives, and the ones we've seen look desperate enough to eat gigis. They're dangerous and likely lolling around the trails stalking easy prey."

"City folk, then." But they were far deep in the green for stragglers.

"That's what I think," Mem agreed. "And that's the big problem. We've got to answer for these people, can't keep pretending the jungle will solve our problems or that it's right letting the green kill them. There's too many. They won't just keep politely dying in Capitol and Second City for our convenience. We're the landholders, the First Families. We have the vote. We're responsible for this mess." Mem's hands gripped the reeki rail.

"Giving the crazies tech won't help, Mem. Governor Wally thinks every citizen should have the vote. But if we want those city grunts and fourth-family tech laborers running the government, Ol' Wally's an example of that."

"Naia." Mem's head jerked. "I don't even trust most First Settlers with the vote. But somehow we best treat all these people better. Because we own the land don't mean it's right to lock them up dying in the cities."

"We ain't. They have the same chance of making it in the jungle as the rest of us. Look at this newbie I'm dragging around.

He's been out here three years. Imagine that. If people have sense, let them use it. Feeding them free and letting them breed up brainless young doesn't help them or us. Letting them poison the planet with tech kills us all. I don't know an answer to any of this, but the Liberalization Act ain't it. And no one can solve others' problems for them. They've got to do it themselves."

"That's what scares me," Mem said somberly. "Maybe they figure fighting greenies for the land is their solution."

Sal stared into the dark, surrounded by rustling and peace. Was Ver Day that far gone? Were the cities—all two of them—that crowded and desperate? Or were city livers just blind and wanting and greedy? Ma always said the dangerous part about tech was that you never noticed the harm it did until you'd already hurt things. Tech fooled you—made life so easy that you didn't see the bill coming due.

"You be careful pulling up this trail, Sally-aia. These people have riled the whole jungle. Mistwalkers have been popping up everywhere. And the gigis . . . they're always bad this time of year. You be careful. And I could wish you a better partner than a newbie."

The plank walk swayed in the breeze, uncertain footing.

Raschad never stirred as Sal slipped into the room and shucked her clothes. City crazies. She tumbled into bed. Mistwalkers and gigis. People had warned her about the trail since before she left Tumble Town. Maybe if she'd listened, she'd have looked harder for someone other than Raschad to pull with her. Then again, if she lost him, he'd already lived long past anyone's expectations.

The thought turned her stomach and promised nightmare. He was her responsibility, and the idiot trusted her. He'd warned her today that he was dangerous. She should warn him not to depend on her.

Sheets slid across her, as fine as George's. Sal opened her eyes.

Raschad sat in undershirt and pants on the edge of his bed. She stretched, and he glanced up from oiling his boots. He looked rested and was using his injured hand this morning.

"I'd best tend that cut," she said.

"When I finish the boots." His eyes returned to his work.

She levered herself upright, holding the sheet about her. Dawn light glowed through the windows, and a fine chill rode the air. By the time they ate and climbed down this tree, it should be light below. Time to pack.

Still holding the sheet around her middle, she retrieved yesterday's dirty clothes and pulled them on. Raschad's eyes stayed on his work. The bastard could be polite.

"How you feel?"

"Fine," he said.

He looked fine, but then he still had to climb down this tree. A tap sounded at the door and he glanced up.

"Won't be breakfast, yet." She stood.

A flush rose from beneath Raschad's shirt and he bent over his boots again. Shrike, she hadn't meant to embarrass the man.

Opening the door, she found Mem looking grim. "You're early, come on in."

Raschad quickly pulled his field shirt over his head. *Manners,* Sal thought—his showed up in different ways at different times than her own, yet he meant well. Mem didn't miss the gesture, or the two rumpled beds and that meaning, either.

"Sal, I'm sorry."

Her heart near stopped. With her and Raschad both safe in the top of this tree, Mem could only mean one thing.

"How bad are they?" She reached for her netting and gear.

Raschad stuffed his feet in his boots.

"Only one of them." Mem grimaced. "Aireils took apart the outside load. I doubt anything's missing. They just like to look. Everyone's down gathering things up."

A chill slipped through her. "That safe in the dark?" You didn't want to blunder into an Aireil.

"Aia." Mem shrugged. "The fleepas are waking, and everything sounds normal. Mistwalkers don't like zassas. Sitting on them hurts their importants, I guess. They've kited out the other end of the grove by now."

Sal grabbed her gun belt and almost dove out the door. Mem followed. Stumping along the plank walks, Sal held down a scream. Going to be *real* late now. Panic slithered about her heart. Here she had help. But here she didn't expect mistwalkers.

Mem scooted around her. She stretched her legs, paced the woman. Racing out of the house, they dropped off the porch. Halfway down she remembered Raschad.

Looking up, she saw him coming down on her head and wondered where he'd found his courage. Then she figured it—action was his answer to fear. *Stick your hand in the scriar's mouth and fire. Climb down the tree as fast as you can.*

They hit the ground panting. Raschad looked shaky, but nodded reassurance.

Aireil stench still rode the morning mists. Stomach cramping, Sal panned her headlamp, cutting the forest floor's murk with a bright arc. The zassa hollow that had sheltered her sleds gaped open, its solid burntwood doors shattered. Packing crates lay strewn from the opening. McDonnels wandered through the grove, collecting her scattered cargo by the light of headlamps. And the freight would all have to be reinventoried.

Raschad moved past. His hand caught her elbow, gave it an encouraging squeeze. He disappeared inside the zassa.

"I'll find another lamp." His words drifted out to her.

"Hand me a maul to hit myself with while you're at it."

"You don't get off that easy."

She smiled in spite of everything.

By the time real light came, her freight sat in a mound next to Raschad's sled. Bent over the pile, he called off numbers from shipping containers and individual package invoices while Mem checked the numbers against Sal's load sheets.

Sal busied herself reloading, trusting the newbie and Mem to do a better job of reading than herself. But maybe she shouldn't trust them. The way Raschad fired off numbers, all careless-sounding, she worried that he didn't understand the importance of what he was doing. How could anyone read that fast?

During the few years Sal had attended Tumble Town's one-room native school, Coach Grimey had told her, in her gravel growl, that letters were important. But packers didn't bother with reading. The government color-coded crates according to destination and coded the load sheets to match, so a packer could get by only knowing colors. But the codes changed each time a crate changed destination. So the markings weren't big, and after the Aireils' banging, scratching, and ripping, half her codes were missing, with some crates only held together by reeki twine. Of course, she could read the *numbers* on the packages. Just not so fast.

"Sal?" Raschad angled a package for better light. "What's this?" He motioned to her, and with a finger on a line of print she couldn't half read, whispered, "What are psiittines?"

She stared. He bit his lip, and she swallowed a smile.

"Tell you later."

He rolled his eyes, and loading went easier then, the newbie's innocence acting as salve for her temper.

Mid-morning found them harnessed in and pulling, with McDonnels pushing the sleds from behind to hurry them out of the grove—good people doing what they could to help. Mem clipped on outside Sal's steering bars and pulled beside her.

"Not good." Mem's eyes roved the forest floor.

Sal ducked a branch. "Easy prey, we ain't." Her voice sounded more confident than she felt. "Especially not Raschad. If they got tech, I imagine he knows how to handle it."

Mem nodded, looking as if she hadn't put the idea of Raschad and tech together before. His collapse last night had made him appear vulnerable, something expected of a newbie, and the McDonnels interpreted that as helplessness.

"Have I used up my personals?"

"Naia. Go ahead," Sal said.

"I know you aren't meaning to get him killed."

Sal held her breath, then let it escape slowly, swallowing a flush of anger. If Mem weren't a friend . . . But then Mem *wouldn't* mention it.

"Naia." She pulled harder. "I don't mean to use him. I told you, I got cornered into hiring him."

"Sorry for asking." Mem looked distressed. "It just isn't like you."

"Aia. I know it. You ain't the only one wondering about it. *I* wonder. But I ain't used him harder than myself."

"It's just he seems decent." Mem groped for words. "Only hurt, sort of clip-winged. But ain't newbies all the same."

"He's tougher than you think." Sal's breath puffed between taut lips. "Must be, to have survived so long out here. You've watched him. Except for his talk, he acts mostly greenie, knows the jungle. Shrike, just two days on trail, and I'm as comfortable with him at my back as I ever was with Chic. Just wish I knew what to think about him. Wish I weren't taking him into trouble. But there's no help for it, nor any place he'll be safer. Klinker would of kept him, but not long. No one wastes much on a newbie."

"Aia. Well . . ."

"Don't offer. I can't spare him, and you ain't going to loan me family for muscle."

Mem hunched. "Don't have family to spare now, anyway. Your sled getting torn apart is a warning. The Aireils are angry. These newcomers are raising hell. Forel found some bodies next that mine hole. The mistwalkers are already thinning out the bastards. You be settler careful from here on."

Sal clenched her teeth and nodded. Aireils scared her more than any strangers. Pulling quiet, they each chased their own thoughts. Then Mem cleared her throat.

"You seem to like this newbie."

Sal wasn't offended. "Aia." She smiled. "Sometimes."

Mem smiled back, shrugged. "Can't be no harm in it. If you're gentle."

Sal snorted, and they both laughed like kids over candy. She shook her head. "He don't want me."

"Bet you're wrong."

"Squat." She gave the sled a heave, stared up at a tapestry of green. "He talks about himself, but leaves me so far from understanding him, it's like he's lied."

"Well . . ." Mem bumped her shoulder. "How's he going to make a greenie understand newbie thoughts? Don't expect the world of him."

Chapter 9

They walked and ate lunch while the McDonnels pulled the sleds. Afterward came good-byes. Nexis, who'd teamed with Raschad all day, faced the big newbie. The tree man had warned Raschad about city crazies running loose in the green, and Sal wondered as Nexis swatted the newbie's shoulder what else they'd talked about. Nexis's expression said he didn't expect to see Raschad again—another reason for hating newbies. Who could afford affection for anyone going to die so soon? Which reminded her of how it felt holding Raschad last evening.

Walking with her, Mem had said, "Be careful, gal." Then, "What could it hurt?" Sal knew what would hurt.

Mem hugged her and headed down the trail. A last wave, and the McDonnels faded into the green. She was alone with the newbie again. Leaning into harness, she pulled hard, trying to forget the sadness in Nexis's eyes.

They met heavy understory growth, mudpots and swarming, fire-stinging jet bees. But nothing out of the ordinary slowed them until Sal saw the human dung pile in the middle of the trail.

Her eyes flicked right, left, up, down. A crumpled rations packet stuck from a crack in a log, and undergrowth lay trampled and tattered. She listened, watching micro wrens flit through the undergrowth; everything seemed safe enough. With a whistled caution to Raschad, she pulled over the pile, unsettled by the useless newbielike fouling of things. But these people weren't newbies, and couldn't be shipped home or counted on to die fast.

She kept her senses peaked. Mem was right. Greenies couldn't ignore city livers forever—the city livers wouldn't let them. Times grew dangerous.

* * *

Afternoon brought drizzling rain and a relief from bugs. When the rain let up, Sal called a rest and studied the sky through a break in the tree canopy. Shredding cloud bellies shone white, and the weather promised to clear. She prayed it stayed that way. They'd regained some time, but not enough.

Raschad climbed over the back of her sled and lay faceup, lengthwise on the load, his head just above hers as she sat on the traces. "You are a tough human being, Banks." He breathed hard. Water dripped and plopped on his slicker.

"Thanks much." She stuck a ripe yellow mi fruit—a lucky find—beneath her soggy netting and took a bite. Juice ran sticky down her chin, and seeds gritted between her teeth. "Compliments ain't going to buy you extra rest."

"Don't make me like you, woman."

"Ain't got time for it if I wanted." Sal swallowed. "Usually, I haul from McDonnel's to the Forks and stop. If I'm pushing it, I can reach a fair campsite farther on. But *if* I'm pushing it, I'm usually at the Forks by now." Her eyes roved the green and snagged on a mound of new growth beneath a big scaly-barked, needle-leaved tree. "There's a mound beneath that taponica."

"The white tree?" Raschad angled his head.

"That's a meltdown, a lost sled."

"Sled?"

"Aia. Taponica sap is real acid—leave green tech under one for long, and the finish melts. Then mold and rot sets in. The botafab makes good growing fertilizer."

"It sat here a long time." He spoke slower than usual, working out the proper way of stating his mind, she thought, without demanding an answer from her.

"Naia. A packer took a break here, same as us—and within this last month, or I'd have been warned of the loss."

His expression turned strange, and he glanced back at his own sled as if it might disappear before his eyes. "That fast?" His manners were slipping again.

"Aia." Best that she educate him, rude or not.

"But why would anyone leave a sled?"

"Naia a good reason."

Splush. A wall of silver fell before her eyes, and she flinched back. Water splashed and streamed off the sled. A tubular funnel leaf, nearly as big as her body, bobbed upward, freed of its weight of trapped rainwater. And Raschad sat up snorting and blowing spray.

"Second best shower I've had this trip." He shook his head, spattering her with water and reeki sap.

"Haia, there." She raised her hands in front of her face. "Get. Get gone."

"Good for you."

"I'll *good for you*." She threw her mi core. He ducked, and she swore he smiled as he slithered backward off her load. Just as well he found humor in things, because the mound beneath the taponica had shaken her gut. "Hook in, lazy."

She wiped mi juice, spit sand-sized seeds, and hauled, aching tired, but with no choice but to move before he ran her over.

They neared the Forks with sunlight slanting brilliant beams through the thinning tree canopy. Scrub replaced tall growth, and fallen jemson leaves coated the trail, matting the sleds' treads with gold.

Sal hoped Loomis Twoteeth had room for company at his trading post. They could pull farther today if they had to, but it would be another hell haul. Stopping, still out of sight of the post, she whooped, then repeated the call twice, warning Loomis that she was coming. No answer sounded.

Stomach knotting, she pulled on through a golden glow of sunlight off quivering jemson foliage. The scrub thinned, giving way to reeki vine and ferns. She creaked to a stop at the lip of the rise above the Forks.

Below, cradled in the heart of a grassy bowl, a tall longbuilding shingled with rock-hard ironwood shakes stood on the west side of the triple crossing of the Plateau, Pike, and River jog trails. All three routes stretched vacant. The post's front porch hunkered low and abandoned in the mud. Nothing stirred about the frond-thatched outbuildings, and only a thin skein of smoke rising from the post's chimney hinted at occupation.

Beyond the post's muddy yard, meadow spread up the sides of the hollow, and a lone tan-pelted fuuli doe grazed the opposite jungle verge. The doe's antler rack scythed grass, dropping it beneath her black muzzle.

Where were the Twoteeths? Sal chewed the inside of her cheek. Where were the porch tramps?

She whistled a *be ready* to Raschad, her eyes still on the buildings below. If Loomis had met trouble enough to stop him from answering her call, then she didn't want to walk into it. But he would leave a warning sign—something. That many Twoteeths wouldn't be caught by surprise. So more likely Loomis awaited trouble, and she'd best not stop between it and him.

Her scalp twitched, and sweat ran on her ribs. She eased her sled down winding switchbacks into the bowl. Brae ferns, weighted with clinging raindrops, lined the trail like huge glittering bird feathers, and emerald-hued carpet moss grew in the ferns' shade. The moss offered better footing than clay mud, but she stuck to the center of the trail, away from dripping fronds. A big midas, hidden by grass, slipped off a rock at their approach and slowly lumbered downhill. What else had she missed?

Everything looked peaceful as bliss. She stopped just shy of Twoteeth's yard and warbled a whistle.

Still no answer. But they couldn't see her well yet from inside. Her mouth felt dry, her bladder heavy.

Out of choices, she pulled into the yard. Raschad followed, faithful as a lizard, if not as trusting. They braked to a halt in front of the main building. Its shingled walls dripped moss and rain, and its shuttered windows stared back at them blind.

She slipped her harness clips. "Twoteeth!" Her hail rang loud and startling in the surrounding silence.

Thump.

Her hand dropped. Her legs tensed.

The front door exploded outward. She vaulted her steering bar and ducked for the far side of the load.

"Banks!" The bellow frightened purple larks from the meadow. "Be damned, it's Banks!"

"Twoteeth!" She froze in place, gripping her chest.

The old man limped into the open, a gangling, mustachioed skeleton dressed in stained brown overalls and a ragged undershirt. A rifle rode the crook of his arm. His boots, big and battered, clumped on the log porch, and two of his sons straightened from behind rain barrels at opposite corners of the building. She heard a third on the roof. Bad times when Twoteeths were scared.

"S'all right, Banks. Jest didn't know who t'expect. We figured ya dead days ago. Figured some sherk might try foolin' us pullin' yer sleds in. Ain't never seen ya this late."

"Long story, Loomis." Keeping her voice low, Sal searched the yard. "Looks like you've got a story yourselves." She slipped her Camm back in its holster and waved Raschad over to her, seeing that Loomis's big boys had their sights on him. "This is my temporary." She spoke loud enough for all to hear. "Name of Raschad. Please don't shoot'im. He pulls good, and even the McDonnels approved of him."

Loomis's mouth twitched. His eyes slitted. But Raschad squatted at her feet like a hired-on might, making himself vulnerable to them, waiting their judgment. Shrike, he could show good sense. Just don't open your mouth, newbie.

"Ain't real partial ta strangers jest now, Banks." Loomis stepped down from the porch, eyeing the crown of Raschad's hat. "Ya don't usually bring any."

"Hard times. Packers in town cheating on my contract. If I hadn't taken him on, I might have lost this one."

"Aia?" The old man chewed his reeki-stained mustache. "Been crazy goings on lately, gal. Ol' Dotti Tarpin's shack burnt. Ain't no one seen him since." Sal's stomach clenched. Everyone liked Ol' Dotti. "Seegie, my youngest, found a sled been raided last week. Nobody around. It looked that gigis been through and maybe done fer the hauler." Loomis gave Raschad another long stare. "Reckon yer word's good 'nough, though." He met her eyes. "Know'd yer pa and all. We'll talk."

"Wish I had time." She tried to relax and speak steady. "But hope to make the Junction campsite before it's too dark."

Whatever she wanted from Loomis, it was best to let him sell it to her, let it be *his* idea. Things came cheaper that way. If she asked for a place to stay, it would cost double. But his usual avarice failed her, and his expression just turned grim. Her stomach knotted tighter. She didn't need this kind of trouble, the kind the McDonnels feared.

"Clive. Delbert. Ya help unload." Loomis jerked a hand over his shoulder. The two wild-haired sons on the porch leaned their rifles against a wall and strode down the porch steps. "Ya work, and I'll talk at ya, Banks, and hope ya listens with more sense than yer usin' now."

Raschad straightened beside her and turned, loosening load straps, moving slow, saying nothing. He obviously had the proper sense of things, so she followed Loomis off a bit, and the Twoteeth boys moved past her. Built like their mother, both stood taller and broader than Sal and heavier than Raschad. Lying about the station with plenty to eat would turn them fat. Now, they were just big.

Pulling out her load sheets, she watched the Twoteeths edge up to her load as if Raschad smelled rotten. They couldn't know he was newbie, could they?

He ignored them—again the wise choice. A body didn't mess with Loomis's kids. When they were all being born, the trader had needed watchdogs, and he'd made little else of them. The girls, just salable goods, were past gone, of course. Sal got along with Loomis, but he wasn't anyone likable.

"Cain't go on." The old man spoke stern.

"I'll call out the numbers, Raschad." She flipped through her load sheets, ignoring Loomis.

Raschad climbed atop her load and opened the canvas. Loomis chawed and spat.

"Jungle's full of arse'oled strangers, gal. Leavin' squat ever'-wheres, cuttin' *nest* trees. They've got the mistwalkers haunting the trails. Ya'll get yer throats slit, lose yer loads, or be torn ta bits at night camp."

Everything going from bad to squat. Twoteeth might just want a night's lodging fee out of her, but for once she figured it was more than greed.

"I hear you, Loomis. You talk sense. We'll likely stay. But it's hard after what we've done to get here even this late." She didn't dare give in easy. "We could use a meal, rest . . ." She should warn him about the meltdown, too.

A movement caught her eye. She glanced toward the sled.

Loomis's boys went for Raschad.

"Shr-ri-ike!" She dropped her load sheets.

The newbie dove for the far side of the load. Delbert caught Raschad's boot, and the newbie disappeared off the sled headfirst as Clive dodged around the load in pursuit.

Sal jerked her maul from her belt. Loomis clumped at her side, and they rounded the sled together in time to see Raschad lash out with a boot.

Delbert dropped flat in the mud, and Raschad danced away. A blade flashed.

"Clive!" Loomis's bellow half deafened her. "Ya leave off. Man didn't say or do nothin' I saw, an' I was watchin' y'all."

Clive stopped, chest heaving, eyes wild, his skinning knife held high. Delbert staggered up, spit muck, and lunged for Raschad.

"Delbert!"

Del froze, too. Striding between the three men, Loomis stared hard at his boys, then glanced at Raschad. The newbie straightened, his stance easy. Sal let her breath out slow, but couldn't take her eyes from Raschad. The whole set of him said, no bragging, that handling Clive and Del didn't worry him. Just then she figured he could handle them—tech weapon, wounded hand, or not.

So did Loomis. "Y'all thank this man fer not killin' ya, an' trot yer arses inside."

The brothers stared, mouths half open, as understanding slowly lit their faces. They'd tackled Raschad with fists and blades when he wore a full holster. Grabbing their hats out of the mud, they stomped off, grumbling and dripping.

Sal relaxed, not forgetting the movement she'd heard on the post's roof. Loomis had three more sons, and odds said all three had a bead on her and Raschad. Couldn't stay here now. What had Raschad done to set off the boys?

"Sorry, Banks." Loomis shook his head. "They was jest all primed fer a fight."

"Can't blame them for being nervous." She did, but politeness was safest. "Partner?" She moved past Loomis.

"S'all right." Scraping mud out of one eye, Raschad slurred his words, mimicking greenie accents.

"C'mon." She caught his harness and pulled him to the sled, glad he didn't say more. "Loomis." The old man paced them. "I hear you read real good."

"Read numbers good," he agreed.

"Then would you call off those marked on the load sheets in blue? That's your color. Aireils got into this sled this morning and made a mess of the markings."

The old man shook his head. "So ya've met'em already. Whole shriking jungle's gone to squat."

Evening light slanted red-gold across the shadowed hollow. Dumping the last of Twoteeth's order in the grass, they retarped Sal's load.

"Don't do this because of me." Raschad's expression turned grim beneath sap, muddy netting, and a coating of bloodsuckers.

"I ain't." She cinched a cover strap on her load and whacked mud from the sled's wide treads. "You can stay if you want. But I ain't being part of a killing tonight."

"They won't kill me." He lifted one of Loomis's pestering little chichi lizards off her load and followed her around the sled, stroking the lizard's pink scaly head while holding it up to eat bugs from his netting.

"I ain't worried about *you*." She gave him a sour glare. "But I'd have to leave the jungle if I was cause of a newbie killing a greenie." She glanced around, making certain they weren't overheard. "That's what it'll be if you stay. I won't blame you, but I'm not waiting to see it. We can camp in this meadow here tonight." She'd already suggested this once.

"Are you going to kill me first?" He snuggled the lizard.

"You talk shriking crazy."

"I'd just rather not experience being eaten alive." He ducked a swarm of cheese gnats. The evening bug flight was truly magnificent after the afternoon rains.

"We ain't got much choice, then, do we. Either it's the bugs—which I agree with you about—or the trail."

"Or I take the trail and you stay."

"Maybe I *should* kill you. How would I move these two sleds alone? I'll lose my contract." She yanked a load strap and its tip snapped up, rapping her chin and startling tears from her eyes.

"You have other contracts, Banks. Only one life."

"And I spend it the way I choose. You coming or staying? I'm hitting the trail." She rose on her toes and glared him as near straight in the eye as she could manage.

His mouth twisted strange. He walked off and began checking his own load while she half slumped on her sled. Going on wasn't smart. But there weren't any smart choices left.

Raschad limped around his load. He had to ache from his tussle with the Twoteeth boys. Doubts tugged Sal one way and the other. With a new split in his lip, he was wide open to infection; the jungle was no place for him tonight. What idiot would've brought him along at all?

"Gal." Loomis strode up. "I'll ask once more."

"It's honest of you, but it's that late I am." She clipped her traces. The old man knew why they were leaving.

"I'm sorry, sending ya out with a new packer an' all." He looked to mean it.

"Don't worry on nothing." It made her nervous to have Twoteeth apologize. "The man's tougher than dried gigi squat. He's wearing that glove because he stuck his hand down a scriar's throat. He won't be killed easy."

"Aia." Loomis glanced at Raschad. "I heard this newbie be unnatural hard."

Her breath caught. Their eyes met, and she nodded.

"Took the chance that you knew." She kept her voice steady. "The way you was acting, I was afraid your boys would shoot him straight off if I admitted what he was."

"Well ..." Loomis's hard expression turned strange. "I was afraid they'd try. Like they did anyway. So I didn't say myself, hoping maybe they wouldn't remember his name. The rockies what come through here ain't got no use for him. They say people who go in where he's claimin' don't come out. I didn't believe it till I saw him put down Del."

The old man looked even more uncomfortable. "I thank ya,

Banks, fer goin' on now. Lost my eldest this spring." She'd heard
about Marty passing of a fever. "His dying made me see what the
boys mean ta me. Don't want no fight here with this bastard's
hard tech. But run low, gal, run quiet. The green's killin' mad."

Sal let her breath out slow and nodded. Loomis turned away.
The stoop in his shoulders scared her as much as anything.
Loomis was getting old. Would she?

She whistled *move*. Raschad whistled back *ready*, and they
hauled for the long rise out of the bowl.

A scriar roared on their back trail.

"This morning." Sal shivered.

Eyes strained by failing light, she squatted over the carcass of
a lipis. Carrion scorpions coated it, their iridescent pincers glowing dull orange. Mouth stalks, arched over the scavengers' backs,
were buried in the deer's rotting meat, and glowing red eyes
stared at her from armored abdominal segments.

The scriar roared again, nearer.

Stomach cut open, the lipis lay beside the trail, its body howler-
chewed. Sal would have thought it a natural kill, except for the
human dung beside it and the five more dead deer littering the
open glade beyond.

"They're ahead of us." Raschad stared uptrail.

"Aia." *Meat* eaters. The thought turned her stomach. "Maybe
they went on to Noca Tana or took the Ebbid to D'arnith's." Or,
if they weren't laid out sick from the handcount of diseases wild
game carried, the poachers might be watching them right now.

"Getting closer to them all the time."

"Aia. And we can't stay here now. Either we turn back or push
on to the Junction. There's a big meadow there, drier than
Twoteeth's. Makes a decent camp this time of year."

A third roar rumbled through the dusk, nearer yet, still on their
back trail.

"I don't want to tackle another scriar." Raschad's voice quavered.

"Best move uptrail, then. He won't pass up carrion."

Chapter 10

Sal's machete arced and dropped, and reeki vines slumped, spraying sap. She took a breath, took a step. Her sled crept forward at her back, and she took another night-blind swing at the trail-blocking fall of reeki vine. It was stupid to be out here. She should've figured some other way at Twoteeth's.

Whiool! Raschad's whistle froze her in mid-swing. *Whiool!*

She vaulted onto her load and grabbed her long rifle, then belly-hugged the canvas and stared downtrail. The faintest glow of moonlight sifted through the tree canopy, revealing a shadowy lump atop his sled.

Whee-a. It was him hugging his load.

Wait, the whistle said. So she waited, sweat pooling, the night gummy hot, fear chilling her spine. Leaves rustled and murmured. Not a breath of breeze reached her, but something stirred up top. Heart thundering, everything unnaturally still, she fixed her eyes on a moonlit slit in the high tree canopy.

A shadow slid across it . . . and another.

Aireils. Her lungs emptied.

Going to lose the loads, forfeit the contract. But she had a good record. The government shouldn't dock her. Losing everything would even get her back in good time to pick up the next haul—if she lived.

But she'd lose medicines, ammunition, supplies people needed. She sweated. Scollarta might raise a stink, say she lost the loads on purpose so as to pick the next up on time—if she lived. And Twoteeth had said the mistwalkers were roused. Mad mistwalkers she didn't want to meet.

More shadows above. Aireil musk carried to her, diluted by reeki stench. Too many mistwalkers. She'd never seen so many at

once—moving spooky silent, the way they always moved. She
held her breath. They rustled past. How had Raschad spied them?

Be still, she wished him. Be still and wait.

She counted thirty shadows, then one more. Insects weighted
her back, stinging right through her shirt padding. They must be
eating Raschad alive, just like he'd feared. But not a sound came
from his sled. Maybe the bloodsuckers had carried him off.

Leaves rustled. She shivered and waited until everything stilled
except her breathing. No more shadows. She counted to a hundred, counted to a hundred again, counted to forty-two . . .

A fleepa chirped. Sixty-two. She waited. Eighty-nine. A howler
whooped tentatively. A second answered, more confident than the
first. One, two, three . . . A queeg frog croaked, and the howlers
broke into full chorus, complaining about the interruption in their
routine.

She whistled high and sharp, hoping Raschad could hear her
through the racket. His answer pierced the howlers' calls, and her
lungs emptied in a rush of relief.

Rolling over fast, she grunted as a solid crunch announced one
less beastie to plague her. Raschad whistled again, nearer. She answered. The sled rocked, startling her gut.

"Me." He stepped up the back of her load and dropped beside
her. "What now?" His whisper carried disembodied in the dark.

"Wait." She slumped. "Let them get ahead. They look to be
moving along the trail."

"Aia."

He swatted the back of his neck and wriggled alongside her,
then stretched out and went limp. Bugs or no bugs, she could just
go to sleep. Her head drooped, but jerked up again as the sled
shook.

Raschad wriggled, rocking the load, his back arched as he
scratched against a tarp strap.

"I could help," Sal said.

"Would you?" He sounded desperate.

"Over." She straddled his hips, freed her hardwood tread rake
from her belt, and ran it up and down, back and forth across the
triple thickness of his shirt back.

"Scu—" He caught himself. "Shrike." He added greenie drawl.
"That feels good."

She snorted, but gave him two more strokes before she stowed
the rake. "C'mon. Best move or they'll eat you bloody."

"Too late."

"Shrike." She rolled off him, booted his hip, and was startled when he tumbled off the load, limp.

But she heard him land easy on his feet. "Cruel, Banks." He straightened.

"Get."

She pulled out slowly, spooked by the Aireils' passing. Old Loomis hadn't exaggerated the creatures' numbers. Not good, not good. Coach Grimey had taught her about the Species Wars—Aireils against humans—and she'd heard worse tales from Pa and Morrie, stories that had given her nightmares as a kid; tales of people's heads torn off, their bodies swollen with poison until they exploded.

Sal shuddered, imagined nightmare and real, each muddling the other. Aireil hands were soft, so soft. She'd been touched by them more than once, working the green all this time. But she'd never stopped fearing them.

In the eighty-first year of Ver Day's settlement, two sisters and their single husband had filed claim on a homestead along an unnamed creek just south of Old Gorge and southwest of where Tumble Town would later stand. A gatherer found their bodies a week later, bloated and blued, but preserved by the Aireil poison that had killed them. Five ompha pines, cut for cabin building, lay on the ground unused.

The next spring, the Aireils killed five more humans, and a fool newbie killed an Aireil. Four long months later, the toll stood at ninety-six humans dead and fourteen mistwalkers. Humans were losing the war.

Then a smart settler figured out that there were certain places the Aireils wouldn't tolerate disturbance, certain trees they wouldn't allow to be cut. And one of their favored places was right where the government had begun building the third Industrial Zone authorized under the Terms of Settlement. Building was stopped, and the killings stopped, too.

After that it was law—greenie law, the strongest kind—that no one messed with the Aireils. Whatever the creatures wanted, they got. And all they really seemed to want was to be free in the green.

Sal took a swig from her belt canteen, sweating faster than she could drink. It was going to be a long night.

Of course it would have been a short one if Raschad hadn't spotted the mistwalkers in time. Startle an Aireil and it would scratch you with its hook claw, condemning you to writhing death. Harm a nest tree and you died quicker, but uglier.

She shuddered. If these crazies had cut nest trees, the jungle faced another war, and the mistwalkers just might solve Governor Wally's population problems quick. Tech weapons or not, greenies didn't stand a chance against Aireils. The big beasts could come at you before you even knew they were about. Raschad was a shriking lucky newbie to have spotted them in time.

The first moon set, and the jungle lay black on black. Sal's legs numbed. Her back spasmed and throbbed. She trudged head down, following the slender beam of her headlamp.

"Aa-ah-ghee-ee!"

Hair rose on her scalp. Her skin prickled.

She froze, forgetting to brake, and her sled bumper juiced her. So she hit both brakes at once. *Thunk.* Raschad's steering bars rammed her sled in the dark. Jammed him up good that time.

"Aa-ah-ghee-ee!" The unseen woman screamed again.

Sweat flooded Sal's armpits and ran between her breasts. A weight landed on the back of her sled. She killed her light, breath deserting her.

"Sal?" Raschad swarmed over her load, smelling of panic.

"Easy." But her own voice scaled upward.

"What?" His whisper quavered.

"Don't know. Squat. Where are we?"

"Don't *you* ask *me*."

"Hush." Her eyes adjusting to the dark, she made out a splotch of light ahead. "See that? Too bright for moonlight."

Raschad hesitated. "Aia."

"We must be close to the Junction. Looks like our lipis butchers didn't find D'arnith's or Noca Tana, either." Loomis had warned her. "Best check it out. Get on back to your sled."

Her load wobbled, and he was gone. She took a step, two, then stopped. Everything felt wrong. The light ahead was too small, the darkness around them too *solid*, too close.

She flicked her headlamp's beam to the right and it bounced off slab-thick bark. She angled the light ahead of her. Broken branches and shattered wood stretched as far as she could see, walling in the trail. Her stomach cramped her lungs. Trees fell, but not many this time of year, with the ground drying.

Forcing a breath, she shifted her beam left. It met more branches, more debris, and a second tree down on its side.

Walked right into it, didn't you? she cussed herself. Just like being stuck in a funnel—no place to move now but ahead. Slipping her harness, she skidded over her load back to Raschad.

"What?" He spoke low.

"Trap."

His traces chinked free. He slid against the end of her load, standing beside her. "You see anything?"

"Naia."

Bugs whined. Fleepas chattered in the distance. Faint and distant, harsh laughter carried downtrail. A chill slid up Sal's spine. More laughter, lots of voices—a big camp. No wonder they had killed all those lipis.

Teeth gritted, back aching, she nudged Raschad. He moved right. She split left. They crept along opposite sides of her sled, moving uptrail step by step.

The laughter grew louder, then became screeching, yelling, and yahooing. Music sounded beneath the ruckus. Fools—they'd draw in every critter from here to the Forks. Sal sweated. Where had the mistwalkers gone?

Firelight glowed ahead; the clearing was nearer than she'd thought, the usual view from the trail reduced by the downed trees' brushy tops. Light showed through only in odd, narrow patches.

Raschad rejoined her, and she tugged him near. "Boost," she whispered and wedged a foot against a limb stob on the downed tree. "Follow me."

Lifting her, his grip wasn't polite. But dried leaves and wet moss slipped beneath her fingers, and she needed his help however it came. Scrabbling, she wriggled onto the log. At her back, with his greater reach, he vaulted up unaided.

Off the log's other side, she sensed the jungle thick and tangled, but didn't dare risk using her headlamp here. She nudged Raschad, and he dropped to the ground. Vines tore. Brush snapped. He steadied her as she landed at his side.

She pushed him forward. He bulled through the scrub. Slimmer, she bobbed and dodged. Just don't meet a moa in here, she prayed to fate. All she needed now was her eyes spit full of acid. Brush clawed her bushwhackers and bruised her arms, threatening to pin her. She swatted and scrabbled, deafened by whining bugs. Tiny jaws clamped down on her gloved fingers, but she fought a scream and pried the monster loose with her belt knife.

Raschad had disappeared. Sweating, she homed on firelight, wriggling double time, her insides aquiver. Lost . . .

She crawled out at his side. He rolled over to make room for her to peek through a veil of reeki. Cheers rocked the night, and the shriking woman screamed again.

Panting, Raschad eased over her for a better view, and his chest bumped her back with every hot breath he breathed in her ear. Ignoring all that, she blinked back her own sweat and made out a bonfire blazing at the Junction clearing's heart. Ragged, shouting figures laughed and jigged around the fire, their elongated shadows dancing like boogies over the encircling brush. A child screeched.

Sal tensed—scarlet blood on a little pink dress ... Raschad rained sweat down her neck.

She steadied, concentrated, and studied the camp and the trampled jungle verge. From a knot of huddled tech-style tents, a boggy path—picked out by the glint of firelight off water—snaked into the surrounding scrub. The stench of fresh squat and old urine rode the air. Any more rain and the clearing would go pure bog and swallow the whole mess—that was one small blessing. But it would be another season before the spot was fit for use again.

Her eyes flicked back to the drunken melee surrounding the fire. You're a fool, Banks, letting these idiot-minded bastards catch you so easy. With their camp stretched right across the Pike and the tree falls stopping sled turnarounds, trail traffic was forced square into the middle of them.

She bumped Raschad's shoulder, signaling him back. He moved, and she slithered around and followed him. The racket from the camp combined with the usual bug din covered what little noise they made, but her back felt vulnerable.

Limb-whipped and bug-gnawed, they tumbled back onto the trail. Their sleds sat unharmed. The drunken would-be-ambushers hadn't spotted the prey in their trap—yet.

Raschad staggered past her and slumped against her load. It had been another way-and-gone too-long day. She swatted a bomb beetle off his back and ducked as it detonated above their heads. The stench didn't bother her just then, but she hoped it had a sore heinie for a week.

"All right?"

"No." He breathed deep. "Shriking tired."

"Aia."

He lay his head on his arms, shoulders slack. She leaned next to him, chin on her crossed wrists. Now what, gal? Got yourself and this newbie stuck good.

A seeg pride yowled northward. Gigis yammered to the south. The noise and the stench ahead was attracting dangerous attention.

Raschad's arm slipped around her. What possessed him?

But it felt good, comfort in a desperate situation. After a moment he let loose and squatted. Checking his weapons, he cleaned his gun grip, straightened his belt knife, felt under his shirt, then loosened a boot blade. The night she'd stripped him at Klinker's, she'd been amazed he could carry so much weight in weapons and still pull. Now she wished he carried more. Squatting beside him, she checked her own gear. It was as good an idea as any other just now.

After a bit, they climbed onto the load and leaned against each other's backs. Maybe at dawn they could switch tread direction and pull backward. But there was no hope of it in the dark, and no real hope of it at all. Sleds did back, but not fast enough to run away from trouble.

"We can leave the sleds." She spoke low. "Hide off the trail."

"We'd be eaten before dawn."

"Aia." She breathed out slow. "We can go back the way we came. That scriar'll be full by now."

Raschad scratched, swatted, rocked. "Too many Aireils. Or if not, more voles. Leave the sleds, and we have nothing to put our backs against."

"Aia, what I figured." She'd given him his outs. He was a smart man, for newbie or greenie. There was just nowhere to go, nothing to do but wait for daylight.

A drunken roar sounded in the distance. Sal flinched. "You'd think they was in the middle of Tumble Town. I never seen or heard anything like them."

"They're Mafeezie's spawn—Runners."

"Aia. I figured." Runners from the Run. She gnawed her lip. "Governor Wally's work, *resettling* the bodies he don't need to work his factories, pushing city folks onto jungle homesteads just to clear the tenements." Remembering Mem's fears, she hunkered her head between her arms, scared, angry, and aching.

Raschad didn't say anything. The noise from the clearing went on. The seeg pride moved farther off—circling, Sal figured, intent on the noise and the fire, not them.

"Sleep, Raschad." She was too keyed up for resting.

"Can't." His back against hers felt taut as a drumhead. "Why do you live with Morrie?"

She half looked around, surprised by his bald questioning. But she decided he meant to rile her, to take her mind off other things and occupy his own.

She answered him straight. "I live with Morrie because the old cuss took me in when I needed it. Because he's as near kin as I got. Sort of maybe my granda, like *maybe* Dancer's son is *maybe* my cousin or my uncle." She rubbed her forehead again. Shrike, she didn't want to die with this newbie. "And Morrie's getting slow, needs a hand now and then."

"You're altruistic."

"What?"

"Caring. Generous," he said.

She snorted. "Well, he grows on you."

"More like things grow on him."

"You know . . ." She chuckled. "You giving him that bath was about worth getting my head cracked."

"The bath was an alternative to cracking *his* head."

"I noticed you ain't an easy forgiver," she said.

"But I'd happily listen to his snoring just now. I'd even give him another bath if that would get us out of here."

"Aia. I'd help." She sagged. This was her fault. They should've braved the bugs in Twoteeth's meadow.

"Banks." He swatted her hip. "Forget my complaining. Just something to say. It's my fault we're stuck out here."

"Aia. It is."

He swatted her again, harder, so she knew he understood her teasing. She relaxed into his broad back. "Do we talk plain tonight, newbie?"

"Aia, greenie. Ask away. Talking's better than sitting here imagining *what ifs*."

"Aia. I'm curious why you ain't with your family."

His head rocked back over hers, his shoulder muscles tense against her back. "Don't complain about this later."

"Fair warning."

"MB-2's not much of a planet. Cities and factory farms."

"Make money off the farms?" He'd said to ask plain, after all.

"No. They don't even feed us. The economy's based on chemical production, mineral export—which is failing—and mercenary supply."

"I suppose you was into mining there, too."

"My grandfather is, among other things."

"Your govies cause you trouble?"

"In different ways. The two main political power bases have been destroying each other for eight generations. That keeps the families busy and the population down, or we'd have outgrown the place long ago. My family's population was reduced to four." He spoke hard and low.

"Sorry." She gnawed her lip and stared into the night.

"It's all right." He leaned away a little. "I need to think about it sometimes just to realize that it didn't happen yesterday, that time passes and things change."

She couldn't let it be. "So you ain't got much family left."

"On the Raschad side I do. But I'm not a Raschad anymore by lineage or affection."

"Count things through your mother's side, then, like we do?"

"It depends." He drew a deep breath. Seegs bayed in the distance, moving nearer again. "Did you grow up happy, Banks?"

"I thought we was talking about you."

"We're talking plain, remember?"

"Aia." She scraped bugs from her face net. "I grew up hard, newbie. That's how I grew, the greenie way. Ma and even Pa loved me. I loved Ma more than anything, and Pa as much as he'd let anyone. But our shack wasn't much better than Morrie's. We passed the old trail to it coming out of Tumble Town down the hill. Ma built it off in the scrub before she married, lived out there alone, made a living gathering herbs and medicinals like my granna before her. She, Granna, and Dancer were real close.

"Then Ma let Stillman Coars spend a night. That was my Pa, a jungle tramp through and through. He wandered in and out, ate up her food, spent off her credits if she let him.

"About the time I come, the monsoons failed, and Ma couldn't feed me right, working scarce pickings in the jungle with a babe in arms. Granna and Dancer helped. But Ma finally turned to cleaning hotels. She hated it, but the income was steadier, and when Pa needed bailing out of one trouble or the other, she managed." Swigging from her canteen, Sal cleared her throat. "I never talked this much about myself to anyone before."

"Don't have to," Raschad said softly.

"Well, maybe you're right. Remembering things can put them better in place. Lots of things have eaten my gut for a long time. Ma worked her hands bloody, broke her back. But Pa just lived as he wanted, never mind if I ate or Ma, never mind that we might ever love him."

Sal sighed. "One night when I was maybe eight, Slick Clay come out to the cabin from Heaven's Rest. Slick just earned wages then, didn't own anything. Pa thought I was asleep. Ma was working up to the Sundowner. Pa drug out his pack and sold Slick a bundle, big around as my thigh, of scatter bark. There was enough to give every govie on the hill waking dreams for a month.

"Everyone knows that selling dream wood is how Slick made his fortune, but doesn't anyone know Pa was the fool that sold it to him for nothing and a promise. Pa sold his soul to hell, and Slick cheated him out of the devil's reward atop that. And no one ever caught Slick selling—no one who'd tell. George become sheriff mostly because people were sick of old Dully Akbauck looking the other way from the tech trade passing between the likes of Slick and the depot. These days now, Slick's *respectable*. He don't dare cross George, and George ain't stupid or greedy." She sighed again. "That answer your question yet?"

"No."

"Naia. Say 'naia.' Don't talk spacer to me. Learn right."

"*Naia*, then. Were you happy?"

"I was happy with Ma. Never was a better ma. But one night at the Sundowner a govie fired on one of the ladies, caught Ma instead. Losing Pa later was mostly just relief."

Bugs whined. Frogs croaked, peepers peeped, and a scriar roared far off. Sal's gut knotted another notch.

"How about you, newbie? You like growing up between mining pits, poison dumps, and killers?" Wasn't she nasty.

"I didn't see that, didn't understand it, until later. If everything around them is just the way they want it, kids don't look deeper, don't want anything scaring them."

She remembered a bit of that feeling. But the facts of life rode the surface in the green.

"Father was rich," Raschad went on. "Mother was powerful. And I was their oldest child. My grandparents on both sides doted on me. Grandfather Raschad even presented me to the Emperor at court.

"But Father was Hail Safer-tol Tarsian. I inherited his looks and stubbornness. The Tarsians were new money; Mother's name brought him respectability. But he never bent knee the way Grandfather Raschad expected of him. And I grew just as proud.

"I was twelve when Grandfather Raschad took me on vacation to KalMinot. We rode a Raschad spacer for a week going and a week returning. I still don't remember what we saw on KalMinot. Back at home, all I could talk about was stars and space. I'd been up before for short hops around MB-2. But this struck me so hard. I *loved* spacing.

"I begged Father to send me to Academy, let me learn anything that would keep me spaced. He agreed—he wanted me off-planet. Axial—Grandfather Raschad—laughed. It hurt worse than anything I'd ever felt. After that, nothing could have changed my mind. Nothing did. Mother pleaded reason with Father. But in the end she loved him more than she feared Grandfather, and agreed I might be safer beyond Axial's reach. All of us knew she was afraid. Still, Father wouldn't give me up to the Raschads' plans."

Slap. Slap. Raschad swatted bugs so hard that the force of his blows vibrated through his body to hers. "The Tarsians sponsored me at Academy, paid my way. I loved Grandfather even after he abandoned me."

Shouting sounded from the camp clearing, and a man squealed as if knife-stuck.

"I graduated from Academy and went to work for the Tarsians. By then they'd made several bad investments, lost money. They couldn't afford to save me for polite assignments. I spaced, and I fought for the highest bidder.

"Then Father died protecting Grandmother from an assassination attempt. Old Axial never even attended the funeral. I did, on a medical carrier, wounded. When things go bad, they go bad in bunches. I couldn't space anymore—twenty-one years old, torn up, and I'd lost my dream."

Sal rocked her head against his, half wishing he'd shut up. But she'd asked—twice—and owed it to him to listen. She was a fool for asking at all. Losing a stranger was one thing; losing someone you'd gotten to know . . .

"I guarded the family after that. The mansion was an armed camp. One night sirens sounded. I stood my post outside Mother's chambers. All the Tarsians except Mother's children died. No one even claimed honor for the victory.

"Mother still had certain uses to the Raschads, and her death would have carried repercussions for them better left unfaced. So the four of us were taken alive, and eventually given to Axial. He claimed he ransomed us, and made it clear that allowing me and my seven-year-old brother to live was simply practical."

Raschad's words rang bitter beneath his calm, and his muscles were slack now against her back. Maybe he no longer recognized his own pain.

"If he killed us, every blood cousin of the Tarsians could claim death rights and compensation. Keeping me, the indisputable heir, alive was cheaper. He drove me off MB-2, won't ever let me return, and only lets me live so long as he knows I'm no threat to his plotting. I keep my appointments with Rimmersin, and Rimmersin verifies to Axial that I'm where I'm supposed to be. If I'm not, every Tarsian or Raschad enemy goes after my brother. But Mother can still cause Grandfather trouble, and will if Mickel dies. So I'm the decoy, the heir who can't cause anyone trouble from this far away."

She stared at nothing, feeling like an innocent and glad of it. "I'd hate them all."

"Aia."

"You hate it here?"

"Naia." He chuckled, no humor in his tone. "Ver Day suits my circumstances. I like to be alone. Things could be worse."

"Might be before morning."

"Don't worry for my sake." He leaned his head against hers again. "Everyone rests eventually."

Her throat ached. How did a newbie stay alive this long thinking like that?

"You miss your family?" His voice had roughened; the bastard wasn't so tough after all.

"Aia." She breathed deep, realizing that she missed both Ma and Pa. "I had a baby sister for a couple of years." Her heart misbeat. "I just barely remember her." She swallowed to steady her voice. "I like the McDonnels' real sweety, proper family stories." She pulled a twig from the mud caked on her boots and flipped it into the dark. "Wish you had better ones to tell."

"Aia."

She picked blindly at her soles, ears full of the Runners' drunken madness. Raschad scratched, rocking her gently. Her eyes closed, weighted with fatigue.

High above, tree frogs chirped from rainwater pools in the hearts of hollow knooje leaves. She floated. Wild figures flitted across the curve of her closed lids. Spiraling, she rose above Ver Day's beautiful green glow. So beautiful . . .

Her stomach dropped out. Her head spun. She plummeted, sucked into soup-thick air. Sonny screamed.

She woke, her throat raw, falling, yanked by her harness.

"Get'em!" Brush cracked. Voices shrieked.

She hit the ground, hard muscle under her—Raschad. Torchlight flared. Shadows swooped. Bodies crashed in the brush.

She pulled her Camm and fired. Raschad's hellish weapon detonated. Dual screams split the night.

"*Runners.*" Raschad's bellow sounded muffled and distant, her ears blast-shocked.

Sweat blinded her. Blurred, lantern-lit figures closed in. Shadows writhed, and she saw blades and truncheons.

Tech light stabbed the dark. She fired one-handed from the hip, a tread maul gripped in her other fist. Runners swarmed over the top of her load in attack.

Raschad fell, weapon roaring, spraying the night with fire trails, stunning her deaf and blind.

The pack faltered. Raschad struggled up. She put her back to his. A blow clipped her shoulder, doubling her over.

Raschad grabbed her harness.

Bellowing sounded above. Runners rained from the trees. Shrieking, they crushed her against Raschad.

Raschad fired. A blow hit Sal's ribs. She lost her maul and struggled to pull her knife. Deaders. *Going to die.* A Runner screamed in her face—Sonny screaming. She screamed back.

Lights strobed wild. A lantern crashed off the sled. A body thumped beside it. And an Aireil grounded.

Sal's heart seemed to stop. Her hair bristled. Her ears rang. And the Runners ran.

Don't! She ducked. The newbie curled over her, pinned her in his arms against the sled. He knew . . .

The jungle went mad. Panicked Runners crashed through underbrush. Screams echoed, rose and fell, death cries merging and swelling on and on until Sal would've screamed herself if Raschad weren't squeezing the breath from her.

Her lungs ached. Her crotch was soaked with sweat—or worse. Her stomach roiled. Then a soul-tearing screech stabbed her eardrums and choked off.

Not a jungle thing stirred. Not a voice cried out.

Aireil stench rode the wind. Brush crashed, and a bloody misshapened lump flew through the wide beam of a fallen handlight. Droplets pattered, struck her cheek. Iron stench.

She gagged. Bodies flew into the scrub, tossed by Aireils. Going to toss us in the jungle, too. *Sally! Sally!*

Sara! Annie! She strained against Raschad's grip. He held on, joints creaking.

Screams rose in the distance. Fingers clawed her thighs. *Annie!* But Raschad's heart pounded her shoulder right through their harness padding, and she knew it wasn't Annie screaming.

Feet pounded the trail, headed their way. Raschad nearly snapped her spine. The shriek stabbed her gut and disintegrated into gurgling.

A second silence fell. Raschad didn't breathe. Sal couldn't.

Wind sighed—only not wind—Aireils. *Thump.* Her sled rocked, rocked again.

Feet landed in the light beam next her head—six-toed, green, furry feet. The sled load creaked, and another set of feet landed near the first. Mold and sap scent mixed with the stench of human blood. Her throat knotted to stone.

A shaggy shadow crouched down and hairy hands brushed her fingers. Raschad dripped sweat on her head. *Where's my hat?*

A grunt sounded next to her ear. She wanted to look, but only sensed a third Aireil move behind Raschad, pinning them. And all three creatures leaned nearer.

What did they want?

Raschad's harness creaked beneath the Aireils' weight. Oh, newbie, please. He didn't move, didn't make a sound, except his breathing wheezed. Please, no fits now. Visions of McDonnel's played through her mind, images of Raschad curled into a lost and panicked heap, images of Sonny, bleeding. She couldn't breathe.

The sled rocked again—once, twice, three times.

She blinked. Raschad wheezed.

Gone. Her eyes closed and her mind slipped away.

Sal woke curled over, lying in Raschad's lap, panting into his side. After the scent of the mistwalkers, his stench was blessedly welcome.

"Up." Her voice was a croak.

"Uuunnh." He shoved her off and dragged himself to his knees. Then he tugged her against him again and stood. "What? What? Don't . . . don't . . ."

She shook him. "Shut up."

Scrabbling, she climbed atop the load, grabbed his harness and pulled until he followed her up out of the mud and the gore. They shivered and clung. She blinked at the red-tinged foliage—everything covered with blood. Her brain cleared. Not blood, idiot, fire. She breathed smoke, heard flames crackle.

Raschad raised his head. His arms slackened. She leaned back and blinked up at his face, painted with red glow and shadow.

"What?" She couldn't look.

He swallowed, his chest pumping against hers. "The tents are burning."

She closed her eyes, her vision spinning. The Aireils had passed them by, not even touched the load. She jerked to her knees and stretched above Raschad, staring away from the fireglow. The other sled squatted behind them, its load intact. Why?

She slumped stomach-down over his shoulder. He leaned into her hip. Feeling him go, she wrapped her arms behind his head so he didn't hit too hard, then tumbled atop him.

"Sal?"

"S'all right." She didn't want to know what he was asking. "Easy." She hugged him, needing time to recover.

"You ever—" His voice shook. When she touched his bare hand, it was cold. "—ever see anything like this?"

"Naia. Never."

Chapter 11

"I can't imagine space." The fire had burned down to a distant
ed glow.

"It's beautiful. Nothing hems you in. Stars burn. Only your ship
and equipment keep you alive. But with them, you can travel forever and never be the same place twice."

His words staggered her shock-numbed mind, and she didn't try
understanding what he meant, only what he felt, an echo of her
love for the green.

Cr-ra-ck!

"Naia—" She startled up.

"Easy." He held her. Her lungs labored, the reeki-tainted smoke
thicker than ever. "Be still."

"What?"

"Aireils, I think."

Cr-ra-ck!

She only breathed. He lay against her side, trembling.

They harnessed in at first strong light and moved out in drizzling rain. Sal held the Camm in her right hand, steered when she
had to with her left, and kept her head up, wary of everything. A
gigi gang had come calling and yelping around the clearing
earlier, firing her blood, making her think crazier than Raschad.
But something had spooked the nasty beasties off. She didn't find
that luck reassuring.

When she glanced back over her load, Raschad looked like a
wild thing scenting blood—body tensed to spring, head up and ac-
tive. The strangeness of the night still gripped her heart.

The rain had arrived before dawn, and the clearing fire had died
out. They'd traded watches after that, and she'd snatched a bit of

real sleep. Then he'd rested, and awakened with puffy eyes above
hollow cheeks. She didn't suppose she looked any better. Her
nose ran, and her throat ached raw.

Slowing into a curve, eyes on the foliage canopy above, she
holstered the Camm in order to steer. Rain dripped from feather
ferns. Fronds longer than she was tall trailed from overhead
branches. On the ground, pea-sized burntwood cones made every
step hazardous and kept the sled fighting her lead.

Sweat ran on her sides. Ahead, a gnarl of branches marked the
end of the Runners' trap; any planned attack would come here.
Raising the Camm's barrel against her shoulder, she rounded a
slight bend in the trail, heart thumping.

Only the tree's shattered crown, trapped in silence and rain,
greeted her. And the trail ahead lay clear except for a single torn
body. Her gut knotted and roiled, but the real shock lay past the
corpse.

Beyond the downed tree bordering the trail, an ompha pine,
propped on an axe-hewn stump, stood tethered by living reeki
vines to the branches of surrounding trees. As if it had never
fallen, the pine's crown soared out of sight, hidden in mist.

Her sled treads clicked to a halt.

Mud squished.

She dropped, spun, and nearly killed Raschad as he slogged up
beside her, weapon raised, expecting trouble. Seeing the tree, he
slowly lowered the gun.

"Scut." He shivered. "What did that?"

"Aireils." She swallowed hard. All that cracking and creaking
last night made sense now. Mistwalkers favored omphas for nest-
ing. "Naia a problem for forty, fifty mistwalkers."

"Scut damn." His face net hung open—smoke and reeki sap
keeping insects at bay—and he looked pale through his coating of
grime. "Banks." His voice barely disturbed the jungle's hush. "I
feel just like a newbie."

"Aia." Her laugh came out a bark, startling her, no humor in it
at all. "Best keep moving."

"I'll clear the way."

"I can." But her voice caught in her throat, and besides, he was
already out of the traces.

"I've done it before." He moved uptrail.

She drew her Camm. Movements wary, Raschad plucked a giant dew leaf and approached the body. Covering the bloody lump
with the leaf, he scooped it off into the brush. She wanted to

uke, but he straightened and made a little sign with his good
and.

Shrike, he had soul religion.

He strode past her, eyes averted. Waiting for him to hook in,
she stared ahead at the clearing. Steam and mist rose from it in
puffs like monstrous exhalations.

He whistled *go*; she pulled.

With daylight brightening in spite of the rain, a fleepa chattered, one good sign. But Sal's muscles remained knotted and
tensed, and her lip quivered as she pulled past the leaf-draped
Runner's body. She'd seen worse. Gigis ate people.

Panic threatened. She fought it, refusing to look too closely at
its source. Ahead, the clearing opened before her.

Mangled, charred bodies dotted the mire, others just bloody
smears. Fear knotted tighter, blurred her vision. She'd never erase
the sight or smell of this morning from her mind, never forget that
other morning . . .

Hot spots smoldered in the duff and threw off oily smoke,
forming clouds beneath clouds. During the night she'd imagined
Aireils spreading the flames—a crazy thought. Mistwalkers hated
fire. Seeing this mess now, she figured the Runners had panicked
and started the tents burning themselves, which made more sense.
But any sense behind all of this was more than she could reckon.

Eyes frozen on an unburned shelter, she stopped. Twisted on
the ground, bloody lumps showed beneath the tent canvas.
Raschad stumped up through the trail's churned mud.

"I'll check for survivors."

"Aia." She reached for her clips.

"I can do it. You guard the sleds."

"I ain't no innocent." Sal unclipped. "Done as bad before, and
with folks I knew. Ain't time enough for you to sort this mess
alone. Stay in sight of the sleds."

She pulled her long rifle from its rack, her heart hammering,
head twinging. They slogged off in different directions, weaving
between bodies, scorched patches of ground that had been reeki
mounds last night, and still smoking logs. Sal walked, and she listened. But she didn't look too close, and covering the east side of
the camp, she spied not a single body intact enough to even
check. She did pry open not one standing tent. It was empty.

Winding her way back toward the sleds, she saw Raschad
straighten from next to a man's rigid-armed body. She waved, and
he moved for his own sled with a shake of his head. She hadn't
expected anything different.

Anyway, they'd done the proper thing. But she kept seeing double, bodies over bodies, Sonny's . . . She clipped onto her traces. At least they didn't have wounded to deal with this deep in the green.

Rolling forward, the sled felt three times as heavy as yesterday, and it took all her will to force her leaden legs to pick up speed, running away, running on.

At the far edge of the clearing another body blocked the trail—a small, stick-limbed lump.

That one froze her, looked like . . . looked like her little sister Annie. Annie? She couldn't ever remember that child's name exactly right.

Raschad whistled, questioning. But she stood paralyzed.

Got to move it, can't pull over it.

She unclipped in a panic, grabbed for the nearest big leaves, marched up the trail, and imitated the wrap and roll Raschad had done on the other corpse. Except she didn't have any soul religion, and it was a very tiny body, looked more like Bobby now, little Bobby after . . .

She dumped it off the trail, then straightened and turned for her sled. Her legs went. She crumpled, puking in the mud.

"Sal?"

She raised a hand to ward him off—hadn't even heard him coming. He caught her fingers, knelt in the mud and cupped a palm under her forehead, holding her face out of the muck.

With a final retch, she straightened and leaned back into him. "S'all right. Just surprised me." Bobby? She fought that down—no good use in remembering everything.

"Aia." He helped her to her feet. "I can lead. You don't have to take it all."

"Naia." She shook her head. "That's the last."

"Should we . . ." He hesitated, eyes flashing white within the shadow of his slicker hood, and looked toward the jungle, then back across the travesty of the clearing. "Should we check the scrub?" The tremor in his voice told her what answer he wanted to hear.

"Aireils don't leave survivors."

"They left us."

For a breath she felt air-headed again. Raschad's hand steadied her. Alone or even with Chic, she might have survived last night. But she'd lived through this with a shriking newbie, a fact strange beyond grasping right now. A shriking newbie . . . his big body sheltering her from the Aireils.

Getting soft. Getting old early. Mem's words—too much time spent in the green.

She looked up at Raschad and all of a sudden wanted to cry. She didn't. But enough must have shown in her face, because his arms folded around her, pressed her near. Finding him trembling, she hugged him back, fiercely. She would have hugged Scollarta this morning just to have someone alive beside her.

Raschad was a sight nicer than the contractor, and his lips when they found her cheek were gentle and warm.

That fast she forgot mistwalkers, bodies, and everything except the look in his eyes, the feel of his muscles against her thighs, his need. Rain trickled inside her hood. His chest moved against hers in short pants.

She took things the next step, came up on her toes and kissed him full on the mouth.

It was good, dizzying. Her body flushed . . .

A gigi shrieked.

They exploded apart.

Squealing mayhem rattled her brain. Her breath caught. Ice shivered her joints and cleared her head. He hesitated, every kind of wildness in his eyes.

He spun away, running for his sled.

She dove between her steering bars and clipped in, frantic, the load dead weight as she lunged for the cover of scrub and the short stretch of trail between the clearing and the Ebbid junction. The treads skidded, fighting her.

She let up on the steering bars. Don't be so scared, gal. Use sense. Tread cleats bit into mud, and relief flooded her spine. She sprinted beneath tall trees.

Boom! A shot cracked—*boom* again. Not Raschad.

She skidded to a stop, leaning on her brakes. A thump and jolt announced Raschad's arrival, following too close again, too fast, going to loosen his teeth yet.

Sal's pulse thumped and thundered. But the gigis weren't after them. The shrieking came from north on the Ebbid.

Blood rushed, reddening her vision.

Her sled rocked, and the newbie vaulted onto its load, weapon drawn, looking like retribution.

"Stay!" She barked it loud enough to be heard over all the racket, then slipped free of her traces and lunged into the scrub.

Glancing back, she thought he would disobey and follow her. But then he settled down, crouched and coiled, his slicker billowing like a demon's wings. Nothing short of Aireils could take that load now—that was one comfort as she bulled into heavy growth and fresh gigi squat. Shouldn't be in here—craziness, crazy gal.

But the Runners had made little paths between the two trails. Following one, sweating and shaking, she ran out of cover, broke into the clear, and then crawled onto a long open stretch of log. Tech wrappers littered the landing. A poaching blind, so the Runners could stalk the Ebbid side of the junction.

Boom. Boom-boom.

Brush shredded. Bark sprayed. Sal crouched and waddled, peeking over the top of ferns and tiger grass.

A gigi screamed. She screamed back. But the sight below her perch froze her.

Two sleds sat on the Ebbid, surrounded by screeching, spike-furred, knee-high beasties. Dug in, weapons blazing, the packers down there wouldn't last long with the smell of carrion from the Runners' camp attracting every gigi this side of Tumble Town, every one of the devils in a blood frenzy.

Run. Raschad sat back there alone. But heat flushed her head to toe, rage blossomed in her gut, and a gigi landed at her feet, wailing and shrieking.

She fired on instinct. The beast exploded into bloody rain, and there was no time to run.

Spinning, she let madness take hold. She sprayed a gang at her back with fire and laughed. But the leaf canopy above the trail writhed and wriggled, and vermin boiled out of the trees.

Blasts sizzled and ricocheted around her—the trapped packers were as like to kill her as the gigis. She jammed a new clip into the Camm, her sweaty fingers fumbling it, and blasted back, catching the gigis in cross fire.

Sh-hee-ing! A shot hit the log. Splinters sprayed out. Pain shot up her leg, and a gigi squealed behind her.

She whacked backward with her tread maul and heard a squashy thump, then twisted and sprayed the forest with fire until the Camm struck empty.

Her stomach lurched. She jammed the useless weapon in her belt and split a pointy skull with her maul, then split another and another. Blood coated her bushwhackers. She fought for footing but the log was aslither with gore, the gigis never retreating—too many—their wailing driving her insane.

Going to die, you . . .

An inhuman scream tore it all—a screeching ululation that froze Sal's spine and sent her belly down on the log.

Off a ways.

Rolling into a fern bank, she rammed a clip into the Camm.
he clearing. Shrike.

She swung up, weapon raised. But her targets kited into the
ush, whooping and barking, abandoning this attack to explore
e larger excitement farther on. She thumped a gigi as it scuttled
ast—too single-minded to defend itself—and lay sweating and
embling while rage deserted her.

Gigis everywhere. And from the sound of things, they'd discov-
ed the dead Runners—which at least would occupy them a bit.
ory bastards. She'd best run.

Ba-am-mm! Raschad's cannon roared, echoing and rumbling
t of the rain. Her gut froze. But after two shots it fell silent,
aybe just potting gigis going past.

She clutched her Camm, and the jungle around her hushed as
new, more distant din rose. The packers below remained hidden
hind their loads, cautious even of benefactors so deep in the
een. Letting them be, she whistled down the wind.

Rain pattered on leaves. Her pulse thundered.

Raschad's whistle carried full and strong with that fluty tone his
d: *safe*. Shrike. Good.

Sal straightened into a crouch, leg throbbing, and studied the
ads below. The lead sled's cover tarp was printed with the Silver
lls' depot flag, a rare sight so far north. But this time of year,
me packers hauled beyond the government routes, moving pri-
te trade goods to markets too hard to reach when things were
et. Tipping her head back, Sal whistled to the packers. They
dn't answer. She whistled again, then twice more, adding her
rsonal warble at the end. Anyone she'd ever packed around
uld recognize that.

"Banks?" A deep-throated roar sounded from the lead sled.

"Aia!"

"Nuke and Haze."

Silver Falls packers, all right, and her with a newbie—but there
asn't time to worry about that. "Got a partner on the Pike." Her
gs quaked—too much use, too many shocks. She stood up slow,
ving them time to see she wasn't a threat.

Emerging from behind their sleds, weapons still raised, heads
, the two flexed solid, massive muscle—Haze just a shorter ver-
n of Nuke Jagger.

"You're squat crazy, Banks!" Nuke cupped his hands to am-
ify his yell. "Those gigis could've shredded your ass."

"Then we best light hell out of here before they remember
Meet you at the junction."

"Can't. There's a tree fall ahead. We were cutting around whe
the shriking gigis hit."

Another Runner trap.

"We'll come up on the other side then, cut to meet you."

"Naia. Run. Whatever those critters are fighting over, it won
keep 'em long."

"Longer than you want to know." She shuddered, her upper li
curling. "If we can cut you out, we'll all be safer together."

"Aia." Nuke hesitated. "What the hell was it last night?"

"Aireils."

"Squat." She'd shaken the big man. "You saved our haunche
already. Run."

No sense in arguing. Sprinting for her sleds, she whistlee
Raschad answered—another big relief. She dove onto the trail.

"Haia, move."

He spun off her load. An axe whumped up the Ebbid. Sh
lunged against harness and hauled. The newbie pulled alongsid
her at the junction.

"Runners blockaded the Ebbid." She ducked clear of her stee
ing bars. "Two packers are trapped on the other side, sled
jammed up like we were last night, can't turn around."

She flipped open her left storage locker and reached for a
axe—that was ten tech things. On the other side she heard h
chain saw rattle—eleven—as Raschad lifted its coils.

They hit the trail at a trot, and he didn't even mention runnin
Ahead, axes thumped a desperate double rhythm.

"Get through before we get there," Raschad begged aloud.

"Aia." Sal ached. Gigis' wails skinned her nerves, and sightin
the barricade, she stopped stone still, the axe thumping carelessl
at her feet. "How we going to clear that?"

Three bristling webb trees blocked the trail, their branche
wedged and snarled in the underbrush on either side. Sal's voi
sounded like a stranger's.

"Have to blow it." Raschad, forgetting what he carried, hugge
the razor-toothed chain saw against his chest.

"Ain't got explosives."

"You're packing damping gel."

"That don't blow anything."

"This is a Morven-4dr." He dropped the saw, drew his b
weapon, and ejected its ammo. "Strip a tube, put an igniter on

seal it with gel so the explosion experiences a thirty-second containment time. We can reduce this mass to splinters."

"You'll blow your hands off and poison the green." Her gut felt like shattered glass. Gigi wailing spiked in the distance.

"We get them out now or we're all dead." He met her stare.

Her sides heaved. "Haze!" she screamed above the whump of axes as loud as she could. "Nuke!"

The axes stopped. "What?" Their bellow barely carried above the gigis' caterwauling.

"Get away. Way back. Going to blow this squat."

She hoped they heard. Raschad was stripping his ammo.

Bolting for the sleds, she tore into the load and popped a crate already Aireil-damaged. She grabbed a square of damping gel. *Shrike*, was all she could think, nothing useful at all pushing past panic as she lit back down the trail.

Raschad met her halfway. "Between the sleds. Don't peek. Don't come out."

He was a fool, depending on tech. And she didn't know three things in a row about creating the kind of explosion he meant to blow. But Nuke and Haze hadn't another chance. She turned tail without a word, skidded belly down over her load, and buried herself between the sleds. Come on, newbie.

His boots pounded the trail, running hard. The sled rocked. He crashed down on her head.

The world went roaring deaf.

A *whumpf* emptied her lungs, stunned her ears. Chunks of wood and rot rained over the sled. Hanging head down, one leg wrapped on the load, Raschad weighed on her shoulders. Mud and leaves splattered on top of them.

She couldn't breathe. Survived the explosion, but going to die hiding from it—a distant part of her found that funny.

Raschad shifted to drag his weight up onto his arms. Sal sucked air, and, through the ringing in her ears, sensed more than heard *silence*. Even the gigis' yammering had stilled. For a moment the only sound was their own gasping breath.

"Get off me." She shoved. He pulled. Between them, they rolled his body onto the load, and she crawled out beside him.

"Haze! Nuke, you sumabitch!"

Ferns stirred down by the blasted mound of earth where the blockade had been.

"Banks? What th'ell you do?"

"My partner!" Sliding off the sled, she hoped they didn't mind owing their lives to a newbie—because they did.

They all dripped blood and sweat by the time they wrestled
Nuke's sleds free. Sal felt like dying, and Raschad looked dead,
except he still moved. He favored his healing hand, and seemed
to have lost pounds just since dawn. His belt, pulled tight, ran
near double around him, and his leathers hung loose all over.

But gigis jabbered, rivering jitters through her gut. Howlers
hooted. A scriar roared. No resting now.

"Move." She grabbed the newbie's elbow, and they stumble-ran
for their sleds while Nuke and Haze clipped in. With her sled
blocking the others, she had to take lead. Clips barely set, she
leaned into the harness and hauled uptrail, knowing she'd never
go fast enough to suit Nuke's long legs or outrun a gigi ganger.

Hitting the first rise, her thigh shot fire. She'd forgotten the tear
in it. Pain left her gulping air, spots floating in front of her eyes.
But a gigi shrieked from a too-near perch, and cold, tearing panic
drove her up another rise.

She hauled on, thinking that if Nuke pushed for more speed
Raschad would take the brunt of that—she had to hold her pace.

The clouds cleared off. The sun rose higher, and sweat blinded
her. Bloodsuckers, biting flies, cheese gnats, and wigglers whined
and stooped, snatching a meal from her bleeding thigh, worming
beneath the netting over the back of her neck.

And the trail kept climbing—had to climb, headed for the Rise
and Glory's Roost.

Her chest ached, knotted tighter, and topping out on the steepest
grade they'd met yet, she just stopped. After two days without a
break on the trail and shock after shock, with next to no sleep, she
had nothing left. When had they even eaten?

Raschad came. She couldn't see him. But she knew his smell—
nothing pretty now. He pried her fingers off the steering bars, unclipped her traces, and eased her back on the sled. Then he
dropped into the mud at her feet, spent.

She heard Nuke and Haze moving up, and wanted to at least
stand, embarrassed to be caught sitting. But she couldn't budge,
concentrated just on filling her tortured lungs.

"Banks?" It was Nuke.

She panted. He panted too—that was one blessing. At her feet
Raschad wheezed and snorted, and Haze stumped up, sounding
like a squeeze box.

"Ya . . . ya . . ." Nuke gasped. "Gonna kill us before the gigi
get a chance."

She laughed, but it sounded like a whimper. "Fi . . . fi . . ."

Raschad leaned his head against her legs, coughing his lungs clear. The dimness narrowing her vision began to lift.

"Here." Haze's voice sounded far off.

She blinked and focused. Haze offered her a canteen. She fumbled it, but he held her hand. She got it to her mouth and gulped. Surfacing, she slipped the canteen down to Raschad, his hands no steadier than hers.

"Wha . . ." Nuke snorted. "What you do back there, Banks?"

"Not me." Wheeze. "Partner. Damping gel, an ammo tube."

"Shrike." Nuke's breath whuffed. "Thought we was dead."

She pulled Raschad's head back, sealed his face net, and slapped the bugs that had gotten inside while he drank. "Me, too." She picked up Raschad's right hand and examined it, then his left.

"Wha . . .?" he asked.

"Counting fingers."

Raschad laughed, and half choked. They all laughed, silly, glad to be alive even if it hurt.

"Sal." Raschad sobered and tapped her leg.

She glanced down, knowing he was afraid to say anything in front of these men. Blood stained the whole front of her thigh. She hadn't realized it was that bad.

"That's a fine one." Haze bent over her, examining the hole in her leg.

"One of you near made gigi bait of me," she said.

"You were doin' your best in return."

"Kind of difficult to aim with the little bastards clawing my heinie."

"Squat, I guess."

Raschad wriggled against her traces, scraping his back up and down. Haze reached for him. "You'll rub it raw."

"Too late." She answered for Raschad and grabbed his shoulders, stilling him, the shriking bugs racing the gigis for his hide.

"We'd best know what's back there." Nuke nodded downtrail, and his tone froze her gut.

She blew out her breath. "A big camp of city scum has been ambushing both trails." She figured he suspected as much. "All dead. K-Kill—" She saw little stick limbs over everything. "—everyone. The Aireils took objection to the squat awful mess they were making of things." She shuddered.

Haze sat down in the mud. Raschad picked splinters from her thigh. Nuke passed his aidkit to her.

As Raschad cleaned her wound, Sal told their new partners about leaving the Forks, skipping her reasoning for heading out so late. She told them about the night before and listening to Runners die, then that morning and the clearing.

"Gigi's ass." Haze's eyes danced, watching for trouble. "We heard the screams."

Sal stared at the top of Raschad's head. What did this alien ex-soldier think? He'd seen slaughter before. Was the gore nothing to a space warrior? But she remembered him signing a blessing over that first body, and her hand dropped onto his shoulder before she thought.

That little move showed more to the other packers than she wanted to be seen. Worse, Raschad looked up, and the concern on his face betrayed them both. She closed her eyes. When she opened them, his head was bent back to his bandaging, and she knew he understood they'd made a mistake.

"Banks?" The strangeness in Nuke's voice forced her to look up. "Trade you sleds." His eyes probed hers.

She couldn't let them think she was slipping; she didn't want sympathy. But Nuke saw that, too, damn him.

"You're gonna kill us if I don't," he added. "My load's lighter."

She nodded. Raschad helped her stand, and she tested the bandage he'd put on her thigh. Most times, anyone steering her sled would receive a lecture on the peculiarities of its brakes or the fragility of its gears. Now she turned for Nuke's sled without another word. No need to make a point of anything just now. Staying alive was point enough.

Watching Nuke Jagger and Meesha Raschad eat hampered a person's breathing. In the twilight hush, Nuke and the newbie sucked down packets of trail slop as if racing death.

She ate her share, too, and no one spared breath for talking. Just as well. She hoped Raschad *didn't* say anything. The more time passed before Nuke and Haze discovered Raschad's origins, the longer they could all pull together and guard each other's backs. Once they realized he was newbie, things would be uncomfortable at best. And owing Raschad their lives would only make the packers hate him more.

She'd pulled with Nuke and Haze before. But that had only taught her that Haze led with his left, Nuke with his feet, and a body didn't want to be on the receiving end of either. Their patience this afternoon while she limped and lagged had more than surprised her. But the men were spent, too. All of them were so tired that they'd crammed into a clearing not big enough for three sleds, let alone four, leaving just enough space for others to get around them—with some heavy cutting. But they wouldn't meet anyone else out here now.

Raschad surfaced from feeding. "Leg hurt?" Speaking low, he kept his words properly accented.

"Aia." Shut up, idiot.

He nodded back, lips sealed, and her nerves relaxed a twist. But his eyes widened. He grabbed his back and spun off Nuke's load to slam against the sled.

"Raschad?" She dove after him, muscled him around, and tore his shirt up. In the dimming light, green goo dripped from the right side of his pale-skinned rib cage, and a billipede's legs and hide bristled from the mess like a piece of wire brush.

"That were a big one." Haze's handlight flared, lighting the newbie's back.

Sal dropped Raschad's shirt before she could think—which betrayed them as much as anything.

"Squat." Haze hissed in her ear. The beam dropped.

"Bad?" Nuke sounded sympathetic.

"Aia. Real bad. Real squat pale, bad. No shriking wonder he's scratching his yellow hide."

"What?" Nuke shifted on the load, still eating.

"Banks." Haze's voice threatened.

"So, truth." She faced the two big packers. "He's newbie, Nuke." There was no profit in denying it. With a ration tube halfway to his mouth, the big man stilled. "I needed muscle fast," she added before they stopped her. "We been together clean from Tumble Town. He ain't given me reason to regret bringing him." Piss, that was a lie.

"Newbie?" Nuke eased from his seat, keeping his voice hushed in the dusk.

"Aia." She tensed, expecting Nuke to slap Raschad, and she'd be damned if she let him.

But Nuke looked to Haze. "I ain't got a complaint about him savin' our arses." The pair stared at each other.

"Squat." Haze spat into the scrub. "Naia. I wondered how any packer'd know to blow hell out the jungle like he did. Squat crazy newbies."

Sal's breath sighed out, and most of her strength followed it. They were taking this well.

"Crazy newbie." Haze spit again.

"Aia." Nuke glared at Raschad. "Get off my sled."

Raschad straightened, his eyes on Haze more than Nuke. "Ride, Banks?" He didn't hide his accent.

"Just an arm."

He flipped her over one shoulder anyway, saving her the pain of stumbling on her injured leg, and trudged uptrail for their sleds. Her head swung toward Nuke and Haze.

"You sleep, Banks," Nuke called after them. "*If* you trust us. We can't trust either one o' you—not your shape or his origin. So's we're awake anyway, and we'll keep watch."

"I hear." She grunted. "Wake us if you want. This be an uncommon newbie hauling me. His sense will surprise you."

"Don't need no more surprises today. Sleep."

"Aia."

Raschad tottered to his sled—second in line and nearest—and dumped her atop the load to dig out his sleep roll. They stretched netting over the hollow at the center of his load, covering her as they worked. Tying off the corners, he crawled in beside her, too spent to bother fixing a second bed. With Nuke and Haze standing watch, he was safest within reach anyway.

"I'll get that billi off you."

"Naia." Raschad turned on his side, facing away from her. "Scraped it off with a stick and threw it at Nuke's load."

"Don't tempt them."

"Sometimes, Banks, I just have to."

"Aia." Like her dealing with the government dockers, you just couldn't let them stomp you all the time.

Chapter 12

Wind woke her. Leaves sifted downward, settling on their sleep net. Stirring air chilled her throat, cool relief from heat, wet, and insects. She sprawled, barely noticing that her arm rested across Raschad's chest, that their legs lay entangled. Fresh air crept through soggy clothes and dried sweaty skin creases. Opening her shirt, she faded back to sleep.

Whack.

Sal startled, flipped a pale yellow thumb-thick vine snake off her chest, and sat up still groggy, the netting tented over her head. Dim light filtered through the canopy far above, dawn approaching, but the jungle floor was still murky. A light flicked on and off downtrail—someone stirring around Haze's sled.

They let us sleep late.

At her side, Raschad breathed deep, still far gone. Easing out of their tangle, Sal slid beneath the net and over the edge of the sled, careful not to startle him. Getting shot this early in the morning would be a damned inconvenience.

Her leg flared pain as it touched down. She limped between the sleds—no hiking into the scrub this morning. Not with gigis lurking and her leg ready to buckle. Instead she used her tread rake to dig a deeper-than-usual hole and tended her needs right in the middle of the trail. Squatting proved tricky. But with her circulation waking up, the leg wound felt to be healing. Raschad made a good nurse.

Buttoning her pants, she slumped onto the back of her load, listened to jungle babble, and scented the air. There wasn't a hint of gigis this morning—the varmints must be too full to mess with tough-hided packers—

Let that be. She breathed deep and relished the breeze stirring even this low down. It signaled weather change, the dry season arriving. The jungle needed it—it was a time when rot died back and the air turned more breathable. She needed it, too—firmer trails to run on, fewer bogs. Raschad needed it before he faded right away. His face looked all bone this morning.

Standing, she limped around her sled, examining the treads. Someone had already washed them clean—another favor from Nuke and Haze, another payment against her and the newbie having saved their lives. But washing the treads was practical, too. Pulling this morning would be hell with wind-dried mud caked in everything. And since her sleds blocked the trail, keeping her moving was just smart.

Light flickered downtrail again. She headed for it.

"Nuke?"

"Aia." His voice rumbled out of the dark.

"Should of woke us."

"Didn't figure it would save time. Ya both been pushed too hard already. That newbie dead yet?"

"Naia." She let him be rude.

"Should be." She didn't try to interpret that. "Still sleeping?"

"Aia. Best stay back from him. He's touchy when he's down. And you're right, he needs the rest. Neither one of us left Tumble Town real healthy."

"You going to tell us about that?" No politer than Nuke, Haze sat up on the other sled, sounding sleepy.

"Aia, guess you should know."

"Sit, then."

Again, Nuke wasn't stupid, and wouldn't let his dislike of newbies ruin common sense. She sat on the rear bumper of his sled, facing Haze, and told them about Scollarta's plotting and the haul out of Tumble Town.

"You ain't alone with your contract troubles, Banks. I heard a sherk jumped a load over to Minit's substation a month back." Nuke spit sideways. "Jungle's going to hell. Rimmersin's doing. Get us another Supervisor, we'd be fine." What would Raschad say about his friend if asked? Sal wondered. "Another Governor would be better yet."

"Reckon you'll vote Liber now, Banks." Haze swung his legs off the side of his load. "Go all tech since you've took up with a newbie."

Sal swallowed, forced a breath. Haze had no right treating her this way. "I told you how that come about."

"Easy to get fooled over a pretty one, ain't it?"

"Don't make me sorry I risked my ass saving yours, Haze."
Her fists balled so tight her knuckles ached.

"Aia, right." Nuke shifted his bulk between her and Haze.
"Naia cause for insults. We've all used newbies sometime."

She cringed. "Don't mean to use him more than I pay him for.
So long as he's honest, I'll be honest with him. Let the jungle take
its due, but I don't put his blood on my hands."

"Only right, I figure." Nuke nudged Haze's knee, and Haze
grumbled in the lightening murk. Nuke clapped Haze's shoulder.
"This be a fine wind, aia."

"Aia," she and Haze answered in unison.

Standing, Sal glanced uptrail at the rear of Raschad's sled.
Shadows had begun to form on the jungle floor. Nothing showed
distinct yet, but there was light enough for her to see him sit up
on his load and slump in a black mound of netting.

She whistled, not wanting him to worry where she'd gone. He
whistled back, then unwound from the sleep net and disappeared
off the front, smart enough not to join them.

"I'll hold my pace as best I can." She limped past Nuke. "But
when you see a way around us, take it." The clearing was too
tight a fit to change their pulling order here. "Tough as the newbie
is, we're spent, and my leg will slow me."

"Banks?" Haze's tone stopped her. "You been sampling the paper?"

The back of her throat tightened until her ears ached, and she
turned—moving slow, every nerve and muscle tensed. Nuke
touched her arm, warning her. She stopped, so mad she shook.
But shutting Haze's squatty mouth wasn't worth adding to her in-
juries.

"What I do with him ain't none of your business, you swine-
headed lecher." Her breath hissed out. "Ain't nothing you done in
your life give you the right to judge, if I was."

She sloughed off Nuke's hand, moved up against Haze's knees.
She'd spent too much time lately running and cowering. "What'sa
matter, Haze, hurt your feelings I ain't never offered you?"

"Banks." Nuke shifted.

Haze tried to knee her—his second mistake. She dropped, re-
versed, came up with her shoulders beneath his calves. She caught
his ankles and flipped him backward into the brush.

"*Bank—*" Haze's scream choked off as he landed with a crash
in heavy growth.

"Shouldn't have done that." Nuke peered into the scrub.

"Neither should he." Gigi's ass, it felt good.

She limped uptrail, sweating—no way to start a morning. Raschad scratched against his load, his gaze on the other sleds.

"Socializing?"

"Aia." She snatched her hat off his load. "You're gonna scratch your back bloody to the bone."

"Too late."

She opened her mouth. Her lungs filled.

But this wasn't his fault. Nerves fluttering, she whipped the netting off his face and kissed him long and hard. And when she let up, he blew out his breath between limp lips.

"Shrike, Banks."

"Your language is deteriorating, newbie." She smiled. Surprised *him* for once.

"Squat."

She laughed. Damn, he was good for her. "I reckon you want breakfast."

He mimed fainting, and she swatted his leg. "A'course. So get these sleds ready. Haia?"

He bent to work. She dug out food and cooked it over a little clay burner fueled by reeki vine while she watched Raschad by the growing light of dawn. He moved sure, quick. She'd never packed with a harder worker. Why'd he have to be a newbie?

"Food."

He left off checking the canvas ties and squatted with her over a pot of quick-fried roots. She slopped a serving onto the pot's lid and passed it to him.

"Sorry to cause trouble."

"No avoiding it. To make Haze happy, you'd have to drop dead. That would be real inconvenient for me. So just haul fast today. Give 'em no cause to complain."

"Aia. We can lighten your load onto mine, save your leg."

"I can pull it."

He didn't argue, smart as always. "Banks?"

"What now?"

"That Runner camp . . ." He jabbed mushy roots with his scoop fork. "Maybe I was wrong. Maybe I'm causing you more trouble than I expected."

"What's that mean?"

"I counted five dead off-planeters in that camp. They may have been hunting for me."

"You're crazy. Newbies and Runners ain't an unlikely mix. Why would they be after you?"

"Used to be—" He shook his head. "—no one dared challenge

the Raschads. But Axial's mines are played out. He's vulnerable, especially with platoons of ex-Tarsian mercenaries working free-lance. His enemies could find uses for me."

A hunk of root stuck in Sal's throat, and she stared at her plate, figuring all the twists and turns in what he said.

"Still no reason to think these newbies were after you."

"They had lots of tech. Long-range communicators."

She breathed out slow, her heart speeding. "Tech comms don't last out here." Her voice sounded hollow. "They were rotted already after coming this far into the green. Fungus gets inside anything with parts." She tried to sound confident. Newbies with money for tech that expensive stayed in the city, didn't chance a jungle death.

"They were after me."

"Piss, they were. It's just Governor Wally sending more fools into the green. He wants to prove that even newbies can survive the wild with tech."

"But wouldn't the government rescue those people? They must have called for help."

"Old Wally don't care about them. Besides, I told you, their comms couldn't have worked. And you ain't so important that you have to be to blame for everything."

"I found those comms by ear," Raschad said. "Someone was calling. I heard ship's chatter. Those newbies had contacts in space."

She stared at mud-caked boots and couldn't make sense of things. *Here*, the green, was real. *Space* was just a word. Why should those Runners die so someone could find a lost newbie?

They finished eating in silence. Raschad gathered their dishes, and she limped back to talk to Nuke.

"You remember what I said." They stood at the rear of Nuke's load again. "You go around us when you can. That won't hurt Haze's feelings."

Haze glared up from working on his steering bars, and Nuke's lips twisted, fighting a smile. At least he didn't hold the newbie personally against her.

"Ah, Haze's been too cocky lately any—" Nuke's eyes rounded. His mouth froze open.

Chill slipped down Sal's back, and she reached for her Camm. Nuke grabbed her arm in one big paw and pinned it against his side. Following the direction of his stare, she froze rigid.

Aireils surrounded them—just there—a dozen heads hanging

beneath the leaf canopy. One big male dropped heavy and silent to the ground. Beyond it, Raschad froze next to her sled, alone.

Don't panic, newbie.

Aireils flowed down the tree trunks, materialized out of the scrub. String-limbed bodies filled the trail. And Nuke's eyes flicked to hers, flicked away to Haze.

They breathed. They blinked. Nothing more.

Her head twinged. Her thigh cramped. She tried not to breathe mistwalker scent—not too hard with Nuke's armpit at nose level. The creatures touched, soft leathery hands all over her, on Nuke and Haze. Uptrail, a press of bodies hid Raschad.

Be still, newbie. Be . . .

Feathery fur tickled her throat, and she looked up into a mistwalker's face. Wisps of pale yellow-green hair fluttered about its muzzle. Deep-set eyes blue as the sky stared at her, their intent fathomless.

She'd been touched before, but never so studied. Its eyes asked questions. She breathed in, breathed slowly out. How could she account for herself to an Aireil? How many thousand years had mistwalkers roamed this planet? And in all that time, they'd not harmed Ver Day one hundredth as much as humans who tried ever so hard not to harm it.

Her stomach ached. Her leg throbbed. Her pulse was beating a dull *thump-thump* in her head. Be still, she told herself. But the mistwalker picked up her limp hand and licked it.

She nearly wet herself. Nuke's fingers dug into her elbow. She clamped down on his belly, providing him some distraction.

Snaky fingers tugged at her belt and probed her boot tops. Breathing deep, she tolerated everything, remembering death screams in the dark, and Raschad pinned against her.

Don't lose your breakfast. Don't be an idiot and faint. Standing so still, it was a real danger. She flexed her knees and concentrated on breathing and counting mossy heads.

She'd never seen so many mistwalkers, never even heard of so many in any one spot—more now even than that night . . .

Poison-tipped fingers slipped away. The tugging and sniffing ended, and the mistwalkers began to disappear back into the green. At the sight, her chest lightened a bit. But gray-green bodies still crowded the trail, and two big males lingered. One edged between Nuke and Haze and lay a hand on each man's shoulder.

Real fear took her gut at that, and nearly took her senses, too, as she saw the growing crush about her sleds, the creatures still examining Raschad.

Please! She remembered bodies on the trail. *Please!*

Aireils shifted, and Sal glimpsed the newbie between their gangly bodies. He'd been netted tight earlier. Now he stood barefaced, staring, his eyes desperate, his hair dripping sweat.

What had she brought him into?

Nuke's grip tightened on her arm. Shaking, she closed her eyes, worked at holding still and not getting herself or these men killed.

"Bank—"

Her eyes flipped open as Raschad's yelp chopped off.

She glimpsed his panic-stricken face. Aireils were lifting him off his feet. Thier shaggy hands dropped from the overstory, snagged his arms, and hauled his rigid body straight out of sight—up and up into the soaring green.

She couldn't breathe, couldn't think. Gigi's breath . . .

She half lunged. Nuke's grip near broke her arm. The Aireils *ignored* her, faded away into sun and mist.

She twisted free. *"Raschad!"*

Haze caught her wrist.

"Raschad!" She stared up at nothing but green—the Aireils and newbie, all gone. And there wasn't a thing in hell to do about that. "Raschad!"

"Banks." Nuke shook her. "Banks. They ain't killed him."

"They hauled him off." Nostrils flared, she gritted her teeth. "Use sense." Her voice broke, startling her. "Squat." She looked away. "He's scared spitless of heights. Just taking him up there'll kill him." Her knees quaked, and pain stabbed behind her eyes. "I brought a newbie into this." She swallowed hard, fighting the knot in her throat.

Nuke patted her shoulder. "Ain't your fault. Newbies ain't nobody's fault." He patted her shoulder again.

She hated him for it.

The sun climbed, sifting into the clearing. Sal lay on her load and listened to jungle stirrings and gossip. Bugs whined a maddening chorus in the morning heat until the wind picked up and cleared them away. Feet shuffled in soggy duff. Nuke's broad shoulders hulked over her.

"We're heading out, Banks, even if we have to cut around you. C'mon, now. Ain't no use lying here."

She didn't answer. Her jaw worked, grinding teeth that already ached. Haze came up, and the men exchanged glances.

"Banks." Haze spoke low. "I'm sorry about earlier." He didn't look sorry. "We've packed this jungle with you, around, behind, and in front of you for years now. You're a real-hell hauler. We ain't leaving you sitting like this. Think. He was a damn newbie waiting to die somewhere."

She flipped up, grabbed Haze's shirt so fast he couldn't dodge, and twisted it tight around his throat. "You freaking pile of squat. He ain't *meat*. He ain't paper. He's a man."

"Banks." Nuke's growl stopped her. Haze's face had begun to darken. "Now, you got more sense than this."

She let Haze go.

"Good gal." Nuke sighed. "Your muscle is dead."

She tensed. Haze backed a step, sucking air.

"Aireils got him." Nuke's tone was infuriatingly calm. "That ain't your fault, just no help for it. Banks . . ." He shook his head. "We gotta go. We'll help you with the load. You're packer. But we got to move. We can take what's due Noca Tana on our sleds. You carry as much more as you can, and we'll pick up your sled on the way back. But we ain't leaving you here." He leaned near. *"Move!"*

Her head jerked. She stared, face stretched to bone, and *heard* them.

Forgive her, she'd killed the newbie by bringing him into the jungle. Knew it would happen. Why should it surprise her? But it left a stone-hard weight in her chest that made it difficult to move, think, breathe. Raschad had handled himself so well, survived so much, he *believed* he could live out here. And, damn him, he'd begun to make her believe it, too.

Nodding into Nuke's hard stare, she slipped to the ground. The newbie was gone.

In a haze of unreality, she brushed past Haze, calculating how she could shift Raschad's load without making any one sled too heavy. Noca Tana was a dead-end spur; if they took her deliveries for the guano town, she could backtrack and catch the Ebbid to D'arnith's. She shuddered at the thought of pulling back to the junction, pulling back alone.

Sucking in a breath, she held it. With his load lighter after Noca Tana, Nuke could haul her extra sled at least as far as the junction, and she could send someone back for it from D'arnith's. With luck she'd still make it to Tumble Town in good time to pick up her next contract.

Luck? She didn't deserve luck.

Nuke and Haze trudged back to their sleds, keeping an eye on her. She wondered how much concern they would show if she wasn't sitting with two sleds in their way. She'd have to dump the lighter one in the brush; she couldn't leave it blocking the trail.

She worked, ignoring their looks, avoiding any thought of why she did what she did or what it meant. But then she opened a locker and Raschad's pack fell in her arms and jammed beneath her chin, smelling of him. The morning came rushing back—her mouth on his.

"Nuke!" She startled fleepas, even startled herself.

Unraveling, you idiot. Damn newbie! He'd got to her, inside where she didn't let trouble like him.

"Banks?" Both men came wide-eyed around the sled, weapons drawn, heads up.

"Take this." Her voice tore. "Ain't got room for it. Won't leave it."

"Aia." Haze's eyes rolled warily as he grabbed the pack, giving his partner a hard look.

"Banks." Nuke squished mud. "I been thinking on things. He wore his weapon. A newbie wouldn't just let them kill him so quiet. Maybe they dropped him. He could be alive."

She swallowed and closed her eyes. "I don't know. He's Meesha Raschad, been tramping near three years." She looked up as the men exchanged surprised glances. "He's picked up a lot of proper ways. I don't know. He might hold out until too late, doing it all greenie, honoring the Aireils' rights." She shook her head. "Don't know."

"Squat, Banks." Nuke looked more uncomfortable than ever. "He can't of been here three years."

"Twoteeth was scared of him." She sensed the conversation wandering from its proper point.

The men exchanged glances again, and Haze stood a little straighter. "I heard of a somabitch rockie tramp south of Tumble Town." Sal nodded. "Squat." Haze rolled his eyes. "They say he buries city folks' heads around his claim to keep the gigis coming, keep everybody else off."

"I don't know where you hear such stupid things." Nuke glared at his partner.

"D'arnith's Wood, those rockies."

"I was sleeping."

"Haze." She clenched her teeth. "You're riding my one workable nerve."

Nuke scowled agreement, but didn't let things drop, either. "Banks, you're awful put out over losing a newbie."

It caught her. She tensed, but had more sense even now than to go for him. Besides, the big man wasn't being nosy; he just wondered how bad she hurt.

"I kissed him twice," she admitted. "Yesterday morning with dead people all around was the first." She shook her head. "He saved my life again and over this trip. I can't explain how I'm feeling or why." Black spots floated about her. "It's like killing something by accident." She stared at black. "You feel so damn guilty."

"Aia." Nuke stared past her. "I been there." Shrike. "But let it be now. Deal with it later." Nuke's jaw worked. "We'll help shift the load."

She stared, nodded, and gripped a load strap.

An Aireil stood next to her steering bars.

"Don't move." Her voice shook. A saggy-breasted female sat on a branch above Haze's head.

Nuke's eyes rounded. Sweat popped on Haze's face. The ground rolled beneath her, and she clung to the load.

Thigh throbbing, head pounding, she stood still. The wind died, and the jungle steamed. Sweat burned her eyes. The sun rode higher. The muscles of her calves began to cramp and twitch. Fruit gnats crawled over her bare face and up her nose.

She fought a sneeze. Tears streamed out of her eyes.

"Aaaacchhhhh!" And it burst from her again, a regular fit. *Going to die.*

But the Aireils only watched. She blinked tears, sniffed, snorted. Still the mistwalkers just watched. She rolled her eyes. Nuke frowned.

Squat. Let'em kill her. She gave with the tug of gravity and sat in the mud, her aching legs spradled, too tired to care.

The Aireil nearest her walked away. The old female in the webb tree behind Haze picked her fur, found something tasty there, and munched it. Sal's breath escaped in a long sigh.

The men's eyes rolled from her to the Aireils to each other and back again to her. It took several rounds before they built nerve enough to break the one rule of survival with Aireils.

Haze took a step back to lean against Raschad's sled. The creatures ignored him. Nuke slowly squatted, braced his rump on a tread, and stared questions at Sal.

"What you think?" he whispered. She gave a tiny shake of her head. "Ain't never heard of nothing like it." His eyes rolled toward the green above.

She gnawed her lip. The female mistwalker tucked up her long legs, wrapped equally long arms about her shins, and closed her eyes.

The seat of Sal's pants had grown squishy and uncomfortable.
"I'm going to stand up and get out of here."

"Don't be crazy."

"Too late."

With a shiver at her unintentional echo of Raschad's words, she
eased her feet under her and rolled to her knees. The Aireils
scratched and slapped bugs, their eyelids drooping.

Nuke scowled. She braced a hand on a tread and stood.

Leaves stirred overhead. Sal froze, sweating. The stirring
moved away. She counted breaths—nineteen, twenty. Steadying,
she eased toward the sled's bumper.

The two visible Aireils ignored her. She picked up her harness,
slid into it, backed between the sled's steering bars. Nuke watched
her, watched the Aireils.

She leaned into her harness. The sled creaked forward.

A rotting mi fruit struck her shoulder. A second splatted at her
feet. Leaves and twigs rained on her head. She tucked down and
froze.

The bombardment stopped.

"Nuke? Haze?"

"Fine. Naia thanks."

She breathed out, chill and clearheaded. Stupid stunt. Could've
got others killed. They don't want us to leave. Don't want to kill
us. Why? What have the Runners triggered?

The sun rode higher. Nuke's stomach rumbled and thundered.
Sal laughed aloud, giddy with heat and strain. A twig bounced off
her shoulder, and she shut up, head pounding.

The sun lowered. Afternoon heat rose, stirring up a wind again.
She couldn't feel it down on the jungle floor, hunkered in the mud
against the sled, but the sound of it brought relief.

The female Aireil stirred on her perch and raised her head. A
difference bled through the rustle of leaves and vines.

More mistwalkers.

Sal held her breath, her body rigid. Wood creaked, and her sled
shivered. Haze must have fainted against it. Their Aireil guards
vanished in a breath.

Sal blinked, slowly convincing herself that the staring faces
were gone and the sound of the wind was only that, the only scent
it carried honest jungle rot. A fleepa sounded a nervous chitter.
She stood, bit by bit.

Blood struggled back into circulation, and her muscles
screamed fire. Black dotted her vision. She turned.

Raschad lay sprawled across her load.

Her heart hammered. Nuke breathed short and shocked. Haze's mouth hung open.

Raschad's arms dangled off the edge of her load, his shredded fingertips dripping blood. Leaves matted his shoulders. Trembling, Sal touched his torn fingers.

Cold. Dead.

Claws clamped tight. Pain shot up her arm.

She yelped. Haze startled, and Nuke grabbed the newbie's wrist. The bloody hand drooped limp again, and Raschad whimpered, tearing the last of the breath from her.

"Ahgh!" She slumped against the load, clutching his harness, and choked down a sob.

Alive. *Alive!*

Haze's breath exploded in a whoosh, and Sal's head snapped up. Both men looked greener than greenies, their eyes fixed on something she couldn't see. She lunged onto the load.

"Naia!"

Her chest seized, everything utter madness. Two long, shallow scratches bled down the newbie's cheek, already swollen and festered. Haze wouldn't meet her eyes. The Aireils had brought Raschad back alive . . . to die.

She gulped air, her lower lip quivering.

"Sal?" Raschad's whisper stuttered her heart.

"Newbie? Where you been, babe?"

His eyes were closed, his breathing shallow and too slow. "Climbing. Took me climbing." His words faded into breathlessness.

The wound on his face smelled jungle awful. Ready to rot. It was an Aireil scratch for sure.

"Nuke and Haze are here." Sal's voice quavered. "I'll clean you up. Make you a spot to rest."

He smiled, and broke her heart. "B-B-Be all right. J-Just t-tired. They t-told me—"

He choked, strangling. She grabbed him. Nuke rocked Raschad's head back, straightening his airway. Raschad coughed, breathed scratchy and labored, expanded his lungs. But his heart pounded beneath her hands, racing Aireil poison through him.

"Nuke." Sal sucked a shaky breath. "Thanks."

"Aia." The big man's expression remained grim.

The newbie was dying. Nuke helped turn Raschad on his side, then stepped away a pace. Haze stood blank-faced, jaw clenched.

She ignored the packers as she rearranged Raschad's arms, dug out a pallet roll to put under his head, and snugged a net over him. Nuke helped again with that, and even Haze finally tied one corner. But she could see their eyes wandering uptrail, wanting gone and done with this. They could cut a path around her sleds, but getting her to move her loads would be faster, quieter, and safer—just not easier.

She ignored them. She dug Raschad's medkit from his pack, then dumped her own aidkit from her belt and crawled beneath the netting.

"Banks?" Nuke's voice.

"Go on. Both of you get. I can handle him now."

"The scriars'll come."

"Naia. Too much mistwalker scent. They won't bother until the rain clears that out, and it's too late for rain today."

The men hovered. She examined Raschad's hands. He'd told some crazy truth about climbing—his palms were shredded right through his gloves, and the scriar-bit one bled freely.

Sal's audience moved off.

Using Raschad's medicines as best she knew how, she cleaned the wounds on his face, squeezing poison out and gall paste in and putting seal gel over the scratches. There wasn't enough sealant to heal his hands. For those she used gall and bandages and propped them on the extra clothing from his pack. She hated dirtying it. But what did a shirt matter to a dead man?

Footsteps sounded in the trail muck.

"Banks?" It was Haze. She didn't look up. "You want, I'll make some reeki tea."

Her breathing half stopped. Her cheek twitched. They'd decided to help, which didn't make sense. The sooner he died, the sooner they could move her. But no time for worrying about it now.

"I'd appreciate it."

"Well . . ." Haze squirmed in the mud. "We figure it's too late for pulling out with Aireils around. Might walk into them blind in the dusk." They were even being polite, not blaming her for blocking the trail.

She'd owe for this one. "Thanks."

"We argued it." Haze shrugged. "But you spoke plain earlier. In your mind, he ain't meat. He's a man. So you can't leave him. And in our minds, you're packer, due respect. Can't just shovel you off the trail." He shrugged again. "Morning brings a new day."

He walked away, head down. She knew he was planning a funeral.

"Sal?" Raschad stirred, his voice a reedy whisper.

"Here." She stroked sweat-soaked hair out of his eyes. "Tea's coming. Can you drink it?"

He made a little neutral sound and drifted away again, his muscles tensed, breaths coming faster than she could count. Reeki tea wouldn't cure *this*. Still, there must be something she could do. Granna and Ma knew these things. Only she had never paid enough attention—was always busy chasing fleepas and hunting jig leepers while Ma gathered medicinals.

Raschad shivered, spasms rippling through him, his throat working. Going to die. *Do something!*

Helplessness froze her, numbed her mind. *Think.* Can't just watch him die like Sonny.

Raschad's shoulders curled in. One hand clutched his chest, the way Morrie's did when he took a spell. Lamie sap—Dancer gave Morrie a swipe on the tongue for lung cramps. Sal looked up. Dusk was gathering quick and deep about them.

"Banks?" It was Haze again. "Brought the tea."

"Sit with him, then." Sal stared skyward at sunlight far, far above. "I got to climb a tree."

She shook and ached, and her hands felt as raw as Raschad's. "Hold his head still."

"We're *trying*." Nuke leaned on Raschad's arm.

"You sure, Banks?" Haze panted near as hard as the newbie.

She ignored the packers, waited out Raschad's convulsive shudder, her eyes locked on his mouth. He gasped, and she shoved a dry reeki wand between his parted teeth and squeezed her hardgotten lamie stem. A single glistening drop of sap fell on his tongue. The reeki wand disintegrated, and she jerked its end from his mouth. He choked and gagged. Killed him, you idiot.

But his breathing slowed. His laboring chest rose and fell, rose and fell, each intake less of a struggle. His arched neck went slack. Nuke and Haze eased up on his arms.

"Got it." Sal shuddered.

Raschad whimpered. Nuke sopped drool from the newbie's mouth, using the tail of his ragged, reeki-stained shirt. Raschad's breath sighed out, and he began to snore softly.

"Well." Haze stared down at Raschad's face, haloed by the dim light of her shaded handlight. "Ain't hurting now, anyways. You're damn smart, Banks."

She shook her head, too spent for words.

"Reckon you can handle him now."

She nodded to Nuke, and the men slipped off the sled, disappearing into darkness.

Shaking, she doctored Haze's long-ignored reeki tea with Raschad's tech medicine the same way she had at Klinker's. If she got the chance to use it, she'd count herself lucky.

Having done all she could, she lay at Raschad's side and waited. Lying there, she remembered a hurt fleepa Ma had picked up. They had waited like this for it to die. Whoever had trained it had chopped its tail. A bobtailed fleepa couldn't climb fast enough to escape, and it could barely walk, let alone run. Captive fleepas were the saddest things she'd ever known until now: Raschad, like that critter, too maimed to fly, let alone live.

When he stirred, she stroked his forehead, just as she had soothed the fleepa. It hadn't helped then, and it didn't matter now. Few greenies kept pets. Taking a thing from its wild state was cruel, wrong, and doomed to failure . . . like newbies in the jungle.

Bugs swarmed. Raschad's fever rose. The lamie sap faded, and Sal feared feeding him more, remembering some caution Dancer had once given about dosing Morrie. Raschad writhed; when she touched him, he moaned. When she left him alone, he chattered a stream of off-planet gibberish, ending in a scream.

That woke him, or at least left him sitting erect, eyes wide and circled by white when she flashed her light on them.

"Here, babe." She eased her arms about him, afraid he might slip her off the load. "Drink this. It'll help."

The tea hit his lips, and he went for the wetness—not the taste, from the smell of the stuff—and choked down a swallow. Wheezing, he fell over again, so she couldn't get any more down him. It probably didn't matter, not with Aireil venom in him.

Raschad twisted and moaned, then broke into babbling, someone's name mixed in with that nonsense until his babbling became plain noise, then screaming torment. She couldn't hold him down, so she backed out of the net and let it tangle until it bound him.

Alone, she waited in the bug-shrilling dark. Sweat ran on her ribs. Hands over her ears, she rode out a fevered wail.

He jerked and flopped limp. Her breath caught.

The jungle paused—shocked silent. She reached up to search for a pulse through the netting, expecting none. But he shivered, sighed, and began to snore again. She sagged against the load.

Shriking newbie! Always surprising her.

Chapter 13

She stared at him in the dim morning light and couldn't believe he still breathed. Healthy he wasn't, but the fever had broken. His eyes opened, and met hers.

She couldn't stop staring. Raschad stared back, then reached a bandaged hand to her cheek and let it fall. Stretching, she kissed the clean spot on his face where she'd wiped sap and mud away from Aireil scratches. The wounds, hot and gummy against her lips, were improved from the gaping red slashes of yesterday. But his hair stood out in long sticky spikes, and jungle filth and blood caked his clothes.

Sal wanted to bathe him, comfort and ease him. She'd never felt like this toward anyone, and wasn't certain why she felt this way now—whether it stemmed from guilt or affection. But with the fleepas whistling, howlers rattling the tree canopy, birds screeching, mist dripping, she could do so little to help him that her wants were useless. They should just be moving.

"Don't look scared. Please," a ghost whispered in the dawn murk, his lips not moving at all.

"Don't look so damn beat up." She tried to smile.

"I'm w-working on it." Raschad's eyes closed, granting her a reprieve. "Sal?"

"What?"

His breath sighed, nothing else. She lifted the worst hand to examine the raw, oozing flesh. His fingerpads were gone, and he breathed purposefully, swallowing pain as she changed his bandages. Breaking open his medkit, she applied the last of the sealant gel to exposed bone and examined the lesser cuts where blood showed through tears in his leathers. Those weren't bad, not of Aireil origin—one blessing, with his fancy medicine nearly gone.

"Raschad?" He stirred. "I've some of that tea stuff left from

172

last night." Turning the cup, she examined the slimy green concoction. "Will it have spoilt?"

"No."

"You'd best drink, aia?"

He nodded, so she steadied his head one-armed and succeeded in washing his chin more than anything else. But enough did go down his throat that his eyes unfocused and he gagged and shivered. She held him. His breathing settled, drifting into sleepy rhythms. Easing free, she slipped beneath the netting and slid to the ground. Legs stiff and cramped, she leaned on a tread.

What a night. What a string of days and nights.

"Banks?"

She startled. "Nuke."

"He alive?"

"Aia."

"Aia?"

"You heard me." Sal straightened.

"But who'd expect it."

Who would?

"Didn't expect nothing that's happened the last two days," Haze said, stumping up at Nuke's side. "Got a miracle newbie, Banks. Never seen the like. He's lived through what would've killed any greenie. Be a wonder to know where he's been."

"They took me climbing." Raschad's voice quavered out of shadow. Sal flinched; Nuke and Haze stilled. "They hauled me to the sky."

"Babe, you don—"

"They wanted me to climb." His voice scaled upward, pounding shivers through Sal's senses. "Which is not my favorite pastime lately." His voice quavered about a hint of amusement.

She crawled onto the sled, sweat popping on her upper lip. Raschad had gone squat crazy.

"I was spacer all my life." His head lolled.

Haze glanced to Nuke. Nuke shook his head and leaned against the sled, staring at Raschad.

"Had an accident shipboard." One bloody hand hid Raschad's face, and his words emerged disembodied, like a tech machine talking. "Fell . . . a long way. Left me strange." That was certain. "The meds taught me to manage the vertigo by imaging the confidence I felt while climbing before the accident."

Nuke's eyes met Sal's and she blinked and swallowed. Raschad's babbling made her sick. But Haze wondered what had happened, and she thought, hoped, the newbie was telling them.

"When I'm scared—" His voice quavered. "—I build a climbing dream, float through space in my mind, go away. It took me up McDonnels' tree. Kept me alive with the Aireils, before."

Before?

"They followed me." Raschad spoke as if they knew what he was talking about. "I ran hard." His voice rose, and sweat flooded Sal's spine. She pressed her fingers to his lips, but he brushed them away. "I got so tired, Sal. I got so tired, Boojie's cooking tasted good." He laughed, high, thin, and insane. "They sensed something. I went spacewalking through my mind. And they got so excited, it was hard to concentrate."

His arm dropped. His eyes rounded, two circles of white gleaming in the morning gloom. Sal didn't think he was seeing her or anything about this morning.

"I panicked. They patted me, sang. It was nice."

She shivered, biting her lip.

"I don't know why." He barely whispered, forcing Haze and Nuke to lean nearer. "They all left, but they kept watching me. I saw one as I ran for town. I never moved so fast."

Sal stared beyond Haze's shocked eyes, remembering Raschad packing past Morrie's shack that first day, looking so big and wild. What a thing to live through, being stalked by Aireils.

"I think . . ." His breath sighed out. She bent nearer. "I think yesterday I concentrated so hard on my climbing dream that they sensed what it was about—took me mistwalking. But I couldn't hold onto my visions.

"They knew that, too." His voice was fading. "I fell, and they caught me. I panicked, but they made things nice again. When I climbed the vines, they went wild, swinging and jumping around me, just wanted me to play—I think."

His breath caught on a sob, and he grabbed Sal's arm, his grip hot and sticky with sealant. She nearly wet herself.

"But I couldn't climb anymore. They scratched me. Things were so strange." His eyes closed. His breath puffed out.

Then his head lolled, and fear tore her gut. But he shivered and his eyes flicked open, glowing pale.

"I don't know what's real . . . they told me . . ." He moaned. "They said . . . somehow . . . told me not to be afraid anymore." He blinked. "I knew I wouldn't die then."

His breathing deepened. His eyes closed.

Haze's mouth hung open; Nuke stood chewing a hank of his beard. Sal felt blast-shocked, the explosion still ringing inside. If Raschad said another word, she'd scream.

But he only whimpered, asleep. She bent over his battered, filth-scummed face and kissed his cheek. His every word rang crazy, but whether it was his insanity or the situation, who could judge? The last part—believing he wouldn't die—did make sense. Half of what killed a person, ever, was fear. So believing he'd live had maybe saved his life. Or maybe the lamie sap had.

Nuke's hand brushed her arm, and she looked up into his hairy face. He looked as if he'd seen a vision. He cocked his head; she nodded. Haze followed, and they stopped far enough away from the sled not to disturb Raschad.

"I heard of things like this." Nuke breathed a long sigh. "Heard of people what can walk the jungle not fearing the mistwalkers, once marked by 'em. But I thought it just stories, like the tale of Ol' Mike and the Species Wars." He glanced at Haze. The shorter man nodded. "You don't worry. We'll get you out, ain't going no place until you're ready."

She sank down on a sled tread. Now she knew she didn't face dealing with an ailing man and two sleds all by herself. But why she heard it scared her as much as the looks the two packers had given Raschad. They thought they'd seen a miracle. She couldn't claim them wrong.

"That's sympathetic treatment of a fool who brought a newbie packing in this jungle." Her voice broke. "Reckon we'd be dead if you hadn't been with us and stayed with us."

Nuke squished his huge feet in the mud. "Reckon the gigis would of kilt us. We ain't doing nothing we don't owe." The big man stared uptrail.

Embarrassed! What went on in their heads? She sucked blood from the hole she'd made in her lip.

"What you mean to tell about this?" She had a right to ask.

"Just what we saw." Haze shook his head. "I don't figure he's much of a newbie anymore. That kind of trip sort of rubs on the green. Man deserves consideration, just like you said."

Her cheeks puffed. *Blessed shrike.*

They faced the day then, and all that needed doing. They didn't dare sit in place any longer. After packing her blister-rotted feet with mair moss, Sal helped split the load from Raschad's sled to Nuke's two and hitched the nearly empty hauler to the back of her loaded sled. Nuke would pull both.

Bent over, checking gears, she found herself staring at Raschad's boots.

"What you doing?" She snapped upright, voice squeaking. How the hell was he standing? "You—" She didn't finish. His face looked so strange, she didn't dare.

"I want to walk."

He wobbled, and she caught his arm. But she sensed more strength in him than she could believe. How did he keep going? Was he a hainting specter?

"When you fall, we're going to pack you up." Her words were slurred, her body numb.

"Aia."

They pulled out, with Raschad walking behind her between her steering bars, shuffling along at speed, his gaze on his feet. Sal didn't interrupt his thoughts, whatever they were.

At mid-morning they took a break. Nuke and Haze walked back to check on Raschad and brought some tea berries Nuke had chanced on to. The men's presence roused Raschad. Watching them eat, his expression stranger than ever, he refused his share of the fruit. Haze held out a water tube.

Raschad stared at the tube, stared at Haze, and shivered and shook. The two partners slipped away as Sal wrapped herself around Raschad and held on. His teeth chattered.

"They killed all those people." His voice sounded like dry leaves rustling.

"Aia, they did."

"Why . . ." He shuddered. "Why did you wait? Why did Nuke and Haze?"

"Aireils wouldn't let us go."

"Oh."

She sensed something torn in his tone and owed him a better explanation. "I just sat until the others wanted to get through on the trail. They said you were dead. We tried to leave then."

He took a long, fluttering breath. "Ah, Sal. What would I have done?"

"Died, I imagine."

He laughed, all scary sounding. "That wouldn't have been the hard part."

"Naia? What, then?" She rocked him.

"Missing you."

"You ass'ole newbie." She buried her face in his hair. "Don't you do this to me."

"Too late."

* * *

Raschad walked through the morning, astounding them all, then collapsed near noon, surprising no one. Nuke wrestled him onto Sal's empty sled, and the newbie slept the afternoon away.

They reached the last steep pitch up the Rise at midday. Even for Nuke, the haul was too much pulling a trailered sled. So Sal waited below in the heat and wet with bugs whining and gigis barking downtrail and guarded Nuke's loads while he and Haze pulled her sleds—with Raschad still riding the empty one—up the zigzagging rock-scrabble trail. Haze hiked back down, and they pulled their respective sleds up together.

She struggled onto Glory's Roost as the sun lowered over mountain peaks far behind her. Slanting golden rays streaked the jungle, lighting rainbows in the mist rising from crashing water and painting the river's stone gorge with fire and purple shadow. The sight would have taken her breath, if she'd had any left.

Hanging on her steering bars, weary to the bone, her injured leg aching, she swayed, the thunder of falling water vibrating her gut. Her feet burned fire, and she hadn't strength enough to unclip from her traces. But at least the air up here was clean and good to breathe. A breeze lifted sweat from her scalp, and overhead, rockwings side-slipped, calling sweet dreams to each other. They'd all made it through another day.

"Banks?" She blinked at Nuke's broad belly. "Eat. Sleep. We don't mind watchin' again." Even though they should.

She staggered out of her steering bars, crawled onto her empty sled and lay down beside Raschad. Haze bent near, staring a long moment at the newbie's slack face.

"Be fine." Haze nodded. "I've heard tell if you survive Aireil venom, you won't never catch nothing again."

"People will say anything."

"Aia, some's even true." He smiled a bristly smile.

"Thank you."

"Aia." His smile broadened. "Shrike, if you was cleaner, I'd invite you for a roll."

She swatted his hat. He caught it and shrugged, still smiling, as he moved off. Watching his broad back, she knew there'd been asking in his teasing. And she owed, but it just wasn't in her. Good thing he didn't take it personal.

"Raschad?" Sal snapped up, flung her net-draped head, blinked against morning glare, and her breath rushed out. Spread-eagled in the sun, he lay on a flat rock, soaking up heat.

Safe.

She flopped back on their pallet, fighting the morning shakes—too much adrenaline, not enough rest, unaccustomed chill. Her heart slowed. No place to go this morning—one relief. Her gut relaxed a notch.

Haze had volunteered to make the run into Noca Tana today alone, hauling the mining settlement's deliveries from both her sleds and Nuke's. He should be back by dusk. If no scriar found them by then, they'd stay put another night. It meant tearing up everyone's load, but Raschad would gain a day's rest without costing extra trail time. And they'd lost too much already.

She glanced up. Raschad was wobbling toward the falls.

"Raschad!" She flipped off the sled, scampered after him barefoot, hit rough ground and stubbed her toe. "Raschad!" *Going to jump.* "Raschad!" The pounding of the falls drowned her words, and he limped onto the reeki bridge that carried the trail across the gut-awful gorge below. *"Raschad!"*

He stumped over sap-greasy vines and fell on his face. Hopping and hobbling, Sal saw Nuke and Haze out of the corner of her eye, running for the bridge.

She stubbed her toe again. "Shrike!"

Raschad wobbled to his feet. The reeki span swayed. She didn't dare rock that bridge while he stood.

"Raschad!" She put all she had into the scream, knowing he couldn't hear it—not standing over the mouth of the canyon with falls and rapids roaring below. Her heart stuttered.

"Banks?"

She waved Haze back. He'd knock Raschad off, for sure. How the hell was the shriking newbie controlling himself to get out so far in the air?

Raschad turned, saw them, *waved*, and lowered to his haunches. Slipping his feet through a tangle of vines, he anchored himself, propped his arms on a rope-thick reeki stem, and leaned head and shoulders over the side of the mess, staring into the canyon gorge below. Sal's mouth froze open. Her vision glittered around the edges.

Mist billowed above the canyon's mouth. Rainbows danced. Sweat dripped from Sal's chin and ran between her breasts. Two days ago he could *not* have walked that bridge, could never have sat, legs aswing, staring into this canyon's heart.

Not the same man out there—changed, reborn.

And she had to go after him. Gigi damn, she hated this shivering, stinking bridge. But half her reputation in the green rested on the fact that she braved Reeki Swing. Fighting a quease of fear, she forced herself onto the webbed bridge.

Vines rolled beneath her heels, oily leaves greased her steps, and the whole thing swayed, dipped, and warped.

Raschad looked up, smiled, and stared back down into the canyon. What was he thinking?

She edged outward. Mist soaked her shirt. The river roared, rushing through the gray rock chute below, its boom and growl numbing her ears. Impact vibrated through her feet like electric shock, and she grabbed a vine.

Raschad glanced up. She pulled herself to his side and dropped, shivering and panting.

"You crazy newbie bastard." She couldn't even hear herself.

He smiled and nodded, then stared over the side again. She gave up and peeked between her knees. Far below, a ribbon of white marked where the roiled river reassembled itself after its interminable, crashing drop. Void tugged at her, knotting her gut and leaving nothing but the sure knowledge that everyone died.

She glanced at Raschad. Crazy.

Her gaze fell again, following a rockwing's flight down canyon walls that leaned inward, darkening as they went, stained with mineral deposits from the jetting river. Lance ferns and lace breath grew huge in the shade and constant rain of the lower canyon and dotted the sunnier, drier upper ledges.

Slate-green hoppers played in the mist, their orange feet clinging to sheer rock, their stubby wings flapping and flitting. Miniaturized by distance, they hunted worms and bugs in the pools that collected on every projection, their pointed beaks probing beneath feathery fern fronds and pecking blooming moss mats. Skimmers played in the spray cloud at the base of the falls, from this height only tiny darting black dots against the white froth.

Her senses blurred, Sal looked away and studied Raschad. In morning light he looked paler and thinner than ever. His head turned. His eyes refocused to the short space between them. She rested against leaves and vines, and he looked away, letting her have her fill of staring. But all the staring in the world wouldn't tell her what to do with him now.

He'd survived a hellish string of disasters. Would he survive the next? What did a body do to keep a newbie living long-term? No one lived permanent, but still . . .

She tugged on his arm. Bracing his elbows on a thick vine, he rose, clinging to her as they wobbled off the bridge.

"Sal!" he yelled as they reached solid stone.

"What?"

He shook his head. Mist sprayed from his hair, and he gestured around, eyes glinting.

Aia. *This*, she thought—as she always did, standing here—was the reward for surviving the trail out. Power and glory thundered through the rock; life burgeoned below in the jungle green. And across the river's chasm, the fern-draped canyon wall glittered with diamond water droplets, a living tapestry of green, dotted with scarlet fungi blooms and afire with dawn. All of it—even the damn bridge—was a testament to greenie determination to preserve this world. Better the Reeki Swing than ruin. *The wonder of the way*, that's how the Terms of Settlement said it.

But Raschad's expression—as if he saw everything for the first time, risen from the dead—shivered her gut. His eyes met hers, and she stared into their sun-glittered depths and felt the world slip away as it had that morning at the Ebbid junction.

His hand rose, brushing her cheek with a scrape of bandages. Her chest ached.

"Breakfast!" Haze's yell cut even through the thunder of the falls.

Sal flinched. Raschad stepped back, face reddening. She grabbed his arm and steered him toward the sleds.

Going to kill Haze yet.

Chapter 14

Roaks winged above, a black skein marking the easy way to oca Tana, and Haze shook a fist at the maze of knotted vines at he, lacking wings, had to brave. Packer quiet, he tugged his ed into the bridge's green web, careful of his footing over greasy p, pooling mist, and ankle-catching tendrils.

Haze had grated Sal's nerves since they'd met up on the Ebbid. ut now she sweated his every step. Vines creaked; treads spit aves into the air. And Haze worked his steering bars like the ne-tech instruments they were, easing the sled over knobs and mps, gnarls and twists of vine, over gaps and old growth going rown—maybe dead, maybe weakened.

The sled tilted and rocked. A crate shifted, and Sal's breath oze in her lungs. Nuke took a step forward and stopped. Any elp he tried to give now would only make matters worse.

"Told him to slow down with his packing." Nuke shifted on the alls of his feet.

Haze ignored his uncertain load and pulled on. The crate tee-red back to center. Treads bit into fresh growth, and the hauler umbered off the far end of the bridge onto solid rock. Sal un-lenched her aching jaw and arched her arms, drying dripping mpits. Heading uptrail, Haze waved. Reeki vines stirred in the nisty breeze and waved back.

It shamed her not to make this crossing herself, but she ouldn't trust Raschad's fragile health to anyone else just now. teering him around, she walked out of the falls' soaking mist to-ward camp. Nuke stood watching Haze a moment longer.

"I don't know Noca Tana." Raschad spoke greenie polite, shuf-ling toward the sleds, his eyes on the jungle.

"It's a bog. Stinks worse than rot flowers. They're working the argest mapped roak colony on Ver Day, and they mine the guano

181

hard by jungle standards. Still, it won't give out in my lifetime. Stopping here, you've seen the best of the Pike."

"Will Haze be safe alone?" So it bothered him, seeing Haze leave. Damn newbie, he just kept making her like him.

"He'll be fine. The skids fly in once a month, to haul out guano and bring supplies. But the government makes such a miser profit on air delivery that the diggers couldn't afford living there and wouldn't get mail without sledders. I've worked this run alone for years. No one with sense bothers a packer."

"The Runners had no sense."

"And they're dead."

But she'd told Nuke to go with Haze anyway. He wouldn't, he'd been determined to stay with them, and Haze had been just as determined to haul alone. Nuke still stood surrounded by mist halos, watching Haze, and from the sag of the big man's shoulders, she figured he questioned his choice. Just because she did it, Sal thought, didn't make packing the green alone any safe prospect.

She and Nuke passed the morning gambling for salted pia seeds and watching Raschad sleep. Sal thought of dousing the newbie with fresh reeki sap to keep off the bugs, but they weren't bothering him—which was strange, because the biting flies had found her and Nuke. Not that Nuke noticed. He just kept one arm flopping like a water bov's tail.

She finally stunned a palm-thick chichiua with her hat, pinned the purple bug and held on while Nuke brought a pot. Fat and red-legged, the chichi only made a mouthful each, but it was a tasty mouthful, and their sport broke the tension of waiting. Neither of them was accustomed to sitting still.

She smiled at Nuke, shrugging for no particular reason. He shrugged back, teeth showing in his shaggy beard.

Come afternoon, clouds began to build, and she walked to the upper lip of the canyon. Settling where the rock curved away from the bridge, out of the falls' mist, she studied the sky. A hoval falcon hunted above, red-brown against a patchwork of blue, white, and slate-gray. Just twice the size of a roak, the raptor presented no threat. It was a rare thing, sitting this safe in the green. But scriars didn't like bare rock, nor did gigis nor any large ground hunter. Mostly just bugs and birds and the occasional stone lizard haunted the exposed knob.

Sal glanced back at the sleds, found them safe, and caught Nuke watching her. In the jungle you kept your eye on what you valued. She glanced back again. This time Nuke stood behind his load, and Raschad was missing from the empty sled. They tended the newbie's needs, she figured. His torn hands made him nearly helpless.

Thunderheads darkened above, fringed with glistening white. She watched the clouds roil and build. Rumbles rolled in the distance. Flashes glowed in fraying cloud bellies, and a jagged bolt lit the sky and backed her off her high perch. But the sight at her sleds stopped her.

Raschad stood naked—as much as she could see of him over her load—and a water sack hung from an upright steering bar, dribbling on his head. Nuke scrubbed the newbie's shoulders, his big hands dark against Raschad's golden skin.

She squatted beside a low rock, hoping the lightning preferred the opposite cliff face, and waited, watching like a peeper. Nuke dried Raschad with a big rag, then wrestled the newbie into a clean pair of pants. He was coating Raschad's arms with fresh reeki sap as she walked up.

"Better, aia." Nuke turned Raschad around as she neared the sled. "Looks healthier, anyways."

"Aia." Much, much healthier. Raschad's eyes were clear and bright, the bruised look fading.

"Be right back." Nuke headed for his sled.

Raschad climbed awkwardly onto her load.

"Must feel better."

He nodded, then rubbed one cheek on his bare shoulder. She looked away at that; the move was innocent, yet as suggestive as if he'd called her. Where you get these thoughts, gal?

Nuke returned and tossed Raschad a big white shirt, probably the packer's best. "Be a bit big, but 'ere. It's clean."

Raschad hesitated. "Thank you."

"Just put it on.'"

It fell loose from Raschad's shoulders and billowed about his ribs, more a small tent than a shirt, and its gaping neck bared his fine skin.

"Nice." Raschad smiled.

She laughed, but Nuke knew he'd been complimented.

"Ain't nothing. Loan my clothes to newbies every day." Nuke cuffed Raschad's shoulder.

Raschad ducked his head, swiping at his hair. Clean, it fell feathery soft about his face. She tugged his short bangs.

"Can't believe you let this monster cut it."

Nuke twisted a tuft of his beard, his cheeks reddening. "Shrike, he couldn't hardly see."

"Aia, but now he's too pretty to pack with our likes."

Nuke snorted. "Ain't got a damn lot of choice."

"Aia." She raised an eyebrow. "Let's see your cuts."

Raschad raised a freshly bandaged hand. She stepped nearer, and the clean, strange scent of him hit her.

"You won't be steering by tomorrow." She talked fast, trying to ignore lavender eyes, the fall of his hair, the remembered sight of Nuke's hands dark against a golden body. But she couldn't ignore the fineness of his skin beneath its skim of fresh reeki sap or the heat rising from him. "Those hands have lots of healing to do yet."

"You secure the steering bar to my arm the way you did coming out of Klinker's. I can get along."

"That was one hand, and less damage." She took a breath. "You ain't hauling my sled down this chute like that."

Nuke settled beside Raschad, tipping the sled. She backed away, glad of an excuse to put space between herself and the newbie.

"We take it down empty." Nuke spit. "The way we brought it up. We can reload at the junction. It'll be light. Anyway, we can decide at the junction."

She nodded. Nuke's offer amounted to charity, and she had no choice but to accept. She already owed Nuke and Haze, and they'd collect someday. But what they gave Raschad was pure gift—newbies didn't live long enough to repay debts. But Nuke watched Raschad as if in the presence of deity, believing this battered alien a miracle. By the time he and Haze downed a drink in Tumble Town, Raschad would be a legend. Settlers save him.

She couldn't call them wrong; Raschad had survived what would have killed anyone else she knew. She watched him flip a bomb beetle skyward with a bandaged hand. The bug exploded, a tiny imitation of the lightning playing overhead, and he smiled at its smoking departure like any greenie kid.

A plop hit her head. She looked up into a patter of rain.

"Move it, Nuker." She flipped open a sled bin. "Time to play house."

Working together, they jammed short poles into the four corner stake slots on Raschad's sled bed. On the poles, they hung an extra tarp, letting it hang low on the windward side to shelter them from the blowing rain. The other side and both ends of the sled they left open. Inserting taller poles in the stake holes midway along the sled's sides, they peaked the tent to sheet water off the front and back.

"Do mine, too." Nuke yelled over the rumble of thunder, and wind whipped canvas in her face as they moved to his load.

With the tents up, they hunkered into shelter beside Raschad and broke out food, not caring that they'd eaten already at mid-day. Raschad needed energy, and Sal had reached the last notch in her own belt.

Rain pattered on the canvas. Sitting all together, facing the falls' billowing mist, they downed biscuits, dried fruit, nuts, and a round of cheese from Nuke's share.

For dessert, Sal dug through her pack and found a packet of greasy sweet cakes. Morrie had given her the cakes at Holiday, and she'd been saving them—damn proud of her self-control—for a special occasion. Nuke smacked meaty lips.

She set the opened packet in front of Raschad. Nuke sighed, wiped his stubbled chin, and gave her a scary look. Shifting be-tween the cakes and the big packer, she hand-fed Raschad.

"I'm full." Raschad leaned away after one cake.

Sal glanced quick at Nuke, expecting a grab for the sweets. But the big man swallowed, looking pained, and shook his head.

"Eat it, son. Much as won't sicken you. Your bones is sticking out, and you weren't nothing to haul up this hill. I reckon you got a few years of catching up to do."

Raschad closed his eyes, his expression strange. "All right." He ate another whole cake—even enjoyed it, she thought. But by then he was tired. Finishing the cup of tea she held for him, he slumped back onto his pallet. "Don't fight over that last cake too long. I might wake up and eat it when you aren't looking." His eyes closed. The fine line of his throat stirred with his breathing.

Full, she decided, and clean, with the near cool of the rain a healing thing. She couldn't think of anything else to do except spread a slicker over him.

Nuke swiped her cake. She let him. You are losing all sense, gal. What you going to do with this newbie? What would he tol-erate? He touched, he did sometimes, but did he want a greenie hide?

She reached out snake quick, ripped the cake packet out of Nuke's grasp, and glared him down. But when she dipped inside, there was still a whole cake.

"Jagger?"

"I was only teasing."

She split the sweet the same as they had split the chichiua, and

she ate with her face hot and her mind spinning. The cake would
be long gone except Nuke had been watching her with Raschad
Shrike, deeper and deeper. Finishing, she wiped her hands on her
thighs and noticed what gigi awful filth and gore she wore—
enough to infect Raschad over and again.

Thunder rumbled. Lightning cracked. And the rain sluiced
down, forming a big water spout off the back of the rain tarp.
Nuke sucked his fingers and watched the water.

"I'm thinking that makes a fine shower head." She scratched
beneath one arm.

"Aia." Nuke glanced across to the flood gushing off his tent
tarp. "Pretty fine. You need me, holler." The sled rocked as he
lumbered to his feet. "But don't need me less you want me *nek-
ked*. Thanks for des-sert."

"Enjoy."

Nuke disappeared into the rain, and she glanced at Raschad.
Lips parted, he snored softly, beyond caring if she put on a show
for him or not. So she tugged her pack to the end of the load and
slid straight off under a gush of clean water.

Chilled for once, she dug a brush from her pack and warmed
up scrubbing her leathers. When they looked near new, which
took some effort, she debated a moment, but finally shucked them
and started in on her pants and then her underthings.

After that it seemed silly not to finish up proper, though it
wasn't often she got bare-assed naked in the jungle. She did now
except for her boots. They were wet past worrying about, and
only a hot fire would dry them, which one didn't have often in the
jungle. But she did have two more pairs of boots.

Scrubbing crud out of her hair, she chased bugs from her pits
and privates, and it felt shriking good. She kept herself powdered
with ground bwor leaf so she never caught anything persistent
along the critter line, but bugs were always wandering through a
person's pants out here. Probing her leg wound, she found it had
scabbed over again after splitting yesterday, so she quit worrying
about it.

Thunder rumbled—pray Haze wasn't caught out in this. The
wind picked up. Rain blinded her, and the flood sheeting off the
sled tarp threatened her footing. Scrabbling underneath the shelter
she dropped panting, dripping, and shivering at Raschad's feet.

This big a storm would slow Haze for sure. Rain was expected
but today they didn't need this, didn't need rain-slippery rock or
flooding, mud slides or guano flows.

She pried off her boots, struggling against suction, wet leather and wetter socks. With her towel soaked through and water trickling from her hair and down her back, her teeth chattered. Shivering, she glanced about for something to dry off on and spied the rag Nuke had used on Raschad. It hung from a steering bar lever on the sheltered side of the sled and looked damp. But it was something. So she scrunched along the newbie's body, straining to reach the rag without rocking the sled.

A touch stopped her heart.

Whipping around, knife drawn clear of the string-hung sheath at her neck, she faced . . . Raschad, awake.

His eyes played over her, their expression first startled, then something else, something she didn't know how to read—desire, pain, nerves. She sucked in a breath. What a sight she must look, naked and reared back with her blade drawn.

She let her knife fall and grabbed for Nuke's rag. But it had fallen off into the mud. Shivering, she swallowed, blinked and saw Raschad lifting the corner of his cloth-lined slicker, waiting while she stared and decided.

She wanted to think the cold made her go, but she knew better, and knew, too, that they wouldn't stop at being friendly this time.

His arms closed around her, tugging her chilled body against his. He flopped one leg over her thighs and chafed her awkwardly with his upper arms. The warmth distracted her a breath, but when she flopped over to warm her front, his thighs and chest and throat heated her into other considerations.

He seemed eager and near terrified at the same time. She felt much the same. His body was nothing like George's to touch. George was solid, square-muscled greenie with a layer of soft flesh from comfortable town living. As a lover, he'd complained about how hard she was to hold, too much bone and muscle. Raschad felt like that, everywhere hard and designed for power, but with curves where George just went straight. When she lifted his shirt and wriggled beneath it, the hollow below his ribs was as soft as down. He moaned and shuddered head to toe.

She gave a thought to Nuke. But lost in the drumming roar of rain on the tarp, enclosed by liquid silver walls, all her concerns washed away.

And Raschad drew her nearer, tugging with muscled upper arms, to rub his face in her wet hair. He was gentle, and knowing and considerate. Finding her hollows, he drew trembling gasps from her lonely body, and she knew without any special emotion that Mira Goontz had been far from his first bedding.

Yet as they reached the heart of the matter, he froze up, his muscles tensed. His breathing went ragged, and chill sweat wet his skin. He wouldn't make so far as satisfying himself.

She thought she should hurry, do something. But she didn't know men, and his lips erased all thought. Her back arched.

He tugged her hips nearer, then did things she hadn't known about or ever thought of, until the gray world went colored and she was alone for a long moment inside herself.

He seemed content. She snuggled beneath his chin, feeling small for once against his long frame. His heart raced beneath her ear. His lungs labored. A shudder took him—another.

He relaxed. And the next thing that happened surprised her: all of it beginning again.

He went slower this time, letting her have her way with him, until his control slipped and he mounted her in frantic haste, wild and wanting, rough, but still pleasing.

His loving left her panting blind into his shoulder, left him sucking air as if she'd hit him. And the tears didn't surprise her, not from a man who'd been long years alone in the jungle and come recently so very near dying.

She held him—he couldn't hold her—and stroked his long hair, pulling Nuke's shirt around them for warmth. The rain drifted down, gentler now, as if playing to their mood. The falls roared, and rock reverberated beneath them as the river flooded.

Sal gave another thought to Haze out on the trail, wishing him greenie luck. Raschad snuggled her to his chest.

She woke to the final drip-dripping of the storm. Golden rays of sunlight slanted beneath the clouds and lit the world between ground and stormy sky with rainbows. Raschad lay awake, watching her, his smile tentative.

What were they going to do now? This wasn't just lying down for fun. Whether it amounted to love, she doubted. But it was serious enough that packing with the newbie would be stranger and more dangerous than ever.

She gave him a gentle hug. "I'd best get dressed before Nuke comes visiting."

"I think he's been by already. Either that or a mountain bear."

"They don't come down off the plateau this time of year."

"Then it was him."

She eased away, stared at the newbie, and laughed. He smiled, pleased, she thought, to have amused her.

They dressed and sat wrapped together. Nuke wandered up and

leaned against the side of the load. Water dripped off the tarp and down the back of his huge brown slicker.

Sal choked. "Shrike, you *are* a mountain bear."

Raschad laughed—silliness from them both, another release of tension. She didn't expect to hide anything from Nuke, but imagined the laughter told him things had changed between her and the newbie. His look was worried, that was sure.

"Haze'll be having it tough in this muck," he said.

Idiot, Sal told herself, Nuke had more concerns than her play just now. "You want, we can go across, look." She cocked her head.

Nuke's eyes flicked to Raschad and away again.

"I can sit the sleds." Raschad straightened. "All I need is one movable finger for the Morven. It fires itself."

Nuke looked torn. "I—" A flash of red light lit the ridge line where the trail pulled up the opposite cliff.

"Haze?" She glanced at Nuke.

He straightened, fists clenching and unclenching. A second flare streaked the sky, and he relaxed.

"I'll meet him. You two stay." He glanced their way, his expression saying he'd missed nothing. "Don't get in trouble." He strode off like an ambulatory chunk of mountain. "Haze'll be right dis-ser-pointed!" His backward-directed yell was barely audible above the roar of the raging river.

Sal gave him a sign. He gave one back, turned his head, and hurried toward the swaying reeki bridge.

"And yours, too!" she screamed, knowing he couldn't hear a thing, and sat back smiling. "What?"

"I didn't catch it." Raschad looked embarrassed.

"You ain't seen that sign?" The question just popped out bald, but they were surely close enough for personal talk now.

"I've seen it a thousand times, minimum. I just don't know what it means."

"Then what you do when they throw it at you?"

"Go on. If they come after me, I put them down. One of them did it with a sort of flourish. Don't know why that bothered me, but I went for him. We both spent time in jail, until the sheriff made me wash my face. Then he put me on the street fast. And I'm not welcome in Tauggerville yet."

She half smiled, half frowned, and didn't quite know what to say. It was pathetic, and made her mad to think what being newbie put him through.

"This—" She flipped him the sign. "—means you like your sex

real private and perverted. Only it means a little worse even than that, like you picked up the habit from your parents. Only worse." She shrugged—educating an innocent.

He laughed, though. It didn't even touch him, the way it didn't mean much of anything between her and Nuke.

"While you are explaining . . ." Those eyes turned on her again. "What the hell is a psiittine?"

She held her sides and roared, remembering she'd promised him an explanation days ago. "It's a treatment kit." He looked blank. "For ass mites. Guess you ain't never used one."

His mouth froze open. "Heaven save us." His eyes rolled. "I don't even want to know." And they both laughed.

"How come, since we're asking questions so free, your name sounds like a pretty gal's?" She slapped his leg.

"Named after my aunt. I'm not ashamed of it."

"Didn't mean you were. You're strong enough for it."

"Naia, not quite." His nose wrinkled. His lips twitched.

He slipped his arm around her, and they watched the sun fire the mountaintops and weave a tapestry among the clouds.

Nuke and Haze skidded into sight just as the sky brightened with the sun's last reflection off mist and cloud, in that moment when dusk seemed to lighten a breath before true dark.

Shadows made crossing the bridge tricky, and no time was good to start with. Working it slow, Nuke pushed and Haze pulled. Boots and sled treads slithered and skated in wet reeki sap. Sal watched, weak-kneed and useless; there was no room for a third person on that damn web.

"Yaia." Haze slithered onto stone.

"Late, mudballer." She fell in at the man's side.

"Lucky I bothered coming back at all. Met up with Nicki Regetti in town, could've stayed in style with the govies, too. But I figured you'd be needing dinner and missing me."

Nuke moved up on Haze's other side, and the three of them maneuvered the sled into the wind to shelter their camp.

"I waited to report the Runner slaughter until I could see it was going to rain a swamper." Haze locked his steering bars and unclipped from his traces. "Then I sort of implied that the storm would keep me in town. So they let me go until the Sub-Super could figure out what to ask me." Mud weighted his slicker, and his shoulders sagged.

Sal flipped out a tread rake and began scraping his sled.

"Do a good job, now." Haze limped to Raschad's side, out of

her and Nuke's way. "Regetti lost her sled to the shriking Runners, but come out alive. Reckon the govies will be real fired when they can't find me to talk at. But I figured they wouldn't fly out in a storm like this one."

"They'll be in the sky come first light." She spoke without looking up, busy peeling reeki vines from a tread well.

"Aia, there." Nuke worked the other side of the sled. "We best hit trail early."

"Well." Haze sat in the mud and leaned against a rock. "I was afraid you'd say that." He looked up the newbie's tall frame. "You strong enough to handle a run tomorrow, kid?"

"Aia."

"Then I guess I ain't got no excuse for kicking."

Sal helped Nuke cook dinner—fresh bread and morel from town and some early highland monk tubers Nuke had foraged. Raschad sat beside her while she worked, watching everything, making nervous wanting-to-help gestures. When her hands were free, Sal kneaded the thick muscle of his shoulders to settle him.

Haze groaned. "Me next."

Nuke shot him a look, and Haze's eyebrows arched.

"Shoulders only." She kept on at Raschad's. Haze half stood. She motioned him down. "*After* we eat."

He made a face. Raschad smiled, unthreatened by Haze's interest in her. Uncommon good sense again. But when did it end? How badly would he surprise her with some newbie ignorance like the psiittine kit?

She set the tubers boiling. No knowing what he would bring her, and, damn her for a fool, she had no business taking responsibility for anyone—let alone a newbie.

Dawn emerged like muted fire over Glory's Roost. Fog billowed from the canyon, glowing orange and lavender, shifting through a dozen shades and hues as Sal watched from a rock ledge halfway down the mountainside.

They'd descended this far using shaded headlamps to pick a path through the predawn dark. Nuke trailered Raschad's empty sled again while the newbie walked, arms held to his body by slings. Yesterday's heavy haul had tired Haze, but they'd shifted more of Sal's load back onto her sled. Going downhill, she figured she could handle the extra weight—at least as far as the junction. Her leg was achy, but holding. Another day and it would be fine.

She swallowed the last of breakfast, wiped her hands on her shirt, and leaned against Raschad. "How you feel?"

"Fine." Still chewing, he studied the lightening sky. "Feels good to move. I was getting sick of lying around."

"You *were* sick."

"Just scratches."

"Poison scratches, bone-deep cuts, and killing bruises. Don't forget I've seen it all. You ain't much of a liar."

"I try." He smiled.

She hissed, raised a finger—and saw the skid, like a giant roak against the dawn sky.

"Time to move."

Raschad gulped breakfast and wriggled his arm into a sling. Nuke and Haze slid to their feet without even looking up. Clipping into their traces, they all pulled for heavy cover. By the time the fliers passed overhead, the packers sat tucked up and hidden. Sal counted two haulers and two scouts by sound, but she couldn't see a thing.

When the drone of power cores faded to a whisper, they moved on, planning to hit the junction at dusk. By then the government investigators should be gone; even govies wouldn't camp beside all the gigi bait in the Pike clearing. Scavengers would have been at the gore by now. But she didn't envy anyone cleaning up what was left, just hoped they worked fast and left the trail clear for Nuke and Haze.

Nuke had debated going to D'arnith's then back on the cutoff to the Pike. But the backtracking would take an extra day, maybe two. Instead, he'd decided to chance being stopped by the govies. That wouldn't lose him as much time as detouring, but avoiding the bastards altogether was better.

They spent the morning ducking under cover of webb trees and burr firs and skidding downhill sitting on the sled brakes, willy worms whining. Twice as fast as their plodding pull up the Rise, their descent ran wild. Nuke needed every bit of his muscle to track the trailered sled, and Raschad tried riding it to make it behave. But one breath he was sitting on it, the next he had sailed through the air and bounced into brush.

Sal laid on her brake. Treads skidded, and her overloaded rig shoved her right past him. Haze yelled. Her brakes locked up.

She hit the do-or-die, and botafab wailed. The sled jerked to a stop, her harness snapping her against the sled's bumper.

Popping free, she staggered back, her heart pounding. Haze had hit a rock and hung up.

"Newbie?" Her voice scaled into a screech.

"What?" Raschad stood up out of a mound of reeki vine.

"Newbie ..." She leaned on her knees and hung her head. "You got the damnedest luck, Raschad." He'd lost his hat, but otherwise looked unharmed.

"Luck's not my fault." He scooted against a tree, scraping mud off the seat of his pants. "I *try* to get killed."

"Aia, and you did that bounce just to see if I could run."

"Naia, but it was entertaining."

"Squat." She took one long stride, grabbed his harness, and jerked him downhill. "You stay in the traces with me, where I can keep my hands on you. I'll put a fanny strap behind us. When I tell you, you sit. If that don't keep you out of trouble, we'll tie you to the shriking sled."

He only smiled beneath his netting.

It took a few curves for them to get the hang of braking together, but then their teaming worked so well, Nuke had trouble keeping ahead of them. After lunch, Raschad went up with Nuke.

By midday the strain of moving fast and hauling hard showed on all of them. Haze's eyes drooped, Nuke's head hung, and Raschad limped worse with every step. He claimed sitting on the fanny strap rested his legs. But Sal would've tied him to a sled except they weren't off the mountain yet, and he was safer in the traces than on a runaway. The front bumper was made for flipping bodies out of the way. But without roll bars, a tumbling sled would leave a rider just a bloody smear.

As they moved on, skids whined overhead, invisible from the jungle floor. The govies were hauling out bodies, Sal figured, and the traffic ran steady.

The trail flattened out at last, and Raschad rode the empty sled, admitting weakness and keeping the thing from bouncing on Nuke. Bugs whined, almost driving Sal insane. Her leg throbbed, but she held the pace.

The day wore on, and the shadows thickened. Wedging their sleds beneath an arch of burntwoods, they watched a line of skids whine away south. It looked as if the govies were done for the day.

Haze scrabbled up a tree, watching the fliers. Raschad fell asleep. She and Nuke cleaned treads and waited.

The fliers had stayed late. Roaks squawked in the distance, raising hell with the skids for flying during roosting time. If the idiot govies didn't hurry, they'd face nightbabies by the time they crossed Glory's Roost.

Going into a late haul on the jungle floor was no smart move, either. She and Nuke, Haze and the newbie, should know better by now. But they hadn't a shriking choice—they were safer moving than stopped near anyplace favored by gigis.

They waited until the sky fell silent and the jungle yammer returned to normal. Then Sal and Haze went scouting.

The trail to the junction lay clear. Haze took the Pike. She turned right, onto the Ebbid. The govies had been up it, and the hole Raschad had blown in it was filled. She wondered what the govies had thought of that.

With the light dimming, she stopped at the Runners' shattered blockade. Yesterday's thunderstorm hadn't reached this far north, and Nuke and Haze's tracks of four days ago still showed as if set in concrete. No one had hauled through since them. That could be good news, or bad. But the trail should be clear from there to the hollow where she planned on camping for the night. Turning back, she reached the junction ahead of Haze and debated going down the Pike after him. But he showed up, looking shaken.

"You ain't running steady, greenie."

"Naia." He glanced back toward the ruined clearing. "Banks, you're something, living through that with a newbie." His jaw set. "No wonder he scares the rockies."

"Well, *he* didn't do it."

"But he's tough—survived that, then near blew himself to hell saving us." Haze shook his head. "He's something. C'mon."

Nuke had reworked her loads, shifting crates from his sleds to Raschad's, and the newbie stood with his arms slip-strapped to the steering bars. It was leaving time. Bunched around Raschad, they all shifted awkwardly and stared at their boots.

"You take care." Sal kicked Nuke's heel. "Wish you weren't going the Pike." The men were headed into gigis and maybe worse. Haze grunted.

"You go easy." Nuke's eyes rested on the newbie. "Don't run yourselves into the ground."

She and Raschad were taking the safer trail, but they were both spent and had no business pulling out at all.

Haze yanked his hat off and squashed it nervously, his mouth working. "Care, newbie. Here." He shoved the hat at her. "He'll need this. I got an old one."

She settled the hat on Raschad's head.

"Thank you." Raschad nodded to both men. "Thank you for keeping me alive. Glad you didn't know there's bounty on me."

Nuke smiled. "Ain't enough left of your hide to be worth anything—couldn't prove where it come from."

"Squat, aia." Haze shifted, kicked a mud clod, grabbed Sal, hugged, and let go with a final grope at her pants. She swatted him, but friendly. They both smiled.

"Squat." Nuke spit into the brush. "What the hell." He squashed the newbie's hat down over his eyes, slapped him on the back, and numbed her arm with a pat. "Go on, get."

He shoved Sal toward her sled and bent behind Raschad's to give him a starting push. It was a strange parting for packers, who passed at times without a word. But their four days together and the things that had happened to them would shake this jungle in the quiet way of greenie events.

And wouldn't Morrie take on now.

Chapter 15

Bugs whined and the midday sun burned through limp foliage as Raschad's sled ground to a halt. Sal broke from her traces and trotted around his load. Her back burned and her healing leg ached and itched. But he must hurt worse. They'd found little rest the night before, taking turns at watch while gigis yelped nearer and nearer.

Hearing her bulling through the brush, Raschad called out before she reached him. "I'm fine." But he still stood tethered to the steering bars, his chest pumping, eyes closed, bushwhackers sweat-soaked, hat stained to the brim.

"Should've stopped sooner." She stripped his arms free and eased him back on the sled.

"Wasn't any place."

"*This* ain't no place."

"Doesn't matter." He slumped against her and slowly caught his breath. "I should be stronger than this."

"Idiot. You should be dead."

"Ummhh." He laughed, still slumped, his eyes closed. "Can't die yet. People waiting on me."

She hugged him. "You're flits."

"Aia," he sighed. "Hungry, too."

She fed him, let him nap, then pulled on—no help for anything else.

"We'll leave it." Her voice was firm in the late afternoon hush of heat and chlorophyll-clogged air. "These crates ain't worth killing yourself."

"Your sled and your reputation are," Raschad said.

She touched his healing cheek. "Naia. They ain't."

His bottom lip sucked in. "Are."

She had to move or be run over. "Raschad!" But he was rolling. She let him go. They'd waste more energy arguing than it would take for him to pull the sled on in. Stubborn bastard.

They made D'arnith's Wood at dusk, and found the logging settlement crowded with dry-season travelers. Their sleds coming down the Ebbid brought people out, staring and jabbering.

Sal pulled around Raschad and led the way alongside Scugs's tavern, hoping people would leave her alone if they saw she had business to do. But they only followed.

"Where ya in from, packer?" A gap-toothed old woman shoved right up to Sal's traces, rude as a gigi.

"Noca Tana." She didn't want talk, but avoiding it would invite more curiosity. She unclipped.

"Gigi's ass, gal, the skids has been flyin' that way all day." The old woman followed her as she made her way to Raschad.

"You managing, babe?"

He wavered between standing and sitting. She braced him with her shoulder and freed his arms. Anxious faces surrounded them—too many faces. It looked like D'arnith's had heard of trouble, and everyone was bottled up, afraid to hit trail.

"What those skids up ta, gal?" The woman pushed, too desperately curious for manners.

"Who knows." Sal shook her head. "Govies don't talk to me." It wasn't a lie, but close enough for guilt. Still, she wouldn't discuss an Aireil massacre in a crowd like this. What a mess to bring a newbie into.

"Yer man's done in!" A shout rose from the milling crowd.

She ignored everyone and bumped Raschad back onto his sled. Stretching flat, he hid his face with his arms. She worked his harness off him.

"Ya seen trouble, fer sure."

"Batch o' gigis come at us." That wasn't a lie, either.

"Ya seen Aireils?"

"Aia. A few." She tugged Raschad up and steered him for Scugs's front door.

"Trail open?"

"Ebbid is." She wished people would shut up.

"Ya must've come up the Pike."

"Aia."

She wrestled Raschad onto the front porch, then aimed him into the dark of the tavern. People followed, but the door slowed them. Crowd enough waited inside, anyway. Sal shoved Raschad between people and chairs and settled him at the only empty table in the taproom. Every eye was on them.

"Banks!" She jumped as Scugs himself stomped up behind her. "I figured you dead. Reckon . . . you got my load?"

"All there." She dug his receipts from her pocket and handed them over. "Everything's on the forward sled." She eased into a chair. "I need a drink now."

"Aia." Scugs eyed her, his dark jowls jiggling. "My boys'll take care of this. You rest. We'll talk later. Aia?"

She nodded. "Later."

Scugs's wave brought a broad-beamed waitress running with a pitcher.

"You look like hell, Banks." Scugs waddled off, reading his delivery list.

The brew cooled her soul. Sighing, she watched Raschad lean over the table and slurp without lifting his mug. She didn't disturb him by trying to help. Her own hand shook, slopping brew onto her lap, and there was no sense spilling on him when he was managing that much himself. Finally he tipped the last of his drink down his throat, teeth holding his mug, and slumped back, his eyes closed. She ached for him.

Jo, the big waitress, brought a second round without being called. "Dinner, Sal?"

"Aia. Lots of it."

Jo disappeared toward the kitchen, fighting the crowd. Sal took closer account of what they had walked into.

Outside of a place to sit and brew to soothe her throat, Scugs's tavern offered little comfort tonight. Packers and miners, woodsmen and gatherers filled the steaming room, slopping drinks, dribbling food, reeking sweat, sap, and worse, and attracting too many bugs. With the tavern's shutters flopped down, the top halves of the front and side walls were only screen netting, and she could hear the crowd outside still yammering.

Too many people here. Too many people on the trails. It would be like this for a month or more—folks traveling before the rains hit again.

Curious eyes studied Raschad's slumped shoulders. Most in the crowd were jungle greenies, who either knew or knew of her. And they all wanted to find out what was happening on the trails. She bore them no ill will; but talking could wait until they ate. She glared, and everyone hung back, eyeing Raschad.

Head propped on the curved back of his vinewood chair, he snored away, oblivious. His netting, pulled loose at the throat so he could drink, still hid his face, and she didn't figure anyone had marked him for a newbie—yet. So she sat still, drinking and fretting at the slowness of their food. How would she feed him in the midst of this mess? She should have asked for a room straight off. But coming in, she had only wanted to get away from the crowd at the door and sit him down. Besides, a room would have to await Scugs's approval of her credit.

What a mess.

A knot of muddy packers entered—Sooey Biggs, his two women, and Ti Doogle from up the Plateau. They nodded Sal's direction, and she nodded back. But when they hesitated, hunting a spot to sit, she didn't offer, though she liked Sooey's gals. Ti's eyes took in Raschad, and the group moved on.

Then a hoot sounded from the table at Raschad's back, and her eyes snapped to the group of drunks there, all strangers. She guessed from their gear that they were rockies—stone miners, not guano prospectors. One of them climbed on his chair.

"Hey! Hey, woman!" The rocky waved to Jo, who was clear across the taproom now. "Drinks 'ere. Ain't ya serving?"

The man dropped down, too drunk to hold onto his perch, and the other rockies patted his back. Sal glanced around. Locals watched the rockies with nothing friendly in their stares, which was fine by her and meant they'd watch Raschad less. But she hoped trouble didn't come before they got out of here. Just let it alone till we eat, she prayed, studying the rockies.

Six of them crowded a corner table. Long-haired and dirty, they had a hungry look not far different from the Runners'. They settled down, and she almost relaxed, but caught the bastards studying Raschad. She stared back.

A scar-faced rockie gave her a knowing smile. "Haia, missy, come sit with us." The idiot batted his eyelashes and cooed. She felt for her tread maul, shifted her gun, held her mouth still, and gave the man a look that drained the eagerness out of his face.

One of the two rocky women sent up another bellow. "Need drinks here."

The second woman and one man stood, kicking their chairs hard into Raschad's. His head snapped up; his hand jerked and stopped. He half turned toward the two trapped behind him by the tangle of their chairs.

"Haia, mudballer, move it."

Sal sat forward, hand at her belt, muscles tensed, eyes on the rockies. Shrike.

"Move." The woman kicked Raschad's chair leg.

Raschad slumped.

Sal grated her chair back, clearing her hands. "He can't move." Which was obvious, with them penning him.

The newbie's head lolled sideways.

"Haia!" A rocky grabbed Raschad's hat and netting.

Sal came up with her maul in hand, but the newbie snagged the rocky's feet with his boot and dumped the drunk backward. The bar fell silent.

The rockies stood as one. Local tables stood, too, behind Sal. Sooey's group moved up at her side. The drunks looked nervous at that, but they were too far gone to stop.

"Ya ain't goin' ta fight fer a packer bitch an her Liberalizer newbie whore!" The raggedy woman at Raschad's back screamed her words in a drunken slur.

Murmurs rose behind Sal. Sooey didn't budge.

"You just leave be an' back off." Sal spoke clear and low. How the shrike they know he was newbie? "Ain't no need for fighting here."

"That right, Ras-chad?" The woman leaned over him. "Ya goin' t'apologize ta honest greenies fer sneakin' yer pale Liber hide in here when good folks ain't got room ta stand?"

Sal's stomach flopped. They knew him; they must have gone for the netting just to make certain. Murmurs grew louder at her back. No one in this crowd was in the mood to waste liquor, food, or space on a newbie tonight.

She sensed Sooey ease back a step, and her grip tightened around the butt of her Camm.

Raschad stood. Her heart thumped. He turned on the rockies, half blocking any shot she had and dwarfing the loudmouth causing the trouble. He didn't say a thing or do anything she saw. But the rockies edged away, and he turned his back on them as if they were nothing, and faced the rest of the room.

The sight of the big, angry double wounds on his cheek stopped even her.

Not a person in that room could know or guess what had marked him. But lantern light picked out the claw wounds, glinting off the sealant-packed cuts, and his eyes flicked over the room as if he knew the soul in every one of them. And none of them mattered.

Sal forced her hand out and caught his arm. He was rigid. If he relaxed a breath, he'd fall.

Shoving aside the table, she jostled others, not caring, and tugged him out of the mess. He followed. People gave way as if a plague was passing.

Scugs's boys would have her sleds in the back by now. She headed that way, avoiding the crowd at the front door. Halfway down the hall, Scugs stopped her.

"Banks."

She looked down at the man's bald head and a big shotblaster in his hands. "Going to shoot me for bringing him in, Scugs?"

Some of the hard edge on the man's meaty face eased. He shifted the huge weapon in his hands. "Shrike, forgot I carried it. Let's talk."

When this man spoke soft, it was time to listen—and he didn't forget what he carried. Still, she half thought she would keep going, then drag the sleds to the edge of the clearing and sleep on them another night.

But night here would be long and dangerous with the rockies stirring things up worse than the gigis. Besides, Scugs was tough, but fair. She owed him answers. After all, he was still asking nicely, not making any move for her weapon or Raschad's, saying nothing about his men surrounding her sleds.

"Be fine." She spoke low to Raschad.

He wobbled, his big body radiating heat and stench. Steadying him, she coaxed him down the hall and through a wide door beneath the back stairs into Scugs's office.

She'd been in that little box before. Nothing was changed. Bare ku-soo paneling walled the room, the pale wood naturally speckled with black, but stained a dirty brown around Scugs's chair. The desk in front of the chair took up most of the office's floor space, and only a single dirty, paper-paned window provided outside light.

Raschad glanced at the overflowing disarray of papers and supplies and tried to back out.

"Be fine. Don't worry about it." Sal held onto him. "Scugs only uses handlights, no lanterns. Don't strike a match and we're safe."

Raschad's eyes focused, and he laughed abruptly. Scugs eyed the big newbie slantwise and dumped a stack of towels off a chair.

"You." He gestured to Raschad. "Sit before you fall." Raschad dropped like a stone, and Scugs waved a hand. "Find yourself a spot, Banks. You know the rules."

Raschad's eyes rolled at her.

"No smoking," she said.

He grimaced, swallowing another mirthless laugh—just tension, just too tired to care.

"Sorry about out front." Scugs cleared a path to his desk chair, and Sal half thought he meant his apology. "It's the time of year, and some of this crowd's been waiting on the supplies you brought. Others wait on news that the trails are safe." He laid the blaster across an open ledger.

"Rumors have run wild of Aireils gathering and strangers tearing up the green. Some fool come across the cutoff near a week ago saying a gigi ganger was headed for the junction. Reckon you might know something of that. You're the first packers in since 'then." He arched bristling black eyebrows.

"Aia." Sal eased into a paper-covered chair beside the newbie's. "I ain't meaning to hold back, Scugs, but we're worn out. And I hoped to avoid trouble. Should of known better. This has been a cursed run since before I begun it."

"Come through a ganger with a newbie and expect to avoid trouble." Scugs snorted. "Lost your mind, gal." His big hide chair groaned and squealed as he turned to slide open a wall panel above his head. Kitchen odors and clatter invaded the room. "Vina," he yelled. "You send Banks's order back here. Quick." The grate closed, chopping off the cooking noises. "I've a room for you if you want it."

Sal nodded. Scugs leaned forward, his broad stomach trapped between chair and desk. "Two rooms, I don't have."

"Ain't necessary." It told him plenty that she would share a bed with a newbie.

"So what they said out front's true."

"Aia." She let her breath puff out slow while Scugs's eyebrows imitated a willy worm. "It's true he's a newbie." Scugs's lips thinned. "We weren't trying to hide it." She arched her neck, stretching tired muscles. "But weren't naia reason to advertise. Not to this lot camped here."

"Those are two horrendous cuts on his cheek." The fat man's jowls worked.

"Trail accident."

Scugs's fat-narrowed eyes slitted. He pulled a cigar from a big carved box in front of him, stuck it in his mouth, and chewed. He'd quit smoking them after his first tavern burned.

"You going to talk, newbie man?"

Raschad blinked, head hanging. "What?"

"What's with the hands? The bandages?"

Sal swallowed. Scugs was pushing damn hard.

"Tore the skin off." Raschad's voice was breathy.

"Aia? Where would you do a thing like that?"

Raschad lay his hands on his chest, propped his feet on the free edge of her chair, and settled lower. "Where no human being within screaming distance has ever been."

Scugs's eyes disappeared. "Learn anything worth knowing?"

Sal's hand edged toward her belt. She fought it back. Scugs didn't miss the twitch or her anger. She only hoped he remembered she had limits. What had happened to a squat hauler in this bar two years ago could happen to him, blaster or not.

His expression said he knew it.

Thump. Raschad's boots hit the floor. She startled inside, but held still. Scugs chewed his cigar, dribbling drool.

"Have you ever been touched by mistwalkers?" Raschad leaned over Scugs's desk, returning insult for insult, eyes glinting in the bare white rays of a suspended handlight.

Her gut hurt. Raschad had walked other worlds and taken lives there, plucked them away to nothingness in the cold dry heart of space. She knew *nothing* about how this man thought. And his time with the Aireils didn't make knowing him any easier.

Damn, he was scary. *Be scared*, Scugs, she willed. Made—a—mistake, her mind said to the rhythm of her pounding heart. Made—a—mistake.

Scugs took the mangled cigar from his lips and examined its tip. Gigis, she was scared.

"I been touched," Scugs said. "Not for a long time . . . but you don't forget."

"'Naia.'" Raschad swallowed. "You never forget. I will never forget, ever." And he touched his cheek, and smiled—which was so crazy, Sal knew he'd dropped sanity downtrail. "Do not go where I've been." He used his too-perfect speech. "Not unless you are already insane."

Scugs stared. Raschad leaned back in the chair, rested his hands on his chest and let his breathing go deep. She reached out to touch his arm before she thought, then pulled her hand back, knowing how things already looked to Scugs. But her face screwed up. She gritted her teeth and just looked away.

"He's a strange one, Banks." Something like concern tinged Scugs's voice. "But newbies do ramble."

Her breath puffed out, not quite a laugh.

"Everything's been damn strange around here of late." Scugs spit bits of smokeleaf at the wall behind him. "Whatever your story, I'd best hear it."

She met the fat man's gaze. "Can't have been stranger than hauling with this newbie. I swear."

He laughed—a hard sound, no mirth in it. But he'd listen now. They were safe. She just had to tell him everything. Only, he wasn't going to believe this.

"Found a meltdown out this side of the Forks."

Scugs's expression went even grimmer. "Knobby Brax never come through."

"Knobby?" Her gut ached.

"Nicki Regetti went out to make salvage on the load, if she could. Hasn't come back." Scugs's lips rolled his cigar about. "I figured you'd gone the same way, and I needed those supplies you brought bad."

She stared at her boots. "Knobby's sled was brand new. It wouldn't have had time to melt as bad as this one."

"Neither would Nicki's. Ain't anyone else missing."

"Wasn't Regetti's, anyway. Carl Haze saw her in Noca Tana. She lost her sled to Runners."

"Runners? I warned her things were crazy in the green."

"Aia, and there's more to tell, but my man needs a bed."

Scugs's men carried Raschad upstairs more because Scugs was practical than sympathetic: he knew Sal wouldn't talk until Raschad was settled. So he even helped her with the newbie— tugged off his boots, and sent for towels, bandages, and boiled water. With the newbie tucked beneath bug netting, Sal began her story again as if she'd never stopped talking. Raschad cried out once; she rose, settled him with a touch, and returned to her chair. Scugs's eyes hung on the newbie, his expression uncertain.

"If I didn't know you, Banks, I'd swear you were lying." His fat lips wrinkled. "But it all agrees with what little we've heard. And you'd be crazy to lie about anything involving Nuke and Haze. I warned those muscle dummies not to haul out of here with the Aireils stirred up. Serves them right." Scugs's jaw worked. He stroked his upper lip, still staring at the newbie.

"I'll set you up. Even loan you muscle. I want you gone in the morning. The government's doing better than usual keeping this quiet. But they'll come snooping soon, and people will go crazy once word's out about the Runners. Best you're not here when that happens—someone might decide it's your fault for bringing a newbie into the green, or some other stupid idea." His mouth twitched. "Aia?"

"Aia. Don't want to waste time talking to govies anyway." She closed her eyes. "Thanks."

"You brought my goods through." Scugs sucked his cigar. "I'm grateful. Now head out, and fast. I'll send an order with you. People will want extra supplies if they think there's an Aireil uprising coming."

"There ain't."

"People will still buy."

The barest glow seeped through their window as Raschad rolled out of bed, slow and stiff. Sal knew they should be in the traces by now. But exhaustion held her, and the next thing she heard was him raiding the food pots Scugs's people had left.

"You eat heavy." She stretched, relishing sheets, a soft, big bed, and the absence of Raschad's sticky body.

That last thought opened her eyes and left her staring and stunned by the sight of him half naked in the glow of a handlight—there were no lanterns anywhere at Scugs's.

Raschad moved better today. All he'd needed was rest— amazing fact—and he looked so fine.

"Meesha." The name felt strange on her tongue, and her voice, half whispering, sounded like someone else's.

He understood, but hesitated—which did her heart no good. But then he came, shucked his pants and slid under the sheet.

"We have no business doing this." But his voice sounded as throaty as her own, and his touch was wanting.

She reckoned later it did them good—got their blood up, eased their strain. Besides, she figured he worried not about the loving, but the love. And he was everything nice he'd been in the jungle, and more. She'd never wanted a man so much, though George'd brought her wonder.

"Raschad." She panted into his hair. "Ah . . ." But she couldn't ask him, not what she was thinking—that it must have been a very long time since he'd had anyone he wanted. Mira Goontz was never gentle.

Their leaving later in dim misty dawn was strange and quiet. Two of Scugs's men pulled out with them through the ramshackle knot of wood and palm-frond buildings that comprised D'arnith's. Leading with her sled, Sal spotted shadowy faces at the windows, and knots of packers, peddlers, and wandering settlers watched them suspiciously. But the rockies were nowhere in evidence;

Scugs had promised they wouldn't be. She hadn't pursued the subject. Scugs could be a very hard man.

Watching Raschad—free of the traces, shadowed by one of the fat man's bullybys—she didn't care if a few heads got thumped on their behalf. The other bully pulled Raschad's sled, carrying half her load. Both men seemed half reverent of the newbie. Scugs must've talked to them some. Raschad was already a legend, and none of them understood a damn about him.

She worked downslope between mountains of drying ku-soo logs and into the logging cut that circled clear around D'arnith's. Stacked fuel wood dotted the cut, mounded with reeki. With the trails open, it could be moved now.

She pulled into jungle. Night lingered beneath the trees. Slowly gaining speed, she felt her muscles warm. Her back relaxed. It felt good to be out this morning. She could have put Scugs's man to pulling her load, but she set the pace and chose the best track on the trail.

The Ebbid widened from D'arnith's down. By midday it would be broad, flat, and fast, a highway by jungle standards. Scugs's men were going through clear to Toad Hall—which was worrisome generosity from the fat man, even if he figured a profit on the run.

Sal reached a wide spot on the trail, and Raschad moved up, pacing her. She let him slip between her steering bars.

"You don't help."

He shrugged, his smile barely visible through the new netting Scugs had supplied. Sapped heavy, he looked every bit greenie again. All of them were sapped this morning; the air was full of hell midges and blue gnats. With the jungle drying, the bugs had to fly or die. A few would crawl into the mud and wait out the dry spell, but not enough so anyone would notice. They'd walked paradise on the Pike compared to the insect swarms they faced now. The lower they dropped, the worse things would get, too, and they wouldn't climb again until beyond Pasquel's.

But the bugs weren't bothering Raschad. Some old stories claimed Aireil venom made the chance survivor immune to bugs and disease, but that was beyond Sal's knowing.

They moved down the trail, fast and easy. Rather than stop for a break when she felt winded, she let one of Scugs's men work the sled while she walked behind with Raschad. He pulled a hand out of his harness straps—where he'd anchored it to ease the swelling—and rested it across her shoulders.

"Better?" she asked.

"Aia. Much." He smiled.

They walked that way for a bit. Then he politely edged her around to his other side and traded arms. It was only common sense to accommodate him, but nice, too.

"Those rockies knew you last night."

"We had a dispute once over a bit of rock."

"Guess they lost."

"Nobody won. I took what I wanted and left the rest. They resent that they aren't certain what I got."

She raised her eyebrows. "Can't be resenting it too much if they ain't killed you."

"Well, it confuses them that they don't know exactly what their complaint is. I mine dirt crystals, and my mother sells them to specialty dealers on MB-2. The market here doesn't pay anyone to dig for them. So I took only what the rockies couldn't use, and their complaint is only that I was digging where they wanted to dig and didn't die when they thought I should."

"Seems lots of people hold that last complaint against you. I never knew a newbie to live through what you have. You're a tough bastard, Raschad."

"Naia." He shook his head. "Just hellish motivated."

"Toad Hall will be all primed for us," she said, fanning off a big yellow stink bee. Buzzing like a heavy hauler on the downhill, it flashed its red, double-pincered rump at her before darting into a bank of grit ferns tough enough for scrubbing cookpots. "Scugs sent messengers out last night to tell people the Runners are cleared out, the mistwalkers riled, but the trails clear. We're liable to meet traffic headed back into the green—which is what Scugs is banking on."

"He's a shrewd fellow."

"I ain't never seen anyone worry him like you did last night, Raschad. You be careful if you ever cross him again. He's First Settler, greenie green to the core."

"May I ask what a First Settler is? Or is that rude?"

"Aia, ask." She arched her neck. "I been asking you questions. You don't still have to ask if you can ask. We been more personal than that."

"*I* have to ask."

"Aia . . . well." Him being newbie, she forgave him his uncertainty as to her reactions. But after what they'd lived through, did he honestly expect her to take offense over a common sense question that wasn't personal? "Just ask."

"Then what is First Settler? A political party?"

"Naia. Settlers are the folks that can vote on the Terms. And it burns up Governor Wally's hide that he can't vote on his own Liberalization Act."

"He's Governor. It's his legislation. Why can't he vote on it?"

"Because he ain't a Settler."

"Which is?" Raschad's eyebrows rode up beneath his netting.

"The first wave of people onto this planet were the *first* settlers." Sal breathed deep. "They drew up the Terms and established the government, making it so everyone that come after them could vote in local elections for, against, on, or about everything *except* the Terms of Settlement. To vote on that, you have to be a landholder descended of a First Settler with proof of your bloodline.

"Morrie's ma gave him rights. And my ma got hers from Granna. Some people claim their rights through the male side, but that's chancier. You have to depend on the woman's word as to who's pa, and that can be challenged."

"So Liberals can't vote?"

"Aia, they can, in local elections, like I just said, *if* they're landholders. And a First Settler could also be a Liber. But no Settler would admit it."

"I've heard you talk about voting. But you live in Morrie's shack." It was late for him to be polite instead of asking her direct, but she liked it.

"I own Ma's land, out in the scrub where our cabin stood. I'm a landholder and a First Settler on both sides and can vote any time. Just me alone, though, don't count much compared to, say, Ma Jinkman, who's poorer than a gigi, but packs a wallop with all the votes of all the kids she's raised. And they won't fool her with this Liber Act."

"I don't understand what's so wrong with it. Why were the rockies calling me a Liber last night?"

"I didn't figure you'd remember that."

"I remember it all—sort of." He blinked, fatigue showing. "I assume the rockies weren't being complimentary."

"Not hardly. Governor Wally and his Libers are moas in the grass. Which is what's wrong with their shrikin' Liberalization Act." Talking about politics always riled her. "The Lib Act . . ." She toned down. "Wally says it don't change a thing in the Terms. I say he's carrying around a stinking dead fleepa. Once he makes a way to change the Terms, then he'll find a way to get the changes done—pass laws that will let him tear up Settler-established wilderness, allow more mining than the amount set by the Terms, bring in more tech than what's allowed now. He's already saying more tech will make living *easier*, never mind the cost to the green." That tore her gut.

"And you think he's wrong."

"If you can make everything right by handing out tech, then what did my Granna die of scabby fever for? How come Knobby Brax, Carlos Schwartz—" And Sonny "—and all the other greenies have died out here without no govie giving a never-you-mind? They died for the green, that's what. So the green stays *green*. But all Governor Wally and the other Liberalizers see is that if they can open up more jungle to tech development, they can move more of the city poor away from under their noses. Get folks like the Runners out of sight, and the Libers don't care if the sherks live or die."

"Aia." Raschad spoke low, his tone so knowing and old-sounding it spooked her.

"Wally's in love with tech." She stared at her boots—the last dry pair she owned. Mud stained their toes already and caked their soles. "And his friends are greed-sucking toads. The more tech they sell, the more money they have to buy their own tech toys and impress off-planeters with how fine and smart they are. Tikey O'hoorahan says—"

"Who?"

"The skinny woman in Dig's Den the night of the fight."

"Aia. Remember."

"She says the city govies make out like they know tech inside and out, and the rest of this planet is full of ignorant idiots because we protect what's here. Well, I don't give a piss what people think, only what I know. And I know that tearing up the green and riling the mistwalkers brings only hurt."

Too angry to talk anymore about govies, tech, or any such darkness on a fine day, she swatted a swarm of gnats. This sweet-talking newbie probably laughed at her behind his netting.

But Raschad's wrist crooked about her shoulder, sympathy in his touch, and they walked a moment in silence.

"My planet's a lump of garbage." His voice carried flat and tired beneath the chatter of fleepas and the cheeping of little yellow-feathered caicais, flycatching above the trail. "They've mined, poisoned, burned it, covered it with muck. But the Raschads owned an estate on Forest Rain. I spent summers there running wild, climbing trees, hiking, tracking deer, hunting birds just to see them. Then Axial abandoned me, and I lost that."

He rocked his head back, staring upward. She did the same,

looking up and up through tier after tier of growth—low ferns, air ferns, strangler ivy and drape leaves, black-striped yellow fungus warts bigger around than her head, young trees, low trees, trees that grew so tall all she saw of them from the jungle floor were vine-wrapped trunks.

"You're right. Don't ever lose this." He hugged her.

And she wondered again why she'd survived that night on the sleds with Aireils in a killing mood. What about this man drew them? What did he see in the green? At McDonnel's he hadn't even been able to look up that zassa. Now he stared and stared.

"You understand the jungle better than any newbie I've heard of." She kneaded the small of his back below his harness.

"I've had training. For the Academy survival course they took us to Brox Alpine and threw us into the jungle in flight suits. We were given only what we'd have on us if our fighter crash-landed on a planet. I almost failed that section."

"You? You couldn't figure out how to survive in the wild?"

"I survived. Didn't want to go back. I reached base camp next to last."

"Who was last?"

"The dead kid."

"Aia." She should have known.

"Go ahead," he said, as if reading her mind.

"You're spooky, newbie."

"Hardly. You're chewing your lip as if you have ninety questions to ask."

"A hundred." She let up on the lip. "How come you didn't want to go back to Academy? Me, I'd stay in any jungle anywhere, anytime, rather than live locked up in a tech box like the govies' skids. But you wanted into a starship and into space." Just the thought of that quivered her gut; it was so strange, so lonely.

"I didn't get along with the other cadets."

"They couldn't have been scarier than the jungle."

"Naia. Just worse." He'd told her to ask, but wasn't answering. She let it go—she was that smart, anyway.

"Look at that." She pointed at a big golden plumebrush as it landed in the feathery crown of a half-grown noddy tree. The bird fanned its great purple crest, tripling the size of its head, and whistled a high trill. The call tugged at her heart and brought a smile to Raschad's face. He kissed her. It was best that they'd fallen behind the sleds.

* * *

After hearing out the fat man's messengers, Toad Hall was primed and waiting for them. Old Marty Vinra, gray-haired and littler than a mite, met them at the Toad Tunnel's mouth and led them into the Hall proper. Strangers nodded greeting, and friends called out to Sal—a blessed better reception than the one at D'arnith's, but it made her nervous.

"Don't mind." Marty squeezed her hand. "C'mon."

The dining room crowd gave way before the little lady. The Vinras were an old family, real First Settlers. Marty had married the last son and inherited the Hall, but lost the husband before bearing children. Now she was turning white, and people worried what would become of the Hall when she passed on. But striding after the leathery old woman, Sal figured such worries came years too early. Marty wasn't thinking on dying soon. Don Vinra had known what he did when he married this woman. If he'd lived longer, they'd have built a dynasty up out of the old blood.

Marty ducked through a curtained opening into a lantern-lit tunnel. It stretched long and straight to a curve so distant that the sight bothered Sal's balance.

"They say you're bringin' me a miracle, gal."

"That's not precisely true." Sal glanced back. Raschad rolled his eyes, saying people had lost their minds. Last night it had seemed the other way around. "Just a cussed tough newbie."

Marty spoke to Raschad. "Scugs says you stopped a mistwalker rampage."

"Naia, Mas Vinra. I distracted a few from other business, but didn't stop them or have any choice about what happened."

"Well, Scugs can tell a good story, especially when it attracts business. Just never you mind." Marty patted Sal's arm. "People will say what they want. I chose you a nice private room. Everyone is wantin' to lay eyes on this man." Marty smiled at Raschad. "They ain't gonna be disappointed. Certainly not the women."

Cheeks burning, Sal stared at her boots. She didn't know what she expected people to think, but hated folks gossiping over her private life. Marty reached up and chunked her shoulder.

"Don't take it so hard. People'll fuss, then forget you till the rains come and they're bored."

"I can't wait to hear what they'll say next spring."

"Oh, child." Marty laughed, teeth flashing. "Folks in this jungle's waited years for you to pick a man. Then you bring them him. What you expect?"

Marty laughed and hooked Raschad's arm. "Son." She stared up his long frame. "This be Toad Hall, discovered the year of this planet 64. The old hopper still lived in here then, the last of his kind. There's drawings of him in the big hall, and he stood taller than most men. So the corridors all accommodate me jest fine."

"I appreciate his architecture." Raschad spoke fine and proper to Marty—making no pretense at greenie talk—and patted his head, for once a good length from the ceiling.

Marty chuckled, warming to her subject, warming to the honest interest in Raschad's eyes. Sal smiled, too. Settlers knew, he was a charmer.

"The walls are coated with the cemented excretions of the toad's hide built up over two, three hundred years. Feel it." Marty slowed while Raschad obeyed. "Smooth as the inside of a scriar's ear. You'll like your room."

Raschad smiled, and his eyes met Sal's. She knew what was on his mind; she felt it herself. The man drove her to distraction.

"Sal," he whispered in the dead middle of the night.

"Aia?" she croaked, sleep groggy.

"Why don't we just stay here."

She stretched, relishing the cool, dry sheets and the quiet of the Hall. "It'd be smart. Marty'd keep *you*."

His lips brushed her face. "I don't want Marty."

"You want me?" She rolled over, snuggling into his chest.

"Forgive me, I do."

"You say it like it's a sin."

"For me, it is."

"Because I'm green?"

"Because I'm squat."

She hugged him. His arms tightened about her in return until she thought her spine would snap. The fool idiot, thinking to protect *her* when nine-tenths of this planet would as soon see him dead. But then, he was right. Just their being together—greenie and newbie—was cause enough for some to kill him.

"Sal?"

"Aia, what now?"

"You're right. Don't depend on tech, most of all not on green tech."

"You're wandering on me again, babe."

"Just . . ." His breath puffed against the soft skin of her neck. "Just don't. Things always betray you."

They left Toad Hall in the dark, abandoning its fine, bugless beds with deep regret. Scugs's bullybys headed for D'arnith's with supplies bought off Marty, and two of Marty's men pulled with her and Raschad. At Tumble Town they'd borrow her extra sled and buy supplies to replace what Marty had sold Scugs at a profit. Marty wasn't worried about an Aireil siege and didn't care to earn too much off people's foolishness. Still, with the trails open again, she'd need supplies. The Hall would be full until the monsoons hit.

Better fed and rested than he'd been since Tumble Town, Raschad moved easier this morning. Striding between his sled's steering bars, he leaned into the brake strap, helping Marty's man slow on the downslope. Marty's other bully pulled with Sal.

"I won't dock your pay for riding, Raschad," she yelled around her load.

"You won't have pay for me if we aren't back on time."

"You won't need it if you're dead. Take a break."

"I am, thank you, all the way to the bottom of this hill."

They spent the night at Vicksburg. Marty's men stayed with them in the morning, and they made Pasquel's with the sun still lighting the sky. The thought of pulling into night set Sal's nerves on edge. But the trail here was civilized, and Tumble Town was just up the hill now. She whistled back to Raschad, and he answered with that fluty double note that meant he was still strong. Hoping he didn't lie, she kept going.

Dark fell. The bugs went wild, but not a vole or a gigi stirred. Only a couple of seegs and a piny tarcat sang in the distance. After a break, Raschad ducked into the traces behind her, helping to pull, and they moved like nothing could stop them. Tumble Town looked wondrous good as they topped Border Hill and rolled toward its lights.

Dockers greeted them in the dark at the depot, grumbling and moaning. Sal weighed and recorded in her deliveries, picked up her pay for the Pike pull, loaded on the Plateau cargo—her next contract—and they were gone before day shift and Scollarta even thought of rising. It felt good.

She and Raschad pulled up to Morrie's with two partial moons lighting the porch, everything still and peaceful. But angling her loaded sled alongside the shack, she scraped a tread.

The old man stormed outside, a sleep net draped over his head and his shotgun poking out the front as if his sex life were suddenly dramatic.

"Sal?" his growl was shaky and sleep-slurred.

"Aia, Morrie."

"You look like monsters in this light."

"Just me and the newbie." She kept her voice low. "We'd appreciate something to drink."

"Shrike, gal." He disappeared into the dark shack.

She slipped her traces and dumped her pack on the porch. Inside, Morrie pumped his reeki oil lantern—*his* hard tech luxury. Flame flared so bright she thought he'd lit the table, but he got it under control and hung the lamp on its hook.

"Close one." Raschad spoke in her ear, and they both chuckled as she secured the load.

Marty's men had taken her empty sled already; she didn't need it for the Plateau haul. The route only moved light trade goods between the shacks and settlements along the Climbing Trail, while bigger contractors than her moved the major supplies. So this run was a single. It felt strange to think of leaving without Raschad. They'd only been gone twelve days, but it seemed like forever.

Morrie's eyes ran all over them as they came into the light. Sal helped Raschad with his pack, took his tool belt and holster off him, and eased his big Morven onto a peg. He was done in again, and she felt like lead herself. Marty's boys had dropped off at the Sundowner, but wouldn't enjoy the divies much tonight.

"Here all right?" Raschad sagged onto Morrie's cot.

"Aia." She sat beside him and leaned into the crook of his arm. She expected a smart comment from Morrie, but got none.

"Hungry?"

"You crazed, Morrie?" Raschad's words slurred.

She laughed, crazed herself with the relief of being in this wreck of a shack again.

"I'll cook all I got." The old man set to work.

Watching him, Sal ached, too tired to do more than think on how strange a homecoming it was, how things looked different, as if something had wiped the haze of familiarity from everything. Raschad was part of that, sitting so big and comforting at her side. But it was more. The Aireils had touched her, too, that long, long day waiting in the deep of the green to die.

Chapter 16

"Hissssh!" She stared into liquid midas eyes. The arm-length lizards blinked back. Morrie'd adopted three of Boojie's pups. "Naia." She laid an arm in front of her plate. The triplets blinked, waiting for a lapse in her vigilance. She snarled, but none of them budged. "You're right. They're a fine lot. About as bright as this stump I'm sitting on."

"Ain't got to be bright, just fast. You look around." Morrie sipped his tea. "It's high summer, nighttime and all, and you can walk the floors barefoot."

"If you don't mind stepping in lizard squat."

"Better'n stepping on the baby moa Lil' Jig de-scovered yesterday."

She raised an eyebrow in spite of exhaustion. "He didn't *de-scover* it in here, did he?"

"Where the hell else?"

"Squat, Morrie! You search the place?"

"I don't search for 'em. Don't wanta find no *moas*."

She pushed her empty plate away with a shiver. The little midases lunged for it as one, licking up missed crumbs. She watched them, too tired even to worry about venom-spitting snakes.

"Morrie. Nuke Jagger and his partner Haze were due in here yesterday. They make?" Morrie nodded, and she breathed out slow.

"What they said . . ." Morrie sucked his bottom lip until his chin half disappeared. "It true?"

"I reckon." Sal levered her body up and limped for her hammock. "You keep people back from here."

"Sal." Morrie's voice shook. "I didn't mean to bring any o' this on you. Just figured you was bored."

"Bored." She tugged the netting open over her hammock. "I'll

215

cuss you tomorrow. For now, I got the Plateau load on the sled already. So keep a mind to it."

Raschad stirred in his sleep, and Morrie glanced toward the cot as if seeing a ghost. "You want, I'll sleep on the sled."

"Naia. No one knows it's here—should be safe until light."

"Get some sleep, then." He still stared at Raschad. "You both looks like sticks."

She curled into the hammock, her mind running circles. If she'd thought straight and picked the Pike load up early, even if she parked it afterward, she would've saved herself trouble with Scollarta. Someone owed her yet for that chair leg to her head.

Sal didn't surface until noon, to find that Morrie had gotten food somewhere and was cooking with rare goodwill. She watched him, feeling lazy, hating the way he moved so careful, kept the pots from banging, tasted the food with a spoon instead of his finger. It wasn't like him. She hated it, wanted normal things—nasty looks, lewd laughs, and no sympathy. She wanted him picking her pocket and waiting for her to cook. But he'd even washed his face.

She stretched and sat up. Every muscle in her body protested, and she grunted as she straightened. Morrie brought her a mug of tea and went back to cooking. She nearly threw the cup at the old fool, but was too thirsty.

Sipping, she turned up a foot and examined yesterday's damage. After all they'd been through, four blisters, a black toenail, and a little rot didn't matter much.

Raschad stirred on the cot, flung an arm out beneath his netting and settled again. Sal rose barefooted, checking every step, watching for bugs and worse. But Morrie was right about the lizards. She crossed the shack without a single multilegged or no-legged encounter and peered at the newbie.

He was deep out, looked a wreck this morning, and smelled worse. Sniffing herself, she decided it wasn't all him.

"I need a bath." Keeping her voice low, she limped for the back door. "The barrel full?"

"Can use the new shower if you want," Morrie said. "I fixed a stall so's the neighbors won't peek."

She tucked her head back. "You sick?"

"Can't rightly say." He looked disgusted. "I took it in my head, having heard Haze's yapping, to do something besides drink. So I built a shower. I'll try to re-cover soon's I can."

"Don't rush." Sal grabbed her towel from the hook next the stove. "Ain't no hurry so long as the ab-ber-a-tion's useful."

"That Raschad's infected you with big words."

"Blame him, but I heard it at the Toad." She went out.

Morrie's stall wasn't much. He hated woodworking, and worm holes pocked its sides; unless she wanted him jabbering about her privates with his drunken buddies, she'd best not let him within yelling distance. But the shower's frame was solid enough to support her towel, and that blocked most of the peepholes. The bug netting that hung about the stall covered the rest.

Above her head, a hole-pierced gourd hung from a leaky stave-and-vine barrel. Stripping, Sal opened a spigot. The gourd gurgled, and sun-warmed water dribbled over her head. Morrie could have done worse. Lathering her hair, eyes clamped shut, she ducked her head, hunting a decent trickle to rinse off in.

Creak.

Her heart lurched. She elbowed back, and hit solid muscle.

"Scut, Sal."

"Raschad!"

He laughed, breathless, but not hurt.

"Get me water!" Soap burned her eyes.

"I'm trying. You need a larger barrel up top. There's not enough pressure."

"Amazin' news."

His arm brushed her shoulder. The barrel spigot creaked, and water splattered over her head. She turned her face into the miserly flow and came up blowing spray.

"You'll get killed sneaking around."

"Sorry. Thought you heard me," he said.

"If I'd heard you, I'd have figured it was Morrie and shot your dinger off."

He laughed again, warming her right through. And his eyes played over her, teasing her past warm. Balanced on the scrub pallet, she helped him strip off his water-splattered clothes. Bugs swarmed the outside of the shower netting, and their arrangement was neither safe nor comfortable. But scrubbing his fine body, Sal forgot practicality.

Morrie *did* give them a wise look when they came in this time. But then his eyes settled on Raschad's naked face, and the look faded. If Sal had known two scars would shut the old man up, she'd have cut herself long ago.

"Morrie." Raschad swung his leg over a log seat. "You look uncommon clean this morning."

"Didn't want you to get i-dee-ers." Morrie grimaced.

They all laughed, and the last bit of tension went out of Sal, out of the whole arrangement.

Dancer arrived and doctored Raschad's hands. Afterward, Morrie served up lunch, dumping most of the food on the newbie's plate. Raschad ate everything down past the scraps.

"I think I'd best dig roots," Morrie grouched, watching Raschad. "You'll gnaw the sides off the shack next."

"Aren't there vi-grubs in there?" Raschad gave Morrie a funny look, teasing, Sal knew, but Morrie didn't. Morrie's face blanked, then colored.

"Shee-rike." He grabbed up dirty dishes. "You two can just cook for yourselfs. Damned if I care if you eat worms." He stalked away, which meant, she thought, that Raschad had reached the old man. Dancer smiled. Morrie liked the newbie.

So the day began well enough. Raschad went to sit on the front porch, hands across his chest, guarding her loaded sled while Morrie washed dishes and she cleaned their gear. Now and then she heard a bug slap, but mostly the critters left Raschad alone. Readying to pull out in the morning, she did, too, and felt hollow every time she thought of leaving.

Steady, she told herself. Can't let a man hobble you.

Morrie went rooting, and returned grumpy, reeki-tarred and vine-scratched. Sal finished cleaning, patching, and oiling her leather gear while Raschad sat at the table again, erasing the evidence of Morrie's gathering. The chink of knife against plate was a quiet, comfortable accompaniment to her work, and she thought she'd best claim some roots herself before there was nothing left. But a midas squealed, and she looked uphill to see one of the tag boys from the depot jogging down.

"Haia, Ziggy." She kept her greeting casual, but her gut knotted. Had Scollarta found something in her contract to call exception to her current load?

"Got a message, Banks."

"Aia?"

"Fer that newbie. Fer M. Raschad."

That didn't help her nerves. What did depot want with Raschad? "He's in with Morrie. Go give it." She gave a lazy wave, every muscle prickling. The boy started for the door, but Raschad stepped out.

"S-S-Sir." Ziggy shoved a tech-sealed packet at the big newbie. "From th-the Supervisor."

Locked on Raschad, Ziggy's eyes were as big as a howlers, as if standing in the man's presence was sacrilege. What kind of tales had the kid heard?

"Thank you, son." Raschad fumbled the packet into his bandaged hands. Ziggy stood staring up at the newbie's naked face, his throat working as if strangling. "You need a reply?"

Raschad gave Sal a nervous glance. She shook her head; she wouldn't intervene between boy and hero.

"K-K-Kin I t-touch it, m-m-mas?"

Raschad blinked. "Sal?"

"Let him." She shrugged.

Raschad shrugged back—his expression saying *greenies are crazy*—and knelt, tilting his head so Ziggy could run a shaky finger down each of the fresh scars on his golden cheek.

"Thanks, m-m-mas."

Ziggy scooted off the porch, and a snort sounded from the window as Morrie moved away. Raschad curled his legs under him and sat on the porch's splintery planks.

"Nervous kid."

"Aia," Sal agreed. "But I reckon you made him the bravest soul in this whole mudballer town just now."

Raschad shook his head, amused. "Will you open this, please?" He let the message packet fall into his lap.

She squatted in front of him, staring at the packet's position against his fly. "Which one?"

He wrinkled his nose. "I want to read the message."

"Idiot."

Opening the packet, she unfolded the enclosed card and held it facing him, not bothering to try reading it upside down. Raschad's eyes shifted.

"There's a comm for me at Government House."

"You weren't expecting one now."

"Naia." His shoulders sagged.

"Don't have to go after it."

"Of course I do."

Idiot again. Herself, unless there was a law against it, she'd let that comm lie. It was bad luck. She knew it, but only nodded, frowning her disagreement.

"Don't worry." His tone softened. "My problems. I won't let them touch you."

"Don't be an ass." Sal spun up and grabbed the harness she'd been mending.

He stared as if trying to decide what he'd said *most* wrong, then stood and walked off without hat, gun, or anything. Sal watched him move up the sunbaked street. Stupid newbie. He didn't belong going to Government House today.

"Morrie!"

Like bloody fingers, sunset-stained tree fronds scraped the windowpanes of Rimmersin's study. Raschad fought nausea. When he looked back, the comm shook in his hands. Words blurred and the room went darker still.

"My condolences. Some wine?"

Raschad shook his head and fought down an urge to kill Rimmersin. But for once the man didn't push, just showed him to the door—the kindest thing the freak had ever done for him.

Outside, he stood in the house's dusk-shadowed garden and still wanted to kill—kill something, hit something. But that would only draw more attention to him, give them an excuse.

What a fool to decide now to start feeling again. Damn you, Sal. What now?

Nightbabies flapped overhead, their ropy bodies dotting the sunset. Raschad walked the outer rim of the hill, past Slackets' Garage. The nightbabies swooped on swarming bugs, wings and bodies snapping in air. Their pathetic wails pierced the wind, and he raised his hands above his head, wondering if he could entice the creatures to stoop on them, if tiny stiletto teeth would tear his wrists open. Or would the flying snakes attack with their dagger-long brood claws—lengths of bone that retracted into leathery sheaths during flight, but slipped out again to cradle their young at roost?

His arms fell limp at his sides. Despite razor talons and fierce, whip-snapping bodies, the nightbabies were meek little creatures, not snakes at all, but egg-laying mammals. Scales ruddied by sunset, the mewling insectivores spiraled like red ribbons over the cliff edge.

He imagined that long clean plunge into oblivion. People made that mistake in the dark, he'd heard—walked over the rim. He angled nearer the edge, fighting its tug . . .

The street wound downhill, and he left the cliff behind.

At the Gigi's Eye, he strode into glare and stink and bought a bottle. The greenies kept their distance, disappointing him. A few were even friendly. He stayed anyway, not wanting to take this trouble back to Sal. And smoke and heat and all, the Gigi was at least better than the dark and the beckoning nightbabies.

His gut churned as he found a corner to sit in. Gods. What was he going to do? It had started again. That woman . . . Who did she work for? Who hunted him now?

A complimentary bottle appeared. The damn greenies were making some idiotic legend out of him, damn if he cared.

Something stirred in the dark off the front porch.

"Morrie? I been waiting." Which was stupid of her to say, since he knew that, and she could smell brew on him.

"Don't start. You wanted him found. I found'im."

"Where?" She shifted the holster beneath her arm.

"George has him."

"I'll go get him."

"George won't give him to you. That newbie done broke the eye out of the Gigi's front window. And other eyes will take healin' before they sees right again. The man done wreaked havoc. He's a mean drunk. Let him sit."

"Shrike." She stumped the length of the porch. She'd known Raschad had no business going to Government House. "I've got to see."

She swung down and headed uphill. Dry weather and nervous energy made it an easy walk. The first side trail took her past Dancer's little house of ironwood shingles and lebob palm thatch, and then, braving brush, she came out at George's back door.

The house stood dark. She hiked around to the front of the rammed-earth jail that sat next door. Music and hollering floated up from the bars at the foot of George's alley, but it was quiet here. Raschad couldn't be so drunk that George wouldn't give him to her. But she felt awkward as ice in sunlight to have to call on George, of all people, looking for her drunk newbie lover.

The jail office sat empty. She let herself in the plank door and stood, blinking, trying to frame in her mind what she should say. Then the cell-block door cracked open, and a stomach-turning thump sounded beyond it.

"Here, now." George's growl faded back into the cells.

Standing in yellow lantern light, she felt like an eavesdropper. The stench of previously used liquor floated through the half-open door, gagging her, and someone inside groaned. Someone else cursed. George had a full house. Suddenly, she didn't want to be here or see Raschad senseless drunk, as disgusting as Morrie coming off a binge. She turned.

"Sal?"

She forced herself to face around again. George closed the door to the cells and leaned on it. She heard the lock fall into place and knew from the look on his face that she should have kept on going out the door.

"You all right?" She didn't know why that question came out first of all the ones in her mind.

But the way he looked it was natural enough, and from his expression, she couldn't have said anything better. He sighed, caught a towel off a hook and wiped his hands. Blood stained his shirt, and one cheek looked dark and puffy.

"I'm fine." He sounded tired. "Naia thanks to Meesha Raschad."

She flinched, but let that slide. "Morrie said you had him."

"I'm keeping him, too." She didn't know what her face did at that, but George softened. "At least until morning. You don't want him before then."

"You know I've handled drunks before."

"Aia." He poured water into a crockery washbasin. "But you ain't handled drunks like him. This wasn't one of Morrie's happy times. Your man was drinking like there was no dawn, and I figure that's what he wanted. That was him just now, beating his head against the wall. Don't know why I stopped him—it's the most useful thing he's done all night."

Sal tried to force George's words to make sense with her memory of a man pulling behind her, a man who never made mistakes or a single uncalculated move. "Ain't like him," she said. "He got some comm tonight up to Government House. I knew it was bad news. He thought he had to go get it."

George turned, staring at his feet instead of her. "I read it." He sounded even more embarrassed than she was at the moment. "His sister died."

Lantern light flickered. Her feet seemed a long way off. The door stood open, but Sal didn't remember opening it.

"Reckon I'll call back in the morning."

"I'll keep him safe as I can."

George looked sad and old, which only made her feel worse. This was none of his doing. He was a good man, and every dirty thing that happened was dumped at his door.

Bugs, sweat, and nightmare—gigis, damned gigis—filled her night. Finally she gave up on sleep and had her gear ready and packed before dawn. Morrie rose quiet and fixed her breakfast, which only put her more on edge; he was still treating her differently.

She helped with the dishes, killing time, and finally went back to George's at first light. Could have gone after him right off last night, she thought, slogging through the brush, and none of this would have happened. But she'd worried what other people would think. Too late now, maybe too late then. Her story: always too late and useless. And there was no more time for waiting on him.

Early as it was, George had Raschad awake and out on the back porch of the house and was dumping rainwater over him—clothes, boots, and all. From the smell of things, Sal figured it a blessing that she hadn't arrived earlier.

Raschad didn't look too fine this morning—he had looked better after the Aireils finished with him. At least they hadn't *meant* to hurt him. But she reckoned George was right—Raschad had been out to kill himself last night. There was always that in him, when she thought on it honestly. He did things maybe a saner soul would avoid. A man who worried about living wouldn't have tested Scugs's temper or set off the explosion that freed Nuke and Haze.

She didn't say anything right off, just stared at the big newbie. When he finally looked up, he blinked and cringed as if the dim glow in the sky was still too much to face.

"I got to pull out." She spoke low, and George moved off. "You can come with me if you want."

She had no sympathy for drunks and weaklings—which amounted to the same thing. And she didn't need any man rotting her life, wasn't about to die like Ma. But this was Raschad, and she couldn't forget what they'd lived through, his gentle touch or the look in his eyes when the Aireils brought him back.

He ran a trembling hand through dripping hair. "I best go dig more crystals. I still have family waiting on me."

She wanted to scream at the worthless weight of them dragging him down into their hell because they were too weak to take care of themselves. But it was his brother left now, just a boy, and his mother, who couldn't be young. Sal reckoned she wouldn't walk away from that if she had any family left.

Maybe that was why Pa chose his way, got into the knife fight over to Pasquel's Clearing that done him. He missed Ma more than he'd admit. And the night before he left for Pasquel's, he sat her down and stared long into her fourteen-year-old eyes. *Do better without me,* he'd said clear. Then he'd kissed her cheek, which he never did, and that was the last they spoke. She'd never decided if he planned on dying. But maybe he didn't want her hanging onto an old drunk, didn't want to kill her like he had Ma.

She ended up with an old drunk anyway. But Morrie wouldn't

kill her in some liquor rage, which perhaps Pa would have. And perhaps Raschad might. Maybe it *was* time for good-byes. When you started wanting to keep a man, it was past time for parting, especially when he didn't want to stay.

"All your stuff's at Morrie's." She stared above his head. "Your pay with it." He glanced up, then wrapped an arm over his head and slumped against the porch post. "You go back, let the old man and Dancer take care of you, *heal* before you go tramping again." A towel sailed out George's back door. She snagged it, wrapped it around Raschad's shoulders. "Rest. Hear?"

"I'm sorry." He met her eyes, finally. "I warned you. But I'm sorry."

"Aia," she whispered. "I know." Tears tugged at the back of her throat, and a trickle started in her nose. She bit down hard. No blessed time for that squat. "You take care." She brushed his hair back. "Ain't never had a better partner."

His eyes shut. His face twisted up tight, but she figured that was just the hangover making itself felt.

She squeezed his shoulder, then stood up fast and left. The man wanted to be gone, and didn't figure on seeing her ugly green hide again. Lots of pulling ahead, anyway.

The porch creaked. Raschad didn't look up, but couldn't have seen anything anyway.

"She's a good woman." George's voice was taut. "Deserves better than you." Raschad knew that. "I tried to marry her once. But she wouldn't quit packing. I couldn't quit sheriffing. I been married twice—both died on me young. I didn't figure Sal would do that. She's too cussed tough."

Raschad shivered. How did you lose a woman, let alone two, and still dare to love another?

"Of all of them," George said quietly, "maybe I've wanted her most. But that ain't going to happen. We both know that, though I don't expect she understands why I can't just be friends and content. Still, I won't ever let anything bad happen to her that I can stop. Because I do understand why she can't settle down—at least part of it. I don't reckon she's mentioned her aunt's family, her cousins to you."

"No—naia." Raschad held his head. "She said her only family was her mother and father, a baby sister that died."

"She never had a sister," George said. Sal lied to him? Raschad felt as if he were losing his mind. "She did have an aunt and uncle that loved her like their own, of which they had four—three girls and a boy.

"About the time Sal was eight, and I still just the deputy, not sheriff yet, she was visiting her aunt's. The place was way out east of town, out where everyone told them not to build. But they were doing good there.

"It looked to me later as if Sal was playing in this root cellar her uncle'd dug into an outcrop of calfstone. She'd set up a proper little playhouse inside. Maybe she'd run the younger ones out of it so she could get it just right.

"Maybe . . ." George stomped a roacher on the edge of the board porch. It's black back cracked, and orange innards squirted. "Anyways, this pack of gigis come through, not a real ganger, just a pack hunting some fun. Tore the little girls all to shreds, gutted the aunt and uncle. Sal drug the boy into the cave with her. She was tore up, and the boy died before her ma come looking to bring her home. Sal never once afterward said a thing about what happened—never mentioned her cousins again.

"The *baby sister* that died is them. That's as close as she can admit to what happened. I think she knows, but she won't say so. And gigis spook her crazy. Nuke Jagger says she about killed you all running from them out at the Ebbid junction."

Raschad shuddered, remembering that run. George couldn't begin to imagine . . . If Sal was panicked then, she and Aunt Meesha would have liked each other.

"Well, there's more to her shying away from me than that, I reckon. But you see, she can't bear sitting still in this town, waiting for gigis to strike again. And then about three years ago, before her pack contracts filled in, she short-hired with a little fella name of Sonny Doobay. Gigis cornered them on trail. He died. She blames herself for that. So she keeps moving and tempting fate, running right up against the gigis all the time, never admitting she's scared."

"She's not scared of nearly enough things." Raschad hugged his gut. "She's not scared of me."

George nodded. "You ain't wrong. But that's part of it, too. Knowing inside how scared she is, she has to prove herself all the time. Which is maybe one reason she came to you. Say *don't* to Sal, and she *has* to do it—even if it's herself saying *don't*. And I reckon that all you two lived through together was just like one big *don't* to her." George twisted a towel in his powerful, square hands. "Those things they're saying about you in the bars can't be true."

"Maybe a tenth." Raschad held his head, his toes aching, teeth, hair . . . Everything hurt.

"Reckon that's still more than anyone should have to live through."

Raschad hugged his gut and rocked. What could he say? Nothing that would begin to explain anything to this jungle-bound greenie who had spent his whole life dragging idiots out of trouble. How did he explain that waiting for his comm in Rimmersin's study last night, he'd heard a familiar voice, peeked into the hall, and been scared to the bone by a face?

The porch creaked again. George folded down and sat next to him. Raschad's breath escaped between clenched teeth.

"Anyway . . ." George spoke with maddening nonchalance. "I won't ever let anything bad happen to her that I can help. And I figure you're something I should've stopped sooner."

Raschad swallowed against a churning stomach. "You're wrong." He breathed slowly, head settling. "I'm something *I* should have stopped sooner."

Much, much sooner. He'd seen that greenie woman in Government House's foyer last night, seen her clearly even in the dim light—the same face he'd seen at a card table with Morrie and again at the docks the day Scollarta had tried to steal Sal's load.

He was being watched. And as long as he was with Sal, *she'd* be watched. He'd sensed it that day with Scollarta, and had been as eager as Sal to leave Tumble Town. Now Sarel was dead. Byebye, big sister. And he was dead-dumb scared.

If he gave them cause, let Sal get near, they—whoever *they* were—would kill her. What else they might be about, he hardly cared, except that those Runners at the junction hadn't invaded this jungle on their own initiative, not with spacer contacts.

"As long as you're taking responsibility for this mess—" George spit in the mud. "—reckon you won't blame me for saying I don't like newbies in general. And I particularly don't like you. You're a screwed-up somabitch taking your trouble out on everything you touch. That was fine so long as you didn't touch anything important. But now you can't blame me for objecting."

"Naia." Red blasted his vision. His head throbbed.

"And you won't blame me for telling her exactly when you'll have to be back in town to pick up your next comm."

"You told her that?" He turned sun-dazzled eyes on George.

"Not yet, but she'll ask, and I'll answer."

"You will . . ."

"Aia. Just now she figures there's no having you. But later, she'll decide she gave up too easy, and she'll come hunting you with a vengeance, and nothing will stop her, least of all me."

Raschad braced an elbow on one knee and rested his spinning head against the palm of his hand. "What are you saying?"

"Don't hurt her anymore."

"How?" He swatted at a fly that had already bitten him half a dozen times, and missed. "I don't run my life."

"Past time you started."

"Staying alive." He blinked at George. "I do it just to spite them. But I'm tired, and there is nothing good for me to give her. Other responsibilities come first. And I'm watched. I don't want Rimmersin noticing her or her wasting time on me."

"Then you figure a solution." George reached between Raschad's shaking arms, and the newbie arched back. But George just wiped his nose with the clean towel he'd been twisting. "You figure it out, newbie, because, I swear, if you hurt her anymore, all your precious responsibilities will suffer—and your hide, too."

Sun burned the back of Raschad's neck. His stomach quivered; his head pulsed. George was serious. As silly, ignorant, and confused as it was, George meant for him to make peace with Sal.

Chapter 17

The trail slipped past beneath her sled, her mind and heart churning with her treads. Everytime she turned around, she half expected to see Raschad pulling at her back. She woke each morning with a keen sense of his absence, the lack of his gentle touch. She missed his smiles, his pretty eyes, his voice, the scent of him. She missed the damn man. No matter she didn't need him, that he was trouble by-the-weight. She wanted him.

First she called herself a thousand kinds of fool for leaving him on George's porch, too sick of body and heart to fight her. Next, she cursed him for letting her walk away—worse yet, for *wanting* her to walk away. That was the hard truth: that he wanted her out of his life, one big complication erased.

When she felt charitable, she didn't blame him. When she turned lonely, she hated him. But then gigis barked, and she was glad to have no one but herself to worry about. Later began the harder questions. Had Raschad ever wanted her? Had she just been convenient? How could he want an ignorant greenie when he was so fine and golden, so tech-smart, with his perfect speech, and eyes that had seen things she couldn't begin to imagine?

But she knew her own worth, and relished her muscled body, the intelligence and skill that kept her alive where living was a chancy thing. And recalling what it was like constantly worrying over the newbie, weighted by his needs, she savored her solitary freedom, the jungle's squawk and howl, wind through the trees, even the shrieking whine of insects. She'd lived all her years in the green and would be damned if she changed or thought less of herself now just for a man.

In a haze of inward thought, she covered the long curve of the Plateau Trail, traveling parallel to the Pike, dropping small goods and mail at the single shacks and tiny settlements that lined that

228

prosperous side of the jungle. But as she reached the Forks, the trail climbed enough to keep her mind occupied with problems other than Raschad. She spent a quiet night camped outside Twoteeth's Trading Post and took the cutoff to D'arnith's Wood in the morning.

Scugs was glad of the mail and supplies she brought, but watched her close until finally she told him plain that the newbie had other business and was about it. She didn't know why that should concern the innkeeper, but Scugs didn't take it well. As if she was to blame for something here, she thought sourly, half-suspicious Scugs was right.

Her mind chewed guilt all the way up the long, lonesome grade to Tent Camp, Moon Base, and Zoolyte, and on into the high country. She reached lofty Macao worn-out by thinking and bored with the whole damn bent of her mind. Stumping into Macao's hotel, she rented a cot and enjoyed the coolest, driest night she'd had since Toad Hall. But at the Toad, she hadn't been alone.

In the morning she headed back down the long trail, hauling dried herbs and spices to be shipped into Capitol from Tumble Town, plus trade goods for delivery at all the little stops she'd visited coming up. More rested than when she began this trek, she felt good, and her blood ran high. She was ready for action, her decisions made.

She was going back and going after Raschad. No freaking yellow-pissin' newbie could gigi her off after all she'd done for him—not without better explanation than he'd given so far. The man would be back to Tumble Town, and she'd be waiting.

What she didn't understand was why George didn't fight her about hunting Raschad. He even looked as if he'd *expected* her pestering. That set her on edge again, made her feel like a kid being indulged until she smarted up. Worse, Morrie just shook his head and baked bread. That near sent her over the brink.

George wouldn't let the newbie go in and out of his town without knowing when to expect the man. So Sal trusted his information and decided there were two safe weeks before she need be in town again to catch Raschad. And two weeks would finish up the Pike run.

That settled, she did something she'd never done before—sold her soul to Tikey O'hoorahan for muscle to pull her returned sled. Tikey had a young one, just in, needing experience, and it didn't cost too much for the help. The other favor she asked, Tikey wouldn't set a price on. Since it concerned them all, Sal didn't press. Packers took care of their own—good or bad.

She waited another day, detailing the sled returned from the Toad, before picking up the late summer Pike run at the earliest possible moment. On the way to the docks, she stopped at Bwashwavie's produce stand, bought fruit, and put a word in Mama B.'s ear. No one watched better than Mama.

At the depot, Scollarta approved her papers as if she were plotting against him. But he didn't say a word or make a move of reprisal for the trouble she'd caused him with her earlier run. She figured he was being smart, and knew greenies watched him now. And if the town's packers decided to do something about his bribe-taking and load-stealing, he might take a tumble off the dock—or worse. His cheating had become dead obvious the day she and Dog Girl swapped load sheets. He'd step careful for a while.

With Tikey's big, busty youngster, Sal pulled away from the docks just two days after she'd packed back off the Plateau run. With only a day off here and there, she'd spent more than a month in the traces, and her clothes fit looser than in years.

And she did this for a man?

If she gave herself time to rest, would she come to her senses and decide he was more trouble than he was worth? But this involved pride. She had to know absolutely that Raschad didn't want *her*, specifically her, before she could let him be. Even then, unless her feelings changed, it would be hard forgetting him.

Seventeen days later she took her rest. Tikey's kid had proved even dumber than expected. They'd lost one day to a jammed tread and two more while the girl wrestled her sled from mudpot to mudpot. The last day pulling in, Sal's temper passed its limits. But seeing no use in killing the girl, she let vexation power her downtrail so fast that she lost the idiot once.

The look on the child's face when they parked at Morrie's said she'd learned plenty on this haul—like maybe packing wasn't the life she wanted after all. Sal suspected in retrospect that Tikey had calculated as much before loaning the girl out. Well, she would even up with Tikey.

Morrie shuffled out of the shack while she was still wrestling her harness clips. "Slow down," he said. "He ain't come in yet."

She kept on at her clips. "He's late."

"Not much." Morrie scratched. "Two, three days is nothing if he's mining as far out as I figure."

"If he runs into Aireils, no telling what could happen."

"Never no tellin' in the jungle."

Tikey's girl limped past, nodded to Morrie, and headed uphill without a word.

"Quiet type." Morrie snagged a buzz sucker off his arm and pinched its head. "She don't look so healthy as when you left. 'Course, I reckoned you'd be back three days ago."

"She ain't quiet, Morrie. She's breathless. Little bitch has a talent for mudpots. Thank the First Settler I didn't take her out when things was *wet*. It didn't rain on us two times total, but she just kept finding them."

"Impatience won't get you nowhere."

"It got me here only three days late, which is a miracle."

"C'mon." Morrie shook his shaggy head. "I got some half-spoilt beans I'll warm for you." Sal threw her harness and caught him square in the back of the head. "Be that way," he said calmly. "I'll dig out the real spoilt ones, see if you likes them better."

The green stretched deep and dense, and Raschad's path wound between shin-high root knees and giant orange-gill fungi. Twilight reigned even at midday, the sun blocked by layer upon layer of humidifying foliage.

His boot caught in a thorn vine and he pitched forward. His shoulder slammed a log. His rump settled in mud. A tattered feather floated through a shaft of foliage-refracted light and settled on his mud-caked knee.

Gigis barked in the distance—hunting, north and south, east and west—their cries just audible above the rush of blood in his ears, the sucking moan of his breaths.

Another feather floated down. He looked up, expecting to witness an avian dismemberment, but a mhoie sat perched in a knot of epiphytic bladderwort, shaking out argent wings and zipping ragged feather edges into precise alignment.

Raschad panted. His head pulsed pain. The bird, perched in a halo of flickering darkness, scratched its head with a five-toed foot. His spine burned dull agony, his spasmed muscles throbbed, and his neck refused to straighten.

Six days ago he'd broken camp with a gigi scout watching. He'd known then he was dead, that this was the last pack out—no more worrying about his family, Sal, or anything. He'd run all the same, and dodged gigis, backtracked, floundered lost through head-high reeki to survive both that day and night and the next—

each step confused with the one before and with his previous run for Tumble Town, fleeing Aireils.

Now reality wandered away from him into the green, and his strength followed it. The black-beaked mhoie spread a wing, stretched its ruffled neck, and groomed a big flight feather from downy base to silvery tip, curving it in a shimmering arc.

The bird glowed against constricting darkness. Raschad's lungs labored. His head slipped sideways. And gigis screeched.

If they came just now, would he feel anything? Or would he sleep right through being eaten alive?

He sensed them, but kept his lids closed, lying limp against the mossy log, his head resting on his pack. He wasn't consciously afraid; he had passed beyond simple fear. His netting was gone, lost somewhere. Something multilegged crawled on his neck. That worried him, but not enough to move.

Something else brushed his shoulder, tickled his cheek. The tickling vanished from his neck. A distinct crunch sounded. Raschad smiled, the reaction never reaching his face. If he could find snacks as easily, he wouldn't always be so hungry.

The Aireil shifted against his side, its odor overwhelming. He sucked air, fighting vertigo and nightmare. Then rough fingerpads stroked his cheek, and his head cleared, his stomach settled.

Hello, he thought.

Hello, it thought back, which didn't surprise him.

Out of numbed instinct and exhaustion's fog, he realized the Aireils had been watching him, keeping the gigis off all this time, while he, too stupid, ran from them both.

Hello. The Aireil stroked his cheek and tugged at his senses, wanting . . . What did it want?

His thoughts drifted. The mistwalker hovered. Raschad, unafraid, dreamed of stars. *Yes,* the Aireil's mind breathed, *yes and yes again.* Distant galaxies and stardust rivers rafted Raschad to sleep.

The night stretched long and strange, filled with bizarre dreams in which the Aireils huddled about him. Hands settled on his body, and a set of ropy arms scooped him against a hairy chest. The world swayed.

Dreams eddied and swirled. Sal floated in and out of focus, her shoulders bent to the harness. Her sled, dogging her heels, was first loaded with dead Runners, then buried beneath reeki vines. The sled bed malformed as she walked, melting into a writhing blob from which tendrils grew outward to snag her thighs and ankles. She didn't notice, just pulled on, stubbornly blind and ignorant of what had happened. And, like the sled, her face distorted. Her features blurred and ran, melted down, until she hung from the blobbish mass of what had been her sled, a great white nurse flower. Her mouth sucked and squeaked.

Raschad woke panting, lost in foggy confusion. His back rested against a mossy log. But the mhoie's perch was absent, and all the encroaching jungle about him appeared unfamiliar. Yet no one thing was arguably different, so he thought that perhaps the bird, like Sal and the Aireils' arms, had been only in his dreams.

Rising on quaking legs, he stumbled, but gained speed as his kinks and cramps worked out. His neck inexplicably didn't bother him this morning—a relief from agony that made other complaints minor. Needing food, water, and a long rest, he walked through glittering haze.

Gigis barked in the distance, as they had barked and harried him for the last week. But the calls were all ahead now. He could go as slow as he liked. The day wore on, and the barking grew louder—not nearer, but more voices, more than one gang calling. From the sound of it, more gangs than he wanted to imagine.

His steps slowed. Yet he followed the gigis perforce, having no other way to go but toward Tumble Town.

Stumbling, he squatted to rest. But a hand-sized kiki nut crashed at his side. He startled up.

Hello.

He sat back down and prized the nut apart with his knife, studying the thinning jungle. White roak spatters dotted the foliage. A hint of trail led between two familiar rocks. *Close,* he realized with dizzying relief. He was near the roak colony, with Tumble Town no more than half a day away.

Gigis barked ahead. The kiki dropped from his hands.

Ahead of him. Headed *into* town. The gigi barking died. His scalp prickled as the jungle fell silent.

He ran. Vines slithered beneath his boots. Limbs whipped his face. He slowed when his lungs failed, but didn't stop.

She won't be there—use sense. She'll be hauling. That was what he wanted to believe—but didn't. George had said she would hunt him, wait for him. Be wrong, George. Be wrong. But even if she wasn't there, others had been kind to him—George, Morrie, Tom Bill, who was mixed up somehow in that bar brawl. And he still owed a tab for the window at the Gigi's Eye.

Aireils appeared at his elbow between one lung-wrenching breath and the next. Maybe they had been there all along. Maybe they were invisible when they wanted.

His mind tumbled. A mistwalker caught his arm, and another blocked him from the front. He fell, up and over its shoulder, and was lifted into the trees again.

He should have panicked, but didn't, concentrating on Tumble Town memories. They in turn *wanted*. And he teased them with a single image of space's vast void, then dreamed instead of muddy streets, board buildings, and Sal.

They recognized the vision or understood it . . . or something. Chittering, they lifted him, climbed, danced between limbs, swung from cascading vines—moving faster than he ever could on the ground, flinging him bodily between them, traveling purposefully toward Tumble Town.

Sal spent her first day back on the front porch. Morrie pottered with his usual business, fixing small tech tools for people too cheap or too poor to take them up to the Slackets. Morrie didn't do a bad job of repair, but didn't have spare parts; when folks committed a tool to Morrie, they knew they'd get it back fixed the best it could be without replacing anything. The most to be hoped for was a new bit of tying wire. Still, if you were as poor as the average Tumble Towner, that was better than nothing and more than you could buy otherwise.

Sundown came late, but Raschad didn't come with it. Sal stayed where she sat, half expecting he would slip into town in the dark and tend his business before she could catch him. But the roak colony slept quiet all night, and she met dawn knowing he hadn't entered town by this route. Reaching town from the south any other way was nearly impossible.

She sat on the porch again in the morning, cleaning gear, and glancing up from a boot patch, spotted Tom Bill.

"Haia, Sal." He walked the street, balancing from one dried mud chunk to the next.

"Haia, Tom."

"You waiting on that newbie, I hear."

"This town talks too loud and too much." Sal scowled.

"I reckon." Tom Bill's lips crooked up.

"Well, as you're polite enough to state your curiosity up front, go ahead and ask why I'm waiting."

"I'm more curious about the past done." Tom Bill swung onto the porch, and she motioned him down.

"Past done. Must mean that little slick haul I took Raschad on up to Glory's Roost."

"Oha, you do that, now?" Tom looked coy.

"Aia. Needed peace from Morrie's drunks. Took a trip."

"I heard it was a mite rough for pleasure."

"It was a mite rough." She went serious, unable to keep up her end of the banter. "Shriking rough even for work."

His lips pursed, he nodded. "Heard."

She mended a harness. Tom Bill stared south at the jungle. She knew what he wanted to hear; he wouldn't leave until she explained something about her relationship with Raschad. But since she wasn't anxious to be alone, he could wait awhile.

"Reckon you're still learning about newbies and such." She tugged a greased thread until it lay flat and straight.

"Not near as much as I'd like. Newbies is slippery—talk a lot, don't say much. Except that Raschad and I spoke before he hauled out. And what he said turned my head, opened little windows I never looked through afore. O' course he was stone drunk, but that helped words fall out I reckon wouldn't have otherwise."

Sal's gut tightened. She sliced a thread.

"I asked him what he thought of the Liberalization Act," Tom Bill went on. "He being newbie, I didn't figure he had objections to questions about greenie business." Sal squinted at Tom, and he fooled at prying a splinter off the porch. "Anyway, he played me back, asked me to explain the act, and since I asked first, I couldn't not answer. He wanted to know about the Industrial Zones. So I explained how Governor Wally says since only two of the four authorized were ever built, he's free to develop the others in pockets. Raschad called them sat-tel-ites."

"Raschad can teach a body lots of new words."

"I reckon, and new thoughts, too. When I'd explained it all, he said maybe Governor Wally ain't as bad as we think. I expected that kind of talk from a newbie. But then he says, maybe Governor Wally's protecting us from worse. He says, we can't imagine what a temptation we are to off-planeters with credit and weapons enough to scoop us up a hundred times over—holding companies, he called them. But he says no one wants a war over a dinky place like ours. So they worm their way into our e-con-no-mee." Tom Bill split the splinter free of the porch and jabbed his boot sole with it. "He says, maybe Governor Wally's playing a stalling game, holding these howlers off by pretending to develop more than actually gets done."

"Why would he think that, I wonder." Sal spoke to her hands, not putting Tom on the spot to answer.

"Raschad says he's seen machines sitting idle." Tom answered anyway, ready for free talk. "He's seen mine shafts that go nowheres, and logging operations taking a tenth what they would from another planet. He says greenies don't notice these things because greenies don't know how bad things can really get."

"The hell." She tossed her harness aside. "Don't go believing newbies, Tom. Raschad hates where he come from." She stood, walked to the porch rail and stared south like Tom. "Raschad's planet is ruined, and politics killed his family. So I reckon *he* don't understand how bad things *are*, because he expects worse. Our good Governor's no friend of ours."

"Raschad didn't say that. He just thinks Wally's making it look as if he's developing things. The *bad* stuff, he figures—the real mining, logging, poaching, dredging, polluting—is off-planeters stealing all they can touch. I reckon that could be true, even if Wally's only saving the green for his own plans."

Sal's jaw worked. Her eyes flicked west down the Pike. "The bent of a newbie's mind can twist your own, Tom. Raschad talks slick, and he's too smart for his own good."

"Looked real smart tossing rockies through the Gigi's Eye the other night."

"That's another thing. He acts so smart that when he's an idiot, it takes you all by surprise. Raschad's as like to be wrong about Wally as I am to be right about Raschad."

"I reckon." Tom jabbed his boot sole. "Hope so, because he said some real frightening things about our own tech, how bo-tan-i-cal based industry can be wiped out by mu-tay-shuns. Which is why more places don't use green tech."

"I ain't smart enough to figure all that." Sal's head spun with the thought. "Haia—someone's coming."

She waved west where a dark spot moved against reeki mounds grown pale green and dry in the late summer heat. Tom stood. The dark spot wobbled and flattened out.

"Morrie!" Sal yelled into the shack, sprinted off the end of the creaking porch, vaulted her sled, and hit the street running. Tom Bill's boots sounded behind her down the Pike.

The dark spot grew larger, resolving itself into a man sprawled on his back, his clothes torn and bloodied. *Naia.* Sal gulped for air, running under full sun with no hat in trail boots.

The man struggled onto his knees. It wasn't Raschad.

Her heart did a double slam against the inside of her chest, and she skidded onto her knees.

"Jeff?" She could hardly see a face beneath the blood and mud. But the bushwhackers and bandoliers were Jinkman make.

"Gigis."

"Hush." She grabbed the kid's arm. Where was Gager?

Tom Bill grabbed the other, and they picked him straight up, none of the Jinkmans being much for weight. Gager made two of Jeff.

"Ga-Ga-Gather . . ."

"Aia. You been out gathering." Sal spoke to shut the kid up; he was in no shape for talking.

"Gigis—"

"Run into a pack of gigis." Her insides danced and slithered, making it hard to breathe. "Going to be fine now."

Tom Bill's eyes rolled. She found a better grip on the kid's belt, and they dragged him uptrail fast.

Morrie'd heard her yell, and Greta Gockelman and her scrub boy ran out to meet them. With that help, they carried Jeff to Morrie's porch. The old man carried out rags and water.

"The Noodle boy's run for Dancer and George." Morrie grabbed Sal's hand and clamped it over a wound on the inside of Jeff's upper arm. "Hold it tight."

Sal's teeth chattered and she fought down the shakes. Not now. No remembering. No time for seeing things now.

Morrie's eyes flicked up to meet hers. Tom Bill stared up the Pike. Greta gripped a porch post until it creaked. Where was Gager? But no one asked; with Jeff here, they all knew where Gager was. The boys had breathed one breath, walked one track since they were fourteen, living with the Jinkmans and then the Kos, trading off helping both families. Good boys. Pink blinded Sal.

"Gi-gis . . ." Jeff fought her.

"Easy. Eas—" She held him.

But the boy pushed up and waved south. Her eyes followed his desperate motion. And as if the south grove's roaks sensed them looking, the colony broke into jabbering squawks.

Raschad? What now? Sal saw herself falling in with him as he walked past Morrie's shack. That would be the easy part.

"Reach in the window, Greta. Get my MagEyes." She stared at the lifting birds. "See what the roaks are hollering about."

Greta drew the tech scopes through the window as if they might bite and passed them to Tom Bill, who sighted south.

But even without the scopes, Sal caught a flicker of movement in the treetops that was too big and too green to be roaks.

"Settlers save us." Tom Bill's voice shook. "Gigis."

And a round, furry head popped out of the brush near enough

to be seen naked-eyed. Half a dozen others flowered the scrub behind it.

"A ganger." For a breath, Sal didn't recognize her own voice. "Get this kid to Boojie's."

Eyes wide, Morrie did just the opposite and ducked through the shack's door net, getting tangled in the process. But Tom and Greta grabbed Jeff's head and feet. Sal took a quick wrap with a rag around the kid's arm, and Tom and Greta headed across the street at a run.

She dove onto a sled, tore her long rifle from its rack, spun back and skidded past Morrie as he emerged from the shack carrying three lizards and his big-barreled blaster.

"Be careful, old man." She shoved him off the porch toward Boojie's and bolted uphill.

Bess Toh and Erma Noodle stood on Noodle's porch next to Boojie's. "Sal?"

"*Gigis!*" She waved south. The women snatched up kids and headed for Toh's Bar. She passed them at a dead run. "*Gigis!*" She yelled the alarm in front of the Pink Garter and Dig's Den, and word was out in that part of town. Concentrating on her footing over the dried mud stubble, she ran for the town bell beside the public shower.

Clang! Shoppers ran from the Pannier. Ernesto Chi strode out of the smokeshop, carrying a bloody cleaver.

Clang! Bare-assed townies stuck their heads through the shower walls. And George appeared in front of the Hill House, hat flying, the Noodles' ten-year-old running at his side.

Mid-street he yelled, "Sal?"

She thought how fine he looked—a dark savior. "Gigis! South. Seen scouts. The roaks are raising hell."

George sailed past, headed for the jail. People didn't need directions on what to do about gigis.

Shutters slammed shut on the Pannier and the Hill House. Sal glanced toward Mary's and saw a couple of bullybys sliding wire grates into place over the windows.

"Gigis! Gigis!" A pack of kids gathered at her knees. "*Get!*" she ordered.

Mothers, fathers, friends, and relatives scooped the kids up and stuffed them in bars and stores—whatever buildings were sturdy enough to defend.

A knot of adults gathered in the street, weapons drawn. Hope O'Toole marched out of the Sundowner with two girls and two boys, all in nothing but silky wrappers, trailing behind her.

"George at the jail? We need blasters." It was the first thing the fancy woman had ever said directly to Sal.

"Aia. Go on." She waved them down street, and the parade broke into a trot. Hope's people might look like fluff with ruffles and feathers bouncing, but were jungle-bred, turned to earning dependable meals. They knew how to fight.

Five of Slick Baron Clay's men followed after the divies, loped around Hope O'Toole, and headed for the south end of town. Clay wouldn't leave his fancy hotel undefended to save another soul. But his other business properties were threatened—the Pink Garter, the barbershop—and his men had family in town, so they were fighting for more than money.

Run, you buggers, Sal thought grimly.

Roaks exploded above the south grove, squawking and shrieking, a rain of white visible beneath the rising flock. Sal laid on the bell rope, sending it into a clanging frenzy, then ran for Morrie's. Her sleds, even tarped in and snugged against the shack, weren't safe. A big gang of gigis would tear the place to the ground.

Sweat poured down her back, but she felt chilled all over. She'd only been in town during one other ganger, a little one.

George chugged out of Jail Alley. Three strangers—two women and a man, rockies from their gear—ran at his back, hauling explosives and detonators. They had nerve. Sal was glad to see them. With the town full of dry-season haulers, at least there would be more guns than five years ago when the last gigi ganger had hit. That one had come up the northeast escarpment, missed the south end of town, but had torn up the Pannier and destroyed every shack and tent on that face of the hill. Sal had returned to town to find twelve new stones standing at the Memorial.

She stretched her legs, pacing George and putting distance between her and the rockies' cargo. "George," she panted, lungs full. "What's the depot sending?" George had a tech communicator for talking to the govies in high town.

He didn't answer. She glanced at him, then looked again harder, stumbled, and nearly fell. He caught her arm.

"What are they sending?"

He shook his head.

The bloody shriking bastards! They *had* to come! But George was grim as hell. She loosened her tread maul, gut roiling. The squats were leaving this town to die.

A blaster boomed. Handguns chattered. Slick's boys, she guessed, starting to work. She hefted her long rifle as they passed

Greta's and sprinted. George was too heavy to keep up; the rockies were smart enough not to try.

She broke into the open, scanned the street for a good position, glanced ahead at the jungle to see what was coming—and stumbled on dried mud. For the time it took to straighten up, her heart just froze.

The bush crawled with gigis, wriggling and writhing as far as she could see, trees and scrub coated with greenish fur, more gigis than she'd ever seen in her life . . .

Her vision blurred. Teeth and claws. Blood and gore. Tiny little screams . . .

She snapped her head right, left, forced herself to breathe and focus. Raschad was out there.

Boots thumped. "Can't stop that!" The man's voice broke.

Sal focused on Frim Urt's panicked face. "Shut up."

Grabbing Frim, she drove him onto Morrie's porch ahead of her and shoved him down at the railing. He jerked his weapon up, popping away at the leading fringe of the gigi swarm.

She lunged off the end of the porch, onto her sled, and vaulted to the roof of the shack for better vantage. It wasn't much of a roof, but she stretched out over the pitch of the shack to even out her weight and opened up with the long rifle. Wasn't often a body had sighting space enough in the jungle to use a gun like this. Today presented no end of targets.

Squalling rose in the distance. The gigis scented blood. Hair rose on Sal's scalp. She sucked air, swallowed panic, and *got mad*, the same as at the Ebbid—just let the rage flow through her.

When the long rifle screamed empty, she snapped a new blast clip off its stock and rammed it home. In a glance she spotted George up on Boojie's roof with Slick's men.

The rifle butt heated up. Her hands burned. Sun scorched her backside. The gigis' hellish-awful rotten stench stewed the air, and roaks circled overhead, screeching and spraying squat until she half wanted to knock off the birds first.

"Banks!" Frim yelped. *Thunk.*

Down to hand fighting already.

Three bundles of fangs and claws flew up over the edge of the roof. She dropped her rifle and blasted away quick with her Camm, laying out those three and four more that followed.

Whoooommmppphhhh. Shock slammed her numb. The street disappeared beneath flying dirt and a flash of fire. Smoke billowed. The rockies were at work.

Time to go. She slid down the creaking roof, but snagged on a jagged shingle. Her fanny broke through wood. She skewed sideways, toppled off the roof head first, then flipped and hit the ground on her back with a lung-stopping thud.

Hands pulled her to her feet. She ran, halos dancing around her. *Sally!* a little voice begged, *Sally! Banks! Banks!* Sonny's ghost screams snapped at her back.

Frim ran at her side, all grudges past. Behind them the gigi swarm had recovered its wits and was tearing into the now undefended buildings. If she and Morrie had a thing left to their names when this was past, it would be a miracle. But staying alive was something in itself. She hoped the old man sat safe in Boojie's cellar and stayed there.

She stumbled. Her gut quaked. Rock and gigis. Hiding in the dark, the smell of blood. *Sally* . . .

Frim jerked her toward Greta's.

Her head yawed, and she saw George, leading the greenie retreat. With the rockies at his back, he disappeared behind a barricade in front of the Pink Garter. The makeshift pile of furniture and barrels wouldn't stop the gigis a breath, but it gave the defenders something to lean on.

Frim dragged her past the barricade. Gathering her wits, she scrabbled onto the Garter's roof, and Frim followed.

Throwing herself flat, she fired before she was even set. The blast from Frim's muzzle half blinded her, but she fired again—fired and fired, the sun blazing.

Her tongue began to stick to the roof of her mouth. Her vision blurred. But it didn't take much aim to hit a gigi in this mess.

A squeal sounded behind her. She spun as a gang piled onto the roof like green lightning. Frim went down. Sal lunged, tread-maul thumping, knife slicing, screaming so her throat tore. Frim fought to his feet, and they ran—gigis everywhere.

Whhoommpphh.

Chunks of dried mud and pieces of furniture clattered on the roof, pelted their heads, and filled the air with dust. There went the town's chairs.

Heading spinning, she pulled Frim off the back of the Garter. They dropped onto a shed and rolled to the ground. Clawed bloody, Frim limped and staggered as she towed him along the alley behind the bars.

Then a gigi streaked squealing from beneath a shed, and the little hairy bastards came at them from everywhere.

Sal emptied her Camm again and cleared a path with her tread maul. *Dead*, she thought. *Both dead now. Just like always. Going to kill Frim. Her fault, always her fault.*

But a door opened; an arm whipped out and jerked her through it. Frim followed, still firing.

Their savior was Lucky Mac. He threw himself on the door, and Sal hammered intruding heads and limbs as he and Frim worked it closed and shoved a solid ironwood bar in place.

She slumped against a wall, heart outracing her lungs. Shrike, she was in the Gigi's Eye.

Smoke filled the bar. Her sinuses prickled with the scent of hot metal, and the roar of weapons stunned her ears. But the place looked blessed good compared to the alley outside.

"Mac . . ." She gulped air.

Mac shook his head. "We need your guns."

She limped for the front of the room and threw herself at an unoccupied firing slit beneath the big, shuttered front windows. While she was reloading, blasts blazed from To-pan-i's Barbershop across the street, and muzzles showed at the Pannier's upper windows.

A few hardy souls still made a stand in the street. But as Sal opened up with her long rifle, they pulled back to the Pannier and disappeared inside. A flash of black mustache at the door told her George had ducked in last. Damn him, taking chances.

She tucked down to reload again, but Doonie Effords, Morrie's pal, grabbed the rifle. She emptied her Camm instead, then traded it for the reloaded rifle and fired—there was no want of targets.

She traded and traded, but the screaming beasties just kept coming. The rockies lobbed something into the street from the Pannier and cleared a space; it didn't last.

Roofs crawled with screaming demons that pried at chimneys, ripped off shingles, and lobbed roofing tiles at the buildings' shutters and firing ports. That much intelligence shivered Sal's gut. *Going to die.*

But, giddy from lack of air, she realized the attack was slowing. Distracted by all the easy meat lying around, the gigis were stopping to feed on their own dead.

Taking a deep breath, bleeding off craziness, she forced herself to slow down, mark her targets, and pot sitting gigis.

Her shoulders ached. Her hands shook, their palms blistered. A piece of shrapnel had caught her through the port and left a cut over one eye. Bleeding freely in the heat, the cut blurred her vision and irritated the hell out of her.

She went even slower, saving ammunition. Light firing from

the other buildings said everyone was running low. When she slumped down to wipe her eye, Doonie peeked out at the slit.

"Goin' ta be a helluva night." The old man's reedy voice cracked. "Where them govies?"

Sal shook her head.

"They gots to come." Doonie breathed heavy, his jaw slack. "Don't they know if'n a ganger like this gets past Tumble Town, there ain't nothing to stop it all the way to the wheat fields? I seen the likes as a kid. A big ganger run north, mostly missed town, so nobody even had a chance to stop it. An' it run clear up to the fields. City folks starved that winter."

She fought a pounding head. Was Governor Wally crazy enough to thin out greenies this way? Or was Rimmersin just too greedy to spend depot supplies and muscle to defend his own basement?

Lucky Mac slumped against the wall beyond Doonie. "I was at the Slackets' when the bell rung. The govies come down as I ran and stretched a big power screen across the street like they thought tech would stop gigis from reaching the depot. Idiots. Rimmersin's dumber than a newbie, trusting tech."

Doonie spit. Grizzled whiskers stood out against the dark of his skin, and he looked so frail and old, she reached out and hugged the stinkin' old squat. Doonie stood it for a breath, then swatted her on the back. "I reckon there's gigis up the side of the hill all the way to Rimmersin's garden by now."

"Naia." Sal turned her attention outside again. "He's got a *big* power grid all about Gov'ment House. He figures the gigis will fill up on us and keep on going."

Right now they were filling up on each other. Snorting and squealing, the feeding gigis pulled their dead beneath cover, and the greenies' blasts fell off until only petty squealing and the wind sounded outside the bar. Sal's stomach rang hollow as a drum.

Then, way off, heavy arms fire thundered, sounding familiar. At least it was hopeful. And beneath the report of the big weapon chattered lighter fire. Someone was still alive and fighting at the south end of town.

Let it be the shrike-freaking government boys at last!

Sal slumped. Her head throbbed, and the twist in her gut wouldn't undo itself. Come night, they might all die. But she knew in her soul that Raschad was already dead. Five days late, with a gang the size of this moving up right across his path . . . he was dead.

The big weapon fell silent. She sat up to stare out her window

slit. A dust devil—alien as snow in this town—whirled up the
street. Hair prickled on the back of her neck. Gigis looked up
from their feeding and stirred, restless.

She raised her long rifle, but didn't fire. The silence threatened
something unimaginable if broken.

A gigi whined. The flag above To-pan-i's Barbershop snapped
in the breeze. Down the street, a wail sounded.

Gigis screeched, and death stench blew through her port.

She clamped her legs. Her finger tightened on her rifle trigger.
The gigis outside her window rose on their hind legs, looking like
bloody midgets, fur raised on their backs.

A big female barked, and the beasts flattened into streaks of
screeching fur, bodies flying in every direction. And an Aireil, a
big hairy wisp, waddled down the center of the street as if it did
such things every day.

"What's it?" Doonie panted at her back.

She took a double breath. "Mistwalker."

The inside of the Gigi's Eye hung still as death.

More Aireils. Their big, gangly bodies slipped over roofs and
through alleys and ambled up the street, herding gigis before
them. Arms like muscled vines snagged stragglers, and snake-
fingered hands uncorked the little beasts' heads.

Sal's stomach knotted, but she hadn't strength to puke.

A too familiar, cloying mix of reeki scent, mud, and rot puffed
through her firing slit. An Aireil passed so near that she saw moss
growing in its silvery fur.

The gigis barreled out of sight.

She blinked. The mistwalkers vanished. People hardly breathed.
The breeze blew; flies droned, hard at work.

In the distance, east, screaming rose again—the same as on the
Pike that night with Raschad.

Her lungs seized up. The Aireils had set an ambush to catch
the gigis between the herders and other mistwalkers hiding in the
scrub. The screaming terror spiked and faded.

She slumped against her port.

"Sal?" Doonie leaned over her, peeking through her firing slit.
She didn't answer. "Sal, ya best look."

She did, nerves blipping and cringing, expecting shock.

He walked alone, big and tall, limping, the Morven in hand like
death come visiting.

"That newbie," someone whispered.

Sal broke for the barricaded door and sent chairs sailing back
into the room. Lucky Mac and Doonie joined her, wanting out.

She stepped into long shadows. Gigi gore stained every wall and pooled in brown puddles in the street. Legs numb from squatting, she stumbled downhill. Raschad's pace picked up.

She broke into a run. They hit like runaway sleds, and he held her hard against him until her back threatened to break.

"I thought you'd be dead," he choked.

She hit his shoulder, no force behind it. "You're late." She hit him again, fighting tears. "I *knew* you was dead."

"*Were* dead."

She hit him again. He held her anyway. She needed the holding; her mind spun, and her senses fogged with shock. She felt him trembling and held him back, hard, held him together.

"You freaking newbie, look what you've done now. Mistwalkers in town. Aireils saving us."

"They just followed me home, Mama. I swear."

Chapter 18

By dusk Tumble Town's survivors waded through the wreckage, cleaning and salvaging. Sal helped haul gigi carcasses to the clearing below Morrie's, where Tom Bill was building a pyre.

Limping away from that gory scene, she examined Morrie's battered but still-standing shack. The gangs had screeched by fast and mostly ignored it—not enough food there to attract them, she figured.

She'd been dealt miracle after miracle. Morrie and even the damn lizards had all escaped unharmed. The old man was at Greta's now, helping rig burners, torches, and lamps for the night.

She checked her sleds. They'd need new tarps, but other than that they were undamaged. Again, botafab wasn't of much interest to gigis. So Morrie, the sleds, George, and Raschad were all accounted for. Everything she cared about—in what order, she wasn't sure yet—had survived. A lucky, lucky woman.

But she had work to do before dark. First off, she meant to find George. It was time he visited the Sundowner's infirmary. Hope O'Toole's best parlor had become a hospital of sorts, and Dancer faced more patients than she could handle. Raschad, with his off-planet education, was helping with the wounded.

Sal shuffled up the street, watching shadows, wary of lurking gigis. Two had torn up Mike Slacket when he poked into the remains of Bwashwavie's produce stand, and George was leading a search of low town, poking in every corner for gigis or human survivors.

A movement on Toh's shattered porch caught her eye, and she blinked. A lean figure stood deep in shadow: the load-by-load packer. Waving, Sal walked toward the woman. The packer waved back, her gesture hesitant, as if she hadn't meant to be seen.

"Evening." Sal stopped beside Toh's raised porch.

The woman stepped forward. In better light, her shirt, while far from spotless, wasn't the least bit bloody or smoke-smudged. Her leathers were freshly oiled, and the rumpled scrub hat atop her head was brushed clean. All and all, this stranger didn't look like anyone who'd fought gigis today.

So where had the woman hid? And what the squat was she doing here now?

"Never seen the like." The woman spoke in southern accents.

"Aia. Never." Sal scraped gigi gore off her gloves onto Toh's broken railing. "Reckon the sight of so many gigis flat paralyzed the govies so's they never recovered to lend a hand."

Standing below the woman, Sal had a clear view of her face. At first mention of govies, a flicker crossed it—telltale guilt that Sal didn't imagine.

Holy squat, what was going on?

"Aia." The woman swatted a circling fly. "Piss-diddlin' bastards is cowards."

Chewing one lip to disguise her twisted smile, Sal nodded. Curse until you're yellow in the face, woman, but you been sleeping where you shouldn't, and you're tit-caught now.

"I'm looking for George, the sheriff."

"Seen him." The woman steadied; nothing Sal would have noticed if she hadn't been watching, just relief at the change in their discussion's aim. "Was over behind that shack a bit ago." The woman pointed.

"Thanks." Sal backed away. "Need to round him up. If you ain't all worn frail—" She smiled, splitting one puffy lip wide open. "—they need burners up to the clearing." She waved toward Morrie's, watching the woman.

The load-by-load's expression slipped. The last thing the packer wanted to do was pitch dead gigis. But she nodded, serious-like, and headed downhill. Sal watched her pass Morrie's. If the woman was smart, she'd work her backside off tonight before anyone else saw that she'd been shirking while the rest of the town fought for their lives.

Sal headed for the Noodles' place. The shack's thatch roof was blown apart, half of it standing straight up, the rest splayed to the wind. Its window netting hung in webby shreds, and a blaster round had torn a hole in the front door so the place looked round-mouthed and panicked—a shocked shack.

Rounding to its backside, she spotted Frim Urt's bullybys tagging George's heels. With Frim laid out, she guessed they needed *someone* to follow, or they'd walk up the seat of their own pants.

"George."

He stumped toward Boojie's as if he hadn't heard her.

"George, you stand still, you stubborn somabitch." She reached him in two strides, grabbed his gun belt, and spun him around. "*We* are headed for the Sundowner."

"Take him," a bully said. "He's fallin' in our way."

She glanced at the speaker—Joc something, one of the young brats who'd drifted into town hoping to make a living off the depot. For all Sal didn't think much of his type, she appreciated his backing at the moment.

"George." She spoke quietly. "The town's done been searched. I just come out of Morrie's shack, and Morrie come out of Boojie's. So let the boys double check, but they ain't going to find anything. You and me, we'll get you fixed up."

He stared at her out of red-rimmed eyes and wanted to argue. But he wobbled with exhaustion and loss of blood from a gash in his arm. He nodded.

"C'mon." She dragged George uphill. Orange glinted off walls and shattered glass all around. And above, lit from the south by the gigi pyre and west by the setting sun, Government House stood bathed in bloodred.

Bust'em, she thought at that vision. All those govies, and not one stirred from their nest to help this town. Bust'em! Ten greenies dead so far, including Jeff Jinkman, whose warning had surely saved lives. If it weren't for Raschad and the Aireils, maybe they'd all be dead. She'd like to see Rimmersin run the damn depot without greenies.

She wrestled George up the Sundowner's steps and into the lobby. Wounded townsfolk filled the fancy chairs and slumped on the thick, flowered carpet. Hope's people tended those they could. Sal pulled George on through to the big front parlor, where the seriously wounded rested on wide velvet couches and makeshift cots. She spotted Raschad and Dancer together at a table in the back corner. Ma and Pa Jinkman stood in front of the big newbie, staring at the floor, heads shaking, shoulders hunched. She eased George onto a sofa and headed for the corner. This couldn't be good.

Raschad's head snapped back. He spun away from the Jinkmans and stumped toward the door as she approached.

"Newbie?" She grabbed him.

"Sal . . ." His expression was rigid, his face all bone. He blinked hard. "The girl will die if they don't take her to the depot clinic."

Girl? Hadn't these people got enough hurt? She let out her breath, holding onto Raschad so he didn't run. "They can't take her to the clinic."

"Sal!" He grabbed her arm.

"Newbie." She pressed a palm over his mouth, shushing him. "They got eight others at home." She pushed harder on his mouth. "Listen! They've nothing to their name except kids. If they take this one to the clinic, they'll never pay off the bill. When they can't pay, the government will call them destitute, put them to work, take their babes." She let up on his mouth. "Raschad, the government won't give the kids any good life. And they already lost a son today. Two sons."

His eyes squeezed shut. He looked like a ghost, the scars on his cheek standing out pale and shiny with sweat. She'd stolen a moment with him earlier to talk about his tramp to Tumble Town— gigis and Aireils. It was a wonder he still stood. Her own knees wobbled at the memory of mistwalkers in the street.

"Sal." He looked defeated. "It doesn't have to be the clinic. But I need more to work with, something to stop the bleeding besides rags. Sealant, MSEX—" What was that? "—Fluid pushes, a vitals monitor." His eyes begged answers.

She glanced down at George. He had a look on his face. "You ain't got that stuff, Sheriff."

"Naia, not since this afternoon." George shook his head. "But I know who does."

"I ain't got the money."

"None of us do. But I have the persuasion." George spoke so low that Sal shivered. He drew his big handgun and checked the clip. "Coming?"

"Aia." Her breath whooshed out. "Reckon someone's got to carry you. Come on, too, newbie."

The Apothecary's stone building stood next door to the Sundowner—which was handy for a brothel. Government-licensed and -subsidized, the medicine shop paid old Salmon Deutchek a fair profit. Sal pulled her Camm and beat its butt on the metafab fire doors sealing the shop. A man who lived off others' ill fortune shouldn't batten up tight and leave them to die for fear of losing money.

The boom of her blows echoed through the shattered town like a death knell. She pounded harder.

"Let be." George caught her arm. "I'll dig him out. Deutchek!" George's yell reverberated in the dusk. "It's Sheriff Estevar. Open up or we'll assume you're hurt and blast our way inside."

The door cracked open. "Now, Sheriff, I—" Salmon's breathy voice quavered.

George shouldered the door, and Salmon scuffled back.

"We'll be purchasing on credit, Salmon."

"You know the government don't let me take credit." The white-haired pharmacist edged away. His shoulders were humped by age, and his head just reached George's chest.

"I ain't asking govies." George stood tall. "And I ain't asking you. The freaking cowards didn't send a single gun."

Deutchek started to argue. But his faded eyes took in George's bloody face, and he gave way. "Squat, George." His voice shook, thin and whiny. "Take what you want. But don't make me go outside. I don't want to know. Just don't want to know." The old man slumped through a curtain into the back of the store.

Sal felt sorry for Salmon in spite of everything. Losing stock like this might get his license revoked. But people were hurt and dying; Salmon couldn't argue the right of what they asked, even if it made him another casualty of the gigi assault.

She helped Raschad fill three big bags with supplies. They found everything he needed except the vitals monitor.

"I'll manage." His voice quavered.

They headed for the door.

"Wait." Stooped and pale, Deutchek appeared in the curtained doorway to his private rooms. "Here." The old man pushed a package at George. "But you don't know how to use it."

George looked at Raschad, and the newbie stepped forward to examine what the pharmacist held.

"Thank you." Raschad blinked, hands shaking. "I'll take care of it. I'll bring it back."

The old man gave him a weak shove and almost managed a smile. "Shia, promises from a newbie. What does it matter, anyway." The little man shuffled out of sight.

George locked up behind them as best he could. And she and Raschad hurried for the Sundowner.

Emptying bags while Raschad washed up, she glanced at the tiny, bloody figure on the table beside her. Dancer held the child's chest wound closed, but from the pool of blood beneath the kid, Sal judged they'd just wasted time at Deutchek's.

Raschad came back—stripped to his undershirt, a bar apron draped over his reeki-soaked pants—and went to work. She handed him whatever he asked for, looking away from what he and Dancer did, blinking back old nightmare, little stick limbs.

Just the newbie's directions shivered her gut. But after a bit she couldn't help watching, amazed by Raschad. He stuck med pads behind the girl's ears, stuck tubes into tiny veins. Dancer helped him paste something skin-thin over a sucking chest wound. And they emptied tube after tube of sealant into the child.

How could such a tiny body need all that?

Finally Raschad stepped back, bounced off Sal's shoulder and limped away.

"Dancer?" Sal couldn't catch her breath of a sudden.

"It's fine." The old woman caught her hand. "We'll just wait now. He worked quick and neat—I reckon he's fixed up worse'n this before. It's a sad thing when other worlds' soldiers learn more medicking than our docs."

Sal's breath hissed. Her heart gave a mighty thump and settled. She shook her head. "Lots of things sad in this world." Her voice squeaked.

"At least this one damn soldier saved us a life."

She nodded, throat knotted tight, and Ma Jinkman nudged her elbow.

"We thank you for helping Pia, Sal." Ma nodded toward Raschad, meaning for her to carry him that thanks.

"I'm sorry about Jeff, Mas Jinkman." She couldn't meet Ma's eyes.

"I know, child. But he couldn't of lived without Gage, no ways." Ma's lip trembled.

Sal hugged the big woman, awkward as a midas. Ma hugged her back. A person survived out here by leaning on those that were left—even on a damn newbie. She glanced to Raschad. What if he hadn't come walking in alive today? Her heart triple-thumped and banged her gut.

Ma let her go, and she went after Raschad. She found him sitting beside George, who had either fallen asleep or fainted.

"Newbie?"

"Get me a tube of sealant." His words slurred. "A fluid push. An MSEX."

She brought it all. And with George mended, they treated a dozen more, working until the newbie fell asleep over a twisted ankle. The injured man stared as if Raschad maybe had died. Sal shook her head, rested her eyes, and shouldered the newbie over so she could get at the man's foot. It had been a damned long day.

Sal woke to sunlight on her face, a thousand needles firing off in her hand. Blinking her eyes open, she eased Raschad over enough to work her arm free. The last thing she wanted was to wake him, but he startled and stared at her wide-eyed. Then, as bad as he looked—eyes sunk in dark circles—and as bad as she felt—her rifle shoulder throbbing—he smiled.

"Newbie." Surrounded by sleeping wounded, she whispered, "You don't do that. Don't flash that smile and sucker me back into loving you."

He blinked. His face stilled, and his breath escaped. "That's the last thing I want." His jaws clamped tight. "But, Sal," he whispered, "sometimes there is nothing I want *more* in all the universe." And his voice broke.

She put her arms around him, tugged his head against her sore shoulder, and held him as she'd held him so many times now, stroking his dirty, greasy hair until he pulled free.

"The girl." He eased away.

She let him go, and gathered her things. It was another day, with work to be done. She headed for the door, noting that George was already gone. She'd have to find him and make sure he didn't kill himself trying to right everything. More than once he'd told her some things you just couldn't mend. She thought he'd learned that truth the hard way from losing two wives. But he didn't much listen to his own advice.

Raschad spent the day with Hope O'Toole and Dancer, rebandaging wounds, setting a broken leg, doing what little he could for these people under these circumstances. Nearly everyone in town had one wound or another. Correct treatment protocol included administering mass spectrum expungents to them all— staving off infection before it got started. But there wasn't enough in the Apothecary to do that job, and the Jinkman girl would need medication for days. So he rationed MSEX and sealant, every pitiful little tech advantage he had, and placed faith in Dancer's native medicine to fill the gaps.

He knew he played god, and it frightened him. However much he'd been responsible for his family's survival these last several years, those were remote relationships, memories that lived only in comms. These people bled on his boots here and now, clung to him, begged sometimes, but mostly accepted their fate, proud and stoic.

He liked these people. He shouldn't, but he did—and he saw bits and pieces of Sal in every one of them. What was he going to do about her? How was he going to leave again?

He should leave now—visit Government House before Rimmersin decided he wasn't coming, before any comm alarmed Axial. But more injured came, and he stayed.

Sal checked on him near noon, then went to eat. When she returned, there were still too many people for them to talk. They locked eyes across the room and almost smiled—everything tentative between them. The way it should be with a newbie, he thought as she left.

Late in the afternoon, he finally sat down to a plate of food at Hope's kitchen table and ate, with her jungle-bred cook staring over his shoulder.

"Ya won't et betta' anywhar."

He swallowed and smiled. "Aia. I haven't, not this planet nor any other."

"Ya is'a flatterer, ain't ya." The woman's dark face split, and her laugh was rich, warm, and energetic, bouncing her vast bosom. "I tell Mas Hope be careful ya 'round the gals." She swatted a bug off his back, rattling his brain, then chuckled and bent over her stew pot again.

Hope came for him as he finished eating and led him up the back stairs to a bath. Taking his arm, she smiled.

"Any of my ladies would be proud to share their room. Anything you want. No charge for you today."

He bit his lip, caught between shock and a smile, and shook his head. He couldn't think of anything to say.

"Couldn't be Sal." Hope's eyes rounded as he nodded. "You'll pay hell catching *her*, if George don't kill you first."

Raschad shook his head. "I'll pay hell surviving her."

"That way, then." Hope's expression softened. "And with Sal Banks . . ."

She led him to her personal room, brought him towels and fresh clothes—which looked as if they would fit—and left him alone with his bath. The water was clean and cool.

The hospitality frightened him. He'd been used all his life. But this felt different—how, exactly, he couldn't say. He settled his bruised body into Hope's tub and never wanted to move again. Would drowning in a brothel be a poor death?

But he had to see Rimmersin first. Stars save him . . . the Aireils couldn't help him now.

Chapter 19

Reeking, ripe and dripping vermin after handling dead gigis all day, Sal stumped into the Sundowner late. Outside, the town was wrapped in darkness. But Morrie's shack was uninhabitable, so she'd retrieved her pack from her sled and left it at George's.

Now she wanted to tell Raschad where she would be and get back there for a bath. Like this, she didn't dare go near the injured, especially the Jinkman girl. So she asked one of the fancy girls to fetch him. The woman gave her such a look, she wondered if Raschad were sleeping with the divie.

Dancer walked out of the parlor with her white hair combed, her clothes clean, and her age-paled eyes looking almost rested.

"He went up to Gov'ment House, child."

Not again. Sal sat straight down on a big lobby chair that was so overstuffed it swallowed her.

"Sal?"

She rubbed her face and took a long breath. "Just tired."

"You ought to be to bed." Dancer fidgeted. "He spelled me while I slept. Then Hope fed him, and he took off uphill like moas chased him." Worry creased Dancer's face.

"He'll be fine," Sal lied against a knotted gut. "Goes up whenever he's in town. Picks up comms from his family."

Dancer looked relieved, so Sal smiled, hiding her panic. Every time he went up there, it was bad news. "Morrie says he'll be careful up to your place."

That was a joke, considering what the gigis had done to Dancer's house. But it was more fixable than Morrie's, and he'd been at it all day.

"The old drunk." Dancer smirked. "Tell him to keep the lizards away from my garden."

Sal tried to smile. Dancer loved her herb garden, harvested

most of her medicines from it. But it hadn't fared well. The old woman just shrugged and headed back into Hope's parlor-turned-infirmary, shoulders squared no matter the loss.

Sal chewed her lip. What would this town do when Dancer passed on? There wasn't a young one around learning her knowledge. But they hadn't lost her yet—and they'd survived another ganger, govie help or no. A cold twist snaked around the pit of her stomach. The sherks would sacrifice the whole town before coming down off their perch.

Five years ago it had been different. She went even colder. Five years ago Rimmersin hadn't been Supervisor. Folks said he was city-proud, and if he couldn't use you, then you weren't worth his notice. Sal had seen him just once, and the howler-faced look of him had turned her stomach. And Raschad dealt with that bastard.

Maybe Rimmersin had just forgotten that they existed. But what about that load-by-load with her clean face and polished leathers—where did she fit into this mess? Sal shuddered, her bad feeling about everything growing worse. She wanted the newbie in her arms tonight, safe, where they could forget the world a bit.

"Sal?"

Her head snapped up—to see Hope O'Toole and Slick Baron Clay, together. Now what? She straightened up. These two were nearly as fond of each other as gigis and Aireils.

"Mas O'Toole."

"Banks." Hope beamed, her fine white teeth showing. "We wonder if you'd mind some discussion. We know you're tired, and won't keep you long. Dinner's on me. You eat, and we'll talk."

Hope's eyes ran Sal's length, and the fancy woman looked as if she danced second thoughts even as she spoke. Glancing down at her gore-matted leathers, Sal didn't blame the divie. Clean and pale in a lace-trimmed dress of some shimmery material, Hope might as well be a newbie for all they dressed in common. Slick was no better, his cloth suit brushed to flawless black, his shirt white and starched—not a hint of mildew about it—and his dark mustache trimmed to fine points. What could this pair want from her?

Slick smiled, and Sal's stomach knotted. She and Slick were never friends, not since she'd seen him dealing black dreams with Pa. She could hurt him in this town. Naia, Slick didn't like her. But you couldn't hide from either one of these people. So she shrugged, and Hope smiled.

"Good. Come along."

Hope waved her into the Sundowner's big, tile-floored dining room. Slick walked at her back, where she didn't like him, and they all sat at a lace-covered table in the back. Rough-dressed customers and fancy house boys and girls crowded the other tables. Slick and Hope chatted until her meal arrived.

"Banks, no one in town knows more than you about Meesha Raschad." Hope cocked her head, speaking in the same casual tone she'd been using with Slick.

"Aia, perhaps." Sal chewed brandied roots and swallowed slowly. Good, good food. "We've talked, but I don't know enough about this newbie to guess what he'll take it into his head to do next. Newbies is newbies."

"I've heard strange things about him." Slick tried, but didn't bring off the pretense of casualness as well as Hope.

"Lots of strange things to hear in the jungle," Sal said.

"They say he's friends with the Aireils and been on Ver Day three years. The first's a miracle for anyone, the second's a miracle for a newbie."

"No one is *friends* with mistwalkers." She scooped up bits of candied cram squash. "But they haven't killed him yet."

"Dear." Hope leaned nearer, her mounded breasts resting on the table. "We don't mean to pry, but—" The fancy woman glanced at Slick with nothing of affection in her expression. "—but everyone in town talks about the man. He was a marvel come walking behind those Aireils. He's been a marvel saving lives ever since. This is one newbie Tumble Town needs to keep. And Slick and I are asking, no apologies about it, how can we do that? Will money keep him? I know women won't."

Women won't? Sal started. Hope gave her a long strange look, left her fighting a blush. What was Hope thinking?

"I'll give him work." Slick leaned nearer. "A man who carries tech like his knows how to use it. And Coach Grimey wants him just to read lessons, so the kids can hear words spoken proper. He's valuable, and mainly because he *can* survive out here. Lots of newbies know what he knows. But they're useless, die too fast. I want to hire him. How do I do that?"

She looked at the couple long and close. They were rude, yet cold serious.

"You can't," she said finally. "He's tied up off-planet, has responsibilities. Until those are quit, he'll keep on the way he's been."

"Shrike." Slick's friendly mask slipped. "I can pay him more than he can get for any damn dirt crystals."

"He don't turn the crystals here."

"Squat." Slick's expression turned worrisomely thoughtful, and his rich man's eyes danced. "That's a fair fortune. Takes powerful connections to buy that authorization."

"Aia." Sal laid her fork down. "I reckon."

Hope looked uncertain. Slick looked cheated.

"I'll talk to him." She swallowed. "Thanks for dinner." Rising, she swung a leg over the back of her chair.

Hope took a breath, but glanced at Slick and shut up, distracted by her competitor's distraction.

"Later, folks," Sal said.

She left a message for Raschad with Hope's parlor boss and hit the street, headed for George's. The likes of Slick wanting to hire a newbie? Now she'd heard everything.

Night air washed over her, cool and cleansing. She threw her head back and took a deep breath. The weather had turned toward the monsoon season and wouldn't be this nice again for a year. Stillness crept into her, a relief from the Sundowner's crowd—everything was dark and quiet, even the insects hushed tonight.

But the quiet was also sad. This town would take a long time mending what the gigis had destroyed. Fourteen new names had joined the death roll today, fourteen souls commended back to nature. Losing Earl, Jr., was breaking hard on the Voses.

She blinked gritty eyes. A handlight glowed in the Dileses' tent. It wouldn't stay on long. Tech cost, and not having tech cost. The govies pushed solar gel generators at greenies, but for a price few could afford. So Governor Wally said *buy more* and the price will drop. But increasing manufacturing meant adding onto the Industrial Zones, killing folks with dirt and making free people dependent on factory goods. Naia. Sal didn't need solar gels when a body could park in the sun when chilled or hide in the shade when hot.

She listened to calling roaks and fleepas as they roosted for the night, heard the first cries of nightbabies rising. Howlers hooted; tiki mice and leepers chirped in the dark. Stars spangled the sky above, waiting on moonrise. Doing without tech was worth it. Whatever it cost to keep this wildness, she didn't begrudge the creatures anything. Lots of tech would bring lots of people out here, and her way of life would die.

She regretted the ignorance that might have killed Jinkman's little girl except for Raschad. She regretted those dead by gigi claws. But she didn't regret having the whole living, breathing jungle to roam. It challenged them all to learn to live with it—and live better than their ancestors had, another time on another planet. People would do better here—had to—even if it took forever to rise out of the mud.

She reached George's porch, legs numb with exhaustion. It was late again. Raschad should be back from his visit up the hill. But there was nothing she could do about that. She hit George's back door and clumped into the kitchen.

He stood at the little countertop tech stove the town had bought him for his twentieth year of sheriffing. Half a dozen of Frim's bullies sat at his table. Seeing her, they nodded and went proper. What had got into them? Sal raised a questioning eyebrow to George, but he only shook his head. She returned the nods and went on into the sitting room.

Staying at George's was nearly as fine as staying at the Hill House: running water, an *inside* shower, clean towels, a real bed. Her eyes drooped. She limped past the front door.

Outside, boards creaked.

"George." *Creak.* "You expecting any—"

Crack. Glass exploded inward. She dove for the floor, Camm in hand, as a thud shook the house.

George burst into the room, the bullybys at his back.

Wind fluttered the lace curtains over George's broken window. Seffy, his last wife, had woven them from fern silk.

Flattening against the house's front wall, George eased to the door and cracked it open. The wind stirred. He put his eye to the crack.

"Shrike!" He threw the door open.

Sal followed him out, Camm raised. In a pool of light shining through the shattered window, Raschad lay sprawled—what was left of him—stark naked and bloody.

She didn't realize she'd yelled until, kneeling beside him, she heard her scream echo off the porch. Sliced open by the broken window, his arm spurted blood, and she clamped a hand over the cut, thinking, *Dead this time. This time he's dead.*

"George!" He dropped beside her, his face white in the dim light. "George . . . he's been up to Government House."

George half reached for Raschad, then seemed to absorb what she'd said and bolted to his feet.

"Joc." His voice reverberated in the night. "Get down to the Sundowner. Bring Dancer. Bring his tech medicine. Joc!" He grabbed the kid's wrist. "Don't tell anyone anything. Get Dancer out quiet. The rest of you, let's move him. And hide this mess. We got high town visitors coming, I wager."

They lay Raschad in the jail's only windowless cell, and George left to make sure the bullybys hid all sign of Raschad's visit to his front porch. At any other house they could have blamed the damage on gigis. But it was clear the beasts hadn't gotten this far.

Hurry, Dancer! Sal thought as she bound Raschad's arm with rags George had thrown at her. *Hurry.* He was so cold.

The big depot siren sounded off up on the hill. The bloody bastards didn't make a sound when the gigis tore the town apart. *Now* they screamed.

And they were screaming for Raschad, Sal knew it. No way he went up that hill and came down looking like this without trouble from Rimmersin. And touching him, trying to stop his bleeding, she understood the nature of that trouble more and more. And the more she understood, the colder she went. Shriking freak. Rimmersin's tech power grids wouldn't protect him from her for a minute.

George came back and read her thoughts.

"Don't you worry on it." He looked as dangerous as she'd ever seen him. "And don't make any move. Not yet. We'll deal with it, but not head-on. They want us to give away who his friends are, who has him. Likely they'll come here first for me. I'll leave some of the boys out front."

Her teeth gritted so hard, she thought her jaw would break. But Joc spilled into the cell, towing Dancer, and all her attention turned to keeping Raschad alive.

Dancer turned to work without a word, and she'd learned some things from Raschad. First, she poured sealant into the gushing wound on his arm, then unpacked her old-fashioned needle and thread and stitched the cut closed around the leaking gel. That done, she spread more sealant over the mess. It would leave a horrendous scar, and there was no guessing the extent of the muscle damage.

Dancer straightened. "He's hurt inside, but I can't help that—maybe bind his ribs."

The old woman picked up his right arm to examine the tears on his wrist. Sal's gut chilled to lead. He'd been bound and fought his way free.

"We'll clean him," Dancer said, "we'll feel bet—"

Raschad's good arm shot out, snapping his upper body off the cot. Dancer hung onto his arm, breaking the force of the blow. But his fist caught Sal in the shoulder, and she nearly passed out when she hit the wall.

Through a sparkling haze she saw Dancer backing, hands up. The big man rose onto his knees.

"It's all right now, son. You're safe. You know me, Raschad. Child?"

His head wobbled. His eyes stared wildly, his every muscle tensed and rigid. Sweat streamed in bloody rivulets down his face, and an odd chemical scent rose off him, sweet and cloying.

"They drugged him." Dancer spoke clipped and flat. "He don't know where he is, who we are."

Sal fought for breath and sanity. She was going to *kill* someone for sure.

Then lights flashed through the window of the neighboring cell.

"Sheriff!" A shout sounded outside.

Depot guards.

"Meesha." She rolled onto one knee and eased toward Raschad. He shuddered, muscles bulging, tendons standing out in his neck. "Newbie," she whispered. "Please."

She reached up and touched him, ready to dive away. But he blinked; his breath puffed out. He hiccuped softly. His lower lip trembled, and he slumped against the wall.

"Sal?"

"Aia, babe." Her heart stuttered. "Aia." She crawled onto the cot beside him. "Hush. Be still."

"Aireils?"

"Aia." Anything to keep him quiet.

She gathered him into her arms, and he slumped, his strength spent. Holding him, she worked one hand free, drew her Camm and trained it past Dancer at the aisle between the cells.

Outside, boots crunched on gravel. Voices grew clearer. She heard George.

"He could have headed for Morrie Tous's shack, Sergeant. He stays there sometimes."

"Where do we find a woman named Sal Banks? I'm told he packs for her."

Sal's heart thumped. Her lungs ached. She didn't recognize the speaker's voice, but figured it was Quarel Schuell, the sergeant in charge of the Depot Guard. Who would tell him she'd hired Raschad? Scollarta?

"Right now you'll find her in my bed." George sounded as if he stood right under a cell window. "Go ahead on in, Schuell." George was doing his best to tell her what was happening outside. "Wake her if you want. But I won't. It's the first she's slept in near two days, and you risk your life disturbing her."

"She's in your house?"

"She lives with old Tous. His place is tore up. This Raschad might go there anyway, figuring no one will look in a wreck. But Sal's here, and however close they played on some pack, she's been with me this month. If she's seen the newbie today, I don't know when it would've been. She worked a gathering crew all day, burning gigis."

"Delightful." Schuell didn't sound delighted. "I think we can leave her questioning for later. On your word, Sheriff."

Sal's breath sighed out. Damned close, George.

The group moved on, leather creaking, the guards' gear jingling softly. She waited. Dancer's white hair glowed like a pale halo in the moonlight.

The jail's front door creaked. Her gut tensed.

Lantern light streamed beneath the cell-block door, and a chair squeaked. Whistling sounded: "The Greenie's Dock in Heaven." Sal relaxed. It was one of the bullybys—for certain wasn't any govie. She eased Raschad's head onto the cot, and Dancer bent over him again.

They hand-bathed him. He'd been whipped and beaten. His eyes were swollen shut, his lower lip swollen double. Sal's jaw clenched tighter and tighter. Now and then Dancer touched her arm, made her take a breath. But she felt his every bruise, the pain about to kill her. They bandaged torn knees, sliced soles, and bloody toes, washed away mud and leaves and sap.

"He come down the cliff," Dancer said finally. "Come off that fancy patio and down bare rock."

Sal shuddered. She'd been thinking the same. All the reeki sap on him meant he'd come through scrub, and the only patch of it between here and Government House was from the back of George's to the base of the cliff that rose to the depot. Strong men had died on that cliff in broad daylight. Then again, a blind, desperate man drugged out of his mind had nothing to lose—which was a great advantage to climbing.

Dancer finished with his feet and plastered him with the medicine patches they'd taken from Salmon for the Jinkman girl. Then she shook her head and kissed his cheek.

"Got to get back," she whispered to Sal. "I'm sorry. Pia Jinkman can't be left too long. You manage?"

"Aia."

Sal helped Dancer gather her gear and passed the woman on to Joc at the door. Then she was alone with Raschad and her

thoughts—an ugly combination, but fuel to see her through the
long wait ahead.

She took off her gore-rotten boots, then padded to the neighboring cell to stand at its window, studying the moonlit track beyond.
Nothing moved. After a bit she checked the opposite side of the
building. Again, nothing.

A chair squeaked out front—Joc shifting around. Muted voices
sounded in the office as the bullybys swapped duty.

Things fell silent again. Insects droned a lulling hum, but she
stared wide-eyed, giving no thought to sleep. With the smell of
Raschad's blood heavy in the air, her mind fought old battles by
working cold and clear on ways to reach Rimmersin.

Dawn draped the cell in shadow. She startled from a doze,
heard steps, and glanced at Raschad. Earlier, he'd been fevered
and restless, but he slept deep now.

Slipping to the adjoining cell, she listened at the window, rec-
ognizing George's voice. The bullyby's answer was too soft for
her to make out. The men moved away, and boots thudded on the
jail's porch. A stir sounded in the office. The unlocked cell-block
door creaked.

She squatted, gun ready, just in case.

"Sal?" It was George.

"Here." She straightened.

"How is he?"

"Alive." She kept her voice low. "Better. A little fever." She
couldn't keep the hate out of her voice.

George moved nearer. Pale light painted shadow bars on his
face and revealed his red-rimmed eyes and drooping lids. She regretted her bitter words; George was at his limits. They all were,
and she had no cause to dump her anger on him.

"I'm sorry." She reached over and hugged him.

For a breath he hesitated, then hugged her back, one-armed, favoring the one Raschad had mended two nights earlier. "I'm
sorry, too."

They both pulled away.

She shrugged. "Long night."

"Aia, and the depot boys aren't happy."

"They'll be unhappier once Rimmersin gets ahold of them."

"Rimmersin."

"That's who Raschad goes to see." Sal's fists clenched. "He
told me once the way Rimmersin looked at him made his skin

crawl. But he had to deal with the sherk to get his comms and his diggings off-planet to his family."

George's eyes were sunk in dark hollows. "We got to figure a way." His jaw worked.

"Naia." She shook her head. "You're the sheriff—this ain't for your doing. Bad enough you hid him. That, at least, you can claim truthfully was to keep him alive. You take care of him for me, sit on him. Keep him here and safe. I got business to see after." She glanced toward the cell where Raschad slept. "This might take a few days."

"I can't sit on him that long."

"Do the best you can. He won't be moving today."

George slumped onto a bunk. "I've an old drunk out front that I arrested this morning. He can help me."

She squeezed her eyes shut. "Govies weren't too rough on him, were they?"

"Never saw him. Guess they're the only ones in town who don't know he's sweet on Dancer."

"Reckon they wouldn't search anyplace that looked as wrecked as her house."

"They sent me inside."

She nodded. "I best start."

George half raised a hand, but let it fall. There was no stopping now.

Sal took a last look at Raschad, then knelt and kissed his bruised cheek. He looked worse this morning than she'd ever seen him, his face swollen to bursting, his eyes a mess, his shoulders black with bruises. Damn newbie, always dying on her.

But he breathed deep and regular now, and showed no sign of fever. It looked like he'd give her one more miracle.

Hat jammed over her head, she left the jail surrounded by bullies. She and Joc stood of a height, and Rajmurti Tickweed weighed lighter. No government eyeballer would pick her out.

"Saw Frim last night." Joc spoke around a stick of sweetweed. "He's near healed. The newbie fixed him fine."

"Good," the others answered in chorus.

Her mouth twitched. They meant they were grateful, that there was more to helping George last night than just earning extra money from the town's emergency funds. Well, she'd paid Frim in an unusual fashion for troubling her at the docks, but it grew good seed. Still, she needed more from these boys; she hoped they'd like the game she had planned.

Last night she'd worried that perhaps, wanting to stay in the government's graces, they would turn Raschad in to Schuell's guards. They hadn't, so she figured she could trust them.

"Need someone watched, Joc." Lorri leaves slid beneath her boots. "You boys must've noticed the load-by-load that's been hanging around."

"Woman." Joc answered, sounding interested, but not worried. So whatever the load-by-load was up to, Sal didn't think it involved these bullybys.

"Aia. She played cards with Morrie the night I took a chair leg over the head."

"I saw her," Joc said. "Was hanging around the Sundowner this morning. Ate breakfast inside."

She nodded; that didn't surprise her.

"You work the docks now and then, I notice." All the bullies nodded. "You ever see her haul a load out?" They exchanged glances, and each shook his head in turn. "Then where's she get credit or money to eat at the Sundowner?"

The bullies' eyes rounded.

"We might want to slow her down," Sal continued. "For sure we'd best know where she's roaming."

"Raj-man." Joc chawed his sweetweed and nodded.

"Aia." Rajmurti nodded back, saying nothing.

They led her to the Gigi's Eye and what little she observed of Tumble Town along the way looked more like its normal self this morning. But folks stood on the street and gathered about the showers talking, stirred up again. Only the bold and blind were scrubbing themselves, there not being a rag of canvas left hanging around the showers. The gigis had run wild in that maze of flapping cloth.

Rajmurti continued up the street while the other bullies mounted the Gigi's steps. Eyes watched them go inside. The Gigi didn't usually serve this time of morning, but with so many people homeless and shackless, all the businesses had their doors open day and night. Sal stood alone a moment on the two big logs that served as the bar's porch. The locals understood. She went in, and the room filled behind her.

"Joy." She waved for the barkeep. "I'm hungry."

"Have rice and greens. On the house, for you."

She decided this wasn't charity, since she'd helped defend the place two days ago. "Thanks. And tea, if you have it."

"Make your tail stand up by itself."

Sal half smiled, but the mirror behind the bar reflected a grim stranger. She'd washed her face in the long hours of the night, but never had gotten her shower. When she took off her hat, her hair stood straight up, stiff and spiky as a gigi's.

She ate breakfast, watching the standing space disappear behind her in the dark bar. One front window was still jagged from Raschad's drunken brawl, and the other had been broken while the ironwood shutters were being dropped during the gigi raid. With both shuttered tight now, keeping track of arrivals in the murk was tricky. But when Slick Baron Clay and his boys swaggered to a front table, it was time.

Sal nodded. Joy waved, and her kids squirted out the front and back entrances to keep watch. It was safe then—only locals present, all family to one degree or another, even Slick.

Joy cleared away her plate. Sal turned and slipped up onto the bar, facing the packed room.

"Reckon you all know the depot boys was looking for Meesha Raschad last night." She let her eyes run over the crowd.

Old To-pan-i wasn't here this morning; his pyre had been lit this time yesterday. They'd all go shaggy-headed until someone else learned to cut hair right. And her bottom lip drew in as she saw Earl Vos Senior's black armband. There were other mourners present, other familiar faces missing. She forced her jaw apart.

"I reckon they've nerve, coming into low town now. Last night was way late, even if they hunted a newbie. Their thinking has twisted, and they've forgot who keeps the depot running."

She looked from face to face, judging the effect of her words. All she read was tight-lipped agreement. Dog Girl, who'd come in from a haul in the wake of the ganger, gave her a battle sign. Mike Slacket wasn't up and about yet, but Tiny stood beside Bocho Man and surprised her with a scary little smile. Even Slick Clay gave her a nod.

Govie regulars kept Slick rich; Heaven's Rest was the one place in town they patronized. On that basis, he could run to Government House selling information about her. But the town kept him alive. At worst, Sal figured, he'd sit back neutral and wait for things to settle. At best, he might help her, for the sake of the newbie's opinion.

"I figure it's time their high perch got uncomfortable," she said into the silence, and met Slick's stare. "Naia reason we should carry all the pain. I'm headed up to the depot—going to check the contract boards, see if there's any work, eyeball the govies. Reckon I'll see you all there, too. A crowd of greenies ought to brighten the depot lads' morning, aia?"

Slipping off the bar, she turned and sipped her tea. Behind her there was a brief spate of comment—people angry, but quiet. They had no idea what she was up to, but knew what she wanted from them. So there wasn't much use in discussion. The bar emptied quick. Sal stayed.

Slick Clay filled the space at her elbow. "Can't imagine what you're thinking, Banks." His eyes were calculating, with no friendliness in them.

She eyed him over the top of her tea mug, wondering what he saw in her. He stared into the big mirror.

"I'm thinking it's time to pick up my next contract."

"A little early," he said.

"Aia, trying to run early since I was almost too late once."

"We've never been friends."

"Naia, but you've never come to harm from me." He couldn't say the same, considering all the booze he'd traded Pa.

"Be nice to know I never would."

"You trust my word?" Time to talk plain.

"Aia, Banks. I trust a greenie packer's word." There was no insult in his tone; he meant what he said. Stupid men didn't get rich in Tumble Town.

"From here on, then, I forget what I've seen of you in the past. *If* I know you aren't fighting me on this."

"Fair enough." He met her stare. "Peace, then. Maybe you could deliver a package for me to the depot when you go up."

"Ain't nothing that'll spoil, is it?"

"Only your day if you open it."

Chapter 20

The bullybys fell in around her again as Sal left the Gigi's Eye. She suspected George intended them to watch her as much as help. But if they didn't get in her way, she wouldn't object.

Ahead, she noticed a big heavy-hauler sled headed southwest out of town, raising a plume of dust. Who would leave now? There'd been little traffic in or out the last two days, and for a heavy hauler it moved fast. They were supposed to clear town before powering up. She stretched her legs, eyes on the hauler. It took the curve below Morrie's out onto the Pike.

"I ain't heard of any heavy pulling out today." Heads shook negative around her. She let it go. "Reckon you boys have jobs up to the depot."

"Haven't checked." Benny Issl picked a fingernail.

"When you do, I've something for you to take along."

She led them to Morrie's and set them cleaning her sleds—she'd hauled dead gigis and a few old friends on them yesterday. While the bullybys worked, she circled the shack. Digging beneath its collapsed porch roof, she found Morrie's drying tray in one piece, untouched by gigis. Having remembered it, she'd known just why the devils had shied off from Morrie's—it was no miracle, after all. Finding a reeki-cloth sack, she pried the black, diamond-scaled moa skin from the tray. Fingertip-sized scarlet dots trailed down the skin's back like rubies. She set about making it presentable, and by the time she walked out front again, her sleds were clean. Joc gave her a nod.

"Here." She held her sack open for inspection.

Benny glanced in first and jumped back a sled length. The others crowded around nervously, flinching and grimacing.

"It's dead, guz," Joc teased Benny.

"Still plenty exciting though, eh?" Sal's eyebrows arched.

267

"Aia." Joc looked thoughtful, and the others smiled.

She sent the sack uphill with them, then hooked onto a sled and took her time pulling up to Bwashwavie's, beside Toh's.

Mama B. sat out front of what had been the family's produce stall. Today two stumps and some salvaged ku-soo boards served as a counter. The offerings looked sparse, and Mama was shelling rock-hard que peas.

"Haia, Sal."

"Haia, Mama. Such a fine day."

"Aia. Interestin' goings on up an' down the street." The old woman loved talk.

"Heavy hauler pulled out mighty fast a bit ago."

"Tikey O'hoorahan with the wind up her back."

"Didn't know she was in town," Sal said carefully.

"Pulled in last evening, while you was up the hill."

"You got sharp eyes, Mama, sharp eyes." The old woman smiled. "Wonder what Tikey was on about."

"Naia telling."

"Umh." Sal shrugged. "That load-by-load's still about."

"Aia. I've kept my eye to her, like you asked." Mama nodded. "Hung around a full two days after you left. So'd that newbie, Raschad, the one you took packing." Mama's eyes narrowed on Sal. "Fact be, she pulled out near on his heels as he struck the green."

"Loads have got to move."

"She didn't look to haul much to me. But I couldn't see what was under her tarp. You got questions, gal, feel free, ask'em right out. This business needs questions."

"Aia, then, was she with Raschad?" Sal needed to be sure— there was just too much she didn't know about him.

"Never that I seen. He don't be the sociable type. Buys food and never says a word. But I reckon you know." Mama shelled peas, examining Sal's every breath. "That load-by-load likes to talk, though. I don't pay her no mind. Tumble Town ain't none o' her business."

"I reckon that's best. I've a feeling her business ain't what she wants us to think."

Mama's lips pursed and her greenish-gray head nodded. The whole town would be warned before noon.

"Has Maria been down visiting?"

"Naia, child." Mama's eyes went sad. "That man don't want her traffickin' with low town, not even her own family. That man be evil, I say."

Sal scuffed her boots in the dust and stared downhill at nothing. Mama meant Rimmersin. "Maria talk much about our supervisor?"

"Oh, aia. She hate that man. So sad. She did love workin' for Mas McCauley. *He* was a good man, for a govie."

"A lot of things changed since Rimmersin come. I don't reckon McCauley would've left us fight a ganger alone."

"Naia." Mama's expression hardened. "Wouldn't any decent person not'a helped." She spit to one side.

"Maria ever mention things that Rimmersin don't like, maybe little things that rile him?"

Mama's gnarled hands stilled over her shucking. "What you got in your mind, gal?"

"Mama, if you ain't guessed, Raschad and I come back from that pack close. Newbie or not—" Her face burned. "—that's my man they hunted last night."

"I's afraid of that." Mama's expression soured, and she paused to gather her thoughts. "Maria say Mas Rimmersin don't like his fruit juice warm. Don't like no roak squat nowhere, especially when he's takin' his lunch on the pat-tee-o. She say nightbabies scare little trickles out o' him." Mama cocked her head. "That help?"

"Aia, Mama." Sal smiled, brief and feral, not certain what she meant to do, but entertaining some fine ideas. "That helps."

A single whining crack sounded from above—weapons fire carrying clear in the heating air.

Mama startled. "Now what'ell?"

"Who knows, with govies." Sal shook her head. "Maybe a moa wriggled into their supplies or something like."

"Well." Mama eyed her. "I reckon being as unkind as those depot folks have been of late tempts bad luck." And que peas hit Mama's pan like a rain of hail.

By the time Sal reached the depot, the excitement had died down. But the govies looked nervous, and checked every crate before they lifted it. She kept her face straight. Only a handful of greenies worked the dock today.

"Glad to see you got a job, Joc."

"Aia." The bullyby waved back. " 'Morning."

She went on to the job board and checked it the same as any other day, then stood in the contract line. A couple of independent packers off the Plateau stood in front of her; no locals were pulling out today. She waited her turn.

"Banks, Sal." She dropped her contract sheet on the counter. "Bogbutt-Ebbid-Plateau Run."

The clerk tinkered with his gear, studying an imported hard-tech power screen. "You're early. Isn't ready."

"Thought I'd try." She shrugged.

"Everything is backed up since you greenies decided to take a vacation."

Sal swallowed hard and smiled thin. "Well, reckon ya'll catch up. I'll check t'marra', 'ey?"

"Can if you want. Contractor won't clear it for haul."

She snagged her sheets and turned away. Contractors held loads until they reached seventy percent of average haul weight—fine by her. She wasn't going anyplace.

Walking off the dock to her sled, she retrieved the package Slick Clay had sent from Heaven's Rest. She hoped it was as *special* as he'd implied. At the receiving window she watched dock traffic, noticing more and more greenie faces. Tumble Town stirred in its own quiet way.

"Package from Heaven's Rest fer Gov'ment House. Da Baron say it ordered last week. He give me a bit ta de-liver it."

The skinny man behind the counter studied the hotel's fancy wrapping on the package she held. "I'll send it up."

"Ap-pre-she-ate it."

"Tell them next time to send a personal note if they're going to use strange delivery people."

Strange! "Aia." She'd lived off these docks for nearly seven years now. She stumped off the wooden platform and headed across to Slackets' Garage. Mike sat out front in a chair made from a metafab burn-fuel drum. One arm was wrapped across her broad belly, and both her eyes were blacked.

"Shrike, Mike." Sal squatted beside the mechanic. "You don't look much better than a friend of mine this morning. Reckon you're feeling poor."

"Feeling mean. *Real* mean."

"I saw Tiny earlier. He looked about the same mood."

"Aia. He does seem cranky. Told this govie lad some unkind things when the boy brought a fancy dock trolley across. It went back still broke. It can wait for their own lazy-butted mechanics. But guess I should speak to him about scaring off business." Mike didn't look concerned.

"I reckon you see a lot, sitting here."

"A bit. Gives me thoughts. Like I've had a feeling all morning

about those crates stacked on the downhill end of the main dock.
I swear they're going to fall afore day's end."

"Now's you mention it, they do seem wobbly."

"There was a mite o' fun a bit ago. A docker spied a moa. Ee-
may-gin that, a moa loose in storage."

Sal nodded. "Would put the fear up their shins."

Mike gave her a studying look. But Sal ignored it, busy watching the depot traffic. "Been awfully dry lately." She scratched. "If
I were those govies, I'd clean out that trash under the temporary
dock."

"It is a hazard." Mike rubbed her injured arm. "A sled could
kick up a spark going by. Seen it happen."

"Aia?"

"Aia." Mike nodded. "Ought to get your treads checked, after
the gigis been at them. You pull in, and we'll have a look at'er."
Mike shifted. "Tiny! Get me up here."

They pulled her sled into a bay and shut the doors behind it.
Sal did the work herself, following Mike's directions. It didn't
take much to wedge a sparker flint in a tread well and three
smaller chunks in the tread. Getting them set at the right angle to
spark when she turned was the tricky part.

She worked her sled the width of the garage eight or ten
times—which wasn't easy with the big doors closed—before she
got it right. Then she nearly lit off a pile of greasy rags. If Tiny
hadn't been watching, they might have lost the garage. But the
twins were too pleased with her sled adjustments to mind.

Mike limped back to her chair, and Tiny stood at her side as
Sal pulled out of the bay. An unusual crowd of packers and locals
jammed the street, checking the job and contract boards or just
milling. And lined up at the job counter stood folks Sal had never
seen in high town before. The government hirers probably blamed
the influx of workers on the gigi raid, knowing everyone needed
credit. But three of Slick Clay's boys waited in the hire line, and
for sure *they* didn't need work.

"Lookit that." Tiny waved as Sal stopped beside her chair.
"There be that load-by-load gal again."

Sal glanced up just as the woman walked away from the contract office's side door, the door the clerks used. She could swear
it was just closing.

"Wish I'd an idea what she's about."

"Wish you did, too." Mike shook her head. "She's been here
before and here now. But I ain't seen her take more than half a
load off the docks. Guess maybe she missed a contract."

"My Pike run would make her comfortable, wouldn't it."

"Looks pretty comfortable anyway, which I don't figure."

Sal shook her head. The load-by-load walked along the front of the docks, her eyes flicking through the crowd of greenies. Hand trolleys rumbled beside her at shoulder level, and she dodged around an oversized crate hanging off the dock's lip.

Bam! Two trolleys slammed into each other, locking wheels.

Sal flinched. The outside trolley's load tipped, the inside trolley wedged beneath it.

"Back off, idiot!" Joc cursed Benny Issl.

"Who's an idiot, you gigi mouth!"

The load-by-load reached the commotion just as two buckets tipped off the listing trolley. The woman opened her mouth. Black goo spilled and splashed over her head, dripping down all the way to her boots: brown reeki tar, the kind the depot used to moisture-proof crates.

The load-by-load screeched. Her boots slipped. Her arms flailed, and she flopped on her back in the pooling tar.

Sal's eyes flicked to Mike. Mike's flicked to hers. Their smiles slipped out in unison.

"You gigi-assed—" The packer spit and yowled, choking on hardening tar. Her screeching became a mumble.

Sal grinned, blood running high.

"Judgment." Tiny's jaw set and his little eyes glittered. "Wish you could stay to see it all."

"What . . . Aia."

Taking Tiny's cue, she leaned into harness and pulled across to dockside as everyone surged toward the downed load-by-load. Ignoring that pleasing sight, she worked her sled downhill along what had been the temporary dock for five years. The main dock sat on rock pillars, but the temporary's were wooden. A string of sleds parked against the smaller dock forced her to work back and forth around them, her sled's right tread clicking with every third revolution. She glanced back and back again before spotting a wisp of smoke eddying beneath the dock, trapped below the line of sight from above.

Beyond it, Tiny waved her on. She waved back, and Rajmurti Tickweed trotted up to slip into the traces behind her. She was careful not to make any sharp turns as they pulled downhill.

"Talked to the squat who tackled Raschad in the showers," Raj said.

George hadn't caught the fighter, but Sal didn't ask how Raj knew who to question. "Aia?"

"He says the load-by-load passed him govie credits to take the newbie's tech off him."

"Government?" She'd figured the load-by-load to work for Scollarta, but messing after Raschad's tech wasn't his type of business.

"Don't like govies dealing in low town."

"Naia." She bit her lip. "Raschad has enemies on enemies."

"Well, that load-by-load's been talking up tech, even peddling some. Sold a solar gel to Ernesto Chi cheap. I wonder where she got it."

They parked in front of the Sundowner and "adjusted" the sled's treads. Head down, Sal heard the depot alarm sound off. Too soon. But it would keep the govies busy.

Two of Hope's boys stuck their heads out an upstairs window. "Something's going on up top!"

She straightened and ran a hand through dirty hair. "Looks like smoke. Hope it don't reach the dock storage."

"Reckon it might?"

"Naia." She frowned. "Not enough wind."

The morning still held business. Checking on Raschad, she found the jail swarming with depot guards in spite of trouble up top. She couldn't avoid them forever, but saw no reason to meet on their terms.

She grabbed Marta Woozniack and Tom Bill out of Dig's Den and Davey from the Bwashwavies' stall. Gathering wood as they went—broken tent frames and exploded chairs—they headed for the south end of town. Gigi bodies could still be found if you looked, so she did. Tom Bill, bless his soul, helped her while the others laid a bonfire according to his directions.

By the time the depot guards showed up, her crew had a stack of rotten gigis at one end of the clearing and a fire burning next the wide, safe break formed by the Pike. Sal wrapped a bandanna around her face, hiding her smile. Raj's informing on her had brought the govies in perfect time, and likely he'd earned a bit on the deal, too.

"Reckon that fire's gettin' there," she called over her shoulder as she walked out to meet the guards.

Tom Bill caught her hint and tossed gigis into the flames. The freshly lit fire puffed out a gut-knotting stench.

"Mas Banks?"

"Aia." She'd never been this close to the depot sergeant before, and she eyed him up and down. George's age or a bit younger,

Schuell and his uniform were spit perfect, his rusty hair cut close to his head, his spotless stone-gray shirt and pants cut especially to fit his body. A tech talkie unit rode his shoulder, and in a face formed of clean straight lines, his brown eyes were quick and intelligent. She'd best step nimble.

"I'm Sergeant Schuell, Depot Guard."

"Aia." She laid on the accent. "George said ya'd be by."

"Then you're aware that we're searching for a man named Meesha Raschad. He assaulted Supervisor Rimmersin."

The hell he did. And how could she be anything *but* aware of the guards' search, with all of low town turned inside out and buzzing? Amazing, too, how the thicker a greenie spoke, the more proper a govie talked. She liked that just now—liked making Schuell think on his pronunciation as much as on what he said.

"I 'eard," she slurred. "Thank ya fer na wakin' me t'other night. Was flat fried out."

"Yes." Schuell backed out of the bonfire's smoke. "We were told this man packs for you."

"Naia." She maneuvered into the smoke again, so the sergeant had to follow. The smell made her glad she hadn't eaten lunch yet, and she tried not to breathe deeply. "Nai-naia. Man hauled one load fer me. That all. Shrikin' newbie. Morrie tricked me inta takin' him. Wouldn'ta picked'im maself."

Just then Marta and Tom Bill dumped another scoop of gigis on the fire. The sergeant blinked and wiped his eyes. "I assume, then, that he doesn't currently work for you?"

"Ain't worked fer me fer a month o' better. Mostly he rockies the green. Was up ta the Sundowner afta the ganger." She pushed back her hat. "Ya ask Hope's liadies?"

The sergeant backed again, beginning to look jungle native—green in the face.

"Fire ain't hot enough," Marta called.

"Put some wood to'er. I'll be right 'ere."

When Sal turned back, Schuell stood in the road, and his squad was halfway to Morrie's shack. "Do you have any idea where else he might go in town?" Schuell yelled over the crackling of the fire.

"Be a newbie, Sarge. Ain't got no friends. Don't know where he'd be, less he payin' or layin' down fer it."

She didn't see what Marta and Tom Bill did to the fire then, but the smoke nearly knocked her to her knees, and the depot boys fled with the wind at their backs.

She tightened the bandanna over her nose and smiled in spite of the gut-rot stench. Gigi smoke rose, drifting toward its target. This time of day, breezes flowed uphill—that was the reason Government House sat where it sat, to catch the cooling drafts.

She jogged around the fire, out of the smoke. "Shrike, Marta. Put wood on this thing before trees commence dying."

Chamoun Nunes slammed his office window shut and keyed his atmosphere unit. That cooled the room, cleared out the stench, and, most important, silenced the greenie jabbering from outside. Not even midday, and he was screaming tired of dealing with them.

Yesterday, the day before, he had needed them. This morning he had needed them. Now, he had enough. But the greenies swamped the hiring office, refusing to understand a simple *naia* or even *get the hell gone*. And posting NO HIRING signs didn't work—the greenies couldn't read. If not physically run off, they stood around in the way of those who had been hired.

Then that woman gets tarred—*tarred*.

And fire breaks out—he'd nearly lost the warehouse just from all the greenies gawking. *His* men had doused the flames before they burned into the main storage yard. But the fire had scorched a stack of passion fruit that now spoiled in the sun attracting jet bees, and he had three dockers in clinic with stings already.

On top of that, after two days of burning wreckage from the gigi ganger, the idiot greenies were at it again. Billowing stench blew around the hill and right in his office window. What were they burning? They could at least wait until afternoon.

The dock superintendent slumped over his desk. Damn, he was tired, tired of greenies and idiocy—tired of Rimmersin. The Liber had had the gall to call, screaming because a package of dram wine delivered from Heaven's Rest had exploded over a stack of comms. *He* hadn't told the pervert to open the thing on his desk.

Nunes's lips crinkled. He wondered how fermented wine smelled on top of the smoke engulfing Government House.

His desk pager beeped. "Yes?"

"Dock foreman reports another moa in the main yard. The men refuse to go back in until something's done."

"Squat. Tell him I'm coming."

But greenies blocked the big double dock door. Cursing, Nunes trotted through shipping, upstairs, and onto the roof catwalk. The smoke outside was choking thick, and a blanket of gray wreathed Government House. Served Rimmersin right. Nunes wrapped an arm over his nose and headed for the rear stairwell.

"Ware the crates!" A scream echoed from street level.

What now? He dropped onto the yard dock.

Rumbling sounded out front. Timbers creaked. Planks shook. He grabbed a railing. Quake?

Boom! The foredock crowd broke into yowling bleats. Slumping against a wall, he checked his timer—late for lunch.

Greenie yelling subsided beneath shouted directions. He waited, refusing to be drawn into another emergency until ready. If he didn't reach quarters soon, cook would stick a patty on a plate and leave it for him or the bugs, whichever came first.

A whiff of rotting passion fruit and a puff of burning gigis combined with the aroma of charred wood raised gorge in his throat. The bugs could have lunch.

He started into the warehouse. Maybe the pissin' greenies would leave for lunch and not come back. But that bespoke common sense, and they seemed particularly short of it today. Rimmersin should be helping with this mess. But Rimmersin was chasing a pretty boy who'd tired of games. Effete shriking freak!

Nunes caught himself using greenie curses and tried to stop. But if Rimmersin hadn't sent Schuell to low town this morning, the guards would be *here*, running off excess greenies and stopping fires before they started.

Nunes cursed his way to the front door and fell silent. Tumbled crates blocked the entrance and spread in a jumbled mountain away from him. He nodded to himself, staring, mind spinning slowly down.

A groan sounded at his elbow, wrenched from his foreman. With the temporary dock charred through and crates covering half of main dock, the only usable loading space the depot had left was hidden beneath dirty greenie boots.

"A shriking piss of a day." The dock foreman mopped his forehead. "And barely half over."

Nunes looked slowly up the dockman's lean body. "It's—"

A mass of screeching roaks rocketed over the depot, deafening Nunes. White-green slurry spattered his face.

He met the dock foreman's shocked gaze. Droppings trickled off the man's hard hat and dripped on his boots. The foreman pulled a wiperag from his pocket and handed it to him.

"Day's over now." Nunes cleaned his face, speaking softly "Get these greenies out of here, every blessed one of them, working or not." His voice rose. "Clear the docks." His words sped up "I want our men in the showers, away from fires, moas, jet bees

and every other blessed shriking piece of squat native disaster on
this whole shriking hill!"

He sucked a breath, heard his words echo. "Shri— I mean *cr*—
Forget it." Couldn't even cuss without greenie taint.

Sal stood outside Mary's, chewing a toothpick and watching the
exodus of splattered greenies from high town. The unusual midday roak flight had come off well; if she'd painted a line for the
flock to follow, they couldn't have blanketed Government House
better. It only added pleasure that the docks lay beneath that line
of flight. Still, it was poor revenge by comparison.

Joc and his boys strode up, scraping off bird splatter and smiling. "That was good." Benny beamed. "Should've seen the Dock
Supe. He took it full in the face."

The others crowded around.

"The man lost it." Joc nodded, more thoughtful than the others.
"Cleared the docks and closed down. They even paid us for losing
the rest of today."

"That stuffed moa holding up?"

"Pretty good. We had to get it back into the main yard, though,
after the jet bees showed up."

"Jet bees?"

The bullybys smiled, and Sal's nose wrinkled. It wasn't enough.
None of it was enough. But little things told in time.

"The skin hidden good?"

"Aia." Joc flipped roak slime at the ground. "I shinnied up a
pole while everyone was eyeing those fallen crates. Tacked it so
its tail on one end and head on the other show against the light.
Can't see it ain't alive without climbing. I reckon by the time they
find the nerve, the jet bees'll be at it again."

"Good." The boys showed intelligence she hadn't expected.
"How's the tar baby?"

"Crackling hard, last I saw." Joc's mouth twitched. "The govies
took her off. Reckon they'd have worried over me?"

"Well, it was their tar." The bullies smiled. "Get, now." Sal
waved them off. "I don't want guards seeing us talking. And remember, none of this is for George's hearing. We best keep him
legal. Besides, he can read the signs."

They nodded and trotted off smiling, boys at play. Except she
wasn't playing anymore. Rimmersin still sat safe—if squat
upon—up in Government House, and Raschad still looked like
hell. Neither of those things allowed her any peace.

She wandered back downhill. A crew worked atop the Pannier,

repairing its gigi-damaged roof. She found a ladder, climbed up, and sat with the tile workers. They eyed her, but didn't interfere. No one interfered with her today. She ignored them, too, taking advantage of their view of Government House.

The smoke from the gigi fire had thinned. Best not overdo any one thing, anyway. She studied the cliff face below the house's stone paved patio, cringing at the climb Raschad must have made to escape.

She should eat, but she wanted to see Raschad. Except that govie guards still wandered the town, and she didn't want them following her. She could say she was visiting George, but she could only say it so often.

Best wait. Besides, she needed to think. She climbed down and headed for Boojie's. With the bar not just open, but *too* open—all its windows gone and half its roof—it should be quiet. But as she entered the open-air taproom, Marta waved and kicked a chair out on the shady side of the bar.

"I know. I know." Marta shook her head as Sal hesitated. "You ain't looking for company. Sit anyway."

"Thirsty, Marta. I'm just thirsty." She slumped in the offered chair.

"Well, order. You going to plunk me if I ask a personal?"

"Might."

"I'm real curious about you and this newbie."

Sal opened her mouth, then closed it. Marta's probing bit deep. But she owed her for helping earlier.

"I don't know." She couldn't meet the brewer's gaze. "He's saved my hide time and again. He's tougher and wilder than any newbie or greenie I ever met." She swallowed hard. "He's been hurt so often, I feel it bleeding from him. But he don't let me touch that. He's dangerous as hell. Cornered, he'll drive you away if he *likes* you, I guess kill you if he don't. He makes me crazy. That's all I know."

"Squat." Marta stared. "Well, squat." Marta's nose wrinkled. "I heard crazier reasons for wantin' a man. Squat, can't let the govies have him no matter."

"Not again." Sal's jaw clenched. "Not ever again."

Marta stood and walked behind her, patting her shoulder as she passed. "Whatever you need. Let us know."

She sat alone and stared at her clenched fists. Sympathy—hard to know how to take it. But the anger in Marta's voice boded ill for govies, and Sal welcomed that from anyone. Her bill for bitterness would come due, but today she didn't care.

Jimmy brought her a brew unbidden. She nursed it and thought. Boojie's two lunch customers finished eating and left. What kind of enemies paid government credits to have Raschad jumped? Who paid Rimmersin the most, the government or Raschad's grandfather? Why was that load-by-load dealing tech?

Greta Gockelman clumped in, sweaty, wet, and smelling of soap. She ordered a brew and wandered to Sal's table.

"Finished his laundry." Greta took a pull on her brew. "Just the way he ordered it, smellin' sweet as the clean sky." Greta laughed. "My boy said he was thinking of egging up to the roak colony. Hope he don't set them off again. Supervisor's like to need a fresh shirt. I just seen the squat up on his *pa-tee-o* looking at low town through his long scope like he does."

"Reckon he's looking for somebody particular."

"Hope the gigis didn't mix up my soap none. Mas Rimmersin says my regular stuff makes him itch like the devil." Greta eyed Sal. "That ain't too out of character for him."

"Naia. Not half."

Sal left Boojie's with her night planned—more petty nonsense, but a person never knew what might stir.

She ran some errands, then went on to George's. He sat in his jail office at the battered desk he'd slapped together from packing crates years ago. There wasn't any sign of Morrie.

"You mind if I talk at that old drunk you brought in? Maybe I'll bail him out."

"I ain't letting him go yet." George lay down the rifle he was cleaning and studied her. "But I suppose you could talk to him, see if he's mending his ways."

"Thanks."

"You all right?"

"You asked me that before." Sal gritted her teeth.

"Ain't got an answer yet."

"I'll tell you when I know."

"Schuell didn't bother you, I hope."

"Naia." Her smile was brief and feral. "Naia problem at all. Have you noticed him looking a little native?"

"I don't want to know." George snorted. "Get, now."

She slipped into the cell block, feeling better than she had all day. George was good for her. George was flat good. She wished he didn't sit in the middle of this. She had no idea how nasty she might let things get; wouldn't know until the time came, she supposed.

"E't it." Morrie's growl carried from Raschad's cell. She didn't hear a response. "Told you it was good."

She eased between open bars and watched Morrie coax a spoonful of soup into Raschad's scabbed mouth. The newbie chased the spoon blind, his eyes swollen shut in the heat of the day.

"Good, boy."

She leaned on the bars, keeping quiet. Outside a flock of roaks screeched and squawked; no one was finding any peace today.

"Enough, Morrie." The newbie's head rolled. "It'll come up." His voice was weak and flat, but at least he could talk.

"Wasn't enough for a bug." Morrie sat the bowl down and wiped Raschad's chin. "You got a visitor." The old man shook his head. "Mean as fried piss."

Raschad's head came up. "Sal?" He sounded worried.

"Aia, babe." She slid onto the edge of his bunk. "I was afraid you wouldn't be awake yet."

"They wouldn't tell me where you were. Are you . . ."

"I'm fine. You look like hell." She laid callused fingers on his torn cheek. "Shrike." Her voice cracked.

"Let it be. Not worth worrying over." His voice fell hollow, his expression hidden beneath bruising and swelling.

"Meesha?" She felt mother-tender toward him, but knew she was taking the wrong tone.

He closed in on himself. "I slipped coming downhill."

"Coming down Government Cliff, you mean." He lay slack. "Raschad." Tight-lipped and angry with herself and him, she gripped his arm. "This town owes you. And this town owes the govies a load of pain. Rimmersin won't sit on that hill long unless you tell us you want him there." Her teeth worked her bottom lip. "That what you're saying? You need him up there still? You figure your family's worth getting what he gave you?" She flinched, had spoken too plain. But he was gigi-headed.

"My family's dead, assassinated." His voice betrayed no emotion. He took a little breath. "Rimmersin told me last night. Someone embarrassed Axial, finally."

Her eyes screwed shut. Couldn't they let him take a painless breath?

"Newbie . . ." The hollowness of his voice, the emptiness of his words scared her. She touched his shoulder. He tensed. "Don't go crazy again. I know you loved them, but—"

"I don't." She held her breath. "I don't know that I loved

them." He shuddered. "Do whatever you want with Rimmersin. I don't care. I'm free of him, free of everything."

He sounded like a man waiting to die.

"You can't let this just go, Raschad."

"Yes, I can." He used spacer dialect, rubbing his difference in her face. "I've told you. I know about being used. The boys at Academy taught me that before we ever reached the jungle for survival training. I didn't understand my *worth* until then. But they showed me why Grandfather abandoned me. People are for using. When I wouldn't serve Grandfather's purposes, I was useless to him. I came out of the jungle only to show that I'd survived, that they couldn't use me without paying, couldn't beat me. What a poor, dumb brat." His breath tore.

She swallowed old helplessness, swallowed disgust. Realization danced black spots through her vision.

"That boy died during your survival training."

"Two boys died. Auntie Meesha taught me survival long before Academy. But I didn't come back a boy."

Sal couldn't breathe. How many ghosts haunted this man?

"Meesha," she whispered. "Meesha, I love you."

"No." His breath sighed out. "No. I'm too tired."

She grabbed him, trying to see something in his face that would tell her what to say. But she only saw pain, and she let him go, sickened by the marks her fingers left on his bruised chin.

Freed, he curled up and tucked his head beneath a pillow.

"Whatever you want." She stood. "I'll quit bothering you. Got other things to do. Reckon if you can make it out of that house, I can get something in." She swung out of the cell.

"Sal!" His panicked voice followed her, and she finally heard more in its tone than dying. "Sal! Don't—"

She shut the outside door. Damn if she'd answer a man who'd rather die than look at her.

Chapter 21

Raschad struggled up. Pain knocked him down, took his breath, silenced him. Morrie and George rushed into the cell.

"Damn you." George grabbed at him. "Damn you."

"Hush, George. Up, you squat-faced newbie." Morrie lifted beneath Raschad's shoulder. "Shriking woman."

Raschad's stomach boiled. He flopped on the bunk, rolled over, and heaved on the floor. Morrie and George shut up and tried to make him comfortable, which they couldn't, which didn't matter.

Sal would get herself killed. His doing. Or worse—she would get herself locked up. She would rather be dead. He hugged his gut. His fault, no matter why or what she did. With his thinking cleared that far, he tried to attract George's attention. But the words came out noise; there wasn't enough strength or breath in him for coherency.

He felt chill and realized fever threatened. He had to fight that. Forcing himself to breathe deep, he relaxed beneath Morrie's soothing hands. George hovered beyond focus, a dark presence near the cell bars.

"Morrie," Raschad slurred at last. "Stop'er."

"Don't fret. George's got an eye to her antics. Rest."

The old man's reassurance and a cool cloth eased him toward sleep, where he wanted to go. But Morrie's droning voice woke him to mist and dizzying lethargy.

"Go easy, George. You'll kill him. Whatever your opinion of his doings with Sal, his hurtin's real, and he's real hurt."

"I know." George stood over him. "But how do I let a freakin' paper newbie hurt her? Can't stop them tearing each other up."

Each other?

"Ain't for you to do. Nor me. They's far grown, and she ain't fluff. But I'll give you, this one has as many gigis to fight inside as out."

"At least he's decided to live."

"Aia. It's a start."

When had he decided to live? His gut hurt and other things hurt worse, everything. Sal . . . A moan escaped him.

"Hush, lad. Be fine." Morrie's hands came back, patient.

Sal spent the rest of the afternoon collecting the last necessary items. The bullybys followed her like a pack of lizard pups, so she drew them into diagramming the storage yard, pinpointing the moa skin's position—which she didn't care piss about now—and generally pumped them for information without asking anything special. Then she sent them off spying on the depot guards just to keep them out of her way.

But as she headed for Slackets' Garage with her gear on her sled, Joc shadowed her. How had she slipped up getting rid of him?

Mike and Tiny, through Ziggy, were expecting her. Tiny let her into the garage and showed her where to park the sled.

"You all right, Banks?" Joc acted nervous of the way Mike eyed him.

"Be fine. Just going to sleep here on the sled tonight. Can't make myself go to George's, the way things are. Guess you have dock work tomorrow."

"Aia."

"I'll see you then."

He looked suspicious, but let Tiny shut the door on him. Peeking through a cobwebby window, she saw him wander downhill.

"I'll bring dinner." Tiny stood at her back.

"Naia, thanks. I'm fine." She pulled her shirttail free and began unbuttoning her pants. "Just going to sleep. Been a while since I did it lying down."

"We'll leave you be, then. You'll need your strength." Mike opened the door to the twins' small apartment.

Tiny shifted nervously, eyes darting about the garage, avoiding her. She dropped her pants, her importants still hidden by her long shirt.

"Nighty-night." Tiny's voice cracked, and he fled after Mike.

Not Tiny? What a thought. Maybe he just didn't like her legs.

She broke out her sleeping mat, strung up a bug net, and dropped flat. Gigis raced through her head the instant she shut her eyes. *Sally.*

Startling from a doze, she focused on two nuies—the size of

her thumb, with antennae twice the length of their black-plated bodies—chirping a lullaby from her shoulder. She chased them off and hunted sleep again. But the sled seemed harder than usual, maybe because she knew George's big soft bed was hers for the asking. But she couldn't face George, and at the moment didn't care if she ever saw Raschad again. Or maybe sleeping came slow because this was the first real rest she'd taken since falling asleep in Raschad's arms at the Sundowner.

Why think of that now? She grabbed her pants, balled them under her ear for a pillow, and tugged the bug net tighter. That reminded her of Raschad hiding in his bedding at the jail.

Let it be. He's a piece of gigi bait. Let go.

But it was too late—way too late. He was twisted in her gut, wound round where no one had ever reached before. And she didn't even know how he'd got there.

Easing her feet off the sled, she stared at the grimy floor of the garage. Aching, she remembered how Raschad's hands could take the aches away. Mouth soured, she remembered the taste of him, the smell of him. There was no use in these thoughts. He was a wild thing—shouldn't be kept, going to die from too much attention. Let him be, let him go.

Let him die if the bastard wanted. A body couldn't hold onto a ghost. And from the first, that was more and more what he'd become, each shock bleeding off bits and pieces of him—the scriar, the Aireils, his sister dying, now all this. No matter that he'd survived three years in the jungle; he was a paper newbie, bound to die.

Her eyes squeezed tight shut. She'd kept the tears back all day, but there was no stopping now. The shriking bastard. She didn't know if she meant Raschad or Rimmersin, who had stripped the last of Raschad away, shocked him beyond her touching. *Going to pay for that, Mas Supervisor.*

Face burning, she stood and padded bare-assed to the garage's sink to wash her face and rinse her mouth. Running water. The Slackets didn't wash once in a week, but they loved tech. The roof leaked above their heads, but they had electric lights—when they weren't running something else with their gel cells. The lights would be off tonight.

She coaxed a smile and crawled back into her nest on the sled. Outside, nightbabies cried and stirred. *Going to pay, Mas Supervisor.*

Quarel Schuell sat at his desk flipping message tabs at an open recycler bin. Missed shots littered the floor and piled against the wall. The game kept his hands busy so he didn't break anything, but his mind ran elsewhere.

He glanced through the big one-way view window beside his desk and sent another tab bouncing off the lip of the recycler. He hated this claustrophobic squeeze box with its spy hole into the assay office. Out there, the clerk sat behind a big counter playing with a cell-powered game board.

Everything had gone to hell. First freaking Rimmersin had locked the guard up on this hill and let gigis tear apart low town; then he'd sent his men chasing a newbie right through that stirred hive. It was a wonder the greenies hadn't run them back uphill riding stakes. The damn newbie had likely crawled into the jungle and died by now, anyway. He hoped he never found the man.

Low town felt mean indeed to hide a newbie. Greenies were usually as immediate as a knife. When they turned quiet and subtle, it was time to be scared. And Nunes, the poor fool, thought his day of bad luck was coincidence.

But Schuell had spent all day in low town interviewing greenies, like the sheriff's woman who smiled, played dumb, and smoked rotten gigi carcasses over a cold fire. Every time she'd smiled, he'd felt the knife twist. And he hadn't dared track her—not Estevar's woman, not with low town stalking his men.

He didn't *want* to find Rimmersin's damn newbie.

Schuell threw a handful of tabs at the window. The clerk outside played his game, oblivious to him. The depot's designer had designed one big joke. What good was a security window if you had to run around the whole building to reach assay? Patrol could respond faster than he could.

He flipped up, grabbed his cap, and strode out the door into a claustrophobic hall. In the tiny front office his desk crew was shooting spit wads at a bull's-eye drawn on their security window around the image of the assay clerk's immobile head.

"What's the score?"

"Seven for two."

"Good enough. Tom, find Jaime and run an erratic patrol along the docks, then up top. I'm taking a walk. The greenies aren't done with us yet."

The young officers' faces lit up—anything to get outside.

Tiny woke Sal at midnight. Mike stood behind him, wheezing and groaning every time she moved her wounded arm, but not about to miss anything. Sal dressed and laid out her gear while the twins opened a back window.

Wailing filled the garage; wings flapped and whispered in darkness. And a musty dread drifted up from the caves riddling the cliff face below. Bellies full, the nightbabies were returning to roost after their first feeding. She had to move quickly—once the moons set, the creatures would come out again.

Tiny helped her attach borrowed ropes to Mike's power winch, then coil the lines below the window. Sal checked her ring and harness, put it on, and let Mike recheck it. She hadn't climbed in some time, and she'd never night-climbed. A full moon and a quarter glowed above them tonight, but a person was smart to be nervous.

"You might net them from the roof," Tiny said, looking worried.

"Naia. I tried it when I was a kid. They wrap around your arms, knock you down, and make a hell of a noise. I've got to get these quick and quiet." She threaded a rope through her belt ring, checked her lights and tie sacks, and straddled the windowsill. "Ready?"

"Aia. Go."

A late spring gusher had scaled another layer of rock off the cliff behind the Slackets' place, but it still wasn't quite a straight drop from the garage's rear wall to the valley below. Backing horizontally, leaning on the rope, she oriented herself and dropped over the lip.

Nightbabies flapped by her. One clipped her helmet with a thunk and a scrape of scales, but the rest avoided her. By the time she reached the first cave, the flight was thinning anyway. Snagging a rock, she swung over a stone edge and hauled herself into a crevice. Wedged tight, she tugged for more slack from Tiny and tabbed her headlamp. The beam caught a nest of three babies coiled in a dark huddle. Blinded, they mewled and spit.

"Come here, darlin's. Going to a party."

Sal shook open a wire mesh sack, secured it on a spare rope beneath the huddled babies, and used a small chisel to pry open feet that grew straight from the babies' legless underbellies. They plunked into the sack, spitting a frenzy, but falling helpless on their backs, pinned more by panic than anatomy. Afraid they'd tear each other up, she was relieved that they quieted once she closed the sack.

Maneuvering the bag back over the rock lip, she tugged on its guide rope, and her catch rose into darkness.

One sack collected. She checked her rope rigging by feel and eased down the cliff face. Loose stone slipped and rattled beneath her right boot, and her heart thumped. The damn newbie had nothing on her for crazy.

Two sacks later she sagged against raw rock, sweating, winded, clawed bloody, and hating nightbabies. Her take stood at nine, but one empty sack still hung on her belt. Might as well fill it before going up.

Looking around for roost holes, she spotted a big dark patch on the rock to her right—a likely opening, one she could reach yet keep her rope near vertical. But a big cave meant more nightbabies than she wanted to deal with up close. So she spidered left instead, toward a smaller hole.

Beneath her climbing gloves her fingertips burned, raw and gooey. Jamming herself into a narrow slit, she maneuvered for position. A jerk warned her she'd reached the end of her climbing rope. She tugged back, reassuring Tiny while trying to concentrate on her holds.

Squeaks and clicks sounded from the narrow slit next to her face. She angled her headlamp's beam down the slit's throat, and four pairs of eyes sparkled back. Tired and sore, she strung her bag and pried apart wiry toes. The first baby went fast, but the middle one spit and flapped.

A screech sounded behind it. Stench puffed in her face. *Shrike.* Wings snapped her nose. Bodies slammed her chest. Tails whipped her head, knocked her back.

She tucked down as flying snakes poured from the hole and rose past her head like a column of smoke. Guano stench engulfed her. She'd found a little entrance, but a *big* cave.

Scrabbling on the scaling rock, she tried to pull herself out of the main flight stream. Aged stone and guano slipped and crumbled beneath her grip. The two babies in her sack wailed and fought, weighing her down.

With her rope angled so far from vertical, she didn't dare let go to cut the bag loose. If she slipped, she'd arc into a swing and be battered against the rocks. And for a shriking newbie . . .

Crouched, she clung. The big moon lowered. Tiny tugged. The little moon swung behind her head. Wings flapped. Her legs cramped. Her arms numbed. Tiny tugged.

The breeze from inside the slit fell off.

Squeaks and flaps died away. A solitary body launched itself with a mewl, and then everything stilled.

Sal swallowed, forcing dried spit past the bulge in her throat. Her legs shook. She thought again of dumping the nightbabies in her sack. But her hands felt like steel claws embedded in the stone. Ignoring a squeak from the gathering sack, she forced her legs up straight, worked her numbed fingers, and clawed her way out onto the slight slope of the cliff, fighting fresh, slick guano and loose rock.

Sweat ran into her eyes, but there wasn't enough moonlight left to see by anyway. She depended on memory and the faint sensations read through her toes and reawakening fingertips. Going to make Rimmersin eat a nightbaby. She concentrated on her rage, on hating the Depot Supervisor, on hating gigis, on Raschad's panicked yell when she left the jail.

Sally. Sara/Annie's little voice echoed through her thoughts, confused with Bobby's wails and Sonny's screams. Sometimes she couldn't help remembering, seeing it all again, knowing exactly what happened and what didn't.

The gigis had caught Sara, Annie, and the baby before they reached the cave. Bobby had made the entrance. She'd whacked the beasts off him with a rock, but too late. And Sonny, poor big-little man—they'd fought back to back. She'd barely taken a scratch, but a gigi had torn his neck open. He'd screamed, begged, then died of fright before the bleeding killed him.

She had tried to help them. She'd *tried*, and it did no good. But tonight Raschad had begged, and she'd walked away. Her staying wouldn't help. And she hoped he was mad, hoped he was scared alive by now.

Crevice by crevice she worked across the cliff, the constant tension of her climbing rope reassuring her that Mike and Tiny still waited above, doing what they could to help.

Hitting a ledge, not much of one, but one she remembered from her downward traverse, she squirmed onto it, leaning into the cliff and taking most of the weight off her legs and arms. Slumped against the slope, dizzy with relief, she glanced at the little moon and reoriented. Maybe she'd live after all.

Taking a deep breath, she filled her lungs to the limit, emptied them, then repeated the process. When her head cleared, she tugged on her sack line. Tiny tugged back, and her catch bag rose straight above her head. At least she knew which direction to climb now. She edged up again and began.

The first step went fine. The second was shriking *long*.

Slack rope fell on her head. Her stomach headed for the valley, followed by her feet.

She screamed. Her harness slammed into her back. Rope whined, arced . . . her handlight crashed into her leg. Rock slapped her helmeted head. The moons went out.

She woke in whirling, screeching darkness, with nightbabies everywhere. Her head was flopped back, and her harness dug into her crotch. *Lived through it . . .*

She tugged herself erect on the rope and braced a foot against the cliff to stop her spinning. But the rock kept slipping away from her. She concentrated, her head pounding.

The palms of her hands felt mushed. She took long deep breaths, and her vision cleared, her teeth stopped chattering. She was going up, she realized—Mike and Tiny were raising her. Settlers forgive her, she was glad of tech just now. Only it was damn jerky tech: one pitch, a stop, then another pitch.

The cliff face closed over her, a darker shadow above. She found wit enough to reach up and grab stone as the winch, on the upcrank, almost cracked her head again.

"Naia!" She yanked on her safety line.

The pull stopped. She hung like an idiot, panting and hunting strength. Finding it, she kicked, wedged her boot in a crack, then lunged upward and flung an arm over the stone lip above.

Brute strength dragged her body over, and she lay against the cliff face, her belly scraped and bleeding, thinking she might wet herself. But the climb rope tightened again. She braced her feet under her and walked the rest of the way up.

Lantern light glowed in the garage, and Mike's ugly face hanging out the window was the most beautiful thing Sal had seen in a long time. Tiny reeled her in, his palms bleeding. Shrike, they'd hauled her up by hand! Fussing and cussing, Mike grabbed her fanny and hefted her over the windowsill.

"You let loose the brake." Tiny's voice scaled skyward.

"It holds itself, or else you mess up the tension." Red-faced, Mike spit, hugging her injured arm.

"It didn't hold *nothing*. Near killed her."

"Haia." Sides heaving, Sal waved a hand between the twins. "I'm alive, and you're hurting my head." Her voice rasped.

Tiny panted, overbreathing and turning purple.

"Stop that." Mike clapped a big hand over Tiny's face, blocking his mouth and nose.

His color faded back to green. He raised a foot, kicked the winch and left a dent in the poor tech thing.

"Tiny—what you do?"

Sal was fighting a faint herself, but she thought Mike might just fade away on them. The barrel-chested woman dropped on her knees and stared at the deformed winch. A scriar shouldn't have been able to mark its case. *Don't trust tech,* Raschad had warned her.

"You sit." Tiny shoved Sal onto her sled, setting her head pounding, and went for bandages.

Mike tugged the winch's case open and stared at the gears. The teeth were snarled and twisted as if the cogs had half melted. The big woman's shoulders shook, and Sal thought Mike might cry, though she hadn't cried even at her pa's pyre.

Tiny returned, wanting to bandage Sal's ribs. Between exhaustion and nausea, she beat him off. "I'm fine." Her vision blurred. "How're those babies?"

Tiny peeked in a sack. " 'Live."

"I'd be gigi-eyed if I near died and killed them on top of it all. Shrike." She held her head and rocked.

"You're hurt."

"Don't start on me—I ain't got time. Help me package these critters. I'll make my delivery across the street and be out of your way. Sorry about the winch."

"Winches is fixable. You'll fall on your face and get caught." Mike was recovering, but in an evil mood.

And if they'd kept arguing, Sal might have agreed with the twins. But they hushed, both of them staring at the twisted winch. The pounding in Sal's head eased. Settlers knew, she didn't need another whack on the noggin this season.

Tiny shook his head and helped her pack all the nightbabies in one crate—a tub of toothy snakes. A little gel-cell-powered light scrapped together from a gas bulb, wires, and a food carton was enough to keep the bunch quiet. Sal sympathized with the cowering creatures as she sealed the box; their night had gone no better than hers. And neither she nor they were done yet.

The street dipped away like black ribbon as she slipped out the Slackets' side door. Caught between night and day, disaster and rage, Tumble Town lay silent below. Morrie said that in times past there had been just the depot here, until business-minded greenies moved in downhill, serving packers camped out waiting for loads. Now and again drunk govies had tumbled down to low town. And everyone came to call it Tumble Town. Just now Sal felt like to tumble on down herself.

Sliding her nightbaby crate into deep shadow, she sat on it and watched the docks. Lights glowed in the shipping office, but no one stirred outside. The door, usually open, was closed tight. The govies sure took a little bad luck to heart.

She concentrated on present business. Boots clumped on wood, and two guards ambled beneath the storage yard's big tech lights. Tiny and Mike had advised her to expect the guards, and the boys were right on time according to the tech timer Tiny'd lent her.

They moved on uphill. Checking the street and docks a final
time, Sal balanced the nightbaby crate on one shoulder and trotted
across the street, thinking, *Keep to your schedule, boys, please.*
She hugged the dock's side, hidden in shadow, her heart pounding, waiting for the alarm to be sounded. But everything remained
silent.

She let her breath out slowly and studied the darkness between
the docks. The tumbled crates from earlier in the day were gone,
reopening the alley to the storage yard. She'd only been in the
yard twice; the bullybys' sketch had best be accurate.

Creeping through shadow, breathing heavily from the weight of
the crate, she didn't dare set it down even to rest. Inside, scaly
bodies shifted and claws scratched, and the little vibrations nagged
at her headache. Pain left a film of sweat on her lip—or maybe
that was fear.

She eased off the dock and through the alley to the back gate.
It was locked, as expected. Pulling Mike's loaned whip blade
from a pocket, she sliced through the metafab as easily as if it
were young reeki. But a chain link escaped her fingers, struck the
metafab gate pipe and clinked.

She froze, heart pounding. Nothing happened.

She slipped in quickly, counted bins along the back of the depot, and dropped her package in the fourth one from the side
door—the correct one, according to Joc. It had better be.

Backtracking, she slipped out the gate, slipping the chain into
place so the fence appeared locked.

"Don't move."

Her lungs seized. Her vision blurred.

"Looking for work?" The words slurred with sarcasm, and a
handbeam blinded her.

"Frig, Nicholas." The second guard chuckled. "She's big
enough for a *job* or two."

Sal bit her lip, as mad as scared. Her knees wanted to give, but
she held on.

"Speak up." A third voice sounded out of the dark. "What are
you doing?"

She swallowed hard. "Was comin' up ta check the job board."
She spoke greenie thick. "I heard somethin' in the alley 'ere. A
chink. I come in ta check."

The first guard stepped around her and tugged on the chain. It
fell at his feet.

"I'll bet you were checking."

"Turn around, hands in back."

She didn't fight, just let it all go. Still, they jerked her harder than needed to grapple her. And by the time they finished, her head hurt so bad she didn't care what happened so long as someone let her sit down. Instead they marched her up the street past the CommO and through a door adjoining the assay entrance. She'd never been in the guard box before.

They recorded her name, took one thumb print and some sort of body record, and finally let her sit. Five uniformed govies crowded the little office around her. All looked spit-clean, young as babes—well, maybe her age, but dumber—and sickeningly pleased with themselves.

"You have any more to say than you told the first officer?"

"Naia."

"Sergeant Schuell is on his way." The govie man's lip quirked up in what she thought was meant to be a smile. "All of a sudden we got us a full house."

"Put her in the tank, Nick."

"With him?"

Sal wondered at that, but couldn't think for the pounding in her head.

"*He* isn't going to cause *her* any trouble."

They all laughed. One flounced. Her head thrummed, and she considered puking on their shiny boots.

A hand levered her up by the elbow and steered her into a narrow hall. Offices lined it on either side, all the walls tech-formed from seamless botafab. At the hall's end a broad metafab door blocked their way.

Hanging his hand weapon on a peg, Nick peeked inside the collar of his shirt. What was that for? His hand rose to a blue plate set in the wall. His fingers danced a jig, and the door in front of them opened on its own. Shriking tech. The govies liked to pretend it was magic, as if greenies were too dumb to know better.

Nicky pulled her into a closet-sized space, and the outside door locked automatically behind them. "Arms out."

He searched her again, getting more intimate than she liked. But her head hammered, and she couldn't fight tonight. He finished his search, then opened a second locked door in the same order as the first, right down to peeking inside his collar. The door opened. He shoved her, not rough, but between her wavering vision and a body already in the narrow space, she staggered.

Someone caught her. If the guard heard her yelp, he didn't turn around.

Chapter 22

"Easy." Squinting puffy-eyed at her, Raschad pulled her onto a jail bunk.

"Gigi's ass." She clenched his shirt. "George?"

"He's fine. He took Morrie to dinner, and I slipped past the bullyby they left watching me."

"Why?" She pulled her voice down an octave.

He flicked hair from her face and tensed. "They do this?" A vein pulsed in his temple.

"Naia." With her hand, she shielded her bruised cheek, where the helmet hadn't protected her. "Did it myself. Went climbing after nightbabies, and the Slackets' winch give out."

"I *told* you not to trust green machines." He gripped her arm until it hurt.

"I said I was climbing after nightbabies, the craziest squat thing I ever heard of, and you're worried about the tech?"

"Not the winch, *you*. Ah, Sal, they've been selling this planet cheap sick technology. It will fail, the same as Knobby's sled melted down in half the time you thought it should have."

"You don't know that was Knobby's sled." She swallowed.

"A sled shouldn't melt down—"

"People and gear disappear all the time." Sal's head hurt too much to listen to foolishness. "And Ver Day's making the same tech we've used since the Settlers landed." But she knew from history lessons that their tech had never been fancy and had all been bootleg. "It's served us fine all these years."

"That's the problem." He hugged her, rocking them both gently. "There's another mutation with every replication. If green templates aren't renewed, they grow something different from what you intended to make. But until we found that meltdown, I didn't realize how bad things had gotten.

"Listen to me. Green tech does not *melt down* under natural conditions. Nothing in the green duplicates the degree of heat and acidity necessary to recycle green products as I know green tech. Something went wrong with your manufacturing techniques long ago. And it's worse now. You told Scugs that Knobby's sled was brand new. Yet no other sled is missing. If that melted sled is his, your tech is disintegrating faster than you've ever experienced before. That means a recent manufacturing mutation or contamination with foreign disease or even intentional sabotage." He rocked harder. "Ver Day's tech is sick, and it's going to fail. And nothing can cure it as things stand."

Sal hung limp, her stomach gagging her, her eyes shut, scared to death that she understood him right, scareder yet that she believed him. "My sleds?"

"Depends on when they were made. They should predate any recent mutation. And contamination occurs during manufacture; it isn't infectious outside the plants. You might be safe." Might be? "Your head hurt?"

"You tell me this, then ask if my *head* hurts." She reared up. "You idiot. Hold still." He stopped rocking. "It hurts like hell."

"Looks the same."

"And you look like squat. What you doing here? You ap-pre-she-ate your first visit that much?"

He glared. She glared back, head thundering.

"I hoped to stop this mess before you ended up hurt or . . . this." His eyes flicked away. "I'm sorry."

"Ain't your fault I'm fleepa-headed. Ain't your fault a moa sits atop this hill. And you ain't ever been in a position to protect *me*. Idiot."

"Sal." He put a hand to his forehead and rested his head against its palm. "Nothing ever gets straight. Why did you have to do something stupid tonight?"

That hurt her feelings. "It don't matter to you, remember? No responsibilities. You can just walk off and die now."

He tensed as if hit, and his jaw worked beneath the clawed welts on his cheek. "Don't push that. The hole has been inviting, but I didn't mean to drag you into it with me."

"Then best you stay out of it." Sal sucked her split lip. That rock was damn hard. "That's not a promise of anything," she added. "It's just, your going will leave a gap." Her face screwed up. Her voice threatened to squeak. *Naia, gal.* "You make me madder than a wet scriar." Sick tech? The world had gone crazy.

Raschad's breath escaped in a soft *whuff*. His arm slipped around her. She held him back.

He stank of herb salve and old blood. But beneath that he smelled ... like himself, so strange, so shivery familiar. She breathed deep, fighting rage that threatened to tear her head off, fighting the memories beneath that rage.

"Do you understand that *I* killed them?" His voice shook.

"What you talking about?" Crazier and crazier.

"The day I defied Axial and entered Academy, I killed my family. Mother knew."

"Naia." She went on, talking fast. "Wasn't your fault the Tarsians went broke or made fancy people mad. And no one should own you."

"But they do. Everyone wants a piece."

She remembered Slick's words—that because Raschad could survive in the green, he was *useful*.

"Let it go." She squeezed his good arm. "You're quits with your gramps now. He has nothing to hold you with."

His arm tightened about her. "He'll find something."

"Does he really want you dead?" A thought coiled up out of the pit of her stomach like a nightbaby rising. "He let you live before, kept your mother, sister, brother alive as long as he could. Did he walk away from you or you from him?"

His grip nearly broke her arm. But she had to shock him into thinking different somehow. His breath tore on a sob. She wrapped herself about him and held on, and he reined himself in.

"We all have our gigis, Sal."

"Morrie talk to you?" Acid bubbled in her gut.

"George."

Her hands did a little dance, but nothing needed saying on the subject. So he knew. So maybe he understood to stay out of her way come hard times, like he had without even knowing, out on the Ebbid, when she bulled into scrub chasing gigis.

"You understand about George and me, then."

Raschad nodded, his chin moving against the top of her head.

"Even with Ma alive, George watched out for me after—" Her throat knotted. "But I don't see you staying, Raschad. From what you say, we'll all be using bows and arrows again soon, and torches and wooden sleds. You'll tire of living without tech, miss easy ways. Even George lives with more tech than some govies. So I figure you're right. We don't belong together. When we get out of this, I won't track you anymore."

She heard herself talking from a ways off, her thoughts spin-

ning too fast to pin down. Except that she knew if she clung to
this newbie, he'd be gone like a panicked fleepa. If she clung
to him, she'd kill herself—or him, like Sonny . . .

"You hate tech that much?" he asked.

She arched her head back. He'd taken her speech all wrong.
But it didn't much matter, because he'd also gotten it right.

"You just *told* me to hate tech, you idiot. And this is how much
I hate it anyway. Ma died when tech might of saved her. But we'd
have lost the land to pay for a skid ride to Capitol. She wouldn't
have it. She couldn't have survived them hauling her away from
the jungle to a govie hospital, anyway. We're part of the land. We
don't leave. And we don't sell our souls to tech. But Morrie's
right, and you're right. I been cheating. I've wronged Ma's memory hauling around these tech sleds, accepting George's fancy
gifts."

"No." He cut her off. "Naia. You walk the fine line between
living like an animal and wreaking havoc like an animal. It isn't
technology that's wrong here—it's the type of tech and how it's
used that matters. Just because your green technology is failing
doesn't mean there aren't alternatives. Hard tech might pollute
more in its manufacture, but it lasts forever. This Morven was
Aunt Meesha's, and her great-aunt's before her. So you don't need
to make nearly as much hard tech as you do green. It's a trade-off,
but you can have tech and keep the green whole, too, if people
want to do things right."

"Aia?" Sal rolled her head to gaze up at him slantwise, the
throb easing in her temple. "Well, with Governor Wally running
things, that puts us in real trouble, don't it?" He hugged her. "This
conversation's run a strange long way, haia, babe?"

His face screwed up, but a hint of smile trembled on his lips.
He ruffled her hair and hugged her closer. But then his breath escaped in a rush. "I wish you loved tech. I wish you did, because
I don't know how to stop what's coming down on Ver Day. What
the Terms of Settlement attempt is marvelous. But the attempt is
insane. People are too greedy." He rocked, rocking her with him,
his every muscle tensed again.

"Raschad?" She hugged him back. A drunk fleepa couldn't be
crazier than this man. "What's got you going now?"

"Rimmersin talked while he . . ." He swallowed, strangling, and
his heart misbeat beneath her ear.

"Rimmersin's squat. And Rimmersin's dead. Greenies will see
to him, even if I don't."

"Doesn't matter. I walked into his trap last night on my own, asked the wrong questions. Besides, it's more than Rimmersin. I was right, and you were right about the Runners."

"The Runners?" She pulled back to stroke his battered cheek. "Meesha, they're all dead in the jungle."

"There will be more," he said, and her gut sank at the cold sanity in his expression. "I couldn't get it straight, but Rimmersin knows they were maneuvered into the green." He breathed out through taut, swollen lips. "He talked as if newbies and Libers are working together on illegal mining and harvesting projects. He has more employers than Grandfather and Governor Wally. And one of them wants me dead."

Her chest knotted drum tight. Sick tech? Cheating depot supervisors? Assassins running the green?

"Why?" She forced breath around the boulder in her throat. How could a stump-dumb greenie fight govies *and* off-planeter crazies? "Those kids at the shower were paid government credits to jump you. Why hurt you here? I thought you were doing exactly what your grandfather wanted."

He rocked them, muscles rigid. "Under MB-2 law, a male blood heir can reestablish the family line and file a claim for blood revenge. Should I return to MB-2, my grandfather's enemies could wage legal war against the Raschads under my name. Maybe someone wants me back. So someone else just wants me dead."

"Ah, shrike, Ra—"

Clack. She froze. Raschad twisted to face the cell door.

Clack. Boots scuffed in the space between the outer and inner lockup doors.

"Come—"

Raschad's arms pinned hers. A knife slipped to her throat—a tiny, flat thing that would fit in a boot sole or a pants seam, razor sharp. Her skin pimpled.

"Easy." His breath ruffled her hair. "Be all right."

Of course. But her stomach flopped, and sweat filmed her face though she could knock him out with an elbow to the ribs or even a tug against his bandaged arm.

The cell's inner door opened. She couldn't see the guard, but guessed he had moved back against the first door.

"Come out, Raschad. The sergeant is waiting." It sounded like Nicky again.

"The woman first." Raschad's voice rang dead with chill. Sweat ran on her spine.

"No games. Schuell wants you now. Rimmersin's coming."

"Let him."

What was Raschad thinking?

"I'll throw in a pair of wrist grapples. You put them on. You don't want us coming in after you."

A set of metafab grapples hit the opposite bunk with a chink. Raschad stood, tugging her up with him.

She rolled her eyes back, but couldn't see his face and didn't dare move her head. He eased her to the doorway where the depot man could see them. Nicky's eyes rounded.

"Out of my way."

Raschad's tone flooded sweat down Sal's ribs. Nicky's hands froze. Doesn't know which way to jump, Sal thought—just a city brat with no experience. The kid stared at Raschad's knife and sweated.

Raschad's knee bumped her thigh—once, twice.

He pushed her—hard—out of the cell, right at Nicky. With all his attention on Raschad, thinking her a victim, not the enemy, the kid didn't react fast enough.

Her boot came up. The govie startled. She caught him under the chin just as his hand jerked toward a red plate high on the wall—an alarm buzzer, she figured. He never touched it.

She landed flat-footed and spun toward Raschad. His knife—made of glass?—dropped. A chill ran through her. He was so crazy, he scared her blind holding that blade.

Nicky moaned. She snapped around and landed a knee on his chest. But the kid was out.

Raschad towered above them. "The grapples."

"What good's that when we can't get out?"

But she spun back for them while Raschad bent over the unconscious guard. Snatching the grapples, she skidded back to her knees over Nick, all three of them crammed in the small space next the outer door. Sweat stench soured the air, hers especially none too sweet.

"Good boy." Raschad chuckled, tendons showing in his jaw.

"What?"

"The code." He rolled Nicky's collar back, revealing a string of numbers separated by dashes. "Kid." Raschad slapped the kid's cheek.

"Nick." She slapped the guard harder. His eyes fluttered, rounding again.

"Help me." Raschad hooked his good arm beneath Nick's shoulder, and together they braced the guard onto his feet.

"Don't wobble, kid." Raschad slid his knife against the kid's throat. "I might stick you by accident. I'm not very steady. Ready?" He glanced at Sal.

"Aia, idiot."

Wounded arm raised, Raschad poked the blue plate beside the outer door with stiffened fingers. It opened like magic.

Guards swarmed the office corridor; the sneaky squats had seen everything that had happened inside the cell.

But they were still on the run, and hadn't yet reached the weapons rack. Raschad shoved Nick into them, blocking the hall, then snagged the kid's weapon from a peg and shouldered Sal in front of him.

Now what? They couldn't believe he'd turn on her. But the gun muzzle nudged the back of her poor aching head.

"Don't move." Raschad spoke to the encroaching guards. "No one has to die here. Not her; not you."

"Back off." Schuell pushed forward, placing himself at the head of his men. His expression said he knew they faced more than just some drunk greenie or dreamed-out docker.

"Weapons down. All of you back up." Raschad's voice came out so cold and ragged, Sal hardly recognized it.

Schuell stood rock steady. "You won't chance her life by shooting. We'll just wait."

But Raschad dug the gun into the back of her ear until she squealed—for effect, sort of—and almost wet herself, an effect she'd just as soon pass up.

"You have no idea who or what you are dealing with, Sergeant." Raschad's voice dropped to a growl. "Rimmersin wouldn't have told you, not while you were hunting me. Now, you don't want to know." Raschad eased Sal along the hall toward them. "Move." Schuell's hand motioned, and they moved. "Out front—everyone drop your weapons and lie on the floor, hands behind your heads."

Schuell hesitated, his eyes flicking from her to Raschad and back. She could smell the newbie sweating, and it scared her senseless—a fact she didn't try to hide. Schuell's eyes locked on hers, and she saw him decide that this was no time or reason to die. He backed up the hall, shielding his boys.

Raschad paced her forward—a step, two. She felt his bandaged hand at the small of her back, felt it slip over her hip and snag her pocket. They came abreast of an open office.

"Sorry, Sal." His breath puffed against her ear.

And he shoved her again—hard again.

She hit Schuell and held on. The guard spun; she clung. Over his shoulder she saw Raschad dodge through a doorway.

Schuell floundered. Guards shoved at him from behind, and she and Schuell toppled into the office at Raschad's back.

Raschad dove into a big glass wall, rolling into a web of splintering glass and fiber threads and out again like rolling from a blanket.

The guards dove after him. She did her best to trip them. And Raschad was gone, fast on his feet.

"Out the front!" Schuell broke free.

She scrabbled after the sergeant and raced shock-faced govies out the jail's front door before anyone remembered she existed. She shivered in the dawn air as the guards headed downhill. She slid into shadow. They chased a shadow; Raschad wouldn't go back to low town. She turned toward Government House and stumped uphill into the dim glow of the rising sun.

"Stop there."

Shriking Schuell. She stretched her hands straight out, hoping that would be enough for him, because little warning lights sparkled behind her eyes anyway. If she raised her hands a fraction higher, she'd faint like a sucker.

"He ain't headed to town." Her voice shook.

"I thought he might not be."

"Let me go up with you," Sal said. "You were right about him. He wasn't going to hurt me. I can talk to him."

"Then why weren't you talking back there?"

"I was scared if I did anything wrong, I'd get you killed. He ain't half sane at best, and not at all after what Rimmersin did to him."

"Rimmersin claims Raschad attacked him."

"Aia. That's why the newbie looks like he does."

Schuell snorted. "You lied to me once, Banks."

"Aia. In a way. Raschad's been with George since the first. That's where he ran, right to Tumble Town's law. George filed an action against Rimmersin, too. I saw an empty heavy hauler powering out yesterday morning—the complaint papers are on it. When it reaches Port Jolly, they'll comm it to Capitol.

"This won't stay quiet. Raschad ain't a newbie you can just bury. Whatever he's done so far has been to save his own life, except tonight, and he figured he was saving mine. He's panicked that Rimmersin will get his hands on me."

And she was panicked that Raschad would get his hands on

Rimmersin. Killing the man would get Raschad killed, too, and wouldn't protect either her or the green.

"How do I believe you?" Schuell stepped nearer.

"I swear on my packer code, and greenies don't lie on their honor. Government people just fail to listen. And while you're standing here, Raschad's about to do something that there is no going back from."

He knew that was true. "Come on, then. I'll pretend yesterday was the first time you ever lied to anyone."

"Wrong." She wobbled as the slick cobbles of the Government House's long, climbing drive began. Schuell caught her arm to steady her. "I lied to my pa once when I was ten."

He laughed, soft and nervous. "Damn it, woman, don't make me like you."

She shuddered. Raschad had said that once. Or maybe she'd said it to him.

Chapter 23

Dawn lit the encircling burntwoods' ragged crowns as Sal and Schuell crested the hill and headed up a graveled walk through Government House's fancy flower garden. A statuary fountain burbled, and a passion cock crowed. Everything seemed so peaceful, Sal hoped she'd guessed wrong.

But reaching the pillared porch in pale dawn light, they found a bloody smear on the house's perfect white stone, and the front door hung open, minus its nontech latch.

"Subtle." Schuell fingered the severed lock.

All she could think was that Raschad's blood stained the door—another bit of him gone.

They stepped into a gleaming white-walled entryway, moving as carefully as fleepas hunting howlers. Chasing Raschad was just as stupid. But no one stopped them. No servants showed.

Her eyes followed a polished wooden banister. It curved to an upper floor, and high above their heads, a tech-powered glass chandelier glittered and gleamed even in the dim light. To either side of the entry, side corridors, tiled in polished stone, led into the house's wings. All this was for *one* person?

Schuell motioned. A patch of mud and a trail of wet grass led up the hallway on her left. Easing in that direction, they peeked into rooms and listened at doors. The air smelled of flowers and oiled wood, and the furniture was finished in shiny machine-woven cloth or fine soft leather.

Sal's chest ached from holding her breath. Schuell hung back, keeping her in sight and under his weapon. She peeked at a flat-topped botafab piano and wandered on, wondering which of these rooms Rimmersin had used to assault Raschad.

"The comm."

She froze at the sound of Raschad's voice.

"Don't be a fool."

She nodded to Schuell. Ahead, on her left, light slanted into the hallway. Was the sun up already? Moving quietly, she crept nearer.

Double doors of carved burntwood stood ajar, pushed inward just enough for a person to slip between them. The farthest door was open wider than the nearer, and oval insets of etched glass in the doors' upper halves scattered lamplight from within the room.

Flattening against the wall, she eased forward and craned her neck until she could see through the nearest door's window. Etched flowers and leaves blurred her view, but the room beyond looked like a fancy office: tile floor, heavy woven rugs, wood paneling, shelves of books. Outside double, pane-windowed doors, she spied a stone-paved patio lit by dawn light. A cell lamp threw shadows in the room's corners. Beside a big wooden desk stood Raschad, blood dripping from a hundred nicks and cuts, his stolen weapon trained on Doyka Rimmersin.

Sal jerked back flat as the newbie's head turned toward the door. Schuell did the same.

"The comm." Raschad's voice tore ragged.

"Why bother." She'd never heard Rimmersin speak before. His voice oozed, oilier than Slick's. "You're dead already, Raschad."

"Perhaps. But there are no drugged wineglasses I'm going to drink from this morning, Supervisor."

"More's the pity. I would do you again anytime, darling."

Rimmersin chuckled. Sal's muscles tensed, and Schuell's fingers dug into her shoulder. She stared at him, sweating, nostrils filled with her own stink. He bit his lip and shook his head. If they startled Raschad, Rimmersin was dead.

Raschad's voice remained calm, scarily peaceful. *Who came back last?* she'd asked Raschad. *The dead boy.*

"My comm, if you please, Supervisor. However much I amuse you, I'm not here for games today."

Sal hugged the wall.

"I only want the comm. Unless that was a lie."

"It hardly matters." Rimmersin's confidence turned her stomach. "There are guards on their way. I won't waste time retrieving a comm you'll never re—"

A choked squawk sounded from the room. "Ra-Raschad!" Rimmersin gagged.

"Humor me, Mas Supervisor."

Straining her neck, Sal peeked through the door glass again, and a chill ran down her spine. She raised one hand to mime a gun at Schuell's temple. The guard nodded, peeked over her head, and flattened back against the wall, chin dripping sweat.

Rimmersin, carrying half the newbie's weight and a third his height, stood pinned against a wall, with Raschad's injured forearm across his scrawny throat. The Supervisor's skin gleamed paler than Raschad's in the tech light. And, glancing at Schuell, Sal knew what he was thinking. Raschad would kill Rimmersin, and Schuell would have to kill Raschad. And she couldn't stop it—couldn't.

"Give up," Rimmersin croaked. "Walk out . . . now, and I'll let you run . . ." Raschad leaned into Rimmersin. The Supervisor gagged and struggled.

"Who paid you to have me watched?" Raschad let up on Rimmersin's throat.

"Off . . . off-planeters." Rimmersin gasped for air. "I d-don't know."

"How was it arranged?" Raschad spoke in a low growl.

"A . . . a n-note from Representative Deesin."

"Who is that?"

"The Governor's secondary advisor."

"Are you reporting on the greenies to him?"

"Sh-She wanted to hear about Aireil tr-trouble."

"Why?" Raschad leaned into Rimmersin.

"I don't know. Just more trouble. Maybe the greenies will start fighting among themselves."

"The Governor is behind this?"

"I don't know."

"You seemed to know the other night."

"I was drunk." Rimmersin's voice scaled upward. "Deesin paid for my appointment petitions for this position. If I don't do what she wants, I'm out."

The squat. Sal pressed against the wall, every muscle rigid. If Deesin and whoever she represented thought anyone on Ver Day could profit from rousing the Aireils, they were worse fools than newbies, and a lot more dangerous.

Her hip ached, a bump gouging into it. She peeked into the office again.

"So being in my grandfather's employ is extra?" Raschad's voice shook. He was going to fall on his face.

"They don't object," Rimmersin whined. "They encourage off-planet connections."

"Which off-planeters paid to have me beaten two months ago?"

"I . . . I'm not sure. I . . ."

Raschad wobbled. Rimmersin jerked. The newbie thumbed the power trigger of his stolen weapon, and the hum froze Rimmersin.

"Why ask so many questions? Worried who might be watching your greenie slut?" The govie's eyes, visible to Sal now beyond Raschad's shoulder, danced wildly. But his expression—on a face as narrow as a rat's—was still cunning.

"My comm, Supervisor." Voice impassive, the newbie refused to be baited. "Now."

"It's here." Rimmersin's voice squeaked as Raschad leaned on the man's throat. "Let me breathe." Sal heard more choking.

The bruising lump against her hip registered on her brain. She felt inside her pocket. And she'd thought Raschad was only giving her a nice pat at the jail!

"Point to it." Raschad's words slurred. "This drawer?" Rimmersin must have agreed. "Thank you."

"I'll get it." Rimmersin still sounded choked.

Don't fall for that.

"No."

Schuell moved from behind her in one smooth motion. *Boom!* A blast roared, and shock waves bounced off the confines of the hall, staggering her. Schuell dived for the doors, bulled the right one open, and bellied onto the study floor. "Don't."

Everything froze. Sal swallowed—once, twice—took a shuddering breath, and peeked into the room again. Her heart pounded.

The lamp was out, and she strained to focus in the dim light seeping through the patio doors. Raschad was going to die. She'd failed him—just like Sonny, just as Frim would have died except for Lucky Mac's help.

Schuell lay on the study's floor, his weapon aimed at Raschad. But the newbie still held Rimmersin from behind, his bloody arm about the supervisor's throat. Both men stared at a large hole in the wall behind the desk.

"Really, mas." Raschad glanced at Schuell, his gun boring into Rimmersin's ear. "One should not assume that one's victim will remain a victim." He laughed, a chill, wheezing sound without mirth. "Try for my weapon again, and I'll gift you its butt behind your ear."

Raschad ground the gun muzzle against Rimmersin's jaw until the man squawked. "But I'm so pleased you've arrived, Sergeant. Would you lay down your weapon. My hand is very tired. I don't want to have an accident." He leaned on Rimmersin, bowing the shorter man's back.

Rising to a crouch, Schuell laid his gun on the floor and pushed it away. Sal sagged. Anything she did now would only distract Raschad, and between Schuell and Rimmersin there wasn't leeway for the newbie to blink.

"Thank you." Raschad's voice broke. He cleared his throat. "Now if you would oblige us by finding the comm Mas Rimmersin is holding for me."

Schuell hesitated, stood, and moved warily toward the desk.

"Left hand, bottom drawer," Rimmersin squeaked.

Schuell looked to Raschad for permission, then opened the drawer at the newbie's nod. Keeping to the side of the desk so his hands remained in sight, he removed a communications packet.

"Would you read it aloud, please." Raschad spoke so softly that Sal barely caught his words. "I'm afraid my eyesight is not what it should be this morning."

Schuell raised the packet. "I need light."

"Go."

Schuell stepped nearer the patio doors. His eyes flicked to Raschad and back. His hands shook as he undid the packet flap, freeing the enclosed comm. A tired man, Sal thought, whose degree of judgment might consequently slip.

" 'To M. Noran-tol-Tarsian Ras—' "

"I know my name."

Schuell glanced at Raschad and cleared his throat. " 'From F. Shae-tol-Mex Everer. My sincerest sympathy upon the death of your sister and more recently your mother and brother.' " Schuell's voice quavered.

" 'Knowing your grandfather will have abandoned you and that your situation is most probably desperate, I have arranged to provide credits for your planetary tax. You understand that I am anxious that you should continue to lead a safe and healthful life in your particular location.' "

What did that mean? Sal wondered. Why couldn't Raschad just up and leave now? Broke, that was why—he never had credit except just enough to reoutfit. And all those sherks back on his home planet wanted him to stay put—they would pay his immigrant taxes to keep him legal here, but never give him enough credit to get off Ver Day.

" 'I regret that your mother died merely as a means to embarrass your grandfather's political position. But, I assure you, it has done him harm in more ways than either side has yet discerned.' " Schuell drew a breath. " ' With my deepest regrets and re—' "

"Enough."

Schuell looked up from the letter, expecting anything, Sal supposed, from a man who'd received such news. But Raschad already knew the hurtful parts; he had just needed to hear them from someone other than Rimmersin to accept the hard truth. He let the Morven's muzzle lower, then staggered and slumped down on a couch.

Schuell stared. Rimmersin stared. Raschad raised the gun toward his bloody face.

"Put it down, son." Schuell's voice shivered her spine.

Whether Raschad heard or just ran out of strength, the gun slipped from his fingers and clattered on the stone floor.

Sweat trickled down Sal's neck and dripped between her breasts. Trembling, she remained still, afraid she'd get someone killed. But how did she save Raschad from himself?

"Kick it away." Schuell coaxed. "No one has to get hurt this morning."

Raschad didn't move.

Rimmersin dropped, snagged the gun—his fingers as thin and pale as rain leeches—and stood back. Those hands had *touched* Raschad. Sal's heart hammered.

Rimmersin pointed the weapon at the floor.

Schuell visibly relaxed. "I'll call for help, mas."

"Wait." Rimmersin's command froze Schuell's hand halfway to his shoulder-mounted talkie. "I've something to show you before we're interrupted." Rimmersin raised his gun, letting it waver between Schuell and Raschad. "I've proof that this newbie attacked me." Raschad remained slumped, his head hanging. "Let's go out on the patio, where we had wine."

Sal's stomach dropped out. Schuell stood absolutely still, missing none of the threat in Rimmersin's stance. Her teeth chattered, and she bit down. The Supervisor had to assume that Schuell had heard him confess to triple dealing, and he meant to kill both Raschad and Schuell.

"Up, Raschad." Rimmersin aimed at the newbie's head.

Sal didn't dare move. If Raschad would just look as if he had some strength in him, she could do something—distract Rimmersin. But if he was done, couldn't react, then Schuell's weapon was too damn far for Raschad to reach. She sweated and stared, searching big-eyed all around her for help.

And, gigis save her, there came Tiny Slacket down the hall, his pasty face as big and stupid-looking as a boar in a parlor. He must have witnessed her arrest and dreamed up bighearted plans to rescue her. Sal blinked sweat, certain she hallucinated. Bumping against Tiny's leg was her crate of nightbabies.

She marveled that she could be more afraid. But her hand shook as she waved him back. He paid no attention, just bumbled on up the hall, peeking in doorways.

"Get *up*, Raschad." Rimmersin's voice spiked. "Get up or I kill Schuell and put the weapon in your hand."

Her heart thumped. Rage wouldn't help her here.

Tiny Slacket stopped at the music-room door and stared inside like the goof he was. Sal pressed flatter against the wall, waved again.

The lump in her pocket dug into her hip.

Tiny turned, and she waved. He froze like a startled fleepa. Her heart thumped.

"Raschad!" Rimmersin's voice tore her gut.

"Let me help him." Schuell's voice was strung taut.

"Throw down your comm tab first." She peeked back and saw Schuell obey. "Now." Rimmersin nodded. "Carefully. Forget going for your weapon."

Schuell eased around the desk, keeping it between himself and Rimmersin, offering no threat. With daylight brightening outside the patio windows, Sal couldn't see their faces at all against the glare. But Schuell bent and slipped an arm about Raschad.

"Come on," Schuell coaxed. The newbie slumped against him. "Up. You want to get up. *Believe me.*"

The newbie's head lifted. "Let him do it here."

Rimmersin chuckled. "Don't push me, love."

"Newbie." Schuell gripped Raschad's knee. "I've a fear of dying in enclosed places."

Raschad's laugh, weak and startled, sounded insane, but she was glad to hear it. At least he was that alert.

"Aia." He straightened against Schuell.

Rimmersin's weapon shook and followed their every move. Out of the corner of her eye, Sal could see Tiny Slacket standing slack-jawed in the hall, halfway between her and the music parlor. In the study, Schuell wrapped his arms around Raschad and lifted.

And the way the newbie folded up off the couch told Sal he wasn't as spent as he might appear to others.

"Out." Rimmersin gestured. "Hurry."

Schuell wrestled Raschad's weight toward the patio doors. Rimmersin turned, following their progress, and finally faced away from the inside doors.

Sal glanced down the hall. Tiny tiptoed toward her with absurd delicacy; she motioned him against the wall.

He kept coming.

She glanced back into the room. Raschad and Schuell already stood outside. Shrike. She glanced at Tiny—the crate on his shoulder was no help at all now.

Rimmersin stopped in the patio doorway, still too near for her to chance going after Schuell's gun. She reached for the tiny tech knife in her pocket, fighting for breath.

"All the way to the wall." Rimmersin motioned. "Sit."

Sal couldn't see Raschad or Schuell anymore, and she trembled as Tiny came even with her. If she didn't move, he would force her hand anyway. Easing away from the wall, she faced the doors. His image blurred by etched flowers, Rimmersin was concentrating on his victims.

"If we work this just right, Raschad, you'll live. The reward promised by certain associates ensures *that*. They thought I was too stupid to understand that with your brother dead, you're valuable again. I don't know what their plans are for you, but I've got the price on your pretty head running high. All you have to be is alive. So cooperate, because Representative Deesin will pay only a little less for you dead. She can't have anyone making peace with the damned Aireils now—that would ruin everything. And the greenies think you're some sort of hero. Fools . . ."

Was there an angle this squat wasn't working? Sal wondered. The bastard meant to kill Schuell and get a legal hold on Raschad, then have him locked up for murder, where he'd be at hand for sale to the highest bidder or for a night's amusement.

She opened the knife blade, toying with the slight weight of it in her hand. Rimmersin was a black silhouette against the outside light. If he didn't move . . .

"You, Sergeant." Rimmersin shifted. "Regrettably, you had to die from the moment you arrived. Time to go, darlings. *Push him*, Raschad."

Sal's gut quaked. She pushed the second door open. Her blade glittered as it sailed away from her, a shimmering sliver.

Rimmersin whirled. A shot cracked over her head.

She hit the floor, sliding belly down after Schuell's gun. But the polished stone was slicker than squat; her fingers jammed against the weapon and spun it away.

Dead now. A shot cracked near her leg. *Dead.*

A squarish shadow flew overhead, squeaking as it passed. And Tiny's crate crashed at Rimmersin's feet.

The lock sprang and the lid flapped open. Nightbabies burst into the room, mewling and wailing, their whip tails snapping.

Arm-length bodies arced airward and fell fluttering to the floor, their wings ill-designed to lift from a level surface. Claws skittered on slick stone and caught in carpets. Mewling filled the room.

Rimmersin screamed. His handgun boomed.

Nightbabies screeched, spattering the fancy rugs. Sal hugged the floor, sucking squat stench into her frozen lungs.

Rimmersin staggered out the patio door.

She lunged onto her feet, dodging flapping, writhing nightbabies, and burst onto the patio. Rimmersin backed ahead of her, arms windmilling, feet stamping a frenzied jig, struggling to free himself of nightbabies. The creatures clung to him, using their cradle claws to climb his clothes, fighting for flight altitude.

Backed against the patio wall, forgotten in Rimmersin's panic, Schuell slipped away from Raschad. The newbie wobbled and dropped to one knee.

Rimmersin screamed. Leathery wings snapped his face.

"Raschad!" Schuell's bellow froze Sal. She watched Rimmersin break into a staggering run, nightbabies weighting his legs. He never saw the wall or thought about what direction he ran. He certainly didn't see Raschad crouched low.

He struck the big newbie. Raschad leaned into the man's stomach and stood, trying to fight clear of the patio wall. The Supervisor upended.

Sun shimmered across the jungle. Schuell stood frozen in silhouette, a nightbaby on the crown of his head.

Rimmersin kept running. Backlit by ruddy dawn, feet off the ground, he pedaled up and over Raschad's shoulder.

Raschad wobbled, his head following Rimmersin's weight.

Sal lunged. Schuell lunged, too, and snagged the newbie's shirt before she reached him. She hit them from behind.

Teetering, they yawed against the waist-high wall and stared down at the nightbabies lifting from Rimmersin's falling body.

Rimmersin landed.

"You lose somethin'?"

Sal spun. "Nothing important, Tiny. Nothing important."

Chapter 24

Scrubbed clean, their wounds tended, their stomachs full, they lay naked and safe in one of Hope's beds. Being with Raschad seemed stranger at the moment than all the rest that had happened. Downstairs, George and Schuell were deciding the newbie's fate; Sal stared at him, refusing to think on that. He watched her in turn, peeking through swollen, slitted eyelids. Glass nicks pocked his face. Bandages bound his ribs.

"Why can't I ever touch you." His words came faint and weary. "Why do I always end up like this?" His wrapped, glass-cut hands flexed against his chest.

She touched them gently. "Why do I always fall on my head?"

"Because you lead with it." He smiled. "Thank you for saving my life."

A tiny knot uncurled deep inside her. "I was afraid maybe you weren't so grateful to still be here."

"I am. Not sure why, except for you." He kissed her cheek. She stroked his hair.

"I didn't save you. You're just too cussed tough to die." He grunted against her shoulder. "Meesha." She kissed his cheek. "When you stood up with Rimmersin on your shoulder—" They'd grown very blunt with each other, but this question almost stuck in her throat. "You didn't mean to kill him."

"I don't know." And he sounded as if his indecision was enough to give him some peace.

She wrapped herself about his battered body and let his deep breathing rock them. He'd lived. Mistwalkers, gigis, Libers—he'd survived them all, and mostly on his own. The little she'd done—feeding him lamie sap or plugging up bleeding holes—had only given him a chance to fight. Outside of that, he took care of himself.

And like morning mist rising, a great weight lifted, leaving her lightheaded and giddy. It was too late not to love him, and was now even all right. He'd hurt her. Life hurt. What counted was that he expected nothing of her, blamed her for nothing, and she wouldn't sag under guilt no matter what came. He was as headstrong as a midas, and whatever happened to him was his own fault. Not hers.

The load-by-load's government credit ran out the day Rimmersin's remains were shipped to Capitol, and the depot clinic threw her out. The packer staggered into Dig's Den begging a drink. So George arrested her for vagrancy—never mind that the whole blessed town was vagrant.

George acted scary, and the woman admitted right out that Rimmersin had paid her to watch Raschad and cause him trouble. But Sal figured stealing her Pike load had been the woman's own scheme.

George freed the packer the next morning, and half the town ran her and her empty sled onto the River Trail, sending her south as fast as she could move. Considering the local mood, the woman was lucky to leave at all.

Schuell accompanied Rimmersin's body to Capitol and returned with a crew of five new govies—all women. The green wasn't safe from tampering yet. But Sal figured Nunes had ideas of how he wanted the depot operated in Rimmersin's wake, and Schuell, being First Settler himself, she'd learned, had talked in important ears in Capitol. Rimmersin's ex-bosses were watched now. What they'd do about saving green tech she had no idea, but people in Tumble Town were beginning to carve and weave again, renewing their skills at hand manufacture. All the jungle was just a big factory anyway, turning out raw products for shaping.

So maybe Raschad had figured things right, and the Terms would fail, green tech would fail. But greenies had a habit of surviving. And by standing up for himself—both in deed and in mind—Raschad had stopped some nasty plans, and saved the green that much hurt, anyway. The longer greenies held back the ruin, the better. Sal didn't figure it was the jungle at risk here, anyway. Like whoever had brought the ku-soo trees and milk bovs, it was humans who were most likely to die.

Raschad's second week of healing passed, and Morrie, Frim Urt, and his boys had finished putting the old man's shack back together. Rebuilding and additions made it years better. But Sal wouldn't take Raschad there—not yet, not with rain falling, molds

blooming, and him thin, pale, quieter even than his norm, and still
moving so achingly slow.

Hope didn't charge them room or board. Sal worried about that,
but the woman said it was small return for the two of them rid-
ding the town of Rimmersin.

For his part, George claimed he wanted Raschad visibly at hand
until the newbie sat out his five weeks of parole for breaking up
the depot's jail. That was the only charge Schuell had filed against
him, Rimmersin being too dead to complain.

So in the mornings Sal worked for Slick Clay—putting in
rainy-season ditches and dikes around the man's properties—and
George took Raschad with him. By noon, when she came in mud-
black and dripping, the two of them would be in George's house
with a meal cooked. Most of the food she recognized as George's
doing. But it amused her when an unusual dish showed up, some
familiar edible cooked in a very unfamiliar way. Settlers save her,
George was letting a newbie cook.

They slept in Hope's bed, smiled at noises heard through their
walls, and healed.

Then Scollarta ordered the Sundowner's services up to Heav-
en's Rest, and Hope let Sal pick the fancy to visit him. No one
had ever seen Dog Girl in a dress before. Dog Girl had never
worn one. Actually, she only hiked up her pants legs, borrowed
Hope's town boots, and wore one of Hope's fancy rain capes over
her leathers. Heaven's Rest let her in anyway, and Scollarta unlocked his door for her. That was invitation enough for Dog Girl.

Sal waited outside the hotel in the dark with Bocho Man. Rain,
scary company, and all, the wait was worth it.

When Dog Girl emerged, the three didn't say a word until they
made it back to the Sundowner's bar, but then they laughed so
hard, long, and silly that they started drinking to sober up. Dog
Girl didn't tell the full story of her bedroom encounter with
Scollarta until nearly dawn. Sal passed out halfway through.

Two days later the contract man shipped out volunteer with
Nunes's other labor culls.

The monsoon season struck full force. Clouds tumbled up huge
and black, dumping floods and turning day to constant night. Mud
ran and slithered. Lights burned at all hours in the bars and businesses. And you could gather a breakfast of mushrooms without
leaving the house.

The eye in the new window at the Gigi glowed balefully, great black shadow eyelashes thrown on it from the crowd within. Sitting atop the bar, Sal glowered, feeling as mean as the gigi eye looked.

"I ain't marrying him."

"I'll do ya, then." Frim's yell was only half joking.

The crowd growled. Bocho Man swatted the top of Frim's head, and Marta Woozniack kicked his ankle.

"Freeze in hell," Sal shouted over the drumming of the rain. "I ain't marrying nobody. *Ain't.*"

"Use sense, gal." Morrie's frustration showed, but Sal stared him in the eye, her jaw set. "You been *livin'* with him near a month already."

"Three weeks, and I done that before without killing him. Don't mean I'm going to marry the shriking newbie."

She stared at a room of determined faces and just got madder. What the hell business was it of this town who she married? She glared at Morrie and old Effords, who'd tricked her into this, inviting her to the Gigi "for a drink."

Hope O'Toole and all her girls and boys sat there in their fancy slickers, staring at her. Tom Bill leaned on the tinny-tune next to Dancer and Frim's lot of bullybys. And every one of the Voses and Bwashwavies was present, plus Greta, the Pannier's manager Khon Whon, Armar Toh, Salmon Deutchek with his cane, Ernesto Chi, Mooli, and Lucky Mac. Even Nuke and Haze prowled one end of the bar. About every damn soul in this end of the jungle was present.

It ain't *their* life, Sal thought angrily. Sitting right up front was Mary. Her eyes glowed, overflowing like her breasts—the woman was loving every breath of it.

The wind howled. The Gigi's double doors eased open against the press of bodies, and Sal's eyes whipped over, ready to blast the new arrival to cinders.

But Raschad stepped into the mess, led by George, both of them so tall they dripped on everyone else. Raschad slipped off his hood, and Nike Toon's eyes followed him through the crowd. Those nearest him nodded and smiled, giving him due respect.

Her outrage wavered at the sight of him, then worsened as she took in his confused expression. They had no right pressuring the newbie, or her through him. She glared fire at George as he stripped out of his slicker.

But the door opened again.

And this time her teeth would have fallen out if they hadn't been clenched so hard. Quarel Schuell walked in with Nicky, and no one panicked. They had shrikin' *invited* him.

The sergeant worked his way around to Slick Clay's table and sat. Nicky settled at his back, next to Clay's men. What a sight, low town and high town bullies mixing.

Next the Jinkmans arrived, carrying Pia—not fair at all; the little girl still looked like a ghost. Sal glared at Morrie from her perch. He and old Effords smiled back, smug.

Raschad eased up beside her. Seething, she met his questioning eyes with a brusque nod toward the whole crowd. He glanced around, braced a boot on the bar's foot rail, and leaned on the counter, back to the room, hands clasped. Greenie business, his expression said. Not his problem.

"Don't look so peaceful." She leaned near his ear. Rain drummed on the roof and the crowd shifted, making more room, as if expecting others. "They're trying to marry you off."

He glanced up. Scars flashed white on his golden cheek, and his eyes danced. "To who?"

"To me, you gigi-headed ass." She glared.

"Shrike." He looked relieved, even amused, which did her no good. "I was afraid they wanted me to pick."

She swatted him. Water splattered from his slicker.

"Take that off before you catch cold." He did, giving her a serious and sympathetic smile. "You want to marry me?" she asked.

"Naia."

"Good." At least he was on her side in this.

"He's comin' now." Face pressed to the front window, Jimmy Ko gestured *quiet* to the crowd.

Sal sat up straighter, glancing at Raschad. Who the hell were they waiting on? Mira Goontz gave her a knowing smile, and Sal raised a fist in return. The doors opened.

Winter Appenheimer waddled in. *A shriking lawyer.*

The Voses shooed their younger brood out into the rain to join the Jinkman kids. The littler Bwashwavies followed. Wouldn't *they* have fun, with every adult in town occupied inside this bar?

Coat shed, Winter walked straight up to Sal. "Young woman." He spoke loud and clear so everyone could hear. "Because what we are going to discuss has legal ramifications, the town council has asked me to represent them in this discussion."

Her jaw set. Town council? Tom, Greta, George, Dancer, Khon Whon, and Ma Jinkman? That was a stacked deck.

"Meesha Raschad." Appenheimer cocked an eye at the newbie. "You might as well turn around. You're the heart of all this."

Raschad turned, finally looking uncomfortable. This would teach him to laugh at her.

"First, I would prefer this be a private conversation between myself and the two of you." Appenheimer stroked his broad silk vest. "However, the town council has informed me that they consider you, Raschad, to be altogether too valuable an asset for this community to lose."

Tom Bill, sitting front and center, nodded confirmation. Sal couldn't believe it.

"They further indicated that since either or both of you might strenuously object to what they feel is the only acceptable solution to certain problems which have come to their attention, they wished me present to make their opinions felt.

"Now." Appenheimer puffed at the feathery edges of his reeki-stained mustache. "This is not a terribly complicated matter. But two things need to be discussed and understood. First, as a born alien to the planet Ver Day, you, Raschad, can not remain in residence on Ver Day without first having a sponsor and second paying your alien tax."

Sal chewed her bottom lip, disliking the discussion's bent.

"I have on record," Appenheimer continued, "a communication from a certain party of which you are already cognizant. It affirms that credits have been deposited with Ver Day's government, sufficient to cover your alien taxes for the next eighty years or your death, whichever comes first. As the closest legal representation available to you, I have been authorized by the Office of Immigration to act as the fund's administrator, unless you prefer otherwise."

Spattered clapping and whooping interrupted Appenheimer.

"Why?" she whispered aside to Raschad. "Why do they still want you to stay on Ver Day? Why do they even want you alive?"

"Some don't." He kept his eyes on the crowd, answering both her questions at once. "But my patron needs me to remain the focus of the Tarsian family's enemies. He has grandchildren with Tarsian blood."

Sal shook her head and looked away. She'd never understand that way of thinking. She never *wanted* to understand. What it had done to Raschad made her sick.

"Now to the second item, Mas Raschad." Appenheimer spoke quite loudly, drawing everyone's attention again. "Sheriff Estevar was notified yesterday that you are to be deported."

Sal dropped off the counter, face burning. Raschad caught her arm, but she jerked it free. "What—"

Appenheimer raised his hand. "Please, Mas Banks."

Raschad tugged on her arm again. She hung against the bar, bristling and as likely to hit Raschad as anyone.

"With the death of Supervisor Rimmersin, Raschad no longer has a planetary sponsor." Appenheimer cleared his throat. "A number of persons from within this community have volunteered. However, it takes time to file and have approved any change of sponsor. And certain irregularities in his original application have come to light. If these aren't cleared up, Mas Raschad would be forced to leave Ver Day and reimmigrate."

She hadn't missed the "would" in Appenheimer's speech. Still, her heart thundered. "What's the *but* line?"

Appenheimer swallowed. "Marriage to a born resident provides an alien immediate citizenship, continuing the length of said marriage, assuming joint residency is maintained."

She took a deep breath between clenched teeth, put a hand to her face and pinched the bridge of her nose between two fingers. Settlers above. She looked at Raschad. He looked at her.

"No." He shook his head. "Naia." He snatched his slicker and bulled through the crowd.

Schuell motioned to Nicky. The kid slipped to the door and blocked it, not looking as confident as a man should, facing a moving target. Raschad had put the fear into those depot boys.

Schuell stood. "I'm sorry, Raschad. As of this morning, you are my responsibility. Unless you marry this woman now, you'll be in my custody until turned over to Capitol's Administrative Police."

Raschad tensed, ready to do something stupid. They should never corner him. But then he just sagged, shoved Benny Issl out of a chair, and sat.

So it was left to her, and there wasn't much choice. People cleared a path. She knelt in front of the newbie and stared up into his scarred, unhappy face.

"Babe." She brushed his hand. "I don't mean to pry, but was it somethin' I said?"

He stared as if she'd lost her mind, then covered his face with a wound-stiffened hand and laughed. "Sal." He sighed behind his hand. "They could still come after me—any time. If I tie you to me, they'll come after you, too. If we had children—" She stiffened. "—by some unlikely coincidence . . ." He shook his head. "It never ends. They never forget. If they think up any excuse, they'll be after you as well as me."

She dropped her head on his knee, then looked up, shaking hair out of her eyes and fighting a piss-boiling rage.

"That's *maybes*. If I worried about *maybes*, I'd never leave Tumble Town. Shrike, I'd already be dead. I ain't worried about *maybes*, idiot. I take care of myself. Quit making excuses."

He bit his bottom lip. "You *want* to marry me?"

"Naia. Don't want to be tied to any man. Just a liability and a pain in the trailer. I own my own sleds, my contracts, run my own business. That don't change if we get married."

He closed his eyes. "You're sure?"

"Squat. I ain't letting that thick-headed government guard have you." She reached up and caught his face between her hands. "I ain't losing you just because we're too mean to try." She sighed. "We were good trail partners. Weren't we?"

"Aia." He bit his lip, and glanced away, then back, chin quivering, eyes aglitter ... and jerked her into his arms.

The crowd went fleepa-brained. Bullybys roared; Hope's people squealed. Fists pounded Sal's back.

Make that *twelve* tech things she indulged in now ... and Settlers forgive her, Raschad meant a bigger change in her life than any handlamp.

When she could, she twisted around, still in Raschad's arms, and stared past Nuke Jagger. Morrie stood by the bar, his old face creased with a sad little smile. She endured a hug from Haze, tugged Raschad to his feet, and forced a way through the celebrating crowd.

"Morrie? Some trick you played, old man."

"Didn't figure I'd live to see it." He wiped at his face. "Damn bugs." He wiped again.

"You know this means more baths, don't you, Morrie?" A hint of a smile tugged Raschad's lips.

"Piss on you." Morrie raised his fists, and Raschad hugged him. "Here, now!" Morrie pawed free.

"Frim says your shack has a new addition." Raschad smiled at the top of the old man's head.

"Aia." Morrie recovered, eyes gleaming. "It's a beaut. Good 'nough for a love nest, if you don't mind lizard squat."

Sal caught George staring at them. "Got to get it done," he said, coming up at her side with Schuell at his back.

She nodded. Schuell handed her a fancy tech pen, and she gritted her teeth and signed the records George had prepared.

Appenheimer stepped up. "You take him?"

"Aia."

"You, her?"

"Aia." Raschad's voice caught in his chest, and she elbowed him so hard that he pinned her to keep from being hit again.

"Well, then, in front of this whole damn town—" Appenheimer signaled for silence. "—I pronounce you legal cohabitators."

"What?" She raised a fist.

"You're married."

George hugged her like a father—which he never was to her—and slapped Raschad's shoulder so hard the newbie staggered.

After that the party went gigi-headed.

She felt strange and sad about George all through dancing, eating smoked klimie, and bellowing songs. But ducking out the Gigi's back door for breathable air, she spotted him next door on Dig's Den's service porch with Earl Junior's widow. Things looked to even out. The jungle was a hard, hard place. You took your loving where you found it, even with a freaking newbie.

"Sal?"

She turned. Tom Bill was leaning against the back wall of the Gigi in the rain, his hat running a river off its brim.

"Haia. I should shower all dressed if you recommend it."

"Naia, not much. Just wanted to give you my personal regards for the future, gal."

"Thanks, aia. Being the bride here, can I get nosy rude?"

"Be my weddin' present to you."

"This all your doing, then?"

He shrugged. "Morrie had his say. And Ma Jinkman. Nuke and Haze can't vote here, but wouldn't shut up no ways. And most other folks felt acceptable after being doctored by Raschad. He's likable, for a newbie."

"Don't suppose you had to wrestle Nike Toon for her vote." Tom laughed. "So why, Mas Mayor?"

"Time to learn." He shook his head. "These newbies won't stop coming till we stop them. Best learn what's wrong and what's right with them before we try that."

"Well, nothing you learn about Raschad will teach you what to expect from another newbie. He's a special idiot."

"That's why we're keeping him—because maybe we'd be wrong to stop them all from coming. There's things to learn, more than just tech. That's where Governor Wally's makin' his mistake."

"What you mean?"

Tom shrugged again and wandered off.

"Haia!" She yelled after him. "If you was learning the *enemy* before, who you studying now?"

He turned, his hat swirling a spray of water. "Who's the enemy? It ain't just greenies against newbies, us or them. And it ain't us against tech. It's the good guys—whoever that is, including Raschad—against the baddies, and that ain't simple." He cocked his head toward the depot and started off again. "Got to get more brew." He disappeared beneath soggy lorri trees, headed upslope toward Marta's brewery.

"Wife?"

She spun on Raschad. "Idiot?"

"I'm glad the heart grows fonder." Already slickered himself, he offered her a brand new, shiny green rain cover. The oiled botafab shimmered like a wet leaf.

"Reckon you stole this," she said.

"Naia. It's a wedding present from the Pannier."

"And they didn't give you one?"

"Gave me the one I've worn the last two weeks."

"Near forgot that." She took the fine coat and stared at it.

"What now?"

"I ain't never had a new slicker."

He didn't laugh, just took the coat, spread it open at the shoulders, and held it until she slipped it on.

"Looks nice, Mas Banks."

"Thank you, Mas Raschad-Banks."

He smiled. She stepped into the storm, trying the coat out, listening to the rattle of rain off its hood.

"Here." She drew him into the wet with her, and side by side they slogged downhill. "Wait."

"Aia?" He turned to face her.

Rain pattered. She wriggled under the hood of his slicker so they could hear each other.

"You happy, newbie?"

He ducked his chin and leaned nearer. "You give me hope, a place to be, and a chance to be useful."

Useful, he'd said, not *used*. She gripped his slickered arms. "You made peace with the mistwalkers. Kept the gigis from the wheat fields, which maybe saved Capitol from starving this winter. You rid the town of Rimmersin's poison, made friends in high town, and even have me working for Slick Clay. I reckon you're more than *useful*."

She stretched up and gave him the longest kiss they'd shared since their shower together at Morrie's. Illness played heck with a man's stamina, and this kiss, which had been a long time building, wasn't the same now as at Morrie's. He never would be the same, nor her, nor wanted to be.

Married to a newbie. She hugged him harder.

"What?"

"Seein' if you'll break."

He pulled back, staring at her within the tent of their hoods, and shook his head. "Naia, Sal Banks. I don't break easy."

"I'm gambling on it."

He took her hand and skated her through the mud and rain toward Morrie's shack. "You happy?"

"Aia," she admitted. "Happy I got my hands on you. Ain't happy to be married."

"My apologies."

"Ain't no help for it. Nor any way to tell if it'll be good or bad until we try."

"Can we try right away?"

"Shrike." She swatted him. "We know *that* ain't a problem."

"Then it's a good way to start."

And finally she laughed, from her moldy socks on up, and knocked his hood off. He dropped his head back in the jungle rain, smiling and beautiful. And the sight twisted her heart. Settlers save her, did he look just a shade green?

Everyone knows what happened, of course. It is difficult to look back over the spans of years and remember the uproar of those days. The meeting, which had been planned to last a week in order that everyone could speak, stretched to two weeks, and then three. There were too many candidates, and a consensus could not be found. Every leading family in the land had a daughter or a niece of marriageable age. Every maid had a flawless lineage, flawless complexion, flawless eyes of black, brown, blue, green, gray; flawless hair of gold, brown, black, red; features of surpassing beauty, and sweet breath and a lovely voice. Even Arthur wearied of it and went hawking. Feuds developed, powerful leaders backed one family and then another as the offers of gold increased. Happy was the man who had nothing to gain or lose by the king's decision. And throughout it all, Merlin sat by the High King's chair, old and frail, his black eyes watching it all, saying nothing.

At last, his patience near an end, King Arthur commanded the meeting to close. He would not divide his kingdom over a woman, he said. He would rather die unwed. Only then did a young man rise from the rear of the Welsh delegation, and, having received permission to speak, addressed the High King in a trembling voice. Just as silver was found threaded into black rock deep within the earth, he began, just as gold was sprinkled sparsely over pebbled sands, so all treasures worth pursuing did not come easy; the brightest jewel often lay buried in the darkest clay. As he overcame his fear, his voice fell into the sweet sing-song of the storyteller, and the Welshmen in the hall settled back comfortably to hear his tale. It was, it seems, the tale of the emperor Maximus and how he found his Elen, the famous Welsh beauty with sapphire eyes whom Maximus wed and for whom he foreswore allegiance to Rome. She was, he sang, fairer than the stars among the heavens, more constant than the sun in his course across the sky, sweeter than wildflowers that grace the summer meadows, and ever a true companion to the king. In all his endeavors she was beside him; she brought him luck and victory; he never lost a battle until he left Britain, where she could not follow. The singer paused—Welshmen were wont to attribute Maximus' prowess to the virtues of his Welsh wife, but it was unwise to expect this descendant of Maximus to believe it—he claimed, instead, that hidden in the dark Welsh mountains lay a jewel as bright as Elen, a girl as beautiful, as wise and steadfast, as Maximus' own bride. Like a vein of precious metal lying undiscovered in the hills, she awaited the High King's notice; a word from him could bring her gold to light. A king's daughter she was, descended from Elen, with hair of starlight and the voice of a nightingale. And Gwillim, for it was my old childhood companion who had risen to speak before them all, took a deep breath and held hard to his courage. The maiden's name, he said, was Guinevere.

There was a shocked silence. The Companions froze. Arthur's face was a mask. Merlin closed his eyes. Then the throng found their voices, and angry protests arose on all sides. "How dare the boy?" "What maid is this? I have heard no tell of her." "That he should mention the name before the king!" Then Gwarthgydd rose and clapped a hand on Gwillim's shoulder.

"My lords," he said, and his deep rumbling voice got their attention. "The lad speaks of my half sister, Guinevere of Northgallis. In his later years, my father the King of Northgallis wed Elen of Gwynedd, a beauty of renown. She died giving birth to the lady in question, who was a childhood friend of Gwillim's here. She is now the ward of King Pellinore and Queen Alyse and lives in Gwynedd. Gwillim likes a good tale, but all he has said is true enough."

"Is that the Lark of Gwynedd?" someone asked. "I have heard of her."

"Isn't that the maid the old witch prophesied about, the night of her birth? You remember Giselda—"

"A curse, I thought it was, a spell—"

"Oh no, she prophesied great beauty and great fame—"

"Has anyone seen her?" asked one of the Companions. "Where is Pellinore? Who can attest to the lad's claims?"

But Pellinore, weary of words, was out hunting. It was Fion who stood.

* * *

That winter lasted forever. Elaine lay abed with an illness born of disappointment and envy, and Alyse could barely tolerate the sight of me. Pellinore was proud and conscious of his new status in the High King's inner circle, but he never came to the women's quarters, wishing to avoid Alyse's cold fury at his betrayal, and I saw him only at dinner in the evenings. The queen's ladies kept aloof at the queen's wishes. Only Ailsa, of all the women in the castle, was thoroughly excited on my behalf.

"Just think of it! Wouldn't your dear mother be proud! Her little Gwen to be King Arthur's queen! Why, I just pinch myself when I think of it! How lucky you are, my lady! How happy you will be!"

But I could not see how this unexpected event could make me happy. Already it seemed to have cost me Elaine's friendship, and she was the only real friend I had ever had. Proud as I was to be chosen out of all the maids in Britain, I could not envision happiness ahead. I was to be married to a man I had never met, and because he was who he was, there was no possible way out of it. I did not feel the thrill all Britain expected me to feel; I felt only apprehension and a nagging regret that I had not married Fion.

However much she suffered at the sight of me, Alyse knew her duty. She set all her ladies to work on my wardrobe, and we sat together all winter sewing my wedding clothes, fashioning new gowns, weaving bed linens and chamber hangings. Dear Pellinore ended up spending Fion's ransom on my trousseau. For if I did not go to Arthur surrounded by the most luxurious finery in the kingdom, I would shame Wales. We had the long winter to get ready, for in the spring the King would come himself to take me out of Wales.

I put this from my mind, for I shook with fear at the very thought of it. Wales was the only home I knew. I remembered every word I had ever spoken to Elaine about how dreadful it would be to be Arthur's queen—well, I thought, I was justly served. That horrible witch had been proved right. And poor Gwillim, who I am sure thought he was doing me the finest service of his life, had been the unwitting instrument of my undoing. But there was nothing to do but face it. If I opened my mouth in complaint, I would shame Alyse and Pellinore, I would shame Northgallis, I would shame Wales. So I said very little and let the people take my silence for maidenly modesty if they chose.

In the month before the equinox Elaine finally rose from her bed. She was thin and pale and took the chair closest to the fire, but at least she joined us.

"Gwen," she said on our first night together in four months. "please forgive me for my grief. I wish you all happiness, you know that. I hated you for a while, but that was my unruly jealousy. I have remembered the prophecy at your birth, and also Merlin's prophecy, and I know that it is you who were born for this, and not I. Please forgive me."

"Oh, Elaine!" I threw my arms around her and we cried together for a long time. "Dear cousin, I would give anything in the world to change places with you and give you your heart's desire! Can you think for one moment I would not, knowing how you feel? Oh, Elaine, I do not want to leave Wales!"

"You will not have to go alone," she said. "Mother says we shall all accompany you to Court and see you married."

"Bless you!" I cried.

"And although Mother must return, I will stay if you like. Surely you may have your own friends there, as the High King has his."

"Oh, thank you, Elaine. You warm my heart, truly. You would give up your home for *me*? Dear Elaine, marry one of his Companions and stay with me always!" But I should not have spoken of marriage. She went pale and trembled.

"I will never marry. Never."

A cold breath seemed to breathe upon my neck, and I shivered. "You will not always feel so, I am sure. Listen, Elaine, once you see the king himself you will not be so enamored of him. He cannot be the dream you cherish any more than he can be the ogre I fear." But she did not answer.

Wedding gifts began to arrive in Gwynedd and Caer Camel. King Fion sent yards of the finest, snow-white linen—no one on earth makes finer linen than the Irish, and this must have been bleached and beaten two hundred times to get such softness and lustre. Alyse declared it perfect for the marriage bed and would not let me touch it, but set her ladies to do the embroidery, although my needlework was finer. Fion also sent quantities of jewelry for Elaine and Queen Alyse as well as myself, all silver and enamel, worked in the intricate way of the Gaels, with interlocking vines and queer nested squares. And he sent me as his personal gift a pair of silver earrings worked around dark blue sapphires that caught the firelight and reminded one of the color of the sea in a summer storm. "To wear," said his note, "with sapphire eyes." I missed him dreadfully.

King Pellinore's carpenters were hard at work building wagons to carry all the gifts and all the luggage to Caer Camel. Horses had to be bought from neighboring lands, and trained to pull them, and his stable had to be enlarged to hold them. Food had to be bought from other kingdoms, even from Less Britain, for the High King would stay with us a month, and everyone in his train had to be fed, yes, and housed. Barracks were erected, and more temporary stables. The place was a riot of feverish activity. Men worked through snow and frost, day and night; no one rested. I used to stand by my window and watch them, amazed that this was all for me. At such times I felt the crushing weight of Britain's expectation. I was the chosen of Arthur—I could be no less than perfect. Whatever flaw they found with me would be magnified a thousand times. And there would be many—all the relatives and friends of the maids he had not chosen—looking to find fault. I could take no wrong step, say no hasty speech, or I would cast a shadow across the glory of Britain. These fears usually sent me into a fit of weeping, but the women only nodded to one another and winked behind my back. Even Ailsa said once in my hearing that all I needed was a good bedding and my fears would take care of themselves. I fainted when I heard it, and after that the women were more careful in their speech.

The truth was, I had never stopped to think that I was marrying a man. At twenty, Arthur was already a legend, even among the Saxons. He was an idea, not flesh and blood. I should have to bear him princes, but exactly what that meant I had not considered. As the rains of April fell, and Elaine grew quieter, and the women stitched away madly at the king's wedding sheets, it began to be real to me. And I was terrified.

I escaped to the stables on dry days, and took Zephyr out on the hills, or flew Ebon, or dallied on the beach. They let me go wherever I chose, although I had a chaperone of troopers. Nothing could be allowed to happen to me. I was no longer Guinevere; I was King Arthur's betrothed. It angered me sometimes that the word of a single man I had not even met could so change my life. And it frightened me, also. What was the High King expecting? An ornament to his Court? A broodmare? Surely he must realize that Gwillim's words were poetry and never meant to describe a woman of flesh and blood! Suppose—suppose he frowned on women riding horses? Should I have to take to a litter, like Alyse? Oh, I wept in frustration and pounded my poor mare over the hills in desperate attempts to escape such thoughts, but they were always there when I returned.

Father Martin was useless as a confidant. He could barely hear my confession, so ready was he to bend the knee to me. I prayed to the Virgin, helpmate of women, to give me the strength to endure what was coming. But when I closed my eyes at night, all that came to me was Merlin's face and the gentle, ghostly voice repeating "what will be, will be."

My fifteenth birthday came and went, barely noticed in the frantic bustle, and three days later a royal courier arrived. Elaine and I gripped each other on the staircase as we strained to hear him give his message to Pellinore in the hall. Spring had brought new longboats to the eastern shores, and the northern kings could not hold their defenses against an attack of such numbers, should it come. King Arthur was required to show his face there and deal with them and could not come to take his bride to Caer Camel. But not wishing to delay the wedding, which was set for the summer solstice, he was sending in his stead three of his closest Companions and a troop of horse to take me to Caer Camel to await his arrival there.

Elaine and I turned to each other. On her face was writ her disappointment; on mine was sheer relief. The men would be arriving in three days and would stay until such time as we felt ready to depart. This was wonderful news! The building could cease, the cooks could rest, and everyone except the queen's ladies could be sure that the preparations they had already made would be sufficient. But a trousseau is never finished. There is always one more cushion to stuff, one more gown to stitch, one more slipper to line.

Elaine had made me a nightgown, entirely of her own design and working, of creamy linen lined with silk, and edged with costly laces. On the morning of the third day she bade me try it on for a final fitting. It was a lovely thing, with loose, flowing lines, and a low throat. But Elaine was unhappy with the bodice, which she felt should be tighter. She gripped the cloth at the back until it was tight, and then placed her hand upon my bosom to get the shape. Then an odd thing happened. She hesitated, and met my eyes. We both thought, at exactly the same moment, of where this gown would be worn, and that a man's large, brown hand would be where her small, white one lay, and she jumped away as I gasped, and we both turned scarlet.

"Oh, Gwen, I can't bear the thought of it!" she cried, tears welling in her eyes.

"Neither can I!" I cried, and we fell weeping into each other's arms. This is but one illustration among many of the state we were in.

Unable to stand the castle any longer, I dressed in my doeskin leggings and soft boots and my old green mantle and went to the stable. I asked no one's permission. Today was the long-awaited day, and everyone was too busy to notice me. I took Ebon on my arm, hopped on Zephyr and rode bareback up into the hills. The king's men were not expected until nightfall, and I should be back, bathed, perfumed, and gowned before they saw me.

It was a glorious day in May, golden and soft, and the forests were full of birds returning to their summer homes. We had a good gallop, and then we had wonderful hunting, one exciting chase after another, with five kills to Ebon's credit by midafternoon, when I hooded him because the pouch was full. He could have filled a saddlebag that magic day, had I brought one with me. We stopped at a stream for Zephyr to drink, and I felt it suddenly—the thrill of excitement, the throbbing expectancy of something marvelous that lay ahead, and was coming. It was a wonderful day to be alive. For the first time in months my spirit lifted, and I felt like singing. We stood in the silence of the forest with dappled sunlight falling all about, while cool water dripped from the mare's muzzle and small creatures rustled in the underbrush. In the blessed stillness, the birds began to sing, tentatively at first, and then in full-throated song. The falcon sat hooded and quiet on my arm as the budding treetops came alive with music. I whistled in imitation and then joined in their chorus, and they let me.

The mare walked gently down the forest track while I sang to the birds, happy to be young and alive, glorying in the magic brightness of that special day. We came upon a clearing, and suddenly the mare stopped, threw up her head, and nickered. I looked about, but it was several moments before I saw the young man on the black horse. They stood under the trees where the track left the clearing, and he was staring at me. As I noticed him, he slid from his horse and took two steps forward. He cleared his throat, but no sound came out. He just stood in the clearing as if he had been there always, and my heart began to pound. He wore a strange device on his cloak, and his clothes were cut a little oddly, but that he was a knight there was no doubt. Black hair fell across his brow and shaded his eyes. His face had good lines and would have been handsome if his nose had not been broken and set slightly crooked. It gave an oddness to his face that set his features apart from those of other men. I could not explain why my spirit soared as I looked at him. He was a stranger, but my heart beat painfully in my chest as he took another step forward and tried again to speak. I felt weak inside, as if I would melt like butter in the sun.

"Are you—are you a vision or are you real?" he whispered. The question, spoken low and almost out of hearing, did not seem out of place, for I had wondered the same about him.

"I am no vision, my lord. Where—who—what badge is that you bear? You are no Welshman."

He bent one knee and sank down on the new grass.

"Forgive such forwardness, my lady. I am a poor knight from foreign parts, and this badge is the badge of my homeland. My name is Lancelot."